Redemption's Embrace

THE REDEMPTION SAGA
BOOK THREE

Redemption's EMBRACE

E. L. CROSS

Redemption's Embrace
Book Three in The Redemption Saga

Copyright © 2021 Erin L. Cross

Scripture both paraphrased and directly quoted from the New
King James Version®.
Copyright © 1982 by Thomas Nelson. Used by permission. All
rights reserved.

Cover Design by Erin L. Cross

Ebook ISBN: 978-1-7363603-4-7
Paperback ISBN: 978-1-7363603-5-4

Other Books by E. L. Cross

※　※　※

The Redemption Saga

To learn about new releases and read exclusive content, connect with E. L. Cross at www.elcrossbooks.com

Dedication

"Come now, and let us reason together," says the Lord,
"Though your sins are like scarlet,
they shall be as white as snow;
Though they are red like crimson, they shall be as wool."

Isaiah 1:18 NKJV

※ ※ ※

To my readers, present and future,
who have fallen in love with these characters
and keep turning pages to see all things
work together for their good.
That is my prayer for you as well.

Contents

Part Three - Restored

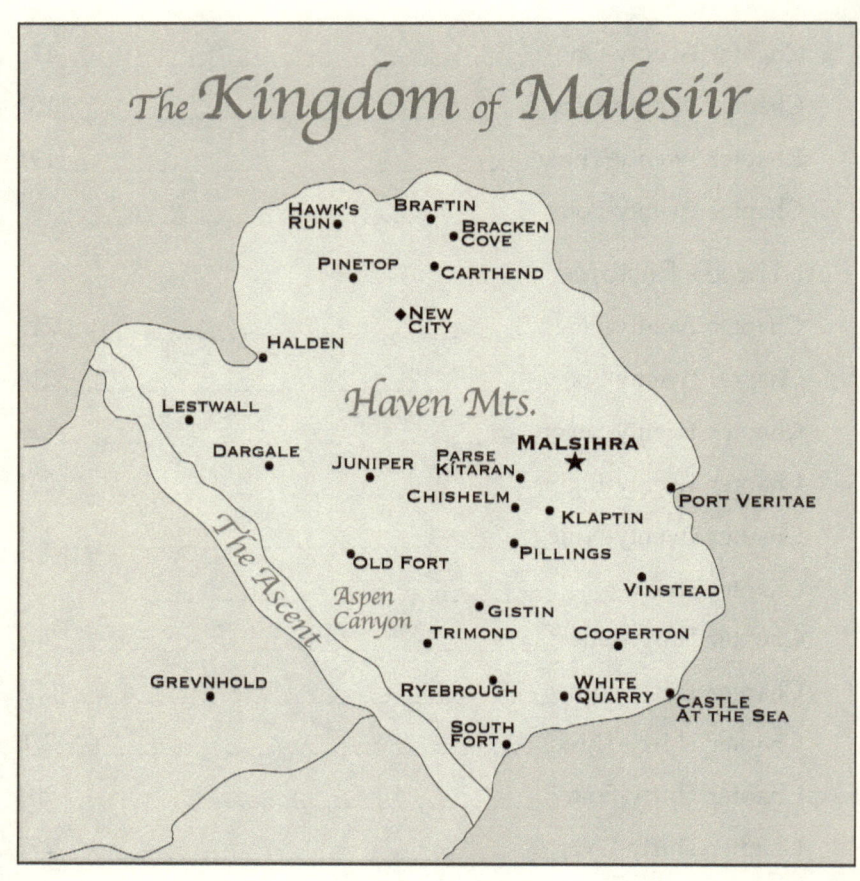

The Kingdom of Malesiir

HAWK'S RUN
BRAFTIN
BRACKEN COVE
PINETOP
CARTHEND
NEW CITY
HALDEN
LESTWALL
Haven Mts.
DARGALE
JUNIPER
PARSE
KITARAN
MALSIHRA
CHISHELM
PORT VERITAE
KLAPTIN
PILLINGS
OLD FORT
VINSTEAD
The Ascent
Aspen Canyon
GISTIN
TRIMOND
COOPERTON
GREVNHOLD
RYEBROUGH
WHITE QUARRY
CASTLE AT THE SEA
SOUTH FORT

PART ONE

FOUND

CHAPTER ONE

VALOR

July 30th

She is gone.

I rise, slowly scanning the clearing. The bent grass next to me evidences that the wraith I encountered was not of my mind's making, but of flesh and blood. Sunlight slants low and golden through the forest as crickets tune their instruments for their nightly chorus.

I breathe evenly, measuring my movements, not allowing the urgency pounding beneath my ribs to manifest in my actions. I spin my gaze back the other way and find who I seek. Swallowing my relieved sigh, I offer her an easy smile. She only blinks.

She looks remade yet again, but this time, not for the better. How many faces have I seen this woman wear? Many.

I saw the broken young woman mistrusting of all save her dearest friend.

I knew the playful yet fragile woman she became as she tentatively began to trust.

I fell in love with the enchanting princess who was quick to smile with a presence like cool water.

I heard tell of the undaunted warrior queen beloved by her people.

I glimpsed the contented wife and soon to be mother adored by her husband.

Then her life took a turn so drastic that she was nearly crushed in the landslide and left unrecognizable from all those other versions. But whether the princess, the queen, or this woman before me I cannot yet name, I name all my friend. It was for this reason I came for her.

Out of loyalty that crossed the boundaries of the grave, I vowed to her slain husband that I would find her, protect her and see her restored.

Before I saw her three days past, I thought the most difficult thing would be finding her. As she crouches in the light that shifts to the violet of gloaming, she appears as unapproachable as any beast of the woods. I realize this will be the most difficult path I have ever walked with her. I am at a momentary loss of where to begin. Oddly, that knowledge sets my feet on the right path.

Spirit of Truth, guide my every step. Guard my every word. Let my very presence be a balm to my anguished friend.

Peace that I had lost hold of when I woke takes hold of me and steadies me.

First, to attend the simplest of things. "Are you hungry?"

She stares for a long moment, then narrows her eyes. She searches the ground behind her without taking her eyes from me. Finding what she seeks, she brings it to hand then sidles closer to me staying crouched low. She stops several paces away and tosses the thing to me. I catch it, and her eyes dart with the movement of my hand.

I spare a glance for what she threw me. It is a nibbled-on smoked rabbit leg so dry and tough it must be nearly inedible. The princess once named the shooting of a rabbit with a bow barbaric. The feral woman before me must have overcome her aversion in favor of survival.

"I thank you, Friend, but I was intending to feed you." I smile and reach a hand back to my pack. She watches all I do, poised to escape if I become a threat. Only a few months back she herself named me the person she trusted most. I hurt anew for her if this is what her trust in humanity has been reduced to.

I locate the hard wedge of cheese wrapped in waxed cloth and toss it to her. She skitters back letting it land on the ground before her as if it may be dangerous, then with tentative fingers picks it up. She lifts the wedge free of the cloth, and her eyes widen. Greedily, she opens her cracked lips to take a bite then pauses, holding it back as if it offends. Accusation glints in her eyes. She tosses the cheese back to me and waits.

I catch it, trying to follow her thoughts, but I am at a loss. This feels more like gentling a wild animal than having a meal with my friend. "I do not understand. What would you have me do?"

She cocks her head to the side and closes her eyes in concentration. I watch her mouth practice the syllables before speaking them.

"Poisoned?"

My face crumbles, and I look down to hide it. What in the cursed depths has been done to my friend that she would think I capable of poisoning her? I compose my features and raise my head. I take a bite of the wedge, chew, and swallow. "It is a bit old and may not satisfy your refined tastes, but I assure you, it is only cheese." When I toss it back to her, she practically inhales it, licking her fingers clean of every morsel.

Taking note of the fading light, she heads to a large densely branched tree. With a jump she catches the lowest limb then swings her feet up to hook them around it and hauls herself up. She climbs nearly forty feet and settles in the crook of two branches, all but disappearing from sight behind the lush foliage.

"So that is how you have evaded me and the Wolves the past week," I murmur to myself. To her I say, "Very clever, Huntress. May I join you?"

Even at this distance I feel her unease before she hedges with another broken sentence, "You...sleep...ground."

"Usually I do. But you seem to think it is safer to sleep in trees, so I will sleep in trees too," I explain.

She points to a large beech tree on the opposite side of the clearing. "Yours."

I decide today is not the day to push this boundary with her and accept her decision. Shouldering my pack, I climb the tree she pointed out to a height opposite hers. I try and fail not to think of when the princess used to curl into my side to sleep at night. If the physical distance she has placed between us is any indication, I will have to span a chasm to find my friend inside this battered creature. I know for certain I am unequal to the obstacle. My arms are not long enough to reach her. Thankfully, I know the One whose arms spanned eternity to rescue us both.

※ ※ ※

The dawn sun warms my brow pleasantly, awakening me this morning. The gentle sway of the tree soothes as does the music of the wind rustling through the leaves. Then the inevitable happens when I look down. The world spins. My mind tries convince me I am unsafe in this perch that previously felt quite secure.

It seems my queen feels the same way. I hear her retching as I clamber from the tree. By the time my feet happily reunite with the ground, she has wandered down the steep bank to the stream. Her latest meal, another overcooked rabbit, is neatly divided into two piles on a rock in the middle of the clearing. I augment her helping with a handful of toasted barley then sit crosslegged, separating meat from sinew and bone while she finishes her ablutions.

Shed of the fur lined cloak that she left hanging on a tree, I take note of the unusual garb she wears. A black skirt of strange fabric flows like water around her legs, covering fine boots. A thin fitted shirt that was white before weeks of grime discolored it peeks out beneath a black leather cuirass with three knives sheathed into the sides. I have never seen a woman's cuirass quite like it.

I return the fourth blade I collected after she hurled it at me days past. She cautiously accepts it with a nod of thanks and sheaths it on her side. Her fingers move to the hilt of an ornate dagger tucked in a belt. The bare blade gleams in the sun. It matches her husband's bespoke sword.

Perhaps that is a good place to begin today. Were I she, I certainly would want to know. I wait until she crouches over her heels to eat her breakfast.

"My Queen, I would like to tell you something that I hope brings you a measure of comfort." I pray this comes out with the sensitivity and condolence due such a thing. The queen continues picking at the grains of barley, consuming them one at a time. "Anders and I were on the road to the seaside castle to visit you."

Her body stills, but her haunted eyes dart up and lock on mine.

"We came upon the battle only a day or two after it happened. We found King Grandileer still resting with the honor you gave him."

Tears rim the queen's eyes as she whispers, "My Leer."

My heart breaks for her again as I recall the love I observed between them. "Anders stayed with the king and ensured he was returned to Malsihra while I came after you. That was about three weeks ago."

She folds in half wrapping her arms around her legs and keening from a pain deeper than any I have ever known. I sit vigil until words form amidst her sorrow.

"Won't leave…Sorry…Sorry…Won't leave," she wails.

"Was it the Wolves?"

"Ruphiri!" She spits back, correcting me, then looks ashamed.

"Did they capture you?"

"Leave chase. Zavaan keep," she replies looking no less guilty.

"Zavaan caught you?" My heart stutters thinking just how awful the last weeks may have been for her.

She nods then as if scolding herself says, "Chases Zavaan. Chases Zavaan."

"Can you tell me—"

"Zavaan *vreh král!*" She slams her fists on the ground, repeating the Limban phrase as she looks at me. The anger contorting her face dissolves into muted surprise. She scans my face, my light armor and weapons then forms my name again without voicing it. Her eyes widen as if realizing who is sitting across from her for the first time. A bloodthirsty smile lifts the corners of her mouth. "*Vreh Král Vragh.*"

"I do not understand." At least I hope I do not.

My queen palms the king's dagger and inclines her head to my sword. I rest my hand on the hilt at her behest. Her grin is all teeth as she lends meaning to the action. "Hunt Zavaan. Kill King Killer."

Her breakfast forgotten, she tucks the dagger back into the worn leather belt and walks behind me to grab my pack, still staying well out of arm's reach. She opens it and sifts through the contents, making a victorious noise when she finds the maps I always keep with me. Unceremoniously, she drops the pack in my lap and spreads the maps out in the grass. Finding the one she searches for, she tosses the others to me. Her fingers crawl over the grass, picking up a few pebbles.

She bites her dry lower lip, not noticing that the act draws blood. She considers the map, cocking her head this way and that. Her index finger traces over the map as she agrees with herself then places a single pebble near the border. She taps it, catching my eye. "Zavaan." Her fingers splay out from it. "Ruphiri." She taps her chest and moves her finger northward from Zavaan's pebble then tosses another pebble to me with a questioning look.

As I lean toward the map, she lunges away. For now, I pretend not to notice, choosing to give her time to remember I am safe. "We are here." I mark our location and drop another pebble where I found the king slain, then consider the place she marked on the map. "Are you certain this is where you last were? I do not think it is possible to travel so much distance in... How long were you with the Wolves?"

Her eyes flash at the term then shutter. I have heard of captives becoming sympathetic to their captors under duress. It bodes ill that she seems offended by my naming them "Wolves." But she wants to kill Zavaan, so I hope she is not so thoroughly lost.

She holds up ten fingers representing ten days then makes a gesture meaning more or less.

"You cannot have gone so far," I contend.

With a stern look, she inches closer to the map and traces a roughly straight line between the two points. "Fast," she assures me. I take a moment to study her up close while pretending to look at the map. Hair that usually shines in the sun hangs in a stringy knotted mess and there is no ignoring the pungent scent of a body in need of a bath. She is really in bad shape if she let go of her incessant demand for personal cleanliness.

I point toward the mountain ridges between the coast and border. "It is just not possible to have gone from—" I am cut off abruptly as a boot lands in my chest throwing me back with a grunt.

My queen flees to the far side of the clearing with knives in both hands and a snarl curling her lips.

"I moved to point to the map!"

Her eyes dart between mine, looking for sincerity.

"I hope you gave them hell for what they did to you," I growl.

She looks at the ground, flushing with shame.

"Come sit down and eat while we figure out what to do."

Her chin quivers as she tests the word. "We."

"Aye. *We*," I assure her.

She returns to the opposite side of the map and crouches rather than sits to give herself an advantage should she need to escape.

Once she begins to chew the barley, I continue our lopsided conversation. "Assuming the Wolves can move as quickly as you claim, they could have gone anywhere in the past eight days. We need reinforcements to find them."

She shakes her head vehemently. "We."

"Why? Why not send for help to hunt them down?"

"Zavaan *vreh král!*" She screams, fisting her hands.

I ask more gently, "Did you see Zavaan kill Grandileer?"

She nods and touches the dagger.

"With his own dagger?" I guess.

She looses a sob, nodding again.

"Then we cannot afford a mistake in apprehending him. We will make certain he is brought to justice, but that means gathering our forces to hunt him down. And we must alert Lorennt that you have been found. I am certain he is worried sick over you."

The queen's face is horrified. "Lorennt chases Zavaan."

"Yes, I am sure Lorennt will want to help chase down Zavaan..."

Another shake of her head, another sob. "Lorennt chases Zavaan!"

"You should tell him yourself that you are safe and seek his help."

She spins her wedding ring around her finger, shaking her head. "Not Lorennt. We."

"You know that I will assist you in hunting down Zavaan, but we must get you to safety first. You are in no condition to pursue him or fight."

"We!" She removes her signet ring and throws it at me. "Hunt Zavaan. Kill."

The queen's ring. The symbol of her power to command. She is making this an order. At least she has not forgotten who she is. "My Queen. I will help you hunt down Zavaan and ensure he is punished for his crimes. But I am still in service to the last vow I made, and I will not break it."

Her brow pinches, waiting for an explanation.

"I swore to the king that I would find you and protect you and see you restored. Do not ask me to break my oath to him." I toss her ring back.

Her eyes glisten. "Found. Protected."

"But not yet restored," I softly state.

She shrugs, fully comprehending how unwell she is. "Broken. Too broken."

"You can be mended," I promise.

The words strike a chord with her, and she hides her face in her hands.

Back to the necessities. I fish in my pack until I find a spare set of my clothes for her to borrow and set them on the map between us. "Here. Go wash out your clothes and bathe before we go. You smell worse than Anders," I tease. The uncouth man is the perpetual end of our jokes, to his amusement as much as ours. Being "as bad as" or "worse than Anders" is not something to be desired.

The queen cocks her head to the side but does not immediately accept the clothes. She seems to be trying to figure out why I would offer her this kindness or, rather, if there are any strings attached. Zavaan's list of sins grows longer by the moment.

"Do you think a few months apart will prevent me from looking after you?" I smirk, hoping to help her remember we are friends. Hesitantly, she gathers the clothes and the bar of soap I set on top. "Sorry, it is the military kind. I have not had the courage to carry around milk soap without you to blame." My teasing smile does not have any effect, but she does head down to the stream, casting me a warning look that I interpret to mean *stay put*. I lie back on the grass to show her I have every intention of doing so.

CHAPTER TWO

ERIANNA

I almost feel human again after scrubbing my hateful clothes and washing my skin and hair three times to rid it of all the filth. *Almost.*

After wringing my hair of excess water and finger combing it as best I can, I pull on the commander's extra shirt. The salty fresh scent of him embedded in the fabric overwhelms my senses. I am flooded with hundreds of bright gilded memories that time did not dull. I let the remnants of that happiness temporarily supplant the darkness of these last months as I braid my wet hair and tie it in place with a strip of my shirt that no amount of scrubbing can return to white. Valor's shirt falls to mid thigh on me, and, if I were alone, I would only wear it until my clothes dry, but that will not do with him here. Instead I pull on his pants and use the worn leather belt to secure them. I stole it from the first blacksmith's shop I happened upon along with a pouch to contain the equally stolen flint, steel, and char cloth for starting fires. Stealing from my people does not sit well with me, so I plan to send payment for the goods once I have funds.

Leer's dagger goes back into the belt as I consider the cuirass. I hate that trace of the deceiver. I recall the feel of Reuel's filthy hands upon me when he laced it and whispered poisoned words into my ears then moved his mouth over mine. A shiver tracks down my spine. I spit in the dirt, ridding my mouth of the extra saliva filling it, and hope I do not vomit again. The past few days my stomach has been as treacherous as during pregnancy.

My thoughts rampage down that corridor, forgetting all the hopefulness and skipping straight to the heartrending conclusion. I am flung from memory to memory of that endless horror—the words that shattered my world, my cold babe, Leer's anguish, Illyanna's too small casket, Mother Celiea's hand reaching for her grandchild, Leer's haggard face, Jaleh's screaming…

I run to the nearest bushes, but the much too long pants trip me. My stomach expels the little I choked down while I shake. My head pounds fiercely. When it is over, I sit on my backside and roll up the long pant legs then pull on my boots.

What was I doing? I run my hands down my sides, trying to ignore the stretch in my palm from the recently healed gash while I reorder my thoughts. Oh, yes. The cuirass. Much as I would prefer to leave it behind, the sturdy light armor and additional weapons provide a tactical advantage I cannot afford to lose. I slip my arms into the thin leather straps then wrap it around my sides. I can only fit the lace through a few of the eyelets, barely enough to keep the cuirass in place.

How appropriate. I curse Reuel the foulest ways I know. He did this on purpose. I have never, *never* seen a soldier need assistance into his cuirass. Cunning Reuel designed my cuirass so that I would need his help to don it. His *permission*, as it were.

I hate him.

The washed skirt and shirt I leave to dry in the sun as I clamber up the bank. The commander is right where I left him, lying in the grass with an arm crossed over his eyes to block the sun.

Some lookout you make, I try to say. All that comes out is a derisive, "Lookout."

"I can keep watch perfectly well with my ears," he rejoins.

I bend over to scoop up a handful of barley and nearly spill out of my cuirass as the wretched thing slides out of place. I squeak and grasp the top of it, righting myself. I fiddle with the laces again, but must admit defeat.

Resignedly, I nudge the commander's foot with my booted toe. "Help."

He lazily lifts his arm from his eyes to evaluate me. His mouth twitches, concealing his amusement at his ill-fitting clothes on me. "I forgot what a small thing you are."

"Oaf," I remark, laying the blame on him, then am pleased with myself for speaking exactly what I intended. I point to the mismatched laces on the cuirass.

The commander rises to his knees then stands slowly, dusting himself off. When he straightens and steps closer, I swallow the fear that coats my tongue. I remind myself that his massive build was once a comfort to me and draw upon the memories of when his arms enfolded me so completely that he blocked out the world.

With a deep breath, I give him my back and feel his fingers moving over the laces, tugging the cord free of the eyelets and righting it.

"Who gave you this?" He deep voice rumbles.

"Reuel," I reply thoughtlessly. It was the wrong path to send my thoughts down.

The tugging at my back continues as Reuel's warm breath blows over my neck and his smokey leather scent fills my nostrils. *"You think you know what I am capable of. But I assure you. You cannot fathom the lows I could bring you to."* Cold steel tinged with our mingled blood caresses my face. *"You are mine, little Queen."*

Run! My mind shrieks. I free Leer's dagger and strike with the pommel at Reuel. His hand shoots up to block. I swing opposite, dropping underneath the fist sure to come at my face. I bring up my knee to unman him, but he blocks that too. I bring my foot down between his, hooking his ankle and dropping him to the ground before I sprint away.

※ ※ ※

VALOR

That went sideways quickly. I watch my queen fly into the forest like, well, like wolves are after her. I scented her fear an instant after she gave Zavaan's name. Actually, she said "Reuel," and said it with much less malice than the name deserves. Almost like he was a friend. It also stands to reason that he was the last person to fit her into the cuirass which itself is not the sort of gift one gives a captive. Come to think of it, if she was only with him for ten days, how did he know her size or that she has a penchant for throwing knives? Furthermore, if her fear convinced her that I was Zavaan, why did she not try to kill me just now? When she rounded on me with a dagger in hand, it was to disable, not to kill. Yet she is utterly resolved on me going with her to kill Zavaan.

More questions, fewer answers, and the answers I thought I held are now murky. I recline in the grass, deciding I will pretend to nap again while I wait for her to return. I know she did not go far since I can hear her retching again. Fear can do that to a person.

My eyes spring open.

Something else can do that to a woman.

I dig the heels of my hands into my eyes while asking for even more sensitivity as I realize I must push my queen where she will not want to go. If she is with child again, be it Grandileer's or Zavaan's—and heaven will have to intervene to spare Zavaan from my wrath if it is his—then I must adjust my queen's plans, whether she likes it or not.

I hear her meander down to the stream and settle there. Close enough. I grab my water skin and make a good bit of noise as I approach to keep from startling her. She sits with her nose buried in the collar of my loaned shirt. I empty the water skin then refill it with fresh water from the spring-fed stream. "Would you like me to finish lacing the cuirass?" I ask casually.

She nods with her nose still buried in the shirt. I scoot alongside her and lace it quickly then place an arm's length between us. More distance than I could reach on my own, but not too much if she reaches for me also.

"Could the reason you cannot keep your food down be due to another babe?" I imbue my words with compassion.

A frown bows her lips and creases her brow as her hand settles over her belly. Silver lines her lashes. "Should be. But no."

Prying as gently as possible, I ask, "You are quite certain? If not Grandileer, then perhaps Zavaan?"

Her chin quivers. "Not my Leer." She does not brush away the tears tracking down her cheek as if they are so often present she has come to accept their persistence. "Reuel did not."

I must have misunderstood. "Zavaan did not force himself on you?"

She shrugs while she searches for the words. "Trespass," she allows then shakes her head, "not more." She opens her left palm and stares at it. A dark pink line from a new scar bisects it. She fists her hand closed. With a measure of pride she glances sidelong at me. "Tricked. Proof… first."

I puzzle at her words until a memory brings clarity to them. Before taking her to wife, Grandileer asked for proof to ensure she was not carrying my child so that he could be certain any children born of their union would be his.

I grin at her. "Very clever, my Queen." My pleasure that she did not again suffer ravishment is dampened by the word she did use. Whatever ways he *trespassed* against her, and there could be many, are so foul that she is skittish of me. Zavaan's days are numbered.

"My Leer's…idea." She returns her eyes to the stream.

"I remember," I acknowledge. I was furious with him at the time. Never would I have imagined good could come from that request, but I have been disproved. "Your husband was a wise man." I inch nearer this underlying pain that is still formless to me. I know something terrible happened between them, but I have no idea what.

She sighs heavily but does not agree with me. So they did not reconcile before he was killed. That is a weighty grief in its own. But he is still *my Leer* to her. What a muddle.

Spirit of Truth, grant me wisdom.

She shakes her head as if trying to scatter the thoughts plaguing her then rises. "Go."

"We must still decide where," I point out. "Will you be convinced to return to your family in Malsihra?"

She shakes her head then says again with conviction, "Lorennt chases Zavaan."

"Alright," I agree since I cannot make sense of that statement. "Nor will I be convinced to take you to hunt Zavaan. Not yet, at least."

She huffs but acquiesces with a dip of her chin.

"Thank you for trusting my decision."

The Creator's ways are beyond fathoming, I once more acknowledge as I decide the only place I can take her is the place I longed to show her a year ago. Though this is far different from what I had in mind at the time. "If you will allow it, I would like to take you to Parse Kítaran. It is my home, and Nev has made her home there too."

The first glimmer of happiness enters her eyes at the mention of Nev, so I feed it. "She is doing very well and growing round these days. But I am put out with you for thinking I need your money to provide for her. I am quite capable of looking after her as a guardian should."

My queen's expression softens. "I thank you."

CHAPTER THREE

ERIANNA

We replenish our supplies and collect Granite from a nearby town where he was stabled. Commander Ironforge was unable to close in on me while mounted. Whenever I heard his approach, I moved far away, thinking it was Reuel on my trail. He tracked me on foot after that and caught up with me.

I ride behind the commander as we once did. Holding to him feels less intimate than being held, so that is what I choose. I would prefer to forget the feel of being in Reuel's arms and preserve only the remembrance of my Leer. I never imagined the day would come that I would trade Valor without hesitation for Grandileer, but every time I wrap my arms around him, I hold back tears from the pain of wishing for Leer in my arms. I would even take back the brokenness of those last few months if it meant his return to me.

Days pass as we trek toward wherever it is we are going. I do not remember at the moment. Nor do I remember the conversations the commander has tried to draw me into. At night, I see Leer kneeling before me, speaking words that I refused to hear at the time and now wish I had. Maybe he would have been able to explain what happened without lying, and I could have believed him. Maybe he could explain in such a way that I could reconcile how the man who ruthlessly let me be shattered was the same man who patiently and gently taught me of a husband's love and sang away my nightmares. I grew to love that man with my whole heart. How could he have done the things he did and lied to everyone for so long? No matter how desperately I try to clear my mind to hear his words, the memory of Leer dissolves and it is the commander kneeling before me instead. I usually walk away from him when that happens to find somewhere to sleep, though sleep is hard to come by, in no small part due to the ache in my head.

It hurts too much to bother fighting through the haze to the present to make the effort worthwhile. Now that I am no longer in mortal danger, my emotions have overthrown the sense of self-preservation that kept me lucid, and I am dragged back down beneath the waves of grief, apathy, and pain.

At the bottom of that ocean is the desire to be returned to Malsihra as lifeless as my family so I may join them beneath the earth. When I sink that low, I find a rope tying me to the land of the living in the form of a promise. I swore to kill the *Král Vragh*. He irrevocably separated me from my Leer. *"We can be mended,"* Leer told me. I wanted to believe him. I wanted him to fight for us and prove me wrong. And fight for me he did. But the cost was his life for mine, not the slaying of our past for a future together.

The tears on my face are cold and too plentiful. I raise my heavy head from where it rests against the commander's back and am dragged above the waves to the present. Is it night already? I lift my gaze skyward and find it darkened and weeping cold tears on my upturned face. The commander veers from the road and follows a game trail through the forest.

Toward a cave.

I tug on a fistful of his cloak. "No." *We must not go in there!* "No!" *It is not safe! They could be in there waiting for us.* I shove against the commander and attempt to slide off Granite's rump to flee. The commander seizes me around my waist and pulls me to the fore of the saddle.

Panic grips me, making an enemy of the one who holds me. I thrash to free myself from his unrelenting grasp. The horse shies at my hysterics. Thunder booms overhead bound to lightning that casts the forest into menacing shapes. The destrier rears, tipping the world. The man cannot hold both me and the horse. He takes the brunt of the fall then rolls me under him in the sodden ground to shield me from the frightened beast's hooves as it dashes between the trees.

I am wild with fear at the heavy press of a body on mine that is not Leer's. The storm breaking over the forest shakes the trees, but it is less violent than my frenzied struggle. The cave ahead is anything but safe. Reuel will not believe my lies this time! He will make me pay for tricking him! I shift my hips to throw him from me, but my feet cannot find purchase on the slick leaves. I whimper when he pins my hands between our two bodies. My face is pressed into his neck. Hot breath tickles my ear, but I cannot turn away. I am caught.

The deep voice of the one who does not lie sends a fissure through my panic. "Erianna, hear me. You are safe."

My sharp inhale carries the smell of salt and sun-soaked days. The fissure splits wide open.

"Valor," I exhale his name as a plea. I pray this is not a dream that will be proved to be another waking nightmare. How long has it been since reality became worse than my dreams?

"Find my eyes, Erianna," he coaxes, pulling back so that I may see him.

Stormy eyes etched with concern hover over me. The fight whooshes out of me. I go limp against the wet ground. Moments later my world is righted as he lifts me to my feet. He braces my arms, whistling for Granite. I step away, wrapping my cloak tight around myself, making sense of the world.

A cave looms further down the path. I draw two knives and feel nauseous at the onslaught of panic.

"What is it?" The commander asks.

"Ruphiri," I whisper, nodding toward the cave.

"Did they hide in caves?"

I jerk my head.

He draws his sword and advances on the maw. I watch his back vanish into the gloom while Granite saunters over as if he would never dare throw a rider. I wrap my fingers in his sodden black mane. Dread makes knots of my insides.

With absolute confidence, Valor returns to me with his ground eating stride and fits sword to scabbard. "The cave is ours, my Queen. Come. Let's get out of the rain."

I walk alongside the stallion and stop just inside the rocky overhang while my eyes adjust to the absence of light. The commander offers me his hand, but I pull away, preferring the horse to being led deeper into the cave.

Without taking offense, he scavenges dry sticks to serve as tinder and finds a half-dry pine log to burn. I lean against Granite's flank, thinking dirty wet horse is not the best smell, but still I prefer it to the one I am desperately trying to forget. The pine log laden with pitch burns hot and smokey. Commander Ironforge bids me leave my cloak with him to dry by the fire and hands me the bundle of Ruphiri clothes. I lock my thoughts to the present by overthinking each movement needed to change into the clean clothes outside the circle of light then hurriedly return to the fire. I give him my back, trusting his long fingers to make short work of the cuirass laces.

"If you like wearing a cuirass, we could have one made that laces at the sides. You should not be dependent upon another to don your own armor." The tightness of his voice conveys that he knows perfectly well why Reuel gave me a cuirass like this. "I have not been able to piece together how he knew your size or skill with knives. Do you know?"

Unfortunately, all too well. "Chase is Zavaan," I explain.

"You have said that many times, but I do not understand." He hands me a wedge of cheese followed by a bit of smoked venison.

I do not understand it myself. I remember dancing with Chase and our many conversations. Other than the singular time he made me uncomfortable and Leer chastised him for it, I thought he was intriguing. "Oh," I exclaim as a piece falls into place. Perhaps Chase was not as perceptive as we thought. Perhaps he knew so much about me because he learned my history in Limba. From Arcto. Why that scheming, manipulative, lying—

"What?"

"Chase and Arcto," I tell him.

He sighs. "I still do not understand."

I glare at him, suddenly frustrated. Maybe if he had had the nerve to come to the castle instead of disappearing for nine months he would understand more! "You... gone... Visit." I grit my teeth, frustrated with the chaos of my thoughts and persistent ache in my head that trips my tongue.

The commander winces then runs fingers through his long hair that has not been clipped since before we met. "Let's wait to have that conversation till you have all of your words."

I roll my eyes, crossing my arms over my knees. The hissing of the damp wood fills the silence between us.

"Granite told me your 'good morning' every day," he says softly. "So even though I could not be with you in person, not a day went by that I did not think of you and pray that you were well and happy."

My frustration abates. As I glance at him from the corner of my eye, I realize I was never angry with him anyway. He was simply the only available target to hurl my words at. A lesson I thought I had learned picking fights with Leer. "Sorry," I murmur, shifting my eyes back to the embers glowing every vibrant hue.

"You have nothing to apologize to me for," he replies. "When we eventually have that conversation, it will be me who has much to ask forgiveness for. And much to thank you for," he turns a grateful smile my way. "Kragorn told me that it was you who insisted I be given another chance as the king's Hand. I owe you much, my Queen."

"Deserve…" I try to tell him, but my breath hitches as I remember that particular fight with Leer. On its heels, memories from that time surface. Playing cards with him in the city. My twin dagger. The month we conceived our daughter. His warm hand in mine and handsome face at our coronation—the singular moment frozen in time when I rejoiced that his was the face I would see upon waking everyday for the rest of my life. But it's not. Just for the short remainder of his.

The wave of grief cresting is not one I am prepared for. I cannot face it. I will be drowned.

I extend a trembling hand to my friend, turning my raw expression to him. He takes my hand in his, becoming my lifeline once again. "Story," I request, catching one of the memories that his touch elicits. "Tell."

"Any story in particular?" He asks.

"Happy." If there is such a thing. I have my doubts, having only glimpsed through windows of happiness before they were obscured.

The commander's deep, steady voice draws me in, letting me see what he sees and put aside my heartache until I am better prepared. That is the captivating power of a good story. It is a window into a life worth remembering and retelling to illustrate something greater. Maybe in the hearing, perspective can be gained or relief can be had from one's own struggles. I have a notion of lying down. This moment soothes my soul and allows me to escape into a sleep blissfully free of turmoil.

⁂

August 4th

I wake slower this morning. The aching in my head has not subsided. But the dread coiling in my stomach is dampened, and I do not have to question why I feel it. I simply know. It is grief for my lost family. I let that knowledge wash through me, but it does not wash me away with it. I am held here, anchored to the present. When I open my eyes, they meet silver. Between where the commander and I lie on our sides, my hand is still encompassed by his, our fingers laced together. His smile is compassionate, giving me permission to rest awhile longer. He always was my favorite person.

"How sweet." The grating Limban words cut through the still, early morning. "Predictable, though."

It is hard to say which of us moves first, but Commander Ironforge and I both stand defensively—knives in my hands and a sword in his. My lip curls into a sneer at the lanky man brandishing two short swords silhouetted in the fog. Jarmuth.

"Took long, Tracker. Pitiful." I mock him in Limban and hope Jarmuth cannot see my shaking hands.

He cackles. "I have had your trail for days. I was just waiting for your master to arrive."

My heart pounds. *Please not yet! I am not ready to face him!* Likely Jarmuth is lying. Reuel would have been the one to confront me if he was here. With a thick varnish of bluster, I rebut, "Never… mine."

"Your joining says otherwise." He wets his lips, jeering, "Do you think we could not all hear your words to him, pathetic as they were? 'Master Reuel,'" he imitates my voice.

I swallow bile, shoving down that memory and am thrice grateful that the commander does not speak a bit of Limban. "Trick."

Jarmuth grins. "I look forward to hearing you explain that to him, Erianna Zavaan."

My eyes go wide as shock tinges the commander's face. He does not have to understand Limban to pick out my new surname.

Jarmuth points a sword at him, laughing uproariously. "You did not tell him! Afraid your Malesiirian lover would not take you back?"

Faster than I can hurl my knife, Jarmuth says with a thick accent in the common tongue, "She wed the King Killer!"

The commander's face tightens, but he does not take the bait. I, however, have heard enough. My blade whirls for Jarmuth's face, but he deflects it with a swing as I sprint for him, drawing Leer's dagger. He will not cut me down. He means to take me captive. It will force him to temper his attack, giving me the advantage.

I, however, have no intention of letting him live.

I dip and spin around to his back, striking for his kidney. He sidesteps, parrying my blade, but I am still moving. I deflect his next swing on the guard of my dagger and advance to slice open his gut with a knife. The cut is shallow and lacks the depth I hoped for. Jarmuth retreats, cursing me in two languages. The commander advances on Jarmuth, but Jarmuth whistles shrilly. The five wolves that I knew were in wait rush past to intercept the commander.

He will be fine. He will be fine, I chant to myself not taking my eyes from my opponent no matter the chorus of growls from man and beast at my back. I angle my knives and assail Jarmuth with a flurry of swipes. When I try to come around behind him, he throws out an elbow that connects with my ribs. Thankfully, the cuirass distributes the force, and my ribs do not crack like they did with Tergehn. Off-balance, I must drop to a crouch before regaining my feet. I use the opportunity to sink a knife into the vulnerable back of his knee. Blood spurts, coating my hand gripping the knife. Jarmuth howls and forgets himself, arcing his sword to cut me down. I merely watch. I feel relieved and grateful that my end will be quick.

Suddenly, Commander Ironforge is above me, catching the downward swing on his blood-drenched sword. He shoves Jarmuth away from me with a roar. I know I will be a hindrance, so I fall back, allowing the warrior take up the fight. He unleashes a fury on Jarmuth I have never before witnessed. I have seen him kill with grim satisfaction while defending me, but this is something else. This is undiluted bloodlust for the enemy that slaughtered the royal guard, that captured me, that killed his king. Slice after slice he imparts to the lamed Ruphiri, my knife still embedded in the back of his knee. His flashing sword knocks aside one of Jarmuth's, sending it clattering against rock. Finally, the commander lames the man's other leg by severing the tendon at the back of his ankle. Jarmuth crashes to the ground and loses his grip on his remaining sword.

Tortured screams vibrate the air. The commander towers over the defeated tracker, surveying him with a trained eye. Realizing what he plans to do, I steel my nerves. He stalks a wide circle around him then in that lethally quiet voice asks, "Where is Zavaan?"

Jarmuth bares his teeth at the warrior.

"I said, where is Zavaan?" The commander grips the hilt of my knife buried in Jarmuth's knee and twists it.

Jarmuth's shriek knots my stomach. On his next breath, the foolish tracker spits in the commander's face. The commander moves the knife with precision to inflict a maximum amount of pain while blood puddles beneath him. My stomach gives me no choice but to turn away, heaving.

"Searching for his wife!" Jarmuth's gutturally accented voice is barely intelligible.

No, no, no! This conversation is not going to happen! "Where!" I yell.

The tracker switches to Limban. "Do not worry, little Queen. He will

23

find you. When he learns you laid with this Malesiirian dog, your punishment will be most severe. Worse than the poison he put in that maid's hands."

The world rocks beneath me. "What?"

Jarmuth cackles. "He planted the idea in that woman's head. It was his idea to rid your womb of the king's spawn."

My ears are ringing, and my vision becomes spotty. I sit down hard, losing my grip on Leer's dagger.

"Say it again so I understand," the commander orders.

Jarmuth throws a punch at his face instead. The commander repays it with another twist of the knife.

My screams overlay Jarmuth's as my mind recalls with horrid clarity the tortured cries I extracted from Jaleh. She was wicked but also a pawn. How many ways has Reuel been jerking my strings to his tune?

"Where is Zavaan?" The commander bellows, his careful control snapping.

"He will find you, Malesiirian dog!" Jarmuth spits again.

Dread pours into me from a depthless cistern. Reuel tracked me across the Continent, beheaded Liddy, massacred our soldiers, stalked me for ten months in Malesiir, made the way to kill my babe, killed my husband, and forced me to marry him. Of course he is coming for me! What a fool I am for thinking it is I who must hunt him! When I am least prepared he will appear and exact punishment for escaping him. Not that it was escape, just running away for a time, a delay of my future of misery. He is going to find me, ravish me, torment me, and use me like a puppet on my throne.

But the commander is not finished with Jarmuth. His next question makes me want to die. "What did Zavaan do to her?"

Jarmuth knows full well his life is about to end, so he decides to make me as miserable as he can in his last moments. "Nothing she did not enjoy. 'Master Reuel' she calls him. The king was not cold before she…"

I cover my ears, drowning out his words with my anguished screams. I will not listen to Jarmuth illustrate what he saw in that cave. I can hardly live with myself for what I did.

My hands are pulled from my ears and held in the commander's. I shut my eyes tightly, unable to bear his disgust. My own guilt is shredding me as it is.

"It is done, my Queen." He speaks calmly again.

"Not! Find… wife!" I argue.

"You cannot be his wife. You are Leer's wife, remember?"

"Sorry," I weep brokenly. "Sorry! Sorry!" I never ever wanted him to hear those things.

"You were his captive. You do not have any reason to be sorry, my Queen."

"Stop! Not queen! Whore!" I spit the indictment that will not wash away from me. I whored myself to the enemy to save my worthless life. I played the whore for the man who murdered my husband.

"You are not!" He declares, shaking me. "Leer's wife is no whore! My queen is no whore! You were captured by the Chief of the Wolves and his pack. You tricked him to save yourself from ravishment. You are intelligent and did what needed doing to gain his trust then escaped and fended for yourself for a week with nothing but your blades."

I fist my left hand at my chest, hiding my shame. I am bound to Reuel. We are wed and joined.

The commander pulls my hand down and uncurls my fingers. Against my will, he reveals the joining scar. "Marrying under duress is not lawful. And this," he touches the scar, "is not the same as consummation. Given the choice, you would not have done any of those things."

"There! Done!" I spread my hand, fully revealing my bondage to Reuel. The ancient custom once bound slaves to their masters. Now it binds a queen to a conquering nation.

"No longer," the commander declares. He takes Leer's dagger from the ground and slices open his left palm then breaks open the scar on mine. He joins our hands together, mingling our blood. With his opposite hand, he cups my neck, bringing my brow forward to rest against his. We are close enough to share breath. "Forevermore, when you see this scar, you will know that it represents my life bound to yours, by blood and by choice. This day, I swear to jealously fight for you, Erianna Valor's Friend, and esteem you so long as there is breath in my body. Nothing that has been or will be can move me from this vow."

The fervor of his words blows heat across my skin even as my tears course onto his face. I am so undeserving of his friendship and loyalty. I am not worth fighting for. There is nothing in me worth esteeming. "Don't. Unworthy."

I feel his smile form. "Erianna. For how long must I tell you of your worth before you know it for yourself? Your worth is not determined by how you feel or what anyone else thinks of you. Your worth is found in the One who made you. The Creator loves you. He calls you His own and made you to be a reflection of Himself. That is where your worth comes from. I see you with His eyes. Yes, you are imperfect. But you are worthy."

Valor does not know what I have done, not everything. The Creator does. He cannot love me after that. Even His love must have limits.

"Until you know for yourself how much you are worth, I will remind you." Valor parts our hands so I may see our bloodied skin. "Do you see this?"

I nod.

"These marks represent love and friendship. You are owned by no one. Zavaan has no claim on you. Do you understand me?"

I return my hand to his. "Thank you."

"Now tell me, what is your name?"

It is the name of my husband. Of my daughter. Of my brother. Of the parents of my heart. A watery ghost of a smile, the first in months, tugs at my mouth. "Erianna Rodiharian."

Valor's smile is lit by a flame of joy that cannot be extinguished. "Good Girl. Do not forget it."

CHAPTER FOUR

VALOR

August 6th

Nearly every waking hour of the day is filled with hard riding. My queen cannot afford to be exposed with only me for protection. The encounter with the tracker, Zavaan's third she later told me, underscores the necessity for reinforcements. I will not be satisfied until she is hemmed in by a fortress and guarded by the best warriors in Malesiir.

The day before we turn onto the road to Parse Kítaran, I feel my queen's temper begin to rise. By noon, when we stop to eat and water Granite, she is in fighting form. Her melancholic irascible temperament is entirely different from that of the princess I knew. Thus, I do not realize her ire is directed at me until she stands before me, glaring balefully.

"My Queen?" I ask pleasantly. As it used to, my politeness irritates her further.

"Lied," she declares.

"I have not, but what do you think I lied about?" The guessing game of interpreting her single word sentences is trying. I drag out my patience by reminding myself she and I once got along quite well without words when it suited us.

She stabs her finger toward the road. "Malsihra."

"Aye, that is the way to the capital, but we are not going there."

"Lies." She turns aside and goes to my pack then begins to separate out a portion of food into the pouch on her belt.

She means to leave me.

I will not allow it.

I rise from my rest and approach her. She brandishes a knife at me without looking up from her task. That statement I understand perfectly.

"I told you I was taking you to Parse Kítaran. This is the way. We are nearly to the turn north that will lead us into the high valley. After that, it is half a day's ride into Parse. I told you this before. Do you not remember?"

She pauses, looking unsure of herself for a moment. She glances sidelong at me, weighing my words.

"Have you forgotten that I do not lie?" I gently remind her.

She shakes her head, returning to task. "Everyone lies."

Instead of simply telling her to trust me as she once did, I ask her to hand me the maps. She acquiesces and, after a stubborn pause, deigns to turn her attention to the path I point out.

"This river will lead us into the high valley. I am not lying to you. I have never lied to you." When she still looks unconvinced, I grin roguishly. "I swear, if I ever decide to take you back to Malsihra, I will warn you first. That way, when I haul you there kicking and screaming, at least I can say I never lied about it."

Her eyes narrow on me. "Dare."

I slap the maps into her palm with a wink. She hits me over the head with them then returns them to the pack.

I chuckle. My friend is still in there somewhere after all.

※ ※ ※

August 7th

My queen is ill at ease until we veer off the road to the capital and begin the ascent into Parse. She lays her head between my shoulders, gazing at the river. Before long, her arms go lax around my waist as she succumbs to her exhaustion. I am not the least bit surprised. I wondered at her never waking with nightmares in the middle of the night. After a few nights, I realized she barely sleeps. Last night, I doubt she slept a bit. I wrap a hand around hers to prevent her from falling. Twining my fingers with hers is unnecessary, but I do it anyway. She tightens her hand around mine in response. The night we spent in the cave, she slept soundly and woke more lucid than before. I hope she is able to sleep deeply until we arrive.

Granite slips into a smooth running walk of his own accord, knowing that home is ahead. My queen stirs awake as we pass through the gorge leading into the valley. I considered taking her to my home for the time being, but I only have one bedroom, and if there is a single thing I learned from our previous time together, it is that I ought to conduct myself in such a way as to be above reproach with my actions. Things would have gone much better for both of us had we avoided even the appearance of immoral behavior.

So to the Tareth's home we will go. If that does not suit her, perhaps she could stay with Nev, but she would be safer in Kragorn's defensible home. I am also hopeful that Leelah will be able to help her.

I hear my queen's breath catch as the valley opens up before us. "Welcome to Peaceful Haven."

"Beautiful," she whispers.

I narrate the vistas, acquainting her with all that she sees. I stop at the bottom of the path that will lead us up to the Tareth's home and point to the end of the valley. "My home is down that way. If you like, I can show you tomorrow. You may also collect Sacha."

Her hand tightens in mine. "Here? Not sold?"

I glance at her over my shoulder. "Of course she is here. I would never sell your horse."

Thank you, she mouths with bright eyes. Getting her back to doing her favorite things has to be of some use. We can even continue sparring if she wishes. Her days are hers to spend as she sees fit so long as she is in Parse.

We head up the path to Kragorn's home and pass beneath the gate into the courtyard, scattering chickens as we go. Within moments Leelah is sprinting out the front door toward us.

"Thank the Almighty! Kragorn received a summons to report to the capital immediately weeks ago because the king had been killed and the queen was missing and we had no idea what happened to you! How dare you not send word to us! After all this time we were afraid that you had been..." Words pour from Leelah in a torrent that causes my queen to stiffen behind me.

"Leelah!" I interrupt her in the authoritative voice she has rarely occasioned to hear from me. It silences her as intended. When I swing down from Granite and she sees that I am not alone, abject shock rearranges her worried expression.

"You found her," she whispers then comes back to herself. She curtsies deeply. "Your Majesty. Our prayers have been answered."

"Queen Erianna Rodiharian, allow me to introduce to you Leelah Tareth, Kragorn's wife," I say somewhat formally. "If it is well with you, Leelah, I hope that you would extend Queen Erianna your hospitality. She has decided to remain in Parse for the time being." I fix Leelah with a look where my queen cannot see that says there is more to the story.

Leelah smiles warmly. "I cannot think of anything I would like better. I have felt cheated that you lot all had the pleasure of Queen Erianna's company while I have not." Leelah extends a hand to her in greeting and waits patiently while she dismounts. Before I can warn Leelah that she might get hit for her presumption, she pulls Erianna into a hug. My queen stiffens but does not fight Leelah which is progress, I suppose. "I am so thankful you are safe, Your Majesty. And I am so sorry for your terrible loss. My heart aches for you."

My queen nods and steps back. "Thank... Thank..." She squeezes Leelah's hand to convey the words she cannot express.

With no sense for the solemnity of the moment, half of Leelah's brood spill out of the house, rushing toward us. I crouch down to greet them and am rocked back with hugs and shouts of "Uncle! Uncle!" They talk over each other, trying to be the first to tell me of their latest adventures.

"I hope you do not mind a bit of noise, Queen Erianna." Leelah comments.

"Not... mind," she replies.

I glance up to see a faint smile gracing her mouth at the children's exuberance. The sight is intercepted by the appearance of a small toad inches from the end of my nose.

Micah pulls the toad back to hug him then extends him again. "Look! He's my favorite that I raised from the tadpoles. He sleeps in my room every night! Isn't he the best!"

Realizing he has an audience, Micah turns to the queen, presenting his pet. "Isn't he amazing!"

"Micah, ladies do not like to—" Leelah's gentle admonishment is cut off by my queen who kneels down to the child and holds out her hands.

"You hafta be real careful with him," Micah sternly warns the cuirass-clad Warrior Queen as he places the toad in her hands.

"His name?" She asks with raised brows.

"His name is Meemp," Micah informs her. "If you listen at night, that's what he says his name is."

The woman with the heart of a warrior who has endured soul-crushing horrors smiles and carefully pats the toad with her index finger. It takes all of one breath for me to know that no matter how I try, I will never get my heart back from her.

Leelah grins at me. "Queen Erianna, I think we are going to be the best of friends," she says to subtly inform me she knows my mind. Not that I would dare think there. For her own sake, I will not drag Leer's wife down that road again.

The queen raises a brow at Leelah then stutters her way through saying, "Not…queen. Just…something…anything." She casts pleading eyes my way.

"What would you like to be called?" I ask.

Her eyes unfocus and flick back and forth as if she is sifting through her memories until she winces.

"Is your given name not appropriate?" Leelah asks.

"She is right," I acknowledge, following some of her thoughts. "Anonymity is necessary for the time being. Would *Anna* be acceptable?"

She hesitates then nods.

Micah sets a hand on my queen's shoulder. "It's alright if you can't talk much. My sister Ivy couldn't talk for a long time either."

The nine year-old girl hangs back near me, warily inspecting the stranger. I lean close to her and whisper, "Anna is my friend. Would you help your mother look after her?"

Ivy nods, bouncing her long brown braids.

The queen gives Meemp the toad back to Micah who takes on the responsibility of introducing his six year-old sister. "This is Lois. She became my sister last year. She thinks of good games to play. And those are my other sisters," he points across the courtyard.

Leelah's eldest and youngest join us. "Thank you Karris," Leelah accepts her infant from the twelve year-old girl and introduces her to Anna.

"And this is Fialla," Leelah turns the babe so she may see her.

My queen is completely still, not even breathing as she gazes upon the smallest Tareth. Leelah is quick to understand her reaction and offers, "Would you like to hold her?"

She searches Leelah's open face as if asking if she is really allowed. Slowly she extends her hands, but pauses, looking at them then down at herself. She frowns at the collection of weaponry. She comes to me, hands me the ornate dagger then sweeps her cloak aside and gestures at the cuirass laces. Only after I rid her of it does she take little Fialla. She cradles the babe close, admiring her.

Leelah asks conversationally, "Do you have any children, Anna?"

I cringe. Leelah knows full well she must have lost her babe.

"Had," my queen sadly replies. "Illyanna."

Her mother's name. My poor sweet friend. How cruel to have lost her mother and the one who was to bear her name.

"I am so sorry. How long ago was that?" Leelah's sincerity and compassion form a bridge between the two women.

My queen frowns. "Don't know."

Leelah rests a hand on her shoulder. "It is challenging to keep up with the passing of time after such loss. It is the second week of August. When did you lose her?"

Tears leave tracks down her face. Without hesitation or stutter she says, "May Fourteenth."

A month to the day after I was at the castle. Why did I not hear of it?

"Nev," my queen suddenly says, then looks to me. "*Nev.*" More urgently this time.

"I can bring her to you if you would like?"

"Now," she insists. "Please."

"Come, Anna. We will go put tea on," Leelah wraps an arm around her shoulders and guides her back to the house with a reassuring glance for me that says, *I will look after her.*

I mount Granite and set out across the valley, wondering how best to prepare Nev for the state of her friend.

※ ※ ※

Leelah and my queen are seated on the couch by the fire when Nev and I quietly enter the great room.

"If you grow tired of holding her, I will take her back," I hear Leelah tell my queen who stares transfixed at baby Fialla nestled in the crook of her arm.

Why, Creator? Why heal her and fulfill that deep desire in her heart only for her to lose her babe? I do not understand.

An answer is not forthcoming.

"Erianna?" Nev speaks from my side. The queen does not look up.

"You must gain her full attention. She cannot hear you otherwise," I murmur, guiding Nev across the great room.

Nev sits next to her friend and gently strokes her head until she looks up, blinking to bring the world back into focus.

"Nev?" She whispers.

Nev hugs her close, simply being with her for a time.

"Valor, will you help me with the tea?" Leelah hooks her arm through mine, not giving me a choice in the matter.

When the door to the kitchen closes behind us, Leelah's expression opens. "What happened?" She hisses, for once speechless.

I tell her the little that I have been able to gather. When she asks why our left hands are wrapped in clean strips of linen, I explain truthfully and with no lack of derogatory descriptors for Zavaan.

"Leelah, I am worried for her," I confess. "I have known her to be introspective at times and thoughtful with her words, but never has she been at a loss for them. I do not know what to do."

Leelah busies her hands with the tea tray while thinking aloud. "Alright. I have some ideas. First, I think the best thing—"

"Valor!" Nev bursts into the kitchen sedately followed by the queen. "Why are you still here? You must warn Lorennt!"

"Of what? I know he must be made aware his sister lives, but Anders would have told him of the attack weeks ago."

Nev is stricken as she declares, "Chases Zavaan!"

"That means something to you? She has been saying that since we found each other."

Nev is dumbfounded. "It should to you as well! Gavin Chase, the man you met in Grass Lake, has been in the castle all winter posing as one of the trade ambassadors from the Commonwealth. He is Reuel Zavaan!"

Chase *is* Zavaan. The snippets my queen has said all fall into place as Nev continues. "Lorennt never trusted him or liked him because Chase was far too interested in Erianna, but Grandileer and Erianna decided he was merely curious about her and did not think he had any designs on her."

"Fools," the queen scolds herself as she passes Fialla back to her mother.

Nev is beside herself. "Erianna and Chase were something like friends. She sometimes included him in her schemes, and he even trained her at knives until she became pregnant." Nev smacks her forehead and turns to the queen. "He was trying to drive a wedge between you and Grandileer from the very beginning! There was that story he told, the dancing, the training Grandileer did not approve of… All of it."

The queen's shoulders slump. Her face burns with shame.

Zavaan had access to my queen all winter.

One curse breeds another in my mind. I turn over the things she said. *Everyone lies. Leave Chase, Zavaan keep.* She must have left the slain king's side when Chase came for her only to realize Zavaan had finally caught her. With the foundation laid, I want to know everything that happened and hopefully better understand what deeper things torment my friend. "Nev, start at the beginning and tell me what happened."

"No, there is not time! You must warn Lorennt! He may not like Chase, but he would allow him into the castle without hesitation. All the Rodiharians are in the gravest danger!"

My queen lays a hand on Nev's rounded belly then turns fierce winter eyes on me. We are of one mind. With the death of Grandileer and his heir, that branch of the Rodiharian line is broken. Prince Lorennt has been moved from the lesser son to the only son—his illegitimate heir from castoff to indispensable.

I return the king's dagger to his widow. "We will not let them fall prey to Zavaan."

She tersely nods.

Leelah stands behind the two women, looking every inch the fighter Kragorn trained her to be. "I will look after them while you ride for Malsihra. We will hole-up here until you or Kragorn returns."

I would rather stay to protect them myself or bring them all with me. The first inkling would leave Prince Lorennt and my kingdom at risk, the second would place these women more at risk than if they remain in this fortress home.

Still, I ask of the woman I am loath to part from, "You are well with this plan, my Queen?"

She rolls her eyes, revealing the imp still hiding somewhere deep within. "Lorennt Chase is Zavaan."

Warning Lorennt has been her idea all along.

I incline my head. "So you have been telling me, and I was too thick to understand."

She looks to the other women then shrugs as if to say, *Do we look surprised? We know how thick-witted you are.*

I grin. "Do you have any message I ought to carry to Lorennt?"

She removes her signet ring and places it in my palm. "Trust you."

The burden of that trust is heavy, especially with my sovereign's death weighing on my conscience. "Shall I convey that you wish to recover here for a time then assist in the hunt for Zavaan?" I do not want there to be any more room for miscommunication when there is already so much.

A terse nod as her hand settles on the dagger, then she gasps. "Give back mine." She points to the dagger and to her skirt.

Nev looks at the dagger. "Is that not yours?"

"My Leer's."

Nev touches the queen's leg through her skirt. "Where are your daggers?"

The queen blushes. "Leer hid."

"Why?" Nev asks, perplexed. The queen averts her gaze, so Nev explains to me, "Grandileer commissioned a twin dagger for her, and she always wears a hidden dagger on her thigh."

"Will Lorennt be able to find them?"

The queen's sharp, threatening gaze makes me conceal a smile. "He better."

"I will retrieve them. Anything else?"

She plucks at her shirt. "Necessities."

"I will do my best."

These are the three women I am responsible for and have vowed to protect. I am leaving them and the children alone with an enemy hunting them. This is ludicrous. "I should not go. Not until Kragorn returns."

"That could be weeks," Leelah argues. "You know that he has built me a fortress so he can be at ease leaving me for months at a time. And we have the Warrior Queen on our side." She winks at that woman who inclines her head. Leelah hugs my side and whispers, "Hopefully, we will be improved when you return, *hmm*?"

"I am counting on you," I reply, squeezing her tightly.

Nev thanks me for rescuing Erianna and hugs me farewell. As promised, I have been a devoted guardian to the young woman. Over the past months I have come to appreciate why Lorennt loves her. In my whole life, I have never met a more guileless, kind, and loyal soul than Nev. I am certain that between her genuine affection and Leelah's expertise they will be able to help my queen find her way out of the darkness she is lost in.

"Walk me out?" I request of my queen.

When we step into the twilit courtyard, I find myself at a loss for words. The thoughts bounding through my head should not be spouted loosely, so I say nothing.

"Gone long?" She asks.

I latch onto that. "I will be gone no more than ten days, hopefully less. Please listen to Leelah and do as she asks. No adventures, are we clear?"

She shrugs.

"I will give Leelah permission to tie you to a kitchen chair if I must. I want your word that you will not leave this home until I return," I insist.

She huffs. "My word."

Granite is displeased when I retrieve him from his rest. He stomps and butts me with his head as I ready him.

I return the cuirass to my queen then exchange the empty water skin and sacks of food for the full ones Leelah provided.

I hold out my left hand to Erianna, and she places hers in mine. "Do not forget."

She brings our bandaged entwined hands to her cheek in farewell. For all the sincerity in the gesture, it serves well in place of taking her in my arms as I long to do.

Minutes later I ride under the gate that Leelah lowers into place behind me. Next to her on the wall-walk, Nev and my queen stand arm in arm.

Creator, protect them all.

CHAPTER FIVE

ERIANNA

"Well it is just us women now," Leelah says brightly, heading toward the stairs. "I have been saving something for just such an occasion."

Her voice trails off as she descends, and Nev turns to follow. I remain behind, watching the storm-eyed warrior ride away until he has passed from my sight. I glance down at my bandaged left palm. Love and friendship. Not bondage. My warrior is trying to drag me from the depths again. Strange that I should feel his absence more than his presence.

Nev returns to my side, wrapping an arm around my waist. "He will be back soon. Come. You will like Leelah. She is high spirited like you. Rather, more so even than you."

The evening is spent listening to the jubilant prattle of Leelah's children and cuddling Fialla. Leelah does not believe in the nonsense of spoiling a babe by holding it too much, so whenever she is not at her mother's breast, I hold her.

It is bittersweet. Had Illyanna not been taken from me in the worst of violations, I would have given birth to her sometime in the next couple weeks. It pains me to hold Fialla, knowing that I will never again hold my and Leer's only babe, but it also soothes my childless mother's heart.

I half attend to Nev and Leelah's conversation after the children are put to bed. I should be happy to see Nev, I did miss her, but that brighter emotion is elusive. At most, I feel an easing in her presence. I do not have to explain as much to her. She knows most of my story and needs little help understanding what happened next. Being with the women is preferable to being alone even though I do not desire to participate. It shows me that the world has not ended. It also distracts, in a minuscule sort of way.

Leelah presents us with a dessert of some kind, but I do not eat any. Nev thinks that is strange which brings to my attention that it is strange. I should want dessert, but food does not have much taste anymore. My stomach tells me I am hungry, so I eat when necessary, but no longer do I enjoy it.

I do not enjoy much of anything.

I drag out bedtime for as long as possible, but eventually, Leelah lifts baby Fialla from my arms, and Nev guides me to the stairs leading from the great room. Leelah loans Nev and I chemises to sleep in. It occurs to me how tall Leelah is when the chemise pools on the floor at my feet instead of ending at my ankles.

Nev and I climb into the bed of our shared room after extinguishing the candles. I lie on my back staring up at the wooden ceiling as Nev speaks softly. A few of her words find their way in, so I turn away from her. But she is Nev. When words fail, her presence alone is enough to speak volumes. She wraps an arm around me, holding me tightly. Her warmth at my back breaks through whatever dam sometimes barricades my tears.

It should be Leer at my back. Leer in my bed. Leer's voice singing me to sleep. Leer's babe in my womb. But he is gone from my reach forever.

His last words repeat over and over. *"Forgive me. This will hurt, but I see no other choice to ensure you escape. Stay hidden, my Dear. I love you."*

I should have held onto him. I should not have allowed him to hide me. I should have insisted we try to escape together or not at all. I should have run between Zavaan and he at swords and done something, anything, to prevent his death.

This does not simply hurt, Leer. This is agony without end.

※ ※ ※

August 8th

I cried the well of tears down to the dregs last night. Not that it will stay emptied. Ever it refills, and I must drain it again.

Leelah sets a plate of food before me at the kitchen table. I pick up my fork but am halted by a small hand on my arm and Nev's larger hand on my other. Leelah gives thanks to the Creator for the bounty, but my memories are louder than the present. I do not hear her words to know when the blessing ends, I only feel the removal of the hands from my arms.

I scoop up the food on my plate, one necessary bite at a time. Nev touches my arm, calling my attention to herself. "You look so thin, Anna. Have you not been eating?"

I shrug. Gestures are easier than words, but I add, "Some."

Nev fusses, "Well, you must eat more." She sounds like Lorennt.

"Tell, Anna, what did you survive on until Valor found you?" Leelah asks.

"Game," I reply, scooping up a bite of eggs.

"Oh, I am sorry, Anna. I do not know you as well as the others. You will have to explain further to me."

I sigh, dredging the tumult to remember what I ate and how I procured it. "Mostly... rabbit. Snared then... roasted."

"Rabbit only?" She exclaims with flashing amber eyes. "You cannot eat only rabbit! You will starve!"

I glance at Nev with a raised brow. Her look says this is news to her also.

Leelah demands, "Tell me, have you been vomiting and has your head ached without end?" At my nod, she slaps her palms on the table and stomps about the kitchen, banging cupboard doors. "That fool man! What was Valor thinking? He knows better! No wonder you cannot string three words together. The first thing to go is your mind."

I fist my left hand at her admonishments of my friend and rise to his defense. "He fed me... other... Asked if... with child."

Leelah stills. "Are you?"

"No."

She resumes her bustle then plunks a mug before me and a slice of bread slathered in honeyed butter. "You will eat all of this and the eggs."

Nev hides her titter at my indignant expression. Queens give orders, they do not take them. The formidable woman only stares me down dictatorially. With a half-smile of appeasement, I set the mug to my lips and pull the thick, rich liquid into my mouth.

"Cream!" I ask of the woman who is clearly more loon than I.

"Mostly. With honey," she affirms.

I look askance at Nev. She offers an encouraging smile. "That is alright, Anna. You enjoy lots of cream in your tea. And did you not say that Valor made you drink fermented milk when you were recovering after Grass Lake?"

I grumble. "Decency of a cookie though."

The women chuckle as I decide to endure Leelah's ministrations for the time being.

※ ※ ※

August 10th

After two full days under Leelah's bossy yet oddly considerate thumb, my headache has subsided, and my thoughts are not so difficult to order. I had attributed the constant ache in my head to anguish and crying, which is true, but eating the rich food has helped considerably.

Leelah and Nev have encouraged me to tell them, together and individually, what happened. I have explained vaguely that the Ruphiri ambushed us, Leer fought Zavaan and died to give me a chance at escape which I could have had by fleeing to the seaside castle, but I placed my trust in Chase who turned out to be Zavaan. I escaped near the Ascent. Valor and I found each other a week later.

I have largely ignored questions about Illyanna and what happened to me while I was Zavaan's prisoner. With intentionality, I speak of him aloud as *Zavaan*, but it does not suit him. *Zavaan* makes him sound like a powerful entity, which he is, but I would rather belittle him. *Reuel* is too personal. It brings to mind murmurs in the dark that he bid me speak while he acquainted himself with my body. *Chase* was the facade of a man whom I thought of nearly as a friend. *Deceiver* is more encompassing of who he is and seems to suit him best, but I would appear weak to not speak his true name.

This is just one of the winding, endlessly looping trails my thoughts run down. I become so lost on those trails that it makes me conversationally useless.

Leelah approaches me the third day after Valor left with a stack of blank paper and pen. "Here. I think this may help you sort through what happened. I know that you are not ready to speak of it, but you are obviously dwelling on it. I would like you to write down chronologically what happened. Then, when you become rutted in thought, write down what you are thinking. Just get it out."

I eye her. "You would read it?"

Leelah presses the stack into my hands. "Only if you wish me to, but certainly not without your permission. This was helpful for Ivy. When she came to us, she could not speak at all. I taught her to read and

40

write, then she filled books with her thoughts." Leelah's fierce expression explains more than her words. "Ivy wished for me to know her story, and so I do. Even if you are the only one to ever see your thoughts put to paper, I believe it will be of certain benefit to release what occupies your mind, allowing you to make sense of it all."

I accept the stack with a nod of thanks and head into the light of day. I plant myself upon the wall-walk under a summer sky, staring across the grassy lawn kept clear of trees for defensive purposes by Leelah's goats. They bleat and grunt, happily wagging short tails while gnawing the bark off trees. A lazy long-haired dog of enormous size watches over them from the shade of the forest edge. My mind draws a comparison between that deadly canine, faithfully guarding his herd and the equally deadly wolf that would seek to devour them. The goats obey the dog who confines them to the edge of the forest, but they have no fear of lying down with him and nibbling affectionately at his coat. Micah says they have never lost a goat in the time Tamraz has guarded them. A warning growl is all it takes for the goats to group tightly while Tamraz ends the threat to his charges.

I pick up the pen and paper to begin writing, hoping that my Tamraz returns before the Wolf finds me.

❊ ❊ ❊

At dinner time, Nev finds me lying on my belly under the blushing sky. A stack of papers covered with writing on both sides is weighted down against the breeze by Leer's dagger. I am nearing the last of the blank sheets of paper Leelah provided. To make sense of things, I went back to the beginning, all the way back to Limba. I lingered over memories of my mother and Liddy then cried my way through their deaths. I glance at the sky above, deciding I have enough light to write for another hour. I was skeptical about the usefulness of this activity, but I can feel my mind reordering itself as I force thoughts to specific moments in time so I may transfer them to paper. I have written my way through my years in Limba and have reached the time I spent with Valor in Grass Lake. Thinking of those weeks is a bright spot in my day, despite the night descending around me. I take the time to describe specific meals we shared, jokes we laughed about, meeting Sacha and learning to ride.

Another chain falls away as I write about it. The commander has again become Valor to me. It seems silly that using his name, such a little thing, brings me tangible relief when the rest of my life is misery.

Valor's name is no longer banished from my vocabulary. We may be friends again.

"Please tell Leelah I shall be in when it is too dark or when I run out of paper. Whichever happens first," I offhandedly say to Nev without glancing up.

"Of course," she whispers and bends to squeeze my shoulder.

I return to my writing, scrunching my letters to fit as much in as possible. Even though there were life threatening and gut wrenching moments with Valor, I am eased by remembering his constancy. I did not hide from him, and he did not hide from me. A fear I have not voiced is dashed apart by remembering his character. Valor was not part of Leer's scheme. He would never have agreed to it. Had he known what Leer allowed to happen to me or known Leer's intentions to prop me up on the throne while making children on Jaleh, Valor would not have taken me to Malsihra. He would have hidden me in the Midlands or anywhere on the Continent rather than condemning me to that existence.

I unwind the bandage from my palm and trace the cut that has scabbed. *Erianna Valor's Friend.* No matter what.

CHAPTER SIX

VALOR

August 11th

To say that Lorennt is angry upon hearing Gavin Chase and Reuel Zavaan are one and the same would be a lie because of how little justice it does to his feelings on the matter. For the sake of ensuring the enemy is not already within these walls, I begin by stating that the queen is alive and delivering her message to him. After watching Lorennt throw a few chairs and flip over the oak table in the war room, I begin to appreciate why my queen insisted I be the one to deliver this news. She knows that Lorennt would never harm her, but she does not well tolerate seeing the full force of a man's temper.

"I should have run him through months ago! I should have run him through the moment I knew his interest in Erianna was far from benign! Why in the accursed depths would she not listen to me!" He hurls another chair into the stone wall. It breaks into kindling. "I am going to tear him apart!"

Lorennt struggles to think past his rage. Unfortunately, this is the mildest of the news. As calmly as I can, I explain what my queen has been able to tell me. The shadows that already line the prince's face deepen as I speak.

For my friend's sake, I skim over what little I know that happened between her and Zavaan. Lorennt will not allow my evasion and pointedly asks, "Did he ravish my sister?"

"She says no, and I am inclined to believe her."

Lorennt's upper lip curls as I elucidate. It occurs to me that he may name my queen the foul thing she called herself. If he does, Lorennt's tangible anger will not be the only ire felt in this room. To help him

43

land on the right way of thinking, I add, "She is disgusted with herself for what she had to do to earn his trust, though I have assured her she acted intelligently, and the guilt rests entirely on Zavaan."

Muscles pulse in Lorennt's jaw as he grits his teeth. "Believe me when I say, had she not given him something, he would have taken everything." He rises, scraping the chair across stone. "I will see her now. Where is she?"

I rest my hands on the arms of my chair, projecting a relaxed posture while inwardly preparing to fend off the punches Lorennt may attempt to land at this bit of news. "My queen refused to return to Malsihra. I tried to reason with her, but she made it quite clear that she would rather spill my blood than willingly come here. I placed her somewhere safe and made certain she understands it is a temporary arrangement."

Red colors Lorennt's neck. "You will bring her to me immediately. I do not care if she wants to be here. She is not in her right mind to make such decisions."

"And why is that, exactly?" I quietly demand. "She was well when I saw her this spring. What happened that so thoroughly broke her?"

"What do you mean *'when you saw her?'* To my knowledge you have not seen her since last autumn."

Without flinching, I explain, "I stumbled across the three of you in the city the day the king asked me to report to him. I did not want to intrude on your party or approach her without Grandileer's permission. Once I determined that she seemed to be happy and well, I moved on to the castle."

Lorennt's eyes narrow. "She lost the babe a month later. She was altered after that and never recovered."

I lean forward on my elbows, staring him down. "I could believe that except I know with certainty there is more to it. As my queen is barely conversant, I need you to fill in the blanks so I may better help her heal."

Lorennt barks a derisive laugh and severs my temper's leash. "You mean so that you may further your ends and sooner see my sister in your bed."

I charge the crowned prince, pinning him against the wall with my forearm pressed across his throat. My words snarl between bared teeth. "I swore to my fallen king that I would protect his wife and see her restored from the wrongs he did her!"

His eyes flicker with disbelief. I release him and withdraw the two letters from my pocket then shove them against his chest. With a glare he takes them. Hagan's letter does not surprise him, but the second letter knocks his feet from beneath him. He stares vacantly through the paper after reading it then tosses it aside.

"What happened, Lorennt? My friend is hurting. She needs help."

He hangs his head in his hands. "I do not know everything that happened. Leer and Erianna were intensely private about their relationship."

"But you know something," I prod. "I vowed to see my queen restored. To her family and to her throne."

Lorennt's eyes are guilt ridden as he fixes me with his weighted stare. What part has he played in this story? Is he protecting himself as much as his brother?

The guilt is deposed by resolve as he shakes his head. "I have no way of knowing what they would and would not want you to know of their sins. Both of them made mistakes, not just Leer. Some of what plagues Erianna is her own guilt." He gains his feet, crossing his arms and throwing up a mask of disdain. "Since you think you know my sister so well, you can deduce what happened or ask her to tell you. I will not speak of it."

My fists curl and uncurl. Then curl again. Challenge lights the prince's face, daring me to throw the first punch and give us both the longed for fight. If my queen did not love him and need me to return to her expediently, I would yield to the impulse.

Instead, I relax my posture then compose my expression. In a polite voice, I respond, "As you see fit, Your Highness. I will aid my queen to the best of my abilities then see her returned to her family."

"You, Commander, will bring her to me immediately. You have no authority to do other than what I order," Lorennt demands, his rage fueled by my tight control.

I smile cunningly and slide the ring from my finger for him to see. "Actually, I have every authority. My new title is *Hand of the Queen*. She has given me three orders that I am in the process of carrying out while fulfilling my last vows to my king."

Lorennt refuses the ring I extend, scorching me with his glare. "What are her orders? If she is so little conversant, I disbelieve they originated with her."

I return the ring to my smallest finger where it fits snugly. "The queen's orders are these, in her exact words. 'Lorennt Chase is Zavaan.' I have informed you and revealed as much as I can on that front. Her second order is to 'Hunt Zavaan' then *'Vreh Král Vragh,'* which translates to *Kill the King Killer*. She is baying for his blood and is determined to help see it spilled, though I will tell you, she is terrified of him and also seems to think I am the only one capable of bringing him down. I told her I would assist in hunting Zavaan and seeing him punished for his crimes, but she must first be recovered. In the meantime, I will speak to whoever is coordinating the hunt for the Wolves and give them them the pertinent information."

Lorennt has never disliked me more than he does in this moment, knowing he cannot challenge his queen's decisions that were logically given, if not spoken. He hates that I am now serving her. "What is her majesty's third order?" He mockingly asks.

I grin fiendishly. "She wants her daggers back. Or else."

Lorennt shakes his head. "Did she tell you why Leer took them from her?"

With a shrug I say, "I do not see how it matters," though I am curious.

"You do not think it matters? This I will tell you. Leer hid them to protect her from herself when she became unstable after the loss of the babe. Ask her what she did when she found them."

That gives cause for concern, but since she has been tromping through the forests with blades aplenty, I am inclined to think whatever harm he feared has passed. "I shall. Now, will you retrieve them or shall I go after them myself?"

Lorennt drums his fingers on his arms, considering me, then acquiesces. "They are in my room. I will bring them."

"She would also like clothing, necessities, and sufficient funds to care for herself for a few months," I add.

Lorennt halts at the door. "A few months? Let me be clear, Commander. She has one month to get herself back here. I need her help."

"She can barely speak, Lorennt!" I exclaim. "What help do you think she will be to you? She needs at least three months."

"I will give her two, then I insist she returns." The prince grips the pommel of his sword. "If she does not, I will upend this kingdom to find her. Starting with Parse Kítaran."

Intentionally, I wrap my hand around the leather bound hilt of my own sword and meet Lorennt's glower with unwavering resolve. "Let me make one thing clear. My duty is first to the one I serve and second to my kingdom. If you think to force her majesty in a direction she does not wish to go, then you and I will find each other at odds."

"It is going to come to that eventually," Lorennt assures me and jerks open the door.

⁎ ⁎ ⁎

ERIANNA

August 12th

I finish drafting Valor and my story, pausing on that hopeful night when he told me he loved me and wanted to be with me. I find it difficult to believe I was ever so callow that I could not see he had fallen in love with me. The seeds were planted in Grass Lake and tended faithfully throughout their growth until blooming on that night.

Of course, the moment when all could have been realized for us was also the advent of Leer into my life. Those memories toss me in every direction.

From the moment we met, Leer was taken with me. I can see it now. Even giving him no encouragement, he knew he had misjudged me the first day we spent in each other's company. For my part, had I not already set my heart on Valor, Leer would have answered my every hope.

I clutch the stack of papers to my chest and stroll along the wall-walk. The Tareth home has proved itself a refuge to me. The seclusion with only Leelah, the children, and my sweet Nev in this fortress home overlooking the peace and beauty of the high valley is a respite in itself. It is quiet up here, excepting the noises of the children and animals which do not offend.

The children are delightfully honest in their speech and actions. They can be excessively happy or outrageously frustrated, and you do not have to doubt that is the perfect truth of what they are feeling.

And then there is Leelah Tareth. She is nothing like what I imagined Kragorn's wife to be. She is strong, determined, independent, and eccentric to a surprising degree while also being equal parts sensitive, understanding, and intuitive. I can see why Valor brought me to Leelah. She has been encouraging and gentle while empowering me to sort through my emotions and giving me the space to do so. But she is unwavering in her demands that I engage with the people around me at mealtimes and sit with her and Nev in the evenings. She will not allow me to give one-word answers to the questions posed to me. She helps me find the words that I need and expects me to use them. If I were not so grateful, I would have stuck my tongue out at the tyrant and holed up in my room until Valor returns.

I try once again to make him appear solely by wishing, but a different form appears. A woman whistles up the path with swishing skirts, bearing a covered basket.

I scan the courtyard below. Ivy is playing with a kitten under the wisteria trellis. "Ivy! Fetch your mother, please. She has company." The quiet girl tucks the kitten under an arm and darts inside.

I await the woman's approach over the narrow iron gate specially designed for Leelah to be able to raise and lower without assistance. There is nothing threatening about the saunter of the beauty with deep brown hair braided into a thick, intricate plait. Nevertheless, my fingers stroke the hilt of Leer's dagger that is secured in a scabbard borrowed from Kragorn's extensive collection of weaponry.

"Hello there!" She calls up to me. "Is Leelah within?"

"She shall be out in a moment," I reply with a polite smile.

The woman openly observes me. "We have not met. I am Tirzah. Are you visiting the Tareths or recently settled in the valley?"

I quirk a brow. "Perhaps both."

She grins but does not inquire further. Instead, she whistles a lilting song that irritates me. People that can whistle seem intent on annoying the rest of us with their skill.

Leelah exclaims happily, "Open the gate, Anna!" while trotting across the courtyard.

I do as bid after scanning the woods for lurking enemies. Once the woman is within, I lower the gate back into place then resignedly descend at Leelah's beckon.

"I was concerned when I did not see you at Gathering yesterday and brought over some remedies in case you or the children were taken ill and some treats in case you had not."

Leelah peeks into the basket and hugs the woman's shoulders. "You are a true delight!"

"Is Kragorn still away?" She asks.

"Alas, yes," Leelah sighs. "But I knew this would be the way of things when we wed. I am proud of him for the work he does."

"*Hmm,*" the woman taps her fingers on the basket's handle. "Is Valor returned yet?"

The obvious interest in her voice slows my steps.

"He is not, but I expect him back in a few days," Leelah replies lightly.

There is an answering smile in the woman's voice at that tidbit. "Good. I know he is a help to you when Kragorn is away. But, oh! I heard something so awful it cannot possibly be true if Valor is expected back soon. I hope you can dispel the rumor before it takes hold in the valley."

Leelah catches sight of me lingering on the stairs. "I hope to be able to, but first, let me introduce you to my friend."

The woman shifts the basket to the crook of one arm and extends a hand to me. I am awkward at this common gesture. People have always bowed to me, or kissed my knuckles if they were favored acquaintances. Queen's do not clasp hands. But I am not a queen right now, so I take the woman's hand.

"Anna, this is my good friend Tirzah. Tirzah, Anna." Leelah's amber eyes glint mischievously as she introduces us. It gives me a moment's pause. What am I missing that is humorous about this situation?

"It is a pleasure to meet you, Anna. How long will you be visiting with Leelah?" Tirzah asks.

"For a time." I fix my appraising gaze on her. Gorgeous violet eyes upturned at the corners return my expression with amusement that places a dimple in one cheek.

Leelah takes the basket from Tirzah and turns us toward the house. "What is this rumor?"

"Oh, that! Knowing Valor is soon to return, I am hardly concerned with it because it could not possibly be true." Tirzah chuckles. "Do not tease me for believing such a thing, but I heard that King Grandileer has been killed."

The grief curled in my belly cracks open like a whip striking my heart.

Zavaan mockingly bows to the king. My Leer roars as he realizes who he battles to save me. Leer fights until his last breath to protect me as the dagger I gave him pierces his heart. It is darkly poetic. I gave him the dagger that would rend his heart just the same as I gave him Zavaan, the enemy that would deal the fatal cut.

His gentle hand is cold in mine that is covered in his blood. The scent of death overwrites the lingering spicy musk of his skin as I plead with him to awake. To open his eyes. To hold me.

Someone *is* holding me. I reach up my hands to grip those on my shoulders, closing my eyes until the warm skin beneath my palms feels more real than Leer's cooling blood.

"Anna. Anna."

I blink, bringing Leelah's face into focus.

"Queen Erianna!" She urgently whispers.

"Leelah." I wrap my arms around her, fighting back tears that I used to be good at damming. "He died to protect me. He hid me, and I watched Zavaan kill him! I should have been at his side! I should have done something! I just cowered and watched him die! I am so sorry!" The words I have not been able to give voice to pour forth in shuddering sobs.

"Shhh," Leelah strokes my hair. "He loved you and did what a good husband should. You could not have affected the outcome. If you had exposed yourself, he would have seen his enemy capture you and then been killed. As it is, he died knowing that he protected his wife and gave her a chance at escape. He died honorably."

"I do not want him to be gone! I want him to mend us and live!"

"I know. I know." Leelah hugs me tightly.

"Is everything alright, Leelah?" I hear Tirzah call from the house.

I turn away, drying my eyes and moving toward my perch on the wall.

"No, you don't," Leelah corrects my path, turning me toward the house then calls back, "We shall be right in."

"I do not want company," I argue, watching Tirzah spare a concerned glance for me then swish back into the vestibule.

"Well, I do. You can do this for me." She leaves no room for argument.

How did I come to have such bossy friends?

※ ※ ※

For hours, I humor Leelah while Tirzah and she talk animatedly about everything and nothing. We take turns snuggling little Fialla who is the most interesting part of the visit for me. It irks me how frequently Valor's name is upon the beautiful woman's lips. When a squabble breaks out between the girls in the kitchen, I spring up to help Nev resolve it, leaving the others in the great room.

The bickering is dealt with, and the girls sent their separate ways. I plop into a kitchen chair while Nev sets more water to boil for another round of tea.

"What do you think of Tirzah?" She whispers.

I arch a brow. "I do not care for her. But that could be my fault."

"Why?" Nev cocks a hip against the sink and dries her hands.

"There is something indefinable in her that reminds me of Lady Silla Hugler. Certainly not in looks but in personality, maybe? What do you think?"

Nev smirks. "I think you have good instincts."

"How so?"

"Tirzah is to you what Silla is to me." Nev drops that vague explanation then waits.

Furrows groove my brow as I puzzle out what she means. Realization moves the creases perpendicular as my brows rise to my hairline. "*Tirzah* has designs on *Valor?*"

Nev winks.

My question pops out before I think it through. "Does he return her interest?"

"*That* is the question we all have." Nev sits at the table with me, leaning into our topic. "Leelah introduced them, and I have seen him speaking with her several times at Gathering. He also asked her to go on a walk with him before he left with Anders to meet you at the coast. More interesting is that Tirzah is one of several eligible friends Leelah has introduced to Valor. Anders says that she is on a mission to find Valor a wife."

I sit back in my chair. An angry flush heats a path up my chest to my ears. Leelah is bossy *and* meddlesome.

Tirzah's interest in Valor is not surprising. I have always known that Valor is desirable. A woman would be a fool not to see it.

"*My beautiful idiot.*" Valor's silver eyes burn into mine, willing me to see what he told me without words.

That was ages ago, but—mess that I am—I cannot stifle the possessive feelings unfurling in my chest.

Valor claimed me as his friend! I clench my fingertips into my scabbed palm. He claimed me, and I claimed him. He is my Hand, the Hand of the Queen. It is part of what he vowed to me on that day and why he accepted my ring and my order to do what he thought was best to achieve my goals. Valor and I are inextricably bound. That entitles me to an opinion.

I gain my feet and drag out my austere queen's mask. "Come, Nev. If Leelah has a say in who Valor weds, then certainly you, his ward, and I, his queen, also have a say. I wish to know this Tirzah who makes designs on my warrior."

There is too much humor in Nev's smile for me to be ignorant of the direction of her thoughts. Though it is not somewhere I could ever go with him again, I know her mind.

Leelah's expression shifts to amusement when I return more determined than miserable. It occurs to me that this is what she found humorous when she introduced me and Tirzah.

I pin her with a look of reproach that she only grins at, daring me to play her game. If she has any sense, she would heed the warning of my sardonically curved mouth. Instead, Leelah nearly dances in her chair, revealing her lack of wits.

Fine. If that is how it must be, then I will play. I may be out of practice, but I am far from a novice. I take charge of the conversation, drawing Nev in as my partner, and set to learning everything I can about Tirzah of Parse Kítaran.

After a lengthy visit with believably false pleasantries on my part, Leelah and I bid Tirzah farewell. From the gate, we watch her turn out of sight with her basket. Leelah nudges me. "I knew you had some spunk in you somewhere. Valor never keeps dull company."

I turn to glare at her. "Just you wait, Mistress Tareth. I am going to pluck you out of your pond and drop you into my lake this winter season at court and see how you fare. I have some friends of my own I look forward to introducing to you."

I spin on my heel and stalk back into the house, sensing her mischievous grin at my back the entire way.

CHAPTER SEVEN

VALOR

August 14th

The quiet of the forest is oppressive. It has been thus since we departed Malsihra. At the edge of a stream, I water the horses, holding Granite's reins and those of Trent's bay destrier. My opposite hand grips my sword, rocking my fingers on the leather wrapped hilt.

Kragorn's destrier bends his head to the clear stream then jerks upward, skittering to the side. Kragorn places his fingertips in the impressions left in the dirt. He shares a black look with me then moves the animal further upstream. "The forest is as strewn with wolf tracks as it is with fallen leaves."

Thus explaining our presence far from the road to Parse Kítaran and my queen. The soldiers stationed in Malsihra reported an uncommon number of wolf sightings. In the market, farmers and peddlers carry tales of being harassed on the roads, some coming from as far as Aspen Canyon near the Ascent and others coming from the southern towns of White Quarry and Ryebrough. Zavaan hunts my queen, and he wishes us to know it.

The thought of her brokenness burns through my chest in a fiery wind, leaving an acid taste at the back of my throat. Zavaan will suffer at my hands for what he did to her. I yearn for him to cross my path. My vengeance will be slow. Creative. Excruciating. If my queen is not present to be hurt by my torture of him, then torture him I shall.

I lost control with Jarmuth. I should not have allowed her to witness those methods of interrogation. Almighty only knows what it unearthed in her memory.

I feel Kragorn's glower like a verbal rebuke, challenging me to be righteous. Since I summoned Kragorn and Trent in the capital, it has seemed our every conversation centers on the Ruphiri and what they did to our king and queen. The conversations are open-ended with threats and curses hanging in the air. Trent has offered many suggestions on how we could repay Zavaan for the evil he did our queen.

Only one thing angers Trent more than the abuse of women and that is the abuse of children. In the past, I have managed to mostly restrain myself at times when I needed to punish men for such abuse. The most bitter fight Trent and I have had was regarding my restraint when he would rather I have been vengeful. He has already assured Kragorn and I that if he is given the chance to work revenge on Zavaan, we had best not stop him. I replied that Zavaan has plenty of blood in which we may both bathe our hands.

Since then, Kragorn has taken every opportunity to temper my vengeful bloodlust with righteous anger, as he does now. "What help will you be to her if you blacken your soul with vengeance? When has piling sins on top of sins solved any injustice?"

I meet his eyes when I say, "For all that Zavaan has done, anything I do would be less than he deserves—a step toward justice."

Kragorn closes the distance between us, lowering his voice that cracks with power not his own. "'As He who called you is holy, you also be holy in all your conduct.' Or are you above the laws of the Almighty?"

I drop my gaze, gritting my teeth.

"'Be holy, for I am Holy.' Is that not what He says?"

"You did not see her," I bite out. "Our Warrior Queen has been reduced to a feral, fearful shadow."

"Does that invalidate the Almighty's commands?" He challenges.

Conviction cracks the shell of malice around my conscience. Through that fracture, the Voice of Truth whispers, *Vengeance is mine.*

My eyes burn with sudden emotion. "You have not seen her," I say again, unable to dislodge the memory of my queen, dirty, gaunt and fearful, asking if I had poisoned the food I gave her. "She needs me to assure her that I have punished them for what they did."

"Punished, aye, but not taken vengeance. We are not holy enough to carry out vengeance. It belongs to the Almighty. This you know."

With a heavy exhale, I repeat him. "This I know."

"Keep it firm in your mind in the days ahead. As more of what was done to our queen comes to light, you must remain firm. For yourself. For her."

Kragorn claps my shoulder as Trent silently emerges from the trees on the steep opposite bank. He drops into the shallow stream, splashing water. The horses startle. "I cannot see a direct way around the Wolves that will not lead them straight to our queen, but I have a plan."

⁂ ⁂ ⁂

We fan out, combing the woods in a southerly direction. Our voices echo on trees and rocks, calling out for our "missing" queen. We spend the remainder of the day in this manner, crisscrossing the landscape, occasionally calling for Erianna.

Our search does not go unnoticed. In my periphery, earth-hued shadows move through the underbrush and dart across game paths. I whistle sharply. The whistle returns to me twice. I continue searching for her, calling for her, all the while closing in on Kragorn.

The Ruphiri remain out of sight. Hopefully, Trent will have some idea of their numbers. At my signal, he would have spurred ahead then circled wide, coming behind my position, tracking those that are tracking us.

I meet Kragorn at dusk. He confirms that he too saw the beasts slinking through our kingdom. We set up camp for the night and eat our rations while waiting for Trent. It is full dark when the clomp of hooves sounds on the forest duff. The flickering light of our small fire bends across the curve of his vambraces as he tends his mount then tosses his saddlebags and bedroll to the ground.

Between bites of dry, smoked venison, Trent says, "Only two Ruphiri. They have four wolves. Made camp in the thicket a short way back."

"They can see us?" Kragorn asks what he already knows.

"Aye. But only just." Trent tears into his last morsel.

"Well done." I recline against my saddle bags. "We move at second watch."

With every indication given that we mean to stay the night, we complete the ruse by lying down to sleep while Kragorn takes first watch. It is trying to wait for the best moment to strike when there are only two swords to oppose our three, but wait we must. A raucous bloody victory is not what will hasten me back to my queen. There must be no doubt that other Ruphiri are not tracking us nearby, waiting to join their companions in the middle of the night, nor can we risk alerting any to our movements. We must make it impossible to be tracked to Parse Kítaran.

Close to middle night, Kragorn nudges me with his boot. The chirping of crickets is an unbroken trill on the air. Trent rolls to a crouch and shrugs into his quiver. I grip my sword. Damp night air has made it slick against my gauntlet. I rub the leather palms on my pants to dry them. Trent leads the way into the forest, an arrow nocked to his bowstring. He goes wide of our destination, posting atop a downed tree to sight his targets.

I swing to the left of the thicket while Kragorn goes opposite. Time to flush our quarry.

Trent fires three arrows in rapid succession into the heart of the thicket. They buzz and thwack harmlessly into wood, but the effect is instantaneous.

The wolves growl and launch into the forest aglow with moonlight. Trent's arrows sing. Yelps of pain punctuate the crunch of my boots on detritus as Kragorn and I rush the thicket.

What should be two Ruphiri has become three, waiting with drawn steel. We adjust our attack plan to compensate. I grind my teeth to keep silent as I break into the midst of the trio, trusting Kragorn to guard my back. The reckless violence of my melee startles the hardened warriors. They spread apart, parrying the downward arc of my blade. A vicious thrust and jerk opens the leg of one man. Kragorn's angry steel prevents retaliation from the other two. I smack my blade against the wrist of my downed opponent. His sword falls impotent to the ground. A backslash spills blood from his neck.

I jolt forward. The jab of a sword glances off my cuirass, sparing my vitals. Kragorn inserts himself between me and the Ruphiri's next lunge and beats his blade aside, giving me time to pivot into the fight, isolating one of the remaining Ruphiri from the other. Kragorn has already dealt a wound to his off arm that causes it to hang limply. Grunts and groans replace harsh battle cries as I advance my attack. With his one handed grip, he cannot parry the push of my sword that slides up his to drive the point into his face. The pain distracts him. Another few cuts delivers him to the Almighty for judgment.

The ring of steel still echoes in my ears when I turn with raised sword to ensure the fight is over. Kragorn's opponent is at his feet. Trent bursts into the thicket to calm the balking horses tied to a tree. I use the grass then my cloak to wipe the gore from my blade before reuniting it with its scabbard.

Our huffing breaths are the only sound Kragorn and I make as we search the bodies for missives or maps that could reveal Zavaan's plans. There is nothing.

Trent cuts the horses free of their bindings. They disappear into the forest, hopefully to be claimed by a fortunate Malesiirian who could turn them for a profit. Though I doubt we will find anything of pertinence, we each take one of their packs to search later.

"All in one piece?" Trent asks as we run back to our camp.

"Aye," Kragorn grunts, hobbling a bit. I assume his trouble to be in a joint or muscle since no blood darkens his pants, leastwise none of his own.

I add my concurrence as I smother our insignificant fire. In moments our horses are tacked and mounted, the extra packs tied securely in place. "Trent, lead on," I order. He will be able to quickly discern the best place to lay a disappearing track through the forest. "We make for the main road." There, our tracks will blend with others on that well traveled artery. I made a promise to return to my queen within ten days. If we encounter trouble or are tracked by more Ruphiri, my word will be broken.

CHAPTER EIGHT

ERIANNA

August 16th

I have spent ten days in Leelah's home. As lovely as the views are, the confinement within these walls grows tedious. I am too familiar with being locked up without end to find perpetual enjoyment behind walls and gates. Too much of my life in Limba was spent in such a way.

Yesterday, Salome Brighton, the aged widow with who Nev resides, came to visit. I appreciated the serenity of the woman's presence. Her quiet joy and abundant wisdom were a blessing to all of us. Leelah and I have begun to chafe at each other, forcing Nev to play arbitrator between my frigid temper and her hot one. The children also are feeling the strain from being confined within these walls that only allows them the reach of the garden, courtyard, and barn.

If I were less frightened of Zavaan or had I not given my word to Valor, I would have slipped out of the fortress home through the cleverly disguised sally port I found two days past. But I am, and I have, so I don't.

I shift my attention from the path into the valley to the paper spread out on the rock wall. Karris showed me how to make colored paints from the flowers and seeds we gathered in Leelah's garden. We spread our art upon the wall-walk, dipping brushes into the watery colors to fill pages upon pages of paper for amusement. We intend to dye some old, stained fabric later to refashion into aprons and various serviceable items.

Karris suggested sewing infant clothes for Fialla, but I cannot bring myself to do that again. In my parlor at the castle is a pile of infant clothes sewn from expensive cloth that Illyanna never wore.

I let myself remember her for a moment on the day that she quickened. There was such wonder on Leer's face when he felt his daughter moving in me. The great king never tired of laying a hand on my belly "to hold his daughter," as he liked to say.

Tears prick my eyes, and I return to swatching the blue paint across my paper before memories of Leer's wonder blend into memories of his horror and grief at finding her dead in my arms in a pool of blood.

Karris asked if we should make red paint, but I have had my fill of red coating my hands and my person.

"This blue is still not dark enough," I comment. "I want deep, sapphire blue, not sky blue."

Karris leans over my paper. "There are some berries in the woods that should darken the shade. Perhaps when Uncle returns he could take us to gather them."

"I would like that," I agree. Inwardly, I have begun to worry. Valor does not break his word. He promised ten day or less. Today is the tenth day. He should be here.

※ ※ ※

I haunt the wall at every opportunity for the rest of the day.

Karris and I dye the old fabrics then hang them out to dry. We bring a sewing basket out of doors then stitch in the sunshine until dark. After dinner, I carry my mug of spiced tea to walk the top of the boundary once more.

Leelah finds me after putting the children to bed, long past my finding of the bottom of my mug of tea. "He will come back. Maybe tomorrow."

"He said ten days. He does not lie to me," I counter. "Something is wrong."

"You do not know that. Maybe he was delayed. There could be bad weather, or a hundred insignificant things could have happened outside of his control." She smiles kindly.

"Or he never made it to Malsihra. He could be captured. He could be dead. He could be bleeding out in the woods. Or—"

"Hush!"

My words break the facade I did not know Leelah held.

"I know what could happen! I watched Kragorn and Valor ride across the Continent to retrieve you! I went almost six months without seeing my husband! Months without letters! Don't dare tell me of all that could go wrong. Well I know it!" Her strident voice echoes in the night air. "He did not even know I was pregnant with Fialla until the few days he broke off from your company upon reaching Chiselm. Then I gave birth to her while he was in the North helping Valor hold the kingdom together."

Guilt niggles at me, but it is quickly dissolved. Leelah had reason to fear losing those she loved, but she did not lose them. I did not have reason to fear, and yet I lost them all anyway. My greatest enemy prowls the mountains searching for more of my loved ones to devour.

I let Leelah's correction stand while inwardly refuting that she has no idea what it means to lose everything.

Her exhale steams the cool night air as she looks heavenward. "I am worried too. We must hold on to hope and pray he is returned to us soon. That is the greatest help we can be to him." With a hand clasped around mine, Leelah guides me back to the house. It is past time to secure the house for the night.

※ ※ ※

I lie awake into the wee hours, counting the seconds that pass then beginning anew when I lose count into the thousands. I am too frightened to sleep. I know what awaits me in my dreams. Valor will join the ranks of my dead loved ones. I do not want to see the creative ways Zavaan will end his life.

I shudder and roll to my side, propping my head on my arm. Something is wrong. I know it. He would not break his word unless it became impossible for him to keep it.

Thunder rumbles in the night heralding rain. The summer showers will soon bring forth the cool days of autumn. Already the nights have grown chilly. It will not be long until the harvest season ends.

The thunder rolls on but separates into distinct booms.

Not booms.

Beats.

I grab my weapons belt and dart out of the room, sliding down the hall to reach the nearest window facing the road. Three riders come into view in the moonlight, rounding the bend in the path, but they are too far out to be certain of their identities. I scramble down the stairs, fling open the door in the great room, unbar the door in the vestibule, and fly into the night. I tie on the belt as I run, the dagger bumping against my hip. The clarion call of a destrier I know well pierces the air. I am up the stairs and hanging over the edge of the wall when the riders call out a greeting. My warrior is at the front with Kragorn and Trent following behind.

My heart drops from my throat back into my chest as I rush to raise the gate. My hands work the crank so quickly that it is open before they cross the grass lawn. I lift the long skirt of the chemise, racing down the stone steps and landing in the courtyard when they enter it.

I search for signs of injury on Valor as my bare feet kick up dust. He looks whole. He sits straight in the saddle, draws Granite up then swings to the ground without a hitch. Discarding propriety in favor of more quickly learning the state of his health, I step into his shadow and let my hands search for what I cannot see. I run them up his chest, over his broad shoulders, and down his strong arms. No blood or bandages mar his body. All my tortured imaginings are swept away as I embrace him. He tentatively returns the gesture.

He is whole.

He is well.

Valor's deep chuckle shakes me. "May I greet you the same way, my Queen?"

I step back, glaring. "You said ten days or less! Do you know how worried I have been?"

He is astonished. Gently, he cups my jaw in one hand as if my complaints are as precious as pearls. "You have your words."

I smile wryly. "Leelah gave me some of hers."

Valor's booming laugh breaks across the night. He drapes an arm around my shoulders, bringing me into his side as he leads Granite to the barn.

Warmth spreads across my skin from the contact between us. I shrug him off with a disparaging huff. "You smell atrocious."

He laughs again. Mercy, it is a good sound! I forgot how often he laughs.

"You expected me to keep my word to you *and* be clean? You expect much." He stops Granite in the aisle of the barn.

"Indeed, I do. My Hand is a representation of me." I pat the destrier then scratch under his mane. He stretches his neck with a grunt of pleasure when I find an itchy spot. "Did all go well?"

Valor takes my right hand in his and slips my signet ring back onto its finger. "Not as well as it could have. We have much to speak of tomorrow."

Fear, my constant companion, scrapes its harsh claws over me, raising bumps on my flesh. "This has to do with why you are arriving like a thief in the night."

"It does, but it will keep," he assures me, taking down a lantern that hangs from a hook in a beam. The sound of flint striking steel precedes light flickering into existence, casting the interior of the barn in an orange glow.

When Valor turns back to me, he chuckles then sweeps off his mantle, dropping it around my shoulders. "You had time to belt on a dagger, but not enough to find a robe? How queenly."

I close his mantle over my loaned white chemise. Both garments drag the ground. "It seemed like the right thing to do. I cannot well fend off an intruder with a robe."

"Very martial of you," he agrees then gives me his saddle bags to hold while he untacks Granite and beds him down for the night.

Cuyler Trent's voice reaches my ears. "Do not tell me the fool woman running about in the dead of night is our Warrior Queen? She should know better."

I turn to clasp his hands in greeting and find a genuine smile to give him. "Tis good to see you, Trent."

"And you." He smiles broadly then says to Valor, "Her fond welcome almost makes up for you pushing us to arrive tonight instead of on the morrow."

"It more than makes up for it." Valor takes his saddle bags from me then slings them over a shoulder. "Besides, I told her ten days and meant to keep my word."

"Well, you did not. You are late," I reprimand. "Ten days was yesterday."

Valor offers a penitent smile. "Ten days and two hours. You can hardly hold that against me."

"You mistake me for someone else." I raise my chin imperiously. "I can, and I will."

"Verily, that is our queen," Kragorn chuckles.

"General," I clasp his hand, "thank you for sharing your home and family with me. Leelah's help has been indispensable."

He pats my shoulder. "I am pleased to hear it. You are most welcome to stay as long as you wish."

"I thank you," I say then allow Valor's hand at my back to usher me from the barn into the night.

I step close to Valor's side as we stroll for the house. There is so much that must be said, but the hour is late, and I think we are both of a mind to defer it until later.

As we walk under the wisteria trellis into the house, Valor stops me a few steps ahead of him and turns me to face him. We are nearly eye level. "Are you well?"

I frown, searching his eyes in the dim light. How to answer? With more honesty than I owe anyone else, I decide, even though it will not assuage the worry darkening his eyes and creasing their corners. "Leelah has helped me to find coherency of thought and word. But no. No, I am far from well."

Sadness marks his expression. I cannot help but ease some of it. "I would be far worse had you not come for me. Thank you."

"Always," he solemnly replies.

Valor and Trent bed down in the great room to seek the few hours of sleep remaining this night while I follow Kragorn up the stairs. He quietly sets two packs of my belongings just inside the door of the room I share with Nev. I thank him and smile as he goes to his wife who will be ecstatic to wake with her husband returned.

I remove Valor's mantle, draping it over a chair. The belt supporting Leer's dagger follows it. As I do every night, I kiss the pommel that well knew Leer's hand. *Goodnight, my Leer.* It is as close to him as I can be.

My heart is less burdened now that Valor and Kragorn are returned, but the deep ache I feel when I lie down in the absence of Leer's arms is no less on this night than any other.

PART TWO

PROTECTED

CHAPTER NINE

VALOR

August 17th

I wake with a start when a bundle of energy lands on top of me shrieking his four-year old battle cry. "Did I scare you? I was very sneaky weren't I?"

"So sneaky," I agree, rubbing sleep from my eyes.

"Make it go away," Trent grumbles.

I throw an arm out to snare Micah before he can pounce on Trent. I hear the clatter of pots in the kitchen and rise with the giggling boy tucked under my arm like a sack of grain.

I push through the kitchen door and plop Micah onto a bench at the table. "Could you not have contained the rascal for another hour, Leelah?"

"I am sure she could have," Erianna says from cookstove where I thought Leelah to be. "But I brought the children down so that she could stay abed with her husband."

"That was thoughtful of you," I say to the queen who wears an apron over her weapons belt. "May I help you with breakfast?"

"How could you help?" Karris enters through the garden door, toting a basket filled with brown eggs and turnips. "If it does not all go into a stew pot then you are useless. Even your potage is terrible."

Erianna pours a mug of tea and places it on the table, motioning me to sit. "Actually, I am the assistant. Karris is teaching me how to cook."

"Thank you," I raise the mug and take my seat. Erianna's mouth bows in a smile, but there is no light behind it.

I watch her go through the motions of setting the table and playing assistant to Karris, but she is not truly here. It is a good show and might fool someone who does not know her, but I see her sadness.

"Should I take a tray up to Mother and Father?" Karris asks, piling biscuits into a bowl.

Erianna's smile is sadder still when she replies, "No. We shall let them rest and come down when they are ready."

Fialla whines from her little bed in the corner. Before I can rise, Erianna scoops her up. She coos to the babe, hugging her to her chest while pouring another mug of tea.

"Mother says you are supposed to have cream first," Karris chides the queen.

"*Mother* is not here," Erianna replies.

Karris brandishes the pitcher of cream. "You still have to do what she says."

"Aye, *you* do. *I* do not." Erianna sets her mug on the table, guarding it from Karris.

I snicker into my mug. Karris glares at me. Though not her blood daughter, Karris takes after Leelah in personality and expression.

When Erianna is busy snuggling Fialla, Karris fills the queen's mug to the brim with cream. "There. Now I will not be accused of allowing you to disobey Mother."

Erianna narrows her eyes at the girl whose bossy expression does not waver.

"Karris, why don't you go wake Trent and your sisters for breakfast," I suggest.

The girl brightens instantly. "Trent is here?"

"In the great room."

She squeals and darts out of the kitchen as I anticipated.

Erianna's brows rise. "Trent has an admirer?"

I wink. "Since you have been holed up for a while, would you like —"

"Oh, no!" Micah shouts as water puddles over the table then drips onto the floor. I snatch the boy back to prevent him from throwing himself at the water while Erianna tosses a rag on the mess.

Cup righted and refilled, Micah attacks his breakfast with the gusto of a grown man.

Erianna gives me her attention, but before I can voice my offer, wailing precedes Ivy and Lois's entrance into the kitchen followed by a cheery, "Good Morning," from Nev.

"What is the trouble?" Erianna asks the girls.

They speak over each other in a muddle of fussing that Nev

translates. "Leelah told the girls she would see to their hair after breakfast and sent them below-stairs."

"That is no trouble," Erianna soothes the children. "Nev and I can tend to your hair."

"You don't know how!" They sob.

"I assure you we do." Nev sits the girls on the bench while Erianna passes Fialla to me then takes up a brush. "I was the lady's maid to the queen and saw to her hair every morning."

"Really?" Lois asks doubtfully.

"Indeed, I did. Well, except for those mornings that the king and queen decided to miss breakfast." Nev's eyes sparkle as she teases Erianna.

Erianna smiles wistfully, running a brush through Ivy's hair. "Breakfast is not so important a meal."

"Says who?" Trent yawns followed by Karris who returns to the cookstove to heap plates of food.

"The women who would rather be skipping it in favor of a meal of a different sort," I explain with a grin, shoving down the unwanted twinge of jealousy.

Those women gasp as if my words offend when they were the ones to begin dancing around the topic.

Trent bats a hand through the air dismissively. "You still need breakfast."

Nev and Erianna exchange a glance that makes the queen blush and the maid titter. Clearly, they disagree.

Lois and Ivy's hair is crafted into a net of smaller braids around the crowns of their heads then secured with ribbons. Nev produces a mirror for the girls and rights their bad moods with a single glance at the court-worthy style.

Erianna steals back Fialla with a genuine smile for the babe then sets to feeding everyone else while her own breakfast grows cold. I hurry to finish my food and start the dishes so she may eat, all the while waiting for an opportunity to speak with her. Just when that opportunity looks probable with Karris taking the girls outside to begin chores, Leelah breezes into the kitchen, her vibrant red hair unbound and mussed. She lands in a chair, and, as if this were some prearranged event, Nev sets to taming her hair while Erianna pours out mugs of tea and retrieves the plates while the women chat amicably.

Kragorn appears looking downright pleasant minutes later. "So, do they approve of the plans?"

I drum my fingers on the table. "I have not had a chance to apprise her of the situation."

"Well, get to it. They need to know," he orders.

"May we speak outside?" Erianna asks me and leads the way through the garden door.

Gladly, I follow her into the garden. She unties her apron and drops it onto a bench as she heads for the stairs to the wall-walk. She comes to a stop overlooking the valley, drawing a slow, steadying breath. "Oh, it can be chaotic in there."

"Without question," I concur. "How have you fared this past week?"

"Well, considering." She rests her hands on the pommels of the twin daggers belted at her hips.

Lorennt provided me with the things she requested, but decided that he would show his displeasure by taking his time procuring them and not answering a single question I posed. He even shamelessly sent the grief stricken King and Queen Abdicàt to shower me with thanks for finding their daughter and plead with me to return her to them as expediently as possible. I found myself unable to do other than assure them I hoped to bring her home to them soon.

"I should not be so critical," Erianna admonishes herself. "Leelah has been an immense help to me, and her children are a wonderful distraction." She affects a smirk. "Besides, it is not all that different from court. The nobility can be as petty and querulous as children."

I frown at her false expression. "Why do you—"

"Anna!" Karris shouts from below.

I groan at, yet again, being interrupted from one of a thousand things I would like to ask Erianna.

"Mother would like to know if you approve and will be available to help with the wash after talking with father?"

Erianna turns her questioning gaze toward me.

"A moment, Karris." In a rush I explain, "Kragorn intends to spend the morning with you putting to paper descriptions of all the Ruphiri you can recall and mapping the roads they used. After that Leelah will fill the rest of your day with chores."

There is nothing false in Erianna's reluctant expression. "I would rather not."

Good. They can have her another day. "Fetch your cloak, riding clothes, and weapons. We are going out. I will handle the Tareths."

Then we can have a nice long talk without interruptions.

"Bless you," she gratefully whispers.

※ ※ ※

The clear summer sunshine gilds expansive verdant fields beneath gloriously blue sky. I hear Erianna's breath hitch. She scoots closer to me atop Granite, setting her thighs against mine and tightening her arms around my waist. I look at her over my shoulder. Her effortless grin draws an answering one from me. This is riding weather.

The valley blurs by while the wind catches every note of Erianna's laugh. Such tangible joy wraps around us that I am certain if I open my hands I could grasp it as easily as the leather reins between my fingers. I never thought we would share such a golden moment again.

How? How is this even possible? If I blink, I know it will dissolve into another dream from which I wake with my head pounding from too much drink. I clasp Erianna's left hand in mine, setting my fingertips to the fresh scar on her palm. *This* is real. *She* is real. And this is no dream. It is not perfect like a dream.

As Erianna closes her hand around my fingers, an unmistakable pang of guilt surges up my arm. I spent months wishing for this, for some way that would make it possible for us to be together. Though I repented of that covetous, sinful desire, I feel like I have stolen something precious from another. I feel culpable for the grief that sharpens the edges of her laughter. But even in my darkest moments, I would not have chosen this at the cost that it came. This moment is mine to enjoy because a depraved man ripped it from her husband. I urge Granite to faster speeds, but the destrier is not able to outpace the anguish feasting on my queen day and night.

I take the turn to my house faster than is strictly safe. Granite slides in the loose gravel. Erianna laughs as his hind legs find purchase. We run up the incline along the narrow road by the creek. Finally, I rein him in when the ground levels out and the fences marking the boundaries of Thad's farm come into view.

I point up the road. "My home is just over that bridge. Thad is my nearest neighbor. I must stop in to let his son know I am home. He looks after things for me when I am away. I purchase most of my food and Granite's hay from their family."

Erianna puts space between us where there had been none. This version of my friend is much more conscientious of propriety.

I spot the young man in the field swinging a scythe, helping put up hay, probably the last cut of the year. At my greeting, he shoulders the scythe to come meet us across the fence.

Quietly, Erianna says to me, "My name is Anna. I am Nev's sister. I work at the castle and am here visiting Nev."

"Concise and plausible," I commend her. "It is also true, in a certain light, which will go down easier when your people eventually learn who you are."

"*That* is to be decided," she remarks. "I have not committed to returning."

"You think you can be *Anna* indefinitely?"

"I have considered it," she says tightly.

I bite my tongue instead of arguing this right here. *Patience*, I counsel myself. This is one of many things to be discussed.

"Valor." The young man wipes sweat from his brow, squinting up at us in the bright sun. "It is good to see you. I hope your travels were safe and uneventful."

Erianna's hand, still held unconsciously in mine, convulses.

Hardly safe. Hardly uneventful. "It is good to see you as well. Col, may I introduce my friend Anna. She is Nev's sister. Anna, this is Nicolas, Thad's eldest son."

Col fixes Erianna with an affable smile. "It is a pleasure, Anna." He blinks, looking closer upon her. His smile shifts to one of appreciation. "Will you be staying here long?"

"A few months at least," she pleasantly returns.

Col grins. "I look forward to becoming better acquainted with you."

Erianna smiles, drawing her hand from beneath mine, subtly resting it upon her thigh to reveal her wedding ring. Col's interest wanes slightly as he catches sight of the ornate ring not befitting a commoner.

Well done, Majesty. "Was there any trouble while I was away?"

Col leans on the handle of the scythe. "Nothing to speak of. The mare was a bit skittish and lost some weight, so I added in a ration of grain and took over a wether to keep her company. She straightened out after that."

"Good. I will bring him back later today. Granite does not like other animals in his pasture." The stallion perks at his name and bobs his head. Col chuckles, reaching to pet his nose. Granite bares his teeth, nipping at the assumed familiarity. "Would you ask your mother if she has any foodstuffs to spare? I will be home for a time."

"I am certain she does. If you plan on being at home today, I shall bring a basket over and get the wether to save you the trouble," he offers.

"That would be appreciated." I clasp the forearm he extends.

"It was a pleasure, Anna. Until later," he smiles broadly.

"Likewise," she politely replies as I wheel Granite back toward the road and set him into a canter that tightens Erianna's arms around my waist.

"I can imagine the stir you caused at court," I mumble to her.

She laughs once. "No, you cannot."

We trot over the little bridge spanning the creek. Granite whistles to let all the creatures know he has returned to his domain. Sacha waits in the corner of the fence then trots alongside us to the barn.

Erianna leaps to the ground as I draw up Granite then climbs the fence to greet her mare. She throws her arms around the horse's neck and is lost in her reunion while I lock the wether in the barn.

"She looks so well," Erianna says leaning against the fence. "I can never thank you enough for keeping her. I have missed her more than words."

I open the gate, turning Granite out. "I could never sell your horse."

She smiles warmly, but it fades to an expression only.

"Why do you force smiles and pleasantness when it is insincere?" I ask what I wanted to voice hours ago.

She drops the falsity with a sigh. "I did it for the children and Leelah initially. Micah noticed how I never smiled and seemed to always be crying. I did not want to burden them with my grief."

"And now?"

"I hope that if I make myself do what ought to be genuine, if I behave how I would if not for..." She pauses, swallowing. "Then perhaps it will become sincere."

"I understand." And truly, I do. I will make my peace with the hollowness of her for now and do all that I can to see her filled with genuine happiness once again. "Would you like to see my home?"

This smile rings true. "I would."

✳ ✳ ✳

Erianna declares everything perfect. She asks if I plan to buy any brood mares or train another destrier when she sees the junk filled stalls in the barn. She is impressed with the few smithing tools I have and encourages me to build a place off the back of the barn to set up a miniature forge. My farfetched dreams are not foolish in her eyes.

As she walks up the steps to my home, I do my best to keep my expression neutral while I unlock the door and let her in. She helps me open the curtains and windows, casting light into the dim interior. Her exclamations over my extravagant book collection make me laugh.

Inhaling deeply, she declares, "Your home smells of books and pine. It is wonderful."

And now it feels complete, I realize. Her presence chases away the loneliness hiding in the corners, waiting to spring on me in the dark. I struggle to maintain the perspective of her loyal Hand as she moves into the kitchen, running fingers over the hewn table. When I planed the wood for it years ago, my thoughts were full of the meals my winter-eyed wife would share with me on its surface. I cannot dwell on those dreams. She is my queen. Grandileer's widow. My friend.

Aye, widow. Wife no longer, the selfish part of me points out. *Think on that.*

I refuse. I will not repeat my past mistakes. I will not allow selfishness and desire to speak louder than compassion, respect, and honor.

Erianna admires the kitchen and taps the copper pipe curled around the flue of the cookstove. She gasps then darts around the corner. Her jubilant cry at the discovery of the tub makes me laugh. I knew she would appreciate that particular purchase.

With a devious grin and hands clasped behind her back, Erianna presents herself to me. "I know what I want to do later."

I cross my arms, forcing a placatory expression and thinking of anything, *anything at all*, but what she wants. "You may use the tub later. I have work to do in the barn."

She grins then continues her exploration into my bedroom. I shut out all thoughts of her being in there. *Almighty, help me be honorable.* I wanted to show her my home but foolishly did not consider the profound impact her being her would have on me.

Taking inventory of my larder wrangles my thoughts onto safer footing. I will need to restock nearly everything. Thankfully, Col cleaned the place and did not leave anything to spoil when I abruptly left. All in all, my home is in fine shape. I start a fire in the cookstove and hear Erianna pass back into the great room.

"Does Tirzah enjoy reading?"

I nearly swallow my tongue at the question and round on the woman cradling a tome in her hands.

She chuckles. "Do not look so surprised. She came to visit a few days ago. Nev told me of Leelah's scheme and that Tirzah has caught your eye."

My mind stumbles downhill while I gape.

She quirks a brow at my dumbstruck expression. With a shrug, she replaces the book and thumbs through another. "She is witty, exceedingly attractive, a bit artful, perhaps, but you like a challenge. Nev and I approve."

Finally managing to speak, I can only repeat her words as a question. "You approve?"

She nods solemnly. "If Leelah has a say in who you wed, then your ward and your queen also get a say. Fortunately, we agree with Leelah's pick. Tirzah seems interested in you."

"She does?" I repeat her again.

"She asked Leelah quite a few questions about you, all casually spoken of course, but her intentions were obvious to Nev and I."

What is happening? I feel like a horse kicked me in the head. Erianna, *Erianna*, is in my home, asking me about a woman that I have considered courting. How did this come about? Leelah's gleaming eyes and crafty smile spring to mind. That woman has much to answer for. What game is she playing now?

Erianna offers me a way out. "If this topic is too awkward for you at present, we may discuss her later."

I quickly gather my thoughts and decide against it. "Now is fine." This may provide a transition into other things. I indicate the armchair near the empty fireplace. She sits primly and crosses her feet at the ankles while I finish with the fire in the kitchen.

Where to begin? I sit on the edge of the chair opposite her, organizing my thoughts. "I do not have to explain that leaving you in Malsihra was painful. Lamentably, I did not cope with it well. I think it was Kragorn who first recommended that I seek a wife and move on. I scoffed at the idea for months, though it was repeated by many."

Erianna's expression is placid. "What changed your mind?"

"You did," I reply.

Perplexed, she asks, "How? When?"

Time to confess. "The king summoned me to meet with him after we rounded up the brigands. While I was on my way to the castle, I came across you, Lorennt, and Nev in the city."

Her confused expression turns accusing. "You *were* there."

"I was," I admit.

"Why did you not come to me? I wanted to see you."

I hate that the hurt clouding her eyes is partly my doing. "I should have, but I saw how happy you were with your family and your husband. You were content. You were with child." I smile sadly. "I did not want to intrude on your life. Furthermore, I felt compelled to seek Grandileer's permission before approaching you. The night he refused to annul the betrothal, he sent me from the castle and ordered me not to have further contact with you." An order I ignored when I sent her letters.

The betrayal she feels coats her tone, her gaze, the stillness of her posture. But it is not directed at me. "Did he deny you permission?"

What did Grandileer do? In what ways did he wrong her? "Had I asked, I believe he would have allowed it. He also recommended I seek a wife of my own."

She starts at this. "Why would he say that?"

"Those fortunate enough to be happily married think everyone should also seek wedded bliss." I smirk.

She sees no humor in my answer. "Leer was not sentimental, nor did he meddle in people's private lives outside of political motives that provided him direct benefit."

The bitterness with which she states the last makes me wonder how far reaching that meddling went beyond what I already know, but we could talk around topics for weeks trying to become reacquainted with each other's lives. I sense she is not ready for me to open up the wounds Leer dealt her and ply needle and thread over them, so I press on. "He was not. However, I will tell you, he was decidedly in love with you, jealously so. He wanted to know if I had made my peace with your marriage."

"Had you?" She asks softly, catching her lower lip in her teeth.

I nod. "The Creator's plans are for the best, even if I cannot understand them. I came to accept that."

Erianna mindlessly spins her wedding ring around her finger. "You made it sound as if I directly influenced your decision to seek a wife?"

"Lorennt came for Grandileer at the end of our meeting when you fell off Sacha. I had never seen the king fearful before, but he was terrified for you. I waited in the corridor with Lorennt and Nev until the physician said you and the babe were well. When Lorennt went in to see you, Nev asked me if I intended to visit you then urged me to retrieve something before deciding." I take the wooden box from its place on my bookshelf and set it in Erianna's hands.

She stares at it then sighs, knowing fully what changed my mind.

"I could only assume Nev knew your heart. Thus, I heeded her caution to wait a while longer before renewing our friendship." I will not compound Erianna's grief by telling her how deeply I hurt at her final rejection. I keep that detail to myself. "I came home after that visit and sought Leelah's help to find a wife. It seemed like it was time. Of the several women to whom she introduced me, Tirzah is the first that I have considered courting."

Erianna rises and replaces the box on my shelf. With disinterest I want to imagine is feigned, she asks, "You are not yet courting her?"

"No, nor will I."

She turns her baffled expression on me. "Why not?"

Because I love you. Because Tirzah will never fit in my arms like you do. Because you need me now more than ever. "Because I have sworn allegiance to you. It would be unfair to ask a woman to be secondary to my position as your Hand."

She frowns. "How is this different than taking a wife while being Leer's Hand?"

I long to point out the inconsistency in her assertions to not return to Malsihra while still acting as queen and making me her Hand, but her thoughts do not seem to be centered in logic at present, and I do not want to anger or estrange her with things she is not ready to hear. "In some respects, being the Hand of the Queen is no different than being the Hand of the King. However, do you not think that it would be unpleasant for a wife to know her husband is at the beck and call of another woman?"

Rage blackens my friend's face into someone unrecognizable. Instinct tells me to reach for my sword—though I do not—as she rises with lethal grace. "You are absolutely right. If it will ease your conscience, I will speak with Tirzah and personally explain who I am and the nature of our relationship. Once Zavaan is drawn and quartered, I shall release you as my Hand." She strides for the door, every inch of her Malesiir's Warrior Queen. "In the meantime, I ought not be in here alone with you. If there is one thing Lorennt managed to instill in me against all odds, it is a sense of propriety."

The door closes smartly behind her, vibrating the air. I stare after her like an idiot. *What in the burning, blazing depths just happened?*

CHAPTER TEN

ERIANNA

I blunt the edge of my frustration with manual labor. My hands lack the callouses for the chores, but they are not as soft as when reading books and needle point was my sole occupation. The days of riding with the Ruphiri then the week spent climbing trees and snaring rabbits thickened my skin somewhat. The viciousness with which I wield a pitchfork to change the bedding in the stalls will leave blisters by evening. I welcome them.

The mindless chore gives structure to my mind, allowing me to come to terms with finding Valor only to discover I will lose him again. Selfishly, I want him to remain my Hand and my friend.

The grooming supplies and halters are neatly stored in the tack room as I expected them to be. I tie Sacha to the fence then set to grooming her.

Valor Ironforge, Hand of the Queen.

As it should be. He is my sworn friend and gave me his unconditional loyalty long ago. I need him to help me kill Zavaan. I cannot do it without him. And if I somehow decide to—rather, am allowed to—remain Queen of Malesiir, I want him at my side, supporting me and being to me what no one else can. My confidant. My counsel. The one who knows all my strengths and weaknesses and will not let me succumb to either.

Valor Ironforge, Husband.

I can make my peace with Valor marrying. I know his heart. He will be an exemplary husband to the woman fortunate enough to lay claim to him. Even if it is not a love match, he would still be devoted and considerate. It is why I knew I could trust him with Nev. *Ugh!* And what a mess I nearly made of that! I cannot imagine having to present Nev to Lorennt as Valor's wife, just hoping he believed me when I said that the child was a Rodiharian. Thankfully, Valor knew better than I how horrible an idea that was and made the better choice. It is a perfect example of why I need him as my Hand. I will make a multitude of stupid decisions without him.

Could he marry and still be my Hand? Doubtful. As he pointed out and I well know, no wife wants to share her husband. I would never put Valor in such a position. If he marries, then he cannot be my Hand. There is no way around it. The question then becomes, which does he want more?

He loves his work. I have seen the passionate way he talks about it. He thrives on the adventure of traveling across the Continent. He enjoys interacting with people of all kinds. He is an excellent mentor to the younger soldiers and a respected commander. He takes pride in mediating disputes and helping people come to resolutions. As my Hand, he could still have all of that. I do not think he would give the position up unless he truly loves the woman he wishes to marry.

So, does he love her and want her more than being Hand of the Queen?

Tirzah Ironforge.

The name sets my teeth on edge and makes me want to hit something. She is accursedly beautiful, plenty amiable, and has the right amount of sass to be truly appealing. If there is a woman that could turn Valor's mind from work to marriage, she is the one to do it. I swear forcefully and creatively while lifting Sacha's hoof to pick it clean.

I do not want to share him. Valor is either my Hand or Tirzah's—

"*Gah!*" I cannot even think it. I mutter curses under my breath while scraping the debris from Sacha's hoof.

"Are her hooves truly that bad?"

Brandishing the pick, I whirl around on the farmer we met earlier. He leans on the fence with crossed arms.

I rest a hand over my racing heart, trying to slow its frantic pace. "How dare you sneak up on me!" I swear again. "*How* did you sneak up on me?"

"I did not mean to. I spotted a hart on the way over and stalked him a ways that I might pick up his trail later." He holds up his hands with a teasing smile. "Do you plan on using that against me?"

I lower the pick from a defensive hold, coming nearer the fence between us. "Are you the hunter in your family, Col?"

He grins wide, revealing a missing tooth fourth left of center. "You remembered my name."

"Why would I not? We met mere hours ago."

"I am surprised your husband tolerates that sort of swearing. Most would find it indecent for a woman."

My expression falls flat. "He thought it was funny."

"Thought?" Col asks gently.

I grimace. I am supposed to be Anna, the mild-mannered sister of Nev who still has a husband. That will have to be amended when I next speak with Tirzah. "He died recently."

"My condolences. How recently?"

"Very recently," Valor interrupts, startling us both.

Col's smile is sheepish as he greets Valor and hands over the promised basket of food.

Valor appraises me with a glance down at my ring. *Why the change?* He silently asks.

I turn back to Sacha as if I did not catch his question. *Tirzah's suitor* should forget that he and I could once speak without words. I huff, picking up Sacha's fore hoof. Leer and I could never communicate so easily. With words or without them, we seemed perpetually determined to misunderstand each other.

How dare Valor remind me of that!

While the men talk, I finish scraping Sacha's feet clean and inspect the mare, trailing hands over her back. She looks very well. The pasture has been good for her. And the grain, I recall. "Thank you, Col, for looking after my mare. She is in wonderful condition."

"She is a fine animal. It was my pleasure." He opens the gate for me when I untie Sacha's lead rope and head toward the barn to saddle her. Col walks toward the house with Valor to collect his payment but calls back to me before I enter the barn. "Anna! May I walk you to Nev's home when you are finished here?"

The offer surprises, not because I am unaware Col finds me interesting, but because Valor is glaring at the young man like he is.

"I will be escorting Anna home," Valor declares, turning for the house as if that settles it.

But the young man has pluck. "Would you like to see my farm after Gathering this week? We will be finished haying the south field by then."

I consider dismissing him, but the hopeful expression in his eyes in spite of the glowering warrior next to him tugs at a corner of my heart. "I would like that."

His boyish smile is unguarded. "I shall see you then. Good day, Anna."

I incline my head and am equally satisfied that Valor seems put out with me. Not that agreeing to visit Col had anything to do with Valor. It had everything to do with the young man himself. He seems so affable that it would have been unpleasant to discourage him roughly.

Valor enters the barn to retrieve the wether from the stall. "Leave off on that," he orders as I heft Sacha's saddle. "We are going to train first, *Majesty*."

I roll my eyes but do as bid, placing Sacha in the fresh stall so I do not have to groom her again before saddling her.

I change into my tunic and wool pants in the tack room. They have become worn, I notice, poking a finger into a hole in the fabric on my thigh. I think it is time for new riding clothes. Since it is only Valor, I leave the overdress in my bag but lace on the altered cuirass. With Leelah's help, I cut and stitched the leather so that the cuirass laces up the front. She encouraged me to wear it when I train to provide my weakened stomach muscles support until they regain their strength.

I replace my daggers then braid my hair tighter. Add a hauberk and I would be passable as the Warrior Queen. Others might not notice the difference, but I feel it deeply.

More noticeable to me than the lack of weighty chainmail is the absence of Leer's gentle hand that was always in mine, anchoring me to him, keeping me from ever feeling alone. Somewhere along the way, I stopped being complete by myself and became one with my husband. That is stolen from me. His hand will never fit in mine again.

I grasp the hilt of his dagger, biting back a surge of tears. Now is not the time for grief. Now is the time to train, to make my body remember dancing with steel and striking with fists so that I may be ready when I face the *Král Vragh*. For that, I need Valor's help.

I grit my teeth, circling back around to being frustrated. There is a time limit on how long I can count on him. He will not hunt Zavaan with me indefinitely when he would rather be with his woman.

I stride into the sunlight, following the sounds of short staves striking a pel. Valor has created a training ring adjacent to the barn complete with pel, weapon stands, targets, and more. It is as well equipped as any in the castle. *Of course it is*, I think, watching the warrior ferociously attack the pel. He never puts a half-hearted amount of effort into anything he cares about, as Tirzah will soon learn.

I sneer then cover it with determination. Training. Only training. I will think on nothing else.

I enter the ring, circling around until I am in Valor's line of sight, though I am certain he already knows I am here. He continues without breaking rhythm, trying my patience. Sakes he moves well! I remembered he was superior to Lorennt, but I forgot the extent of his prowess. Bored with gawking, I select a pair of staves and twirl them, loosening my arms, while I continue circling him until I have a decent chance of smacking him over the head. I rush forward to engage him.

Valor whirls on me at the last second, blocking both my staves—the one aimed for his head and the other at his knees. That trick worked on Lorennt from time to time, but not on Valor.

As we size each other up over our crossed staves, Valor's eyes assess my form, then he smirks. "No overdress today?"

That is what he noticed? Armed with three daggers, four knives and wielding a short staff in each hand, he points out *that* minor impropriety? Unbelievable! "It gets in my way. Besides, the only person here to scandalize is you, and you have seen me in much less," I saucily reply.

He blinks then grins. "There is that." He steps back with a relaxed posture meant to conceal the warrior poised to strike. "Let's see if you earned your title or if you are still the whining highness I remember."

"You will have to try much harder than that to antagonize me." I swing my staves, feeling their reach while casually shifting my feet to attack. "I have heard myself called every name imaginable. *Whining* is practically a compliment."

As he composes his witty response, I strike and land a lucky hit to his shins, but that is the last one. All is a flurry as we dance around each other, clashing staves and blending in a few kicks. My endurance is sadly lacking, but Valor does not slow to accommodate my fatigue. Instead, he pushes me until I can no longer block his attacks. I am forced to yield ground until my back is at the fence. His staff bruises my upper arm then settles across my neck.

"Yield," Valor demands.

Thinking fast, I use the one trick left to me. I curve my mouth invitingly and look up at him under my lashes, stepping forward with his staff still resting against my neck. "There is something you should know," I purr, taking another step, then another.

Curious, he allows it.

I speak slowly, holding the eye contact and distracting him from the ground I am gaining. "I. Will. Never." I lean into him, subtly placing my foot between his.

"Never what?" He murmurs, searching my gaze.

I smile beatifically. "Yield." Viciously, I hook my foot behind his and, at the same instant, throw all my weight into the elbow I drive into his lower abdomen. He grunts, going down hard. Anticipating his next move to trip me, I rap his knuckles with my staff while bounding away.

Safely out of reach, I raise my staves into the offensive position, daring him to see what else I have learned, although my bravado will only hold so long as he does not test it. I am spent.

Valor gapes at me. I cant my head higher, glaring down my nose at him.

He bellows, folding in half and causing me to jump. For a moment, I do not comprehend that he is laughing. He wipes tears of mirth from his eyes. Between broken guffaws, he declares, "A draw then, my Warrior Queen. It is a title you well earned."

I straighten to catch my breath and return his smile, but it is short lived.

If you were a true Warrior Queen, your husband and daughter would still be alive, the Insidious Voice accuses me.

The reminder knocks all the humor from the moment. I turn away from Valor and replace my staves where I found them. *Training. Only training. Do not falter.* But it is too late to fend off the anger and grief.

I stalk across the ring with bared teeth. I draw two knives and spin, unleashing them with all my might. They sink up to their hilts in the target. I free two more, releasing them overhand and hearing the unison thuds. The dagger from my thigh is the smallest of the remaining three. I loose it backhanded. It also finds its mark.

I free my own dagger, the twin to Leer's, the one I should have been able to raise when I watched my husband die. I hurl it haphazardly at the target, screaming in rage. It clatters off harmlessly, landing in the dust. I scream again, gripping the hilt of Leer's dagger until the imprint is marked in my left palm.

Over and over, Zavaan sinks the blade into Leer's heart then rips it out, dripping Leer's lifeblood. My Leer turns his head my direction, searching for me, showing me his love, even unto death.

I weep now as I could not then. "Don't leave me! Please! Please, come back," I sob.

I see his handsome face on the day of our coronation and feel his hand in mine, vowing to never leave me. Earlier that same morning, his brown eyes flecked with black were so rich in the dawn light as he made love to me and told me how thoroughly I had captured his heart.

In the entirety of our marriage, there was not one night we spent apart. Even when I was angry and would not share our bed, he did not leave me. He slept in the parlor, keeping his promise to me. But never again. Now I sleep alone. I wake alone. Because of my selfishness. My weakness. My enemy.

"How did he die?" Valor asks soberly.

"We were ambushed like in Nevermore. I could not warn him fast enough. I was drowning and so tired. He did not hear me until they were upon us. They pushed most of our men over the cliff. Leer was on his gelding. They gained on us when he tried to outrun them. His destrier would have served better, but he had to hold me."

More guilt is heaped upon me. We might have escaped if I had been brave and rode my own horse and Leer his destrier. I was a hindrance. "I did not want to live, but he refused to let me die. He forced me to live, again and again. It cost him his life. He should have cast me to the Wolves and escaped, but he did not. He hid me in a thicket. I was weak and unarmed. I am no Warrior Queen. I am a coward." I recount every horrific moment as I watched Leer fight Zavaan, and he bought me a chance to escape.

"I should not have left him! I gave my word!" My hands grasp fistfuls of dirt. It grinds into my nail beds. "I am a liar just like him. We are the worst sorts of liars."

"What did you both lie about?"

I shake my head. Valor cannot know. I will not tell anyone what Leer did.

"What happened after he was killed?"

This part of the story pours out of me. Valor ought to know how terrible a queen he has sworn himself to. It will make it all the easier for him to leave me. I do not spare myself from him knowing everything. My stomach churns to recount it. I must stop to swallow the bile fighting its way up. How quickly I partook of Zavaan's lies! How quick I was to believe the murderer over Leer, over Valor. I explain how I escaped and the last thing Zavaan said to me. "I was a fool. A stupid, whoring fool. Can you not see that now?" I glance at Valor, expecting the fury in his eyes. Somehow we came to be sitting side by side in the dirt of the training ring.

"Zavaan is an evil man who tried to break you so thoroughly you did not know your own name, but you still saw the truth through his lies, praise be to the Creator. You acted bravely and intelligently. You discovered his weaknesses and used them. You escaped!"

His absolution does not make me feel any less despicable. I wrap my arms around my legs, resting my brow against my knees, trying to hold my pathetic self together. "I am sorry! I am sorry I let your king die. I have failed Malesiir. I thought only of my own pain and left us vulnerable to attack because of my selfishness."

"I do not see it that way," Valor says gently. "I see a woman who was dealt such deep soul-wounds that she could not rise from them on her own. Her husband so loved her that he did everything he could to see her restored and willingly gave his life to protect his bride. Do not cheapen what Grandileer did by claiming responsibility for his death."

This I hear and understand. I will not belittle Leer's sacrifice again.

At my assent, Valor continues. "Zavaan is at fault for trying to tear apart Malesiir, in more ways than one. Lorennt and I need your help to prevent him from doing further harm."

Zavaan must be stopped. It is what rouses me from bed in the morning. The longer he lives, the greater his crimes, the higher the death toll. If Lorennt is working toward this goal too, then we stand a better chance. "What happened in Malsihra?"

"We can talk after you have had a nice long bath. You smell *atrocious.*" He drags the word out comedically. I huff a laugh.

"Good. Now, I am going to help you find your feet." Valor lifts me from the dirt then returns my weapons to me, one by one. "Someday, I want to hear the story of how you two came to have matching daggers in the style of Grandileer's sword."

I trace my thumb over the words Leer had etched into my blade. "Someday."

✲ ✲ ✲

VALOR

I sit on the porch, honing the edge of my sword until it is bragging-sharp. Spent of her words and will, I sent Erianna into the bathing room to soak in the tub. I know that she needs time to come back to herself after losing her control.

My sword whines as I push it across the whetstone. What I witnessed was a mere glimpse into the maelstrom inside her. One moment, she is teasing and almost herself; in another, a commanding queen; the next, a bereaved young widow. I try to organize her looks, her actions, her words into a semblance of order, but there simply is none. What emotion did she not display today? The range of things she expressed ran from polite to terse, calm to enraged, coy to surly. She could not even keep up with herself. The only thing she could not be called was logical.

Spirit of Truth, I am out of my depth. I do not know what to do. Please grant me the wisdom to help her. Please show me what to do.

Perhaps I should speak with Leelah and Nev. We could work together to help Erianna. But how to do that without violating the trust she has given us individually? Lorennt certainly was no help, other than cautioning me about returning the daggers to her. He also warned me to keep her away from heights. When I replied that she had been sleeping in trees for weeks, he visibly paled and told me to put a stop to it but would not tell me why.

Given what Erianna revealed in saying with absolute seriousness that she did not want to live, but Leer refused to let her die...

My heart stops. It is too perfect a fit to not draw a conclusion. Hagan's letter insisting that I come aid her or she would be lost also makes sense. It also explains why Leer took away her weapons.

She was a danger to herself.

My thoughts drift to the deep tub she is currently immersed in... Or *submersed* in...

My sword and whetstone clatter to the ground. I am halfway through the outer door before I restrain myself from hauling her out of the bath. She has had ample opportunity to end her life if she was still of a mind. She has been armed to the teeth, sleeping forty feet up in trees, and practically living on the wall surrounding Leelah's house. Instead, she seems to have set her mind on killing Zavaan.

But she has not made plans beyond that, I realize with a start. She is in a state of indecision and has been evasive about her thoughts, other than insisting that I be her Hand until we kill Zavaan, then she will release me. Because she will no longer be alive?

I jam my sword into its scabbard. That is unacceptable and of next priority to discuss with her.

I do not care what she says. She may try to release me as her Hand, but I will not go. I will follow her indefinitely if I must and not give her a choice. How do I explain that I would rather my future include her, even if only as a friend, than as someone else's husband? She took me so thoroughly off guard with talk of Tirzah, because she has occupied all of my thoughts since I received those summons a month ago.

Woe's sakes! I nearly made a fool of myself when she walked into the training yard. I reminded myself multiple times that she was my queen and that I would not make the same mistakes as before while she circled me. Then she grew impatient and left me dumbstruck when I got a close look at her. I hoped she would be inclined to go find her overdress and save me from the temptation of staring at her beautiful, lithe figure. What did I say after she reminded me at the most inopportune moment that I have seen her in undergarments? Not that I dwell on it or that those moments held anything but the urge to protect her and kill her enemies, but she made me dumb with the casual reminder while wearing garments that hugged every blessed curve. The dozen things I did not say—at least, I hope I did not say—come clearly to mind. Getting knocked to the ground for thinking where I should not was the least I was due. It struck me as hilarious that she played me so well. *I will never yield.* That is the woman I know. Gorgeous, feisty, and quick-witted.

But in an instant she was swept away in anguish-driven rage, and I along with her. When I caught the drift of her thoughts, I sympathized. I feel guilt that I was not there to fight and die alongside my king—if that is what it came to. How much more would she, his wife, the woman touted as the Warrior Queen for her heart more than her ability, feel guilt for hiding while her husband was killed before her eyes. That sort of powerlessness breeds destructive fear. Then to be captured by that same murdering, villainous, ravaging dog… Were I in her place, I doubt I would be coherent either.

By the time I hear her moving about inside, I have finished honing a few daggers in addition to my sword.

She opens the door and steps out, bearing a tray of food. "I thank you for bringing me these dresses to wear. My wardrobe is extensive, but it contains nothing of such simplicity. Where did these come from?"

"Lorennt packed your belongings. My understanding is that they belong to Nev." I take the tray while she settles on the porch steps next to me and scoop up a few oatcakes.

"I thought they looked familiar. That also explains the slender fit." She plucks at the fitted sleeves.

"If you would like to purchase better fitting ones, I can arrange it."

"I would. And new pants for training and riding. Mine are a bit worn."

Hallelujah. "We shall enlist Leelah's help for that." *And ensure these new ones are not so distracting.*

"Will you go with me to visit Col's farm?" She asks between bites of food.

"That you think you have to ask amuses me." I cast my eyes sidelong at her. "Why did you tell him you are widowed?"

She winces.

"That word offends?"

A nod.

Barren, *widowed*, and, undoubtedly, *stillborn* are the three most offensive words to her. I am certain that she will suffer them often in the coming months, but not from me.

"Forgive me." I rephrase the question and add another. "Why did you admit that your husband recently died? Why agree to spend time with Col?"

"It was an accident. He asked if my husband tolerated my salty language. I answered in the past tense."

"Did Grandileer tolerate it?"

Erianna chuckles. "He thought it was funny, especially when it was directed at him. He said it was akin to being heckled by a chipmunk— all bark and chatter but more darling than anything else." She smiles wryly. "Mind you, he was not often brought to swearing himself. He was far too controlled for that. Though, my antics did bring it out in him on occasion, most often when Lorennt tattled or made me confess to something."

I watch in amazement as Erianna's burdens visibly lighten while recounting the worst swearing she brought him to. Perhaps this could be part of the Creator's answer to how I should help her. Maybe she needs to remember all the happy moments to dull the painful ones and show her that life can be worth living.

She laughs brightly. "You should have seen how the assistant blushed when I exited Leer's office. He thought we had been reluctant to answer the door for another reason. Of course, I made a show of straightening my skirt to help along his misperception." She waggles her brows mischievously, demonstrating once again how different her views on intimacy are from a year ago. Nothing of fear or displeasure is carried in her tone. Grandileer was good to her in that regard.

I grin at her impishness. "What was the first of your antics in the castle?"

She scrunches up her face while thinking then gaily jumps into the story. "That would be when Lorennt and I cozened the nobles we did not like in a card game."

We trade stories on the porch for hours, basking in the pleasantness of each other's company and postponing the weightier matters until we have extracted every bit of happiness from this summer's day.

CHAPTER ELEVEN

ERIANNA

I feel more myself in Valor's presence than I have in months. I know it cannot last, but I let his steadfastness help me find center. I recline on my elbows on the porch step, watching the summer sunshine highlight the golden brown of his hair. There is silver at his temples, but I cannot see it with the length falling forward like it is. I drum my fingers to keep them from flipping the locks back to see how much silver is now concealed there.

Sacha whinnies impatiently at being shut in the barn for several hours on such a lovely day. Valor glances up at the sun's position in the sky. His hair falls back revealing more silver than I remembered. The past year has had trials for both of us.

"Would you like to tour some of the valley before returning to Leelah's?"

"Very much," I agree.

He groans while rising, his knees popping after sitting for so long. I snicker.

"Do not laugh." He wags a finger at me. "It will happen to you soon enough."

I am sure. I feel as if the past year aged me a decade or more. At the ripe old age of twenty, I have joined the ranks of the widowed. I wince at the word and accept the hand Valor offers. With all his usual pestering, he pulls me so hard off the steps that I stumble forward.

"At least some things do not change," I grumble.

"You start on the horses while I bank the fire," Valor says, gathering our empty mugs and tray to head inside.

Why would he bank the fire and not put it out? He wouldn't unless he plans to return. "Are you not staying at the Tareth's home tonight?"

He pauses, turning back a step. "I was not planning on it. Do you want me to?"

It is an offer, but there is no sense in it. He has no reason to stay there. He has his own home and his own bed. Kragorn and Trent are able to guard the Tareth home. His presence is redundant. Besides, how would he explain his unnecessary presence to Tirzah? "It does not matter. I had simply not thought about it." My voice comes out too sharp.

"Erianna—"

"I shall do my best to ensure Granite has a proper grooming. It has likely been months since someone has done a decent job of it," I toss wryly, trotting toward the barn.

I set to work on Granite, scoffing at myself for forgetting who Valor and I are to each other. We are not the inseparable more-than-friends we once were. That is over. An afternoon catching up does not change anything. So logical was the assumption that he would stay in his own home that he did not even think to mention it to me. No longer do we prefer to sleep on hard benches next to each other when there are comfortable beds apart. He will not keep vigil with me through the long nights anymore.

My vision blurs as I run soft brushes over Granite's coat. I growl angrily, swiping a sleeve across my face. This is Leelah's fault. She did not warn me I would become trapped in whatever part of my journal I stopped at. I will continue my project after Valor escorts me back to the Tareth home and not stop until I remember that I am the Queen of Malesiir, Leer's Untouchable Wife.

Erianna, Leer's wife.

Valor, Tirzah's suitor.

I grimace and spit in the straw covered floor. *Get used to it.* Valor and Tirzah. Tirzah and Valor.

Valor holding Tirzah close. Tirzah learning that Valor's eyes brighten from stormy to purest silver when he is at his happiest or desirous. Valor bringing Tirzah to this house and making her his wife...

I mutter curses under my breath.

Granite turns his neck to watch me brush his legs. He blows slobber in my face when I find a ticklish spot.

"Thanks for making my bath a wasted effort," I grouse.

I finish grooming the destrier and touch up Sacha's coat, but Valor is still inside. "Likely taking his sweet time so that I must do all the work, *hmm*?" I ask the horses. Granite tosses his head in agreement. I tack both horses and find a stool to climb atop so I may reach Granite's tall back to fit his saddle. I know the meticulously cared for black leather tack as well as Sacha's.

"That must be part of the problem," I tell them. "Familiarity breeds possessiveness."

Lorennt would insist upon sticking to the propriety of titles. I should not have fallen back into the habit of using his given name. I should have used his title indefinitely.

I glance over my shoulder. Valor still is not here. That useless, accursed layabout! Even I know it does not take *that* long to bank a fire. He is probably sitting inside, enjoying a book, waiting for me to lead the horses out.

I relocate the horses to the fence nearest the house and tie them off. Had it been Valor leading Granite, he would have simply dropped the reins and the destrier would have obediently stayed put. Granite chooses not to heed me when I have tried that. He follows me about, nudging my back, until I scratch under his mane, or until Valor catches him head butting me and stomps at the horse who then acts like he would never dream of being rude to a lady.

I march up the steps to the house, but the door opens, as anticipated, before I can enter.

"In a high temper, I see," Valor remarks and hands me my saddle bags.

"I have not said a word," I tersely state.

"Ah, but you never present so well as when you are livid." He winks.

That takes the heat out of me on the instant. Leer vowed that he would be the last man to compliment me on that.

"What is it?" Valor lowers his head to the side to catch my expression. His sensitivity to my rapidly shifting moods frustrates me. He should not care so much! My attachment to him is his fault too. He started this nonsense all the way back in Grass Lake when he claimed me.

I toss my braid, ignoring his question. With the graceful dignity of a queen, I return to Sacha and make ready to leave this perfect cabin in the woods, vowing not to become attached to it. Just as Valor's room at the castle could not be my refuge, neither can his home.

I fasten my saddle bags then take up Sacha's reins and a fistful of her mane in one hand. Before I can mount, Valor's hands grip my waist, lifting me to the saddle. He fits my feet to the stirrups, tucking my skirt around my legs as he goes. He checks the tightness of the girth and all the buckles on the mare's tack. He never entrusts my safety to another. That reminder pains and thoroughly confuses me about where we stand with each other. We must define this new ground we are on before I do something utterly foolish and inappropriate. Like smacking him for being so considerate. Or seeking his arms and pleading with him to do whatever it takes to make the world go away.

"It seems you have not forgotten how to properly tack a horse even though I doubt you lifted a finger to do the chore yourself since being given the opportunity to shirk it with a wave of your royal hand," Valor mocks, brushing back a hank of damp hair that fell in his eyes.

He bathed. That is why he was taking so long. I look closer upon him and note clean clothes and a pack slung over his shoulder. He means to stay with me. He will not leave me.

"No comment? Just as I thought. You have become lazy in my absence."

Ridiculous tears burn the back of my eyes. I bury them with sass. "Actually, I insisted on grooming Sacha myself."

"Did you muck a stall? Scrub a saddle?"

I glance at my nails, pretending they are not broken from scrabbling up trees and are once more long and even. "Such things are beneath a queen." Or so I was told.

He tuts in disapproval. "I almost feel ashamed for getting you out of washing laundry today. I shall have to ensure Leelah conscripts you for chores."

I flick my fingers at him. "You can try."

Valor grins wickedly. "What do you think the chances are that Sacha is in any better shape than you and stands even half a chance at outrunning Granite?"

I mimic his mischievous expression rather than trying to conjure one of my own. "Well, that really all depends on if I cheat, doesn't it?"

I wheel Sacha sideways and cut off his dash to Granite before setting heels to her. I find the rhythm of Sacha's gait as easily as if it has been a day since riding her, not five months. Her powerful hindquarters drive us forward. Col's fence blurs past. I hear Granite's hooves thundering close behind and lean over Sacha's neck.

"Mind the turn!" Valor bellows.

I brace myself and slide Sacha through the loose ground, whooping loudly. We gallop into the field, going wide of the river in the bottom of the valley. I like this place nearly as much as the Hillcountry—maybe more, actually. I slow Sacha to a lope so I may admire the landscape. The valley has plenty of open spaces, providing room to run with beautiful forests to explore and mountain ridges to hem it all in.

A Peaceful Haven it certainly is.

"Tell me about this place," I request as Valor pulls even with me, and we rein in the horses.

With his own brand of enthusiastic storytelling that engages not with animated gestures but with passionate intensity, Valor tells me how the high valley came to be settled by the Judges and what it was like those first few years as they escaped the purge and fled to Malesiir. He points out the landmarks as we pass them and the communal spaces that were the first to be decided upon. A whitewashed, split-log chapel sits upon a hill, overlooking the river that winds merrily through the length of the valley. The Judges gather there on the day of rest to worship the Creator together and be exhorted by the reading of the Holy Texts. After the Gathering, they fellowship over a meal where each family provides what they are able to share. Leelah was quite sad to miss the Gathering and fellowship meal while we awaited Valor's return. There will be another in a few days, but I am undecided whether or not I will attend.

Father and Mother Celiea encouraged Lorennt, Leer and I to attend weekly chapel services with them, but Leer felt it was an unnecessary expenditure of his time that could be better spent elsewhere, and I did what he did. From my understanding, Lorennt attended on occasion and Nev often went, but there was its own strife, because they could not be seen together publicly and were still divided by social class even within the chapel.

"Do you attend the chapel services when you are in Malsihra?" I ask Valor.

He nods his head. "Do you?"

"Leer did not care to," I reply, thinking that explanation is sufficient.

"I know. Did *you* attend?"

"Our time together was limited. I did not wish to leave him ere dawn on a morning we could be slower to rise and breakfast together." I find myself justifying my actions then am not sure why I felt it necessary. I am queen. I may simply say, "No. I did not."

"You will attend with me and the Tareth family while here," he declares.

Oh, will I? I might wish for half a day's quiet with the house emptied of its boisterous occupants.

Changing the subject, "What is that place?" I indicate where a finger of the river has been diverted into a large, low-walled pool then empties into ditches that water an expansive garden.

"Ah, that." He grins. "Had I not snatched you out of Leelah's claws today, you would be well acquainted with the community washing pool. The women meet there twice a week to wash their family's laundry."

"How miserable. Why would they want to do laundry together?"

Valor quirks a brow at me. "To socialize," he drawls.

I shake my head. I simply do not understand the constant need of most women to congregate and cluck without end.

"Did you get along with the noblewomen at the castle?"

"Get along? Mostly."

"But?" He pries.

"I preferred the company of my family, including Nev, to all others. When time permitted, I visited with a few friends I made in the city." It is a succinct answer. It should satisfy, but it does not.

Directly this time, Valor asks, "Do you not have any friends among the noblewomen?"

I consider if I am prepared to explain the dynamic of my place in the castle. I search my thoughts for any pitfalls that would lead me to a conversation I do not want to have or to something I would rather he not know. Nothing stands out, so I attempt an explanation. "Mother Celiea encouraged me to join the women in her solar for daily needlepoint, but it was tedious, and I made excuses for a long time before explaining to her I simply did not want to go. Instead, I used a portion of the time to train with Lorennt. Often, I would go riding or venture into the city to secure Leer's place in the heart's of the commoners. Sometimes, I would hide in my parlor with Nev and read." I smirk. "I took you at your word and smuggled a portion of your library into my own."

He chuckles. "I noticed. It amused me to know you were still taking my dessert in the form of books."

I laugh. "I never thought of it like that. It served me quite well in the end. I learned how to trap small game from one of your books. I just wish there had been one of your notes in the margin warning me too much rabbit could starve a body."

He draws up Granite, his jaw falling open. "Were you eating nothing but rabbit while on your own in the forest?"

I affirm it. "Leelah called you a fool for not sooner recognizing that part of what ailed me was the headaches and madness from mostly eating rabbit. I assured her that you fed me better after I found you."

"*I* found you," he corrects.

"Only because *I* was searching for *you*." I walk Sacha in a tight circle around Granite to pester the warrior.

"*After* I found you, and *you* ran away from me," he emphasizes then asks, "Why did you run from me?"

I stop with my knee against his. "I was on my way to the North. It was the last place I knew you to be. I am no match for Zavaan, but I believe you are and set out to find you."

"*Vreh Král Vragh*," he intones.

The title incites fear, bloodlust, dread, and grief all at once. I close my eyes to get hold of myself so I may dull the emotions and memories hauled to the fore. Valor takes my hand in his where it rests on my thigh, and I am grateful. It makes finding my way back to the present a more direct journey. I trace the pads of my fingers over the scar on his palm. *I do not belong to Zavaan.*

Leer protected me with his death, and Valor intends to fight for me in life.

"He must be killed," I assert. "Thus, I set out to find you. I did not know who else to trust."

"But you ran from me when we found each other."

"Beyond not being in my right mind, it was so sudden to find you before me. I was unsure of what you would do with me. I could not know if you would aid me or drag me back to Malsihra." Shame colors my face. I drop my eyes from his and try to release his hand, but he holds on. "I also feared you would most likely decide that I was undeserving of being your queen after the things I had done. I did not want you to know. I still do not."

Valor dispels more of my fear with his unyielding loyalty. "My Queen. Now and evermore." He brings my hand to his mouth, bowing over it.

He honors me with the fealty of a trusted vassal, but his breath over my hand feels like that of a lover. When his lips touch my knuckles, I inhale sharply at the jolt sent up my arm from his kiss. My heart races. I am snared by the storm of his eyes that is well on its way to being overtaken by silver. He feels it too. It startles. It frightens. It excites. Every reckless bone in my body yearns for him as his rapid breaths caress the back of my hand.

Sacha takes a shifting step forward, bringing me closer to Valor. That is enough for both of us to break free of the momentary trance.

He bows lower, presses my knuckles to his brow. It is more formal. More safe. "My Queen."

"Thank you for your fidelity." I cringe at the word thoughtlessly chosen. Or perhaps not so thoughtlessly...

I smile, thickly masking the stirring in me as his eyes—once again dark—find mine.

"Always." He releases me and nudges Granite forward.

I turn Sacha to follow. What were we speaking of that led to such? I track backwards then forwards and find only his steadfast nature reassuring my fragile one. Nothing there should have given either of us cause to find something of our past lingering in our present. It is a good reminder to tread with caution.

Valor waves a greeting to some folks we pass then turns us toward the river. We stop at its edge, letting the horses take their fill.

"Before we arrive at the Tareth's, I must relate what transpired while I was away." He searches my gaze. "Can you hear it now?"

His warning bodes ill. "Are the rest of my family alive and safe?"

"They are," he assures me.

"Then I will hear it," I decide.

We remain alongside the river, walking the horses at their leisure and using the sound of water rushing over rock to ensure our voices do not carry.

"Your family misses you and longs for your return," Valor begins, then corrects himself. "That does not adequately express how relieved and overjoyed they are to know you are alive, nor how much they want you with them."

"They are devastated by Leer's death. The timing is so cruel, especially to Mother Celiea who was nearly as broken by the loss of Illyanna as Leer and I. To also lose her eldest son..." I try to detach myself from the explanation as a lump rises in my throat.

"You are not the least of importance to them," Valor interjects. "You are not a consolation to them. Had I not known the relation between you all, I would have taken their relief as that of parents who were told their only daughter lives when they were certain she was lost."

Was that where my thoughts were headed? Yes, it was. I know

Father and Mother better than that. Was it then a means of excusing myself for hiding out here and shirking my responsibilities? Guilt attests to the truth therein. "How is Lorennt?"

Valor is slow to answer. "Did you anticipate how badly he would take the revealing of Chase's identity?"

I nod. Poor Lorennt. He more than I probably laments not disposing of Chase the night we met him, or later during the tournament. "We must not allow Lorennt to cross swords with him. I have seen them fight. Lorennt would not survive Zavaan either."

"I would hear the story of that soon," he orders, and I agree. "Lorennt is angered, but he wants you to come home. He has demanded it."

"Then you did not tell him of my faithlessness. He would see it as unforgivable."

"Again, you are wrong. You are misplacing your own feelings of disgust caused by Zavaan's violation onto those who love you," Valor reiterates, trying to make me understand. "I would not have revealed it, but Lorennt insisted on knowing the wrongs Zavaan did to you, so I told what I had surmised at the time. Lorennt froths at the mouth for Zavaan's death all the more for it, but he assured me that had you not given Zavaan something, he would have taken everything." Valor's lip curled while he spoke the last, and he pauses to ease it. His fury, too, is all for Zavaan. "So you see. There is nothing unforgivable between you and Lorennt."

I grip the pommel of my saddle until my knuckles are white. *Oh, Lorennt. I miss you.* "You forget that he does not know that we hid Nev or that he is to be a father. He will count my hiding them from him to be the worst of my sins."

"But was it Lorennt that you hid them from?" Valor challenges my fears. "Was it not mostly from the king learning of the babe's existence? If Grandileer had been of a different disposition and Nev had not had so many misgivings, you would have kept her with you. I know that you would have fought for them. There is still much we have to discuss on that, but without speaking on it extensively, I think we can both agree that Nev must go to Lorennt."

"Aye. She must," I readily concur. "Lorennt needs her, and Malesiir needs the heir to the Rodiharian name."

"Good. We are of one mind." Valor runs his fingers through his hair, forewarning me that what he next needs to tell frustrates him. "At the risk of causing you to do something foolish, I must also tell you that

Lorennt plans on retrieving you himself if you do not return to Malsihra within two months. However," Valor raises a hand, forestalling my outburst, "I warned the prince that if you did not want to return, then I would do whatever was necessary to prevent you from being forced to. So, if you insist on running away, I only ask that you tell me so I may make the arrangements and accompany you."

I fix him with my shocked expression. "If I decide to disappear from Malesiir, to never return, you would go with me?"

He looks long upon me before answering. "I hope that is not what you decide. It would cause your family unnecessary grief, and I know you would come to regret it. But, aye. Where you go, I go."

"Even if I decided to make Grass Lake my home?" I ask softly.

Feeling the unspoken weight behind my question, Valor asks with equal quiet, "Is that truly what you wish to know?"

I cannot hold his gaze boring into mine. "What else happened in Malsihra?"

Valor's tone is no less heavy. "Lorennt cautioned me against returning your weapons to you and told me I must keep you from heights. Will you tell me why he said that?"

Run! The Insidious Voice hisses. *He will not understand. He will condemn you for it and think less of you than he already does. You know he is not as forgiving as he pretends to be.*

I long to clap my hands over my ears, but it will not drown out the voice nor will plucking out my eyes remove the images flashing behind them.

"Erianna, look at me," Valor instructs. "You will find no judgment."

Holding my breath and reserving the right to run, I shift my gaze to his. He did not lie. No judgment. No pity either. Only active sympathy that seeks to climb into my wrecked life with me and make sense of the ruins.

I crack open the door I hide behind and reveal a sliver of the truth. "I did not want to live anymore. I tried to join Illyanna beneath the soft earth. Hagan thwarted my fall from the ramparts."

Valor is not shocked, but still he pales. "Why did you not want to live?"

I shake my head. *Not yet.*

He does not press me, but asks instead, "Do you want to live now?"

Do I? In this moment, riding with Valor or earlier sitting on his porch, I am almost happy. Despite the practical impossibility, I could spend the rest of my days like this. But in the dark hours that stretch out farther than the light ones, life becomes unbearable. If my existence holds nights without end, as it did after losing Illyanna, after Leer's sins were revealed, after I heaped my own wickedness on top of the rubble, then no. No, I could not live like that. Excepting the thing that makes me rise in the morning.

"I want to kill Zavaan. I will live to see it done." Then I can decide about my own life.

A battle rages across Valor's face, but I cannot distinguish the sides engaging in the war. Tightly, he requests, "I would have your word that you will not—" Muscles twitch in his jaw as he bites down on words he does not want to release upon me. He adjusts from a request to an admonition. "You must find something else to live for. Revenge is not enough. It will destroy you between the longing for it and the getting of it."

"You think me not destroyed already?" I stare out from my ravaged, embittered soul.

"I know you are." He doles out the harsh reality then adds a qualifier. "But not beyond redemption. There is life on the other side of this. The Creator longs for you to take hold of what He alone can give you. He can restore you beyond anything you have ever experienced."

"I have had enough of His help!" I seethe. "His sort of help healed my womb then stole my daughter. His help gave me a husband I came to love only to watch his heart be speared in his breast. And what good was it for Him to open Nev's womb and tear a family asunder when she had to choose between her other half and their child? It set in motion events that led one brother to try to kill the other." My bitterness boils over at the one Valor calls Almighty. "I want nothing to do with Him!"

Sacha leaps into a gallop at the booted heels I dig into her sides. I have had enough conversation for one day.

※ ※ ※

VALOR

Erianna was done. I knew she had given and heard all she could manage for the day, but I pushed her in hopes of reassuring myself that she would stay with me. Thank the the Great Counselor that I choked back the desire to extract from her the same promise Grandileer did. *Do not leave me.* I cannot add to what already is crushing her. Every day that I spend with her, I realize just how much that is and how much she is still hiding. Helping her heal is intensely difficult when she has gushing wounds I cannot see. It will be impossible if she does not release her grip on her anger and allow the Spirit of Truth to bring His peace and light to her darkness.

Granite lengthens his stride to gain on the chestnut mare pounding across the valley. Unfortunately, I must catch her before she reaches the Tareth's home. They might ask her about the topic I have needed to discuss with her all day. She is not ready for it, but other than forbidding anyone from speaking to her, I do not see a way to avoid it. Kragorn will want the answers drafted tonight so that Trent may leave at first light. We must act quickly.

If Erianna can hear me calling to her, she gives no indication of it. She does not rein in until the wall comes into view, and then only insomuch as she will not trample any children wandering about. When I lead Granite into the barn, she is hastily untacking Sacha.

I put Granite into a stall and approach the woman whose demeanor could not make it more clear that she wants to be left alone. "Erianna, I would not have this conversation with you now if it was not so necessary, but you must hear this from me."

She hefts the saddle off Sacha with a grunt and carries it to the tack room. She returns with a bucket of brushes and towels to dry the mare but does not so much as glance at me.

Knowing there is a possibility she could be so lost in her thoughts she did not hear me, I repeat myself. "Please listen to me. This should not wait until tomorrow." She ducks under the mare's neck to brush the off-side I stand on. "Erianna?"

She grinds her teeth, working the brushes over Sacha, laying all the hairs of her coat in the proper direction. She can hear me just fine but is choosing to ignore me. With a sigh, I pick up a pair of brushes and start on the mare's legs, assisting her with the chore. I extend her the bucket to drop her brushes in then we take up towels to dry the sweat from Sacha's coat before the day cools into night and chills the horse. I leave her to finish it while I set up a stall for the mare.

Erianna stays to help me with Granite, and he is settled in short order. I toss her a clothes brush while she whisks away most of the hair on her dress. "Loath as I am to admit it, you are a superior groom to me."

Her mouth twitches at the corners, but she forgoes her usual gloating, so I do it for her, pitching my voice high as I can reach. "Of course I am, you oaf. How do you expect to keep a horse in order when you cannot keep your own self groomed?"

Her face splits into a grin. Instead of passing me the brush, she quirks an eyebrow at me and efficiently sweeps the hairs off my shirt.

I continue my dialogue, giving voice to her actions. "Oh Valor, see what a mess you are. You look every bit the mountain goat Leelah declares you to be."

She snickers and drops the brush into my hand so I may clean off my pants while she waits.

"Well, what say you, my Queen?" I hold my arms out to the side. "Is Leelah right? Do I look like a mountain goat?"

She cocks her head to the side, considering me. "Did you spend much time with Anders this past year?"

I grimace. "As bad as Anders? I would rather look like a goat."

"Well, I am afraid it is Anders I am reminded of. You must either tend your beard with the devotion I give my hair or go on looking like a woodsman. Verily, I did not recognize you at first with all that." The twirl of her hand encompasses my longer hair and full beard.

"Are you so familiar with beard care?" I tease.

She nods curtly. "Leer maintained his only a finger width long so that he needed to do very little beyond regular trimming and brushing." Her eyes soften at a memory. "I asked if he would ever grow it out. He said he would do it for me if I wished to see how I liked the feel of it on my skin, but it would mean more work for him."

Curious at this rare glimpse into their relationship, I ask, "What did you decide?"

Erianna blushes deeply, absentmindedly tracing a hand up her shoulder and around the base her neck, remembering. "Changing it was unnecessary. I liked the length he kept it." Her smile wavers. She drops her face to the ground. Tears glitter on her cheeks. Her fingertips dash them away.

I catch hold of her hand as she brushes past, stalling her retreat. Gently, I pull her toward me and bring her against my chest. This is not the Warrior Queen. This is the too young widow who was given much and feels she lost it all. As my arms come lightly around her shoulders, I feel something break in her.

Her hands fist my shirt, and she weeps. "I miss him so much. I was not ready to lose him. I still need him." She shudders on an exhale. "He promised me a lifetime. We did not even have a year."

This precious woman. She may not love easily, but when she finally does, she loves consumingly. "I am sorry. I hate that this has happened. If I could bring him back to you, I would."

"I know, and I thank you for it. And for this," she leans into me. "You still feel so safe to me."

"I am glad. I shall always strive to be a safe place for you to turn." I feel her use the last of her strength to dam her tears. Her shoulders droop, and she sags from the cost this day has exacted.

"Valor, I am done. I have nothing more this day. Please, whatever it is, let it wait till tomorrow. If you have no serious objections, I would seek my bed." She is truly done if she is reverting to asking for my permission.

My concern becomes that of a man for his woman. It outweighs our duties to the kingdom as the queen and commander.

Kragorn wants her tactical knowledge. Lorennt needs her help to lead the kingdom. But who will care for her? "We shall speak on it tomorrow. Can I bring you something to eat?" She shakes her head. "At least have the creamed milk with honey. It will suffice if you do not have the energy to eat."

She sighs, looking up at me with her head still resting against my chest. "If I must to ease your mind."

I smile affectionately. "You must."

"So be it." She steps back.

I offer her my arm, and she accepts, letting me assist her into the house, shielding her from the before-dinner chaos, and guiding her up the stairs into her room. When I return delivering the cream, she has already donned her nightclothes. I assure her that I will be below-stairs when she wakes which she receives with thanks and bids me goodnight.

The schemes of the Wolves will just have to wait.

CHAPTER TWELVE

VALOR

August 18th

The most pleasant smell beckons me from wandering dreams to enjoy the full promise of a summer's day. I smile, searching for the source in the liminal place between waking and sleeping. The sweetness of wildflowers and lavender lead me back into my dreams where I journey willingly. Silk falls across my neck. I reach up a hand, twining it between my fingers. There is much of it. I sink my fingers in deeper.

A bee sting ruins the dream.

I grumble, raising my lids. The chill of a winter's day awaits in the eyes above me.

"What are you doing?" Erianna hisses in the predawn dark.

"Sleeping," I grunt and wrap another length of silk around my hand.

"Stop that!" Her eyes spark annoyance, and her soft lips purse.

"What?"

She rolls her eyes dramatically downward, and I follow their path.

My hand is wrapped in the silk tresses of her raven hair that spilled over her shoulder when she bent to wake me.

"Sorry." I reluctantly slide my hand free as another breath of summer tickles my senses.

She rises, drawing my notice to the riding clothes she wears with the boon of an overdress. "Get up!" She commands then strides from sight carrying my weapons belt and boots.

Groaning, I toss back the blanket and follow her into the vestibule where she hands me my things. The air is unpleasantly cool when she unbars the door, leading me into the courtyard.

I rub sleep from my eyes. "Why have you woken me so early?"

"I need to train, and you are going to spar with me," she declares.

"Wake Trent next time."

She melds into the cobalt hues around her, wearing the colors upon her pale skin in the moonlight. Deft fingers work her hair into a plait that falls to her waist as we enter the training yard. After stretching, she casts aside the overdress and slips into a sparing stance, waiting for me to do the same.

I consider her for a moment. A thrill shoots through my blood and drags up the corners of my mouth. This is the Warrior Queen. "You are terrifying, Majesty."

Her features draw back in the semblance of a smile, but there is ferocity behind it. Without another word or waiting for me to ready myself, she initiates our old routine used to warm our muscles for the exertion. She paces herself today, focused on building her endurance and the correctness of her posture. I hold up my hands when she is winded.

"Catch your breath," I instruct.

She crosses her arms over her head and walks a leisurely circle around the ring while breathing deeply.

We go on like this until both of us are drenched with sweat, and we can no longer feel the cold for all the heat emanating from us.

Erianna's muscles shake from exhaustion by the time Leelah calls us to breakfast, but her spirits are high.

"Absolutely not!" Leelah stomps her foot and blocks our entry through the kitchen door. "You are both filthy and smell awful."

Erianna leans close and sniffs at my clinging shirt then shrugs. "You have smelled worse."

I grin and sniff at her. The lavender and honey are still detectable beneath the scent of her exertion. "So have you."

"You will turn my stomach from breakfast if you come in like that!" Leelah's head bobs as she brandishes a wooden spoon.

"But we are *hungry*," Erianna whines.

"Then you will eat in the garden with the dog!" Leelah slams the door with finality.

Erianna snickers. "Come. Now we need only wait for our food to arrive and may converse in peace."

We settle onto a bench, Erianna more uprightly for the cuirass limiting her movements. She plucks at the laces, loosening them to allow herself more breathing room, then yawns so wide I am certain she dislocates her jaw.

Karris delivers a plate of food for us to share. I accept it and offer Erianna first choice. She scoops a bite of sweetened porridge, leaving me to devour the cured ham.

Erianna finishes the porridge and takes up the water skin we keep at hand while training. "You have my attention. Tell me what needs to be said," she resolves then sips at the liquid.

I lean forward, bracing my arms on my thighs, picking up where I left off in the story yesterday. "When we captured the brigands, there were three women among the men. I am not sure how they became mixed in with the group. They refused to say. They were valuable to the brigands for their ability to persuade reluctant villages to aid their cause, and they made good coin selling themselves to the outlaws. It was clear that they did not hold to the brigands ideals or wish to forfeit their lives alongside them when we took them as prisoners, but, at that time, they were disinclined to reveal anything of import. When we brought them in, the brigands either withstood interrogation or seemed to genuinely have little information on the broader goals of Gires and Brogan beyond stealing coin and creating widespread dissension in Malesiir."

Erianna inclines her head in a perfect imitation of Grandileer's patient demeanor of taking in information to be weighed. I wonder how many other subtle mannerisms of his she has assimilated.

"With fresh questions to ask and after months of letting them fester in their prison cells, Lorennt and I spoke with the brigands and women while I was there. We asked if they heard anyone speaking Limban or had seen men fitting Zavaan's or Jarmuth's description."

Erianna holds her breath at the impending answer. I wish there was something I could do to blunt the coming blow, but there is not.

"The men still did not have anything to say to us, but the women did. They had seen both Zavaan and Jarmuth and provided us with a few details to validate their claims that I hope you can verify. They saw other men in similar dress in their company and heard them speaking the Limban tongue."

"The details?" She asks.

I offer the first claim, hating that she will know the answer. "They say that Zavaan is heavily scarred across his back and abdomen."

Erianna confirms it.

"They say that Jarmuth called them *devkar levnyr*."

Erianna's lip curls. "Are these women unattractive?"

"They..." How to say it without offending? "They were likely attractive at one time, but they have obviously lived difficult lives. Why? What does that mean?"

She snorts derisively. "It means I am glad you ran Jarmuth through. He, the basest of humanity, insulted them by calling them... Well, there is not a direct translation, but it is a slur that means a cheap whore so unappealing she is not worth taking."

And those are the sort of men Erianna was subjected to for ten days. "I need you to sit down with us today and give us all the details you remember of the Wolves. It is imperative that we know who we are looking for to prevent them from hiding in plain sight. Kragorn also hopes you may remember the roads they used between the coast and the Ascent. Every detail you provide will be put to use. Trent shall set out for Chishelm this afternoon to present the information to General Kannik who is leading the search."

"Very well. But let us finish this first." She returns me to task. "What were the Ruphiri doing with the brigands? Or can I assume they were co-conspirators from the beginning?"

"You can assume that. The women told us the brigands have been hiding in the mountains and pilfering for years, but without a goal beyond taking advantage of others hard work. Roughly a year and a half ago, some Limban men made contact with them and set plans in motion to convince the provinces to secede from Malesiir starting with the North."

Erianna turns sideways on the bench to face me fully. Questions leap from her wide eyes, but she bites her tongue on them.

"Without recounting the exchange word for word, Lorennt and I surmised that the goal was the destabilization of the Malesiirian economy and the procuring of supplies and funds for the Wolves. It adequately explains where all the supplies and gold went that were stolen by the brigands. Furthermore, Zavaan's arrival in Malesiir seems to coincide with yours. Trent believes the description Lorennt gave him fits well with the fifth horseman that you stumbled across in the woods during your spy lessons."

"It was him," she whispers. Her breaths become rapid as facts assault her one after another. "Valor, it was Bronis that ran away with me the night that you were away, the one that struck my face. He is Zavaan's second and so atrocious even Zavaan did not let him near me. Bronis had me!"

"You fought him off and escaped," I remind her, but she is not listening.

Fear grips her throat, strangling her. "In Grass Lake, Chase—Zavaan —followed us the day I met him. He saw us sparing. He saw you provoke me to fight then earn my trust. He tried to do that exact thing to me in Malesiir when... when..." She presses a hand to her chest, gasping.

I take her hands in mine. "Slowly. It is just you and I. You are safe."

She nods, striving to calm her breaths.

"What do you mean he did the same thing to you that I did?" Something I still regret.

"He seized an opportunity Lorennt and I foolishly gave him. Leer thought he was just studying me and making sport of my fear, but that was not it at all." Erianna is horrified. "He was trying to be you. In a thousand ways, he tried to side with me, tease me. He even trained me. Valor," her voice quakes, "he must have been watching us so closely."

My mind throws these details into the mismatched jumble she has revealed, trying to keep pace with her.

Erianna pulls her hands from mine and wraps them around her middle. "Oh, it disgusts! He spied on us! How could he have been so near and us not know it?"

I am losing the Warrior Queen. She is succumbing to her fear. Next will be grief, and then she will be poured out for the rest of the day.

"He planned this," she whispers. "He has been planning this for far longer than we have known each other. Before Leer sent for me, Zavaan was planning to move against him. Zavaan played Leer just like Leer played—"

"My Queen!" I shout, startling her, trying to keep her from slipping away on the downward spiral. "I need you to attend. There is more, and it is imperative you hear it." I pull her to her feet and lead her around the garden, using the physical movement to redirect her thoughts. "Aye. Zavaan has been planning this. How much? We do not know. The women overheard him say two things in Limban often. He said *Vreh Král* and *Zajatí Královna*. What does the second mean?"

"Capture the Queen," she replies, stepping closer to my side and wrapping both hands around my arm.

Past and present collide in a way that stirs my own fear. In the dark of the Nevermore Forest, Erianna held onto me, pleading with me to protect her. *"They have found me. Please do not let them take me! Please,*

Commander! They will break me and my kingdom."

My sword hand itches with fear, kindling my temper. A truer presage she could not have uttered. They took her. They broke her. Our kingdom lost its king and was poised upon the edge of civil war. If Lorennt and Erianna do not rally quickly, it is still possible should another family make a bid for the throne. Irrational feelings of being watched raise the hairs on my neck. I clench the leather wrapped hilt in my off-hand as I engage all my senses to scan the walled garden for the enemies I hope I will not find.

I have not yet told Erianna that we found wolf tracks spread liberally on the roads to Malesiir and throughout the forests, nor of the ambush we set for those tracking us who hoped we would lead them to her.

"They did all they set out to do." Erianna's tearful words snap the frayed rope of my control.

"Not yet," I growl, allowing my sword hand the relief of bringing her into my embrace. I bend my head to hers, challenging her despair which is a greater enemy than the fanged corporeal ones. "We are still standing. You are not lost, and the kingdom has not collapsed. We will route these Wolves and see the peace restored that they tried to destroy."

My fingers trace her jaw, lifting her face to mine, willing her to seize my resolve for her own. "We do not yield."

But Erianna has already crumbled and holding what remains of her is like grasping a handful of sand. I cannot keep her together, not when she believes she is irreparably shattered.

Movement near the house catches my notice. My eyes find Leelah dropping to her knees and bowing her head, but not in defeat. She goes to war.

It is then that I am given the words. I place my hands on either side of Erianna's face and fervently demand, "Is there breath in your lungs? Does your heart beat in your chest? Is there strength in your body? Aye. All that you have. We do not yield!"

Her eyes have never looked so desolate or truthful. "There is nothing left to yield. It has already been surrendered. I am only bones, dry and cracked in the sun. There is no life in me."

"Then you need new life. I cannot grant it to you. But there is One who can. His Breath will revive your very soul and free you from the fear binding you more securely than chains."

Bitterness flows from Erianna's mouth. "You think Him capable? He has already abandoned me in the midst of the deepest hell. When I needed Him most, He was not there. So, I will not call out to Him now. He will not answer me."

"I tell you, He was there. As surely as I am with you now, He has never abandoned you."

"Then He is a sadist!" She scoffs. "Taking pleasure in my pain, watching idly while my life was razed to ashes."

"That is the Deceiver's voice you hear," I realize with the guidance of Truth. "He can only tell lies and will whisper the ones most devastating to you, hoping to lead you astray from the Creator's love. He wants to destroy you as surely as he is destroyed. Tell me," I urge. "What does that voice sound like? You have heard the Voice of Truth. Recall it. How long has it been since you heard that Voice? How long have you been listening to the Deceiver instead?"

Creases form across her brow, and her eyes lower as she searches her memories. But too quickly, she casts aside my question. "It makes no difference. The *truth* is my husband is dead. The *truth* is Illyanna died in my arms. The truth is I am half in the grave, and my only aim before I submit to its pull is to drag Zavaan there with me."

Erianna breaks my hold on her and strides from the garden back to the training yard, fueled by hate, exuding malice.

I loose a long, slow breath, watching her until she passes from sight. Leelah joins me, staring after her. "Now we know the real enemy," Leelah declares, "and we can take up the proper arms in this fight."

My hands clasp together, no longer yearning for the weapons of steel to sever flesh but the weapons of the Spirit to sunder darkness.

CHAPTER THIRTEEN

ERIANNA

August 22nd

I can hardly move without groaning in pain. After spending the first half of yesterday training until I could not raise my staff without shaking like a leaf, Valor refused to spar with me anymore. When I asked Trent to train me, Valor gave me the choice of being tied to a chair in the great room or conditioning Sacha. I chose the latter.

Luckily for me, I will not have to admit I overworked myself and cannot spar today. Leelah has conscripted all of us to help harvest the last of her garden, except for Trent who is scouting the woods for wolf tracks under the guise of hunting.

Lois and Ivy bound into our room with ribbons streaming from their hands. "Good morning! Will you please, please, please do our hair?"

After that is done, they keep us company while we dress and ready for the day. Nev obliges the girls by letting them feel the babe move about inside her. Though Nev is further progressed in her pregnancy than I was allowed to, she is still graceful in her movements, and her willowy figure has not filled out beyond the roundness of her belly. The girls jest that she is smuggling a melon under her dress. I laugh along with them and spend a goodly amount of time sharing in Nev's joy with my hand on my little niece or nephew. No matter what, I do not ever let her see my envious tears.

A knock on the door is followed by Leelah's voice that is too alert for the hour. "Do not dawdle! We must get through breakfast and complete the chores quickly to have time aplenty to thoroughly clean the garden."

I look to my companions. "Did she not say last eve that all we needed to do was help bring in the harvest?"

They all shrug, and Ivy explains, "Mother will not waste extra hands on a light day's work. She will have us doing the harvest while Father and Uncle put the garden to bed for the winter."

"That also means cleaning out the barn and adding all the manure and straw on top of the garden," Lois chimes in. Ivy concurs.

Nev giggles. "No day of rest for you, Anna. Maybe next time you will listen to Valor when he says to 'put down the staves.'"

I hold back a groan and stuff an extra change of clothes into my saddlebag along with everything I will need for the day. If worse comes to worse, I will simply escape to Valor's house when no one is looking and soak my aching muscles in his glorious bathtub.

A high pitched *ping, ping, ping* resounds through the misty air. "What is that?" I ask the girls. The pitch is too high to be the sounds from a forge, but it is similar in rhythm.

Lois waves her hand in the air. "That is Father and Uncle peening the scythes. They put a new edge on the blades before each use with a hammer and anvil."

Another knock on the door, this time Karris. "Anna, Mother says she needs your help and to hurry below."

I look askance at Nev and cover Lois's ears. She covers Ivy's. "I am the *blessed Queen*, yet I do not think I have given out as many orders in the last year as *Mistress Tareth* has given out in the last week!"

Nev snickers. "Aye. She is authoritarian."

"She is a tyrant!" I hiss.

Nev shrugs sympathetically.

Down in the kitchen, Leelah presses mugs of tea and porridge cakes into our hands. "What kept you? The day is wasting."

"Apologies, Milady." I mockingly curtsy to her. Nev hides a laugh.

Leelah tosses an apron at my face with a grin. "I like your sass. I would hate having a dullard for a best friend."

"Best friend?"

"The very best. Just you wait." Leelah winks an amber eye and struts into the garden, barking orders.

Nev pops half her porridge cake into her mouth, stoppering her laugh. She ties an apron high over her waist, accentuating Melon's round presence.

The garden resembles nothing of the peaceful, overgrown muddle of yesterday. The girls move through rows of tall plants, filling baskets with the last of the beans and corn, while Micah sits in the middle of a dirt pile happy as can be, searching for carrots, turnips and potatoes. He throws fistfuls of dirt to the side and cheers when he finds an overlooked root, adding it to a growing pile.

"Nev." Leelah waves the woman over. I follow along. "Would you help the girls with the corn they cannot reach? Then I need you to collect all the dead flowers for seeds and the blooms to take to Salome for the Gathering tomorrow." Nev nods and accepts the pair of shears Leelah slaps into her palm. "Baskets are over there." Leelah points to a teetering stack of various size rush baskets.

"*Hmm*." She considers me over crossed arms. "Valor tells me you enjoy hard work, so you can work with me."

Of course he did, the fiend.

Leelah guides me to the stack of tools Kragorn hauled out of the barn. She hands me a long handled scythe and a whetstone stone nestled in a leather water pouch. "We will be inspecting the work the girls have done to ensure they did not miss anything edible. After that, we will cut the rows at the ground. The men will go behind us, raking and hauling everything to the goats and cow. Except for that row." Leelah points to it. "Valor would like those greens cut and carted to his house where he will dry them for Granite to enjoy this winter. Come. I will teach you how to use the scythe. There is nothing to it."

If not an outright liar, Leelah is dangerously optimistic. Every muscle in my back and stomach protests at the wide, swinging motion of wielding the scythe over the garden rows. Holding the blade at the correct angle parallel to the ground to achieve a close cut without digging the blade into the dirt is thrice difficult. I repeatedly forget to hone the blade with the whetstone in my apron pocket until Leelah reminds me every few minutes. I catch my breath while I use my apron to wipe the blade clean then slide the stone off the edge of the blade to sharpen it. Leelah progresses down her row rapidly and is beginning another before I have finished half of my first.

I try to work faster, but the tip of my blade sinks into the earth. I stomp my foot in frustration and pull the blade up to knock off the burs I surely put in the metal.

"You are leaning too far forward," Valor comments behind me where he bundles the cut bean plants. "Stand up straighter and spread your feet further apart."

I do as bid then continue the stroke, swinging my arms side to side while trying to properly grip the snath of the scythe. It pulls terribly between my shoulders, and I grumble under my breath but press on.

"You are still leaning forward," Valor remarks as he returns for another bundle.

I stand up straighter, but the scythe becomes awkward in my hands causing me to raise it too high on the backswing.

"Hold it lower, parallel with—"

"I am trying!" I snap. "Either demonstrate or leave me be!"

He stands next to me and demonstrates the placement of the scythe then hands the tool back to me. I try, but his expression says I am still doing it wrong.

I growl and stomp my foot. "Just fix me that I may do it properly!" When did he become concerned about propriety, anyway?

Valor stands behind me, wrapping his arms around me, and adjusts my hands on the grip and uses his feet to push mine into a wider stance. He guides me through the stroke, but the cut is uneven.

"*Hmm...*" He adjusts my hold again. "This is not right. The grip is too low for you."

Valor takes the scythe, leading me back to the pile of tools. He raises the grip on the snath. "Try it now."

It fits much better, and I do not have to stoop to hold it correctly.

"Did Leelah not adjust the grip for you?" Valor asks suspiciously, eyeing the woman across the garden.

"No." I follow his gaze to where Leelah glides efficiently over a row. Kragorn moves behind her, raking and bundling the fallen corn stalks. "She told me that I will be her very best friend. Should I be worried?"

Valor snorts. "No."

"Why would she say that?"

"Leelah is just being Leelah. Enthusiastic and meddlesome. But she means well. Do not worry," Valor reassures me, casting an annoyed look at the red head. "Come, Majesty. The sooner this is done, the sooner you can have that bath."

"How did you know—"

"Look! Look! I got the giant king of 'em all!" Micah gloats, holding a fat squirming earthworm aloft. "Father is going to take me fishing later if I find good worms, and this is the best one yet! Ha!" The boy kisses the unhappy worm and darts off to show his father. Kragorn pauses to praise his son's find and swoops him into the air, sending dirt flying every direction from the filthy lad.

Scything goes much better for the rest of the morning. I fall into a rhythm with the tool that is mindlessly pleasant. I keep my eyes on the row before me while the girls sing their way through their work. Valor whistles the tune of their song as he goes behind me, hauling away the spent plants, then works ahead of my slow pace by cleaning the overlooked produce from the next row.

At midmorning, we finish up the first round of our assigned chores. Nev and Karris, who are the least dirty of the lot of us, bring platters of food out. We congregate by the water bucket in the shade, passing around the dipper.

"What next, General Leelah?" Valor asks, dusting off his hands then reaching for a slice of peach I had just decided to take. He bites into it while I go after another.

Leelah props hands on her hips, surveying her domain. "The barn needs to be cleaned out and the manure spread thickly over the finished rows. We also need to gather the herbs into bunches and hang them to dry in the larder."

I reach for a slice of melon, but Valor beats me to it, plucking the slice off the tray. I glare up at him, but he pays no mind. Maybe it was unintentional.

"We can help Kragorn in the barn," Valor nudges me. "She has not had to clean a stall in months. It will be character building."

Usually, I would not balk at the labor, but the thought of bending over a pitchfork makes me groan.

General Leelah only nods. "Fine. Anna you…"

"No!" Micah interrupts, tugging on his mother's skirt. "I want Majie to pick herbs with me!"

"Majie?" Leelah asks. "Who is Majie?"

Micha points to me. "She is. That's what Uncle calls her."

Majesty, he means. "It is an endearment," I say, lest someone seeks to explain my title.

"What's a-dear-men?" Micah asks.

Karris supplies, "It's like when Father calls Mother 'Honey-sop.'"

"No," I interject over Nev's giggling, "it is not like that at all."

"It's kind of like that." Valor grins mischievously and swipes a piece of melon from my hand.

I hit his arm and take it back. "Do not confuse the children."

Kragorn takes control of the matter. "It is a term of respect that you may call her if you wish."

I incline my head regally. "Thank you, General."

"Happy to help, Majie," he replies solemnly.

I roll my eyes.

"Do you know how to bundle herbs, Majie?" Leelah snickers on the name. I suppose it is not going away anytime soon.

"I think I remember how. Hellah taught me when we were in Grass Lake."

"Oh!" Leelah exclaims. "I forgot you met Hellah! Oh, I am jealous! I have always wanted to meet her."

"You would get on well," I assure her. "Perhaps I can introduce you. I have promised to bring her to visit once travel is safer."

Valor is all astonishment. "When did you do that?"

"Hellah and I have kept regular correspondence over the last year," I inform him, taking pleasure in his surprise. "We usually send each other little gifts with our letters. In fact," I remember excitedly, "she should have already sent me scarves to wrap—" I swallow my words, looking at little Fialla tied to Leelah's back with a length of cloth. My gaiety vanishes.

Once we were confident that Illyanna was growing in me, I sent Hellah money along with my last letter and asked her to send me a dozen of the brightly colored scarves the women of Grass Lake use to tie their babes to them. Though Mother Celiea said we could find a wet nurse for the littlest Rodiharian and there was no need for the babe to be constantly bound to me, I was certain I wanted my babe close to me always. I am even more certain of it now.

I fist my hands to keep them from reaching to my empty womb. A pall descends over the adults who stare at me with growing expressions of pity. I have ruined the jovial mood again.

Nev wraps her arms around my waist, hugging my side. I force a smile and lay a hand on her belly. "Not a waste at all. Our little Melon will need to be close to his mother. And you, sweet Nev, will be the height of fashion in Malesiir for all your colorful wraps."

I drop my slice of fruit back onto the tray with a frozen smile. "Leelah, where are some more shears and twine? I will start on those herbs."

"I can show you," Valor offers. He guides me past the basket containing those things, through the kitchen door, and into the great room.

Without a word, he takes me against him, hiding me from the world while this fresh wave of grief tries to drown me. Over and over I cry, "I lost my babe."

※ ※ ※
* * *

The others have progressed well in spite of our absence. Micah did not forget that I was to pick herbs with him. He takes me in hand when I return to the garden. I am given a lesson on the proper way to use scissors, how many herbs ought to go into a bundle, and how to tie a smart knot. He also says, "Make double sure you leave a dog's tail of string so Mother can hang the bundles in the rafters."

"A dog's tail?"

"This much," he gestures. "Do not forget." His brows go up and down with each word.

I show him my first bundles and receive his exuberant approval.

"How many worms did you find today?" I ask.

"A giant pail full! Look!" He runs to collect it and stuffs his little hand beneath the thin layer of soil in the bucket, glorying in his fistful of worms. "I will teach you how to fish when we go to the creek after chores."

"I thought only you and your father were going?"

"No, we all go the day before Gathering to bathe in fine weather," Karris explains from across the row. "We usually take our dinner too and eat fish if we catch any. That's why we all hurry through chores. The faster we get done—"

"The more time we get to play!" Ivy, Lois and Micah chant. It is a saying Leelah oft repeats when the children begin to grumble at chores.

"That sounds like a great deal of fun, but Uncle, Nev, and I are delivering all those greens to his home after chores." *And then I'll have a real bath.* I dwell on the evening's plans that Valor told me of to help bring me back to the present and give me something to look forward to.

Leelah, Kragorn, and Valor return with a fresh load of barn litter to spread over the garden. I continue moving along the row of herbs, bent to my task and lost in my thoughts. Something smacks into my skirt, startling me to look around, but I see nothing out of the ordinary around me. I bend over again and tie a few more bundles then see Nev startle, looking behind her.

"Did you bump my skirt?" She asks me. I shake my head and we continue working.

Something solid smacks the back of my leg. Karris bursts out laughing.

"Karris, what did you do?" Nev asks.

"Not a thing! Honest!" She giggles.

In rapid succession, I hear a thump then feel one.

Karris can contain herself no longer. She braces her hands on her knees, guffawing. "It is Uncle! He is throwing horse apples at you!"

Valor whistles merrily, raking the spent litter over a garden bed, but at our feet are round clods of dry horse manure.

"*Ugh!*" Nev gasps in disgust. "Valor, how could you!"

He does a rotten job of maintaining his feigned innocence.

"Because he is an absolute child!" I deride, returning to my task for all of a minute.

The next clod hits my rear. I round on Valor with tight lipped furry. His shoulders shake with laughter.

"Just ignore him, and he will bore of it," Nev suggests.

But that will not satisfy me. I scoop up a handful of the lumps and hurl them at his face. He laughs, dodging the missiles I lob. I huff in indignation and brush my hands off on my skirt.

Leelah chuckles. "I never thought I would see *Majie* in my garden throwing horse droppings! No one will ever believe me."

"My brother would believe you," I snicker.

Nev laughs. "He would probably think you started it. Oh, but can you imagine what Leer would say? He would take you to task straightaway! He did not even let you clean Sacha's stall."

So clearly can I imagine Leer's reaction that I double over with laughter and tell Nev in Leer's patient cadence, "My Dear. Queens do not touch horse manure if it can be avoided."

She sits down in the dirt from laughing so hard. "Then Lorennt would be in trouble, too, for letting you misbehave."

I nod, brushing tears of mirth from the corners of my eyes. Remembering with Nev is so much better than remembering alone. She takes the sting out of it, because she was there and understands the nuances of Leer and I better than anyone else. She also knows the pain from missing her own Rodiharian prince.

"Mother! How come Uncle throws horse apples at them, and they laugh? When I threw horse apples at Ivy she cried, and I got switched." Micah's little bellow draws the rest of the party into the moment, lifting our spirits through the remainder of the chores.

I glance at Valor with a grateful smile, and he winks. This man holds me through my tears then will do whatever it takes to lighten my heart afterward. Even if that means throwing a horse apple.

He is still my favorite person.

CHAPTER FOURTEEN

ERIANNA

We three ride over to Valor's house in Leelah's little pony cart with the greens heaped in the back. The journey takes much longer at such a plodding pace, so I seize the opportunity to rest. I lie atop the greens and close my eyes, content to listen to Valor and Nev talk about the Gathering tomorrow and various aspects of life in the high valley. I am nearly asleep when we reach the turn to Valor's house. For the fun of being a brute, he takes the turn quickly, toppling me from the pile of greens.

"Did I disturb your rest, Majie?" He asks over his shoulder with his trouble laden half-smile.

I sit up from the corner I rolled into. "Banish whatever thought has made you smile thus."

He faces forward with a grin. "I thought you would want to be awake to greet your admirer if he is about."

Nev perks up with keen interest. "What admirer?"

"Thad's eldest, Col. I am chaperoning their first meeting tomorrow," Valor informs her conspiratorially.

I roll my eyes.

"Do not tell me you have snared another!" Nev adds fuel to Valor's teasing.

"Another?" Valor exclaims.

Nev leans close to him. "Erianna had a string of noblemen in pursuit of her affections."

"That is a bounding exaggeration of the truth," I scoff. "The majority sought my company as a means of gaining the king's ear."

"Aye, but the other half wanted *your* ear," Nev insinuates.

Valor's booming laugh bursts forth. "Tell me, did any of them gain her ear?"

"Not a one. Erianna was the picture of devotion to her husband. But that did not prevent Leer from tossing a few over-eager pursuers out of the great hall," Nev recollects. "Lorennt also blocked several men from Erianna's company."

"He did not," I retort.

"Lord Eglon?" She counters, reminding me of the eager young lord who sought my attention for a few weeks after the solstice celebrations.

"Oh. I forgot about him." I cross my arms. "Leer only threw the lewd drunkards out of the great hall. The rest had the good sense not to seek me out when Leer was present."

"Or Lorennt, for the most part," she concurs then sighs dramatically. "Many a man had unrequited love for Leer's Untouchable Wife."

"Nev!" I hiss.

"His what?" Valor asks.

Nev offers me an apologetic glance and moves on. "I jest only. Erianna was not the flirt I make her out to be. Therein lies the humor. But are you truly seeing Col tomorrow?"

I explain, "He invited me to tour his farm, and I thought it a good opportunity to see firsthand how my people live. If I do not understand them, how can I make the best decisions for them?"

"Which is admirable," Valor points out, "except that Col does not know you are his twice-royal queen and have more interest in the farm than him."

"That should not present much of a problem." Nev offers a solution. "Valor will be there and as often as you two are in company, it would be a simple thing to imply there was some attachment between you that could easily be explained away once it is made known that Anna is, in fact, Queen Erianna." Nev pauses for effect then, with a sly glance at me, exclaims, "Oh! But that will not work if you have already formed an attachment with Tirzah. Have you?"

I cover a smile at Nev's blunt question and wait for the answer.

Valor turns the cart onto the little bridge that just accommodates it. "I have not formed an attachment with her. You all think about that woman more often than I do."

"Do you not find her attractive?" Nev prods.

"She is, but I am not sure we would suit each other," Valor replies.

"Then you will continue seeing her until you are certain?" Nev asks.

"I will not. I have a queen and a ward to look after. I cannot imagine taking responsibility for another woman. You two are an absolute handful," Valor directs that at me then returns his attention to Nev. "As for Col, I believe assuring him that Erianna was simply being polite and has no desire to entertain suitors while she is in mourning will effectively dissuade him."

"That is quite true," I say for Nev's benefit lest she acts on her notion to push Valor and I together. She means well, but I do not think my heart will ever recover from the loss of my husband and daughter.

We work to put up the greens so they will dry properly then head inside to prepare dinner while Valor takes the first bath. There is not much to preparing the simple meal which leaves time for us to tend to some of the chores Valor has neglected. He keeps a neat home, so all is done before he finishes his bath.

I search for a book to borrow while Nev rests in an armchair and picks up our conversation in a hushed tone. "I am sorry I said that! I do not know what has gotten into me."

"That Melon has made you daft," I tease. "You rarely ever speak an unintentional word. This is what comes from having Lorennt's child growing inside you."

She sighs, revealing something of her own heart that has still not healed from their separation. "You might be right."

"Do you wish things had happened differently? That you had stayed with him?" I ask gently.

Her deepest blue eyes sparkle with unshed tears. "Of course. He is my other half. I will never stop missing him. I know that he would have been a wonderful father to our babe."

"Aye, he would," I agree wholeheartedly, "and he still could be."

Her eyes become guarded. "What do you mean?"

"I do not want you to give me your answer yet, but Valor and I both think it is necessary for you to return to Malsihra with me in a few months. Please listen," I interrupt the slow shake of her head. "I know that you have made a home here, but everything has changed. Leer is gone," I push past the lump in my throat the declaration produces. "Lorennt was furious with him for sending you away. Nothing we said could convince him that the blame did not rest on Leer. Lorennt wanted to take you to wife and Boldizar sided with him. You know that I wanted it too, but I supported your decision."

"But Celiea and Leer—"

I take her hands in mine. "It does not matter anymore. Leer's branch of the family has been cut off. Illyanna is gone, and I will not be able to give the Rodiharians an heir."

"What are you saying?" Nev's grip tightens around mine. "You could have more children, maybe with one of the cousins or," she swallows convulsively. "Or you and Lorennt could—"

"Absolutely not," I reply unwaveringly. "Lorennt is my brother and ever shall be." I tuck back a lock of her light hair, smiling sadly. "I told you how I lost Illyanna. What I did not tell you was that the physician believes it is unlikely I will be able to carry a babe for the full term. He believes I will lose many more and told Leer there was a great risk to me in trying."

"Oh, Erianna!" Nev is horrified at the thought.

"Hush. I have made my peace with it. Besides, I have no husband to get a child on me, nor do I want one." I lay my hand on Lorennt's babe. "I know Lorennt would claim you both, and our little Melon will be the heir to the throne, the first offspring of Lorennt's branch of the family. We need *you*, Nev. Lorennt needs you. Please think about it."

She nods, and we settle into our private thoughts until Valor joins us. Nev must be made to see the wisdom in this. I am afraid I will be forced to do something as decisive as Leer would have deemed necessary if she does not come around. I hope it does not come to that.

"How did I do?" Valor seeks our approval as he exits the bathing room.

We give him our attention, and my heart jolts.

He shaved off the unkempt woodsman beard and returned to looking like the Valor I knew a year ago except for the long hair he has combed back. I lace my fingers together so I do not stretch them out and trace the rugged planes of his face once more visible.

"Leelah has called you a mountain goat a dozen times. Why the change?" Nev asks.

Valor pulls out chairs at the table for us, and we take our seats. "I was told that I was beginning to look like Anders and my appearance is a reflection of the one I serve. That seemed just cause."

"Ah. I see," Nev drawls, covering a smile.

Heat creeps up my face. He did it for me. "Much better. We approve."

"If either of you are handy with scissors, I could use help trimming my hair," Valor requests.

Thankfully, I can honestly say that is not a skill I posses. Even though my fingers itch to twine in the golden brown locks. "I am not."

"Nor I," Nev says.

"Then it will have to wait." Valor shrugs.

We talk and laugh over the light meal. While Nev takes her turn in the bath, I set the tea on. A tingling awareness tells that Valor's eyes are on me as I move about the kitchen.

"You are staring," I say without turning around.

He chuckles. "I am."

"People usually apologize for such." I pour the water into the pot, wafting delicate chamomile.

"I am not sorry," he replies.

I lean against the edge of the cupboard, facing him and waiting for the tea to steep. We consider each other across the room.

Valor is the first to break the companionable silence. "Would you understand if I said it feels strange to see you in my kitchen?"

"In a bad way?" I ask.

He shakes his head.

"I understand completely." I brace my hands on either side, curling my fingers around the wooden surface.

"What do you usually do in the evenings?" I ask.

"If I am not with the Tareth family? Read. Soak in the tub. Sit on the porch." He stretches his legs out before him and crosses his arms. "Mostly I just pass time until I can reasonably retire for the night."

He is lonely, I realize with no small pang of guilt. He needs a companion. A wife.

"How have you spent your evenings Queen Erianna?"

I instantly blush, making Valor chuckle. I lift the teapot and pour the brew into mugs. I add twice as much honey to my cup as to his.

Once settled opposite him, I reply. "Leer and I were rarely together during the day outside of mealtimes. We retired early and used the evenings to be together, telling each other of our day and the significant happenings within the court and kingdom." I stare sadly into my steaming mug, hating myself for spending the last weeks of our marriage so angry at him that we were not even speaking. I search back further in my memory. "I usually read. Or soaked in my tub. Or tried to learn the game of chess of which Leer was so fond." So clearly can I remember Leer sitting across from me that I almost believe when I look up he will be here. If not for the pain banding my chest, I might try.

"What have you done now, my Dear?" Leer asks.

"Whatever do you mean?" I say innocently.

"Did you think I would not notice that half the pawns are missing?" He steeples his fingers.

"Are they?" I glance down at the board.

"Erianna," he chides in his beautiful voice.

"Maybe you should go look for them if you wish to play." I grin mischievously.

He sighs. "I am tired, Dearest."

"They are nearby," I simper. "I swear it. You will not have to go down to the kitchens tonight."

He dithers but relents to my good humor. "I will need a clue."

"You will find some of them in your second favorite place in these rooms," I supply with a quirked brow.

Leer rises and searches the couch.

I head through the parlor door and call over my shoulder, "That is your third favorite place."

He chuckles, hinting at the mellifluous laugh I hope to draw out presently, and follows me into the bedroom. I stand in the middle of the room, watching as he draws back the covers on the bed revealing half of the stolen chess pieces.

"And for the rest?" He asks silkily.

"They are in your first favorite place—in these rooms or any other." I catch my lip between my teeth as he crooks a finger at me. I draw near to him.

Leer raises his hands to my face and begins a caress that starts by loosening my hair from its braid then travels downward, freeing the laces of my gown and slowly, gently sliding it from my shoulders. "My favorite place, in this room or any other, is in your arms. Thus, I must conclude that—"

My gown drops to the floor and with it, the unmistakable clatter of the missing pieces. Leer's grin gives rise to his rich laugh that could chase away any cloud in my sky. "My Dear, do not ever change. My days were so dreary before you."

"I am sure they were," I complacently remark. "And now, since you have done most of the work already in turning down our bed and helping me out of my dress, why don't you tuck me in for the night?"

His answering smile makes my heart race. "I, too, seem to have lost interest in the game for the evening." He brushes a hand across the bed, scattering the pieces without a care for where they fall.

Another man's hand softly touches my cheek. I blink my eyes rapidly, trying to reorient myself.

"Erianna?" Valor's concerned grey eyes are before me. His hand cups my face. "Can you hear me?"

The memory evaporates on a painful breath. I nod, biting my lip hard to contain the sob searching for a way out. Valor opens his arms to me, and I lean forward to fall into him but stop myself. Leer would not like it. He would be so jealous.

"I cannot." I draw my knees to my chest, wrapping my arms around them.

Valor lowers his arms and settles onto his heels, not backing away from me. "Where did you go?"

"I was lost in a memory," I whisper. That is all I can manage without losing control.

He smiles compassionately. "Should I not have disturbed you?"

I shake my head. "I cannot live in them. They are vibrant yet hollow. And every one of them leads to the same wretched conclusion."

"What can I do for you?"

A tremor shakes me. Sinister memories threaten to unfurl. "Would you—" I swallow the words *hold me.* "Be near me."

Valor looks uncertain how to be nearer me without crossing a boundary that is murky even for me. He turns and sits back against my chair. "Like that night at Grevnhold?"

I release my knees, dropping my toes to the floor. Valor leans a shoulder against my legs, giving me what I asked for.

"Why did you choose this place in the valley to build your home?" I wonder aloud and let his deep voice fill the cracks in my heart.

"I wanted a parcel that was set back from the rest of the community. I needed a quiet place to think and be without the constant passing by of neighbors. This parcel was unclaimed and had several things to recommend it besides its location. The land lays well. It has the creek for a constant water source. Those were good indications that I would be able to sink a well and strike water without much difficulty."

"Could you?"

He huffs. "No. Things usually work out to be more difficult than I envision them at the outset. I ran into a layer of rock that had to be broken through. It was days of hard work just to breach it. But it was worth it. I struck an underground spring beneath the rock and was able to lay the well easily after that."

"And you needed timber for your home," I consider what else would have endeared this place to him.

"Aye. Granite's pasture was mostly wooded when I selected this parcel. I created the pasture by felling the trees for the barn and the home. I tried to train Granite to hitch logs, but he decided he was too noble to be a draft horse. I bought the draft pony out there and gave it to Leelah when I had no more need of it."

Valor tells me how he went about laying the foundation and splitting the logs then hoisting them into place using the pony and ramps. I settle in my chair, relaxing into his story until Nev finishes with her bath. Valor refills the tub with fresh, hot water for me, and I sink up to my chin in the blissful heat.

※ ※ ※

VALOR

I rub my hand over the back of my head, trying to erase the sensation of Erianna's mindless touch. She did not realize she was doing it, but as I talked, she settled and began to comb her fingers from my scalp to the ends of my hair, sending shivers down my spine and making my blood heat.

I do not know why she would not let me hold her when it was so obvious that she wanted comfort, but as I fill Nev's mug with tea, I decide to ask her. I know precisely where to start.

I put the mug in her hands and sit in the chair opposite. "I want to ask you about what you said earlier. Why did you call Erianna 'Leer's Untouchable Wife'?"

Nev winces. "I should not have said that."

"But you did, and now I cannot let it go." I tell her what happened, asking for context.

"Poor thing." Nev sighs, glancing to the closed bathing room door. "I suppose you should understand so you know how best to reach her, though I dislike feeling I break her confidence." She lays her hands on her belly that I can see jumping with each kick of the babe. I do not feel close enough to Nev that I would ask to lay my hand on her, but Leelah permitted me to when she was pregnant with Micah. It was a singular feeling.

"Lorennt and Leer were dissimilar, as I am sure you do not need to be told. But in one area they were identical. They were both possessive and jealous lovers." Nev pauses to collect her thoughts. "Lorennt was terribly jealous of my affection and did not tolerate my maintaining friendships with other men. Not that I sought other men, but... *Hmm...* How to explain?" She drums her fingers on her belly. "Lorennt would see your friendship with Leelah as inappropriate and would not have allowed me to have such a relationship."

"But she is like a sister to me. Her children call me 'Uncle.'" I say, trying to understand, "Is it not the same with Erianna and Lorennt? They are as siblings and quite close."

Nev nods, taking up this thread. "Aye, with very strict rules. Leer and Lorennt were even jealous of each other. Leer entrusted Lorennt with Erianna's safekeeping and was pleased that they were friends, but Lorennt almost never laid a hand on her. He never hugged her or did anything beyond offering her his arm when the situation called for it. For instance, when they trained, Lorennt would only show Erianna what she must do. He avoided touching her or moving her into the correct position. It infuriated her. She did not understand Leer's possessiveness, though Lorennt and I tried to explain it to her."

I frown, recalling how Erianna snapped at me earlier today when I tried to respect her space by demonstrating with the scythe instead of positioning her. "Leer did not explain his feelings to her?"

"It would have caused a fight that brought the castle down if he did. But I cannot explain why, so do not ask. That will have to come from her," Nev declares. "Leer tried to downplay his jealous feelings to her, and actually left it to Lorennt to ensure she learned 'Malesiirian propriety.' Unfortunately, Erianna did not take to their possessiveness well. She began calling herself 'Leer's Untouchable Wife' and felt more isolated from those around her. Not that she sought attention from others, but she could feel the distance even more than her rank caused because of Leer's territorial nature. She said the nobility saw her as Leer's wife or the queen, never as a person."

I grit my teeth. My friend who hates feeling alone was in a marriage that isolated her. "Did Leer not give her the affection she needed?"

"Do not misunderstand me," Nev hurries to explain. "As much as they were possessive, Leer and Lorennt were equally affectionate. Once they began cultivating love between them, Leer was terribly devoted and as openly affectionate as propriety and Erianna's modesty would allow, much more so in private. They were making a good life together."

"But now Grandileer is gone," I begin to understand. "Yet Erianna's loyalty to him continues to isolate her and make her feel guilty for wanting my comfort."

"Aye," Nev concurs and lowers her voice to a mere whisper. "I would hazard that the love she still feels for you is compounding her guilt."

My heart pounds. "You think something of what she once felt for me remains?"

"I am sure of it. But the road to reach her through her grief and overcoming the many obstacles between you is going to be treacherous," Nev cautions me of what I already know.

"I think you know my heart toward her, but I will tell you my mind. Even if she is never capable of offering me more than friendship and the position as her Hand, I shall not willingly leave her," I fiercely assert my claim on the one my heart loves.

Nev's smile is bright. "Good. I want to see my friends reunited and made happy with each other."

CHAPTER FIFTEEN

ERIANNA

August 23rd

"Oh you rotten things! You had baths and did not invite me!" Leelah pouts while serving up bowls of porridge.

"Your baths last even longer than hers." Valor points his spoon at me. "I had no intention of being there till dawn so you could have 'a proper bath.'"

Leelah glares at Valor then swings her gaze to me. "You, I expected better of. You know the esteem a woman places on a tub bath."

I shrug. "You were much occupied with your family. It did not seem right to take you from where you were needed."

"Hogwash," she says tartly.

Nev escapes Leelah's censure by absenteeism. Trent escorted her to Salome Brighton's home so that she could help the aged woman prepare her contributions for the fellowship meal. I should have asked Trent to take me too, but my secret plans of avoiding the Gathering would be foiled.

Valor finishes off his bowl then scoops some from mine. "There is a simple solution for your dilemma, and it does not rest with us."

Leelah's gaze swings toward her husband. Kragorn scowls at Valor with a look that unambiguously says, *Blackguard.*

"I want my own bathtub," Leelah proclaims, witholding the second helping she was about to put in his bowl.

"We must first have a bathing room before we have a tub," Kragorn defers blame.

"Then build me one," Leelah says, still holding back the scoop of porridge. "We could make room for it off the back wall of the kitchen to take advantage of the stove while also watering the garden, saving me countless hours of labor on multiple chores."

"That is a good idea, Honey-sop, but it is a monumental expense. Perhaps someday, when I have more time to save us the cost of someone else building the room..." Kragorn reaches for the serving spoon, but Leelah drops it into the pot and stomps away, plunking it on the stove.

Kragorn glares at Valor, who only grins, then goes to the stove to refill his bowl himself. "It is an unnecessary expenditure since you may use Valor's tub whenever you wish."

I assume Kragorn is being a miser and cannot help but interject on Leelah's behalf, "A woman should have her own tub, Kragorn. Surely, for a beloved wife, the cost is not too high."

"Oh, no?" Kragorn rebuts, and names the sum Valor spent.

My jaw falls open in shock. It is the equivalent of five years worth of wages for a commoner. "You jest!"

Valor shrugs.

"We could cut the costs tremendously if we purchase a smaller tub," Leelah says. "That was Valor's largest expense."

"I stand behind the decision to this day," Valor declares. "If you are going to do a thing, do it right."

"Aye, but even for you that tub is large," I counter. "Are you practicing swimming in there?"

Valor takes my leftover porridge with a sly smile.

Leelah rolls her eyes. "He insisted on having a tub large enough to hold him *and* the future Mistress Ironforge."

"I am certain my wife will appreciate my forethought on her behalf," Valor placidly replies, suddenly very interested in his porridge.

I am taken with the uncontrollable urge to hit him as a picture pops into my head of Valor and the buxom Tirzah enjoying an evening soak in the tub. I shove up from the bench and smack him on the back of his head. "Do not be crass."

He turns his bewildered gaze to me. "What did I say?"

My scolding look rebukes him thoroughly. *I know what you were thinking.*

Valor fights it, but rarely witnessed embarrassment colors his face.

Satisfied, I marshal the girls. "Come. Let us tend to your hair before Gathering."

* * *

※ ※ ※

"What do you mean you are not attending?" Valor asks as Kragorn and Leelah pile children into the pony cart.

"I am of a mind to stay here and rest. I have been putting off a project that I must continue. The quiet will do me good," I explain.

"We will be late if we do not depart," Leelah hurries us.

"Have a lovely time." I wave and head back inside.

I hear Kragorn set the pony into motion and the crunch of wheels rolling through the courtyard. Valor calls out to halt me on the stairs, but I continue upward. "Enjoy your day, Commander. I will be waiting here when you return."

The clomping of his boots on the stairs evidences his frustration. His steps are usually silent. "You know I cannot leave you alone."

"Certainly, you can. If it will set your mind at ease, I will lower the gate behind you," I offer, heading into my room. His broad shoulders fill the frame and prevent me from closing the door.

He crosses his arms over his chest. "Either we both go, or we both stay."

"I make you do nothing. You go or stay of your own will."

"I wish to go. This is something I anticipate every week, but I cannot go without you."

I open the trunk with my belongings, pushing rumpled dresses aside to glance at where I left off in my journal. I replace the pages and take up a stack of blank ones and a pen. Though I try to ignore his presence that takes up too much space in the room, I cannot ignore Valor's arm stretching past me to close the trunk when I straighten.

"Why are you being obstinate? You knew Gathering was today." He considers me from much too close, peeling apart my layers with the windswept storm in his eyes. Accusation snaps in them like lightning. "You never planned on attending. Why?"

I cant my head back to look full in his face, losing grip on my intention to remain pleasantly firm in my address. "I have other things I would rather attend to this morning. You need not hover."

Truly, I need him to *not* be in my room. With Valor at my front and a bed at my back, my mind lists in a dangerous direction. All I can see is him. The world outside this room fades to insignificance. How does he do this to me? It is worse than dangerous. It is tempting.

I clutch the papers to my chest like a shield, edging past him without coming in contact until my foot snags on the blanket hanging off the unmade bed. Valor's hand catches my arm to stop my fall, but that draws me closer to him. The air crackles between us. The storm beckons to me, inviting me to lose myself in this moment, to lean in.

I wonder at the naivety I once possessed that allowed me to sleep upon a bed with him and not even consider its other main use. I recall the moment that I felt something spark between us upon that bed in Grevnhold, the question I saw in his eyes that I could not interpret. If I meet his gaze now, will I see it there again? Or is this all me? Do I imagine desire coming from him because I wish it to be there?

Valor's grip around my arm softens. His thumb strokes my skin through the fabric. I suppress a shiver at his touch, yet I cannot suppress a blinding thought. *What would it be like to be his?*

Valor suddenly pulls me into the hall and firmly closes the bedroom door. "I am disappointed we will not be at Gathering today, but as you seem determined to stay here, then here I will stay."

He strides past me, descends the stairs, and exits into the courtyard.

I collapse back against the door, calming the racing of my heart. Oh, that cannot happen again! My emotions are far too chaotic to be trusted, my heart too bruised to not seek relief.

I find the stairs and hide in the safety of the kitchen. Writing is the first order of the day. Then I will be about the business of a queen, visiting with Col at his farm.

I spread out my papers on the table and take up my pen. Thoughts of Valor's disappointment at not attending Gathering intrude on my quietude.

Not my fault, I reassure myself. *If Valor insists on trying to out-stubborn me, then that is not my fault.*

I begin writing but cannot focus on the task for the guilt that prickles my conscience. Valor has asked for absolutely nothing from me until now. How selfish of me to refuse to give him half a day of my time! That is all he has requested from me, and I refused him.

He does not have to stay here. He is free to do as he pleases, I argue against myself.

He stays for you, to protect you, the other side of me points out.

I tap my pen on the table, vacillating for another moment, then growl, stacking up my papers and abandoning my journal. I dart through the courtyard toward the stables where I find Valor untacking Granite.

"If we leave now will we be too late?"

He pauses while unbuckling the bridle. "Not if you do not mind riding with me."

I nod and retrieve the saddle from the tack room. Valor's smile is wide and bright as he fastens the girth in place. Granite snorts, wanting us to make up our minds if we are going or staying.

"May I ride on the fore?" I ask hesitantly as he mounts in the courtyard. "I do not want horse sweat soaked into my dress when we arrive."

"This morning is getting better by the moment," Valor teases as he takes my hand, hoisting me up and settling me in the comfort of his arms.

Before I can name him a cad, he sends Granite into a gallop that steals my breath. His arms tighten around me so we may move as one with the horse. I stifle the contented humming of my heart.

✵ ✵ ✵

Valor reins in Granite as the chapel comes into view. The doors are open wide, coaxing in the breeze and letting the music pour out. I feel the same hesitation I always do when I descend the stairs into the great hall knowing it is filled with people, but Leer is not with me to steady me. My hand seeks Valor's that is wrapped around my waist as we stop by Leelah's pony cart. Valor swings to the ground and lifts me down after him. He takes my hand on his arm, leading me too quickly up the steps of the chapel. The building is filled with people standing shoulder to shoulder, raising their voices in corporate song. I balk at the door, but Valor draws me before him, propelling me forward. Some heads turn as we enter, but most smile in greeting. Valor guides me onto a bench where Salome, Nev, and Trent scoot closer together to make room for us. Trent elbows my side in greeting.

Valor takes the vacant spot at the end of the row, giving me a reassuring smile then joins in the song. I soon realize that though he may whistle like a songbird, Valor sings in a deep monotone. I catch Nev's eye from around Trent and press my lips into a firm line to conceal my amusement. She winks at me, knowing exactly what I am thinking, then faces forward, singing along. The tune is familiar to me, but I cannot remember the words, so I merely listen.

"What kept you?" Trent whispers in my ear.

"Tried to avoid being here," I murmur back, "but I was guilted into attending for his sake."

Trent nods sympathetically. He goes where Nev goes.

We are asked to be seated, and the teaching elder steps forward to ask for the Creator's blessing on the reading of the Holy Texts. The elder stands behind a lectern built specifically for the weighty tome. The words therein are beautiful. As they are read aloud, I am drawn in.

"In the Forty-sixth Song it is written:

'The Almighty is our refuge and strength, an ever-present help in trouble.

Therefore we will not fear, though the earth give way and the mountains fall into the heart of the sea, though its waters roar and foam and the mountains quake with their surging.

There is a river whose streams gladden the city of the Almighty, the holy place where the Most High dwells. He is within her, she will not fall; He will help her at break of day. Nations are in uproar, kingdoms fall; He lifts His voice, the earth melts.

The Creator is with us; the Eternal King of our forefathers is our fortress.'"

The people respond to the reading in one voice. "It is so."

The elder looks out over his community and smiles. "Friends, let us look to these Words as both an exhortation and a challenge. We have been given a wonderful and unfailing promise that even if all around us gives way, we will be preserved if we seek refuge within the Almighty. It is within His unlimited power that we will find our strength, and it is within His everlasting arms that we find our help. Therefore we will not fear. We know we are safe. No matter what trials we must pass through, no matter the raging of the storm or the upheaval of the ground beneath our feet."

It is a lovely picture, but I doubt its veracity. Even if the world gives way around me I do not need to fear? Truly, it did give way, and I am still drowning in fear.

"These words give us a picture of the holy city. Long ago, this was a tangible place on earth where the presence of the Most High dwelt among men. Today, we know that His presence does not reside only in one city, but within the hearts of all those who love Him and He has called His own. We, His people, are the city, and He is our river."

A murmur of assent sounds in the room followed by Micah's hushed but enthusiastic voice saying, "I *love* the river!"

We all chuckle, and the elder smiles. "So should we all delight in the Almighty as our source of life. In Him alone, we find our sustenance. In Him alone, we find peace. And in Him alone, do we find the only waters capable of washing away all our iniquities and wrongdoing. Those waters are the endless fount of His grace shown to us in His

Saving Son."

I look around the room at these happy people so full of life. They believe they are forgiven, and maybe they are. But my sins are too dark. They are unforgivable. I glance down at my hands to see if the blood on them is still there. No visible evidence of it remains, but I feel it as surely as if its touch was indelible.

Valor's hand covers both of mine. With his steadiness for contrast, I realize how badly I tremble.

"Once again we are promised," the elder continues, "that the Almighty dwells within us, and we will not fall. We are refreshed in His endless mercy that is poured out upon us every day."

His face is somber as he expounds upon the last part of the Text. "'Nations are in uproar, kingdoms fall; He lifts His voice, the earth melts.' Friends, we have this assurance that no matter what transpires in the world around us, our lives are secure in this eternal hope: 'The Almighty Creator is with us; the Eternal King of our forefathers is our fortress.' If He speaks to the raging world around us, His voice will melt away our greatest foes, our most terrifying enemies. But even if He allows the storm to rage on around us, we are safe when we make Him our fortress."

I wonder if these people yet know the uproar of a warring nation or that their earthly king has fallen? Would they be so quick to imagine their lives secure if they knew the failing ledge their home teeters upon?

"Let us take a moment to respond in silent prayer, giving thanks to the Creator for His words spoken to our hearts today. Let us also use this time to confess our sins and receive forgiveness, not forgetting that 'If we confess our sins, He is faithful and just and will forgive us our sins and purify us from all unrighteousness.' Let us pray." The elder bows his head as do those around me.

Valor releases my hands to clasp his own together. His brows fold inward with the fervor of his unuttered words raised heavenward.

I close my eyes, fighting against the strong pull I feel to also raise my heart's voice to the Creator. He did not hear my desperate cries to spare my daughter. He was not there in my horrified silence as I watched my husband breathe his last. It seems He refuses to hear my prayers though He harkens to the voices of others. He heard Valor's prayers to save me time and again. He heard Father and Mother Celiea's prayers to keep me from departing this world as my life's blood rushed out of my ruined womb and the poisons worked their evil. And for what? Why not preserve the King of Malesiir? Why not spare the heir to the throne? I am the least of those that should have remained in this world. If He turned a deaf ear to my other prayers, asking for forgiveness for the vile on my hands certainly seems like something He would be deaf to as well. His love and forgiveness are not meant for me.

"Amen," the elder speaks, and it is echoed in the chapel.

CHAPTER SIXTEEN

ERIANNA

We join with the Tareth's for the fellowship meal while Nev and Salome help a few other women lay out the shared repast upon a large table. Leelah and I spread a blanket over the sun-warmed grass to sit on while the children play with their friends. Having been deprived of her social life these past two weeks, it is not long before she is off visiting with friends.

Trent reclines next to me, lying back on his elbows, waiting for the line around the table to clear. "You will have to give the final verdict, but from what I have experienced, the meals these women prepare are second to none. And they have a penchant for making desserts."

I smile, watching it all unfold, while simultaneously scanning the crowd in the unlikely event I see someone who will recognize me as the queen. Valor and Kragorn have been drawn into a sober conversation with several men that I assume are other elders in the community. The elder that taught today is among them.

"Hello, Anna."

I groan inwardly then look around, composing my face into a pleasant mask. "Hello, Tirzah."

Trent shoots me a mischievous grin and helps me to my feet as the beautiful woman stops at the edge of our blanket.

"It is lovely to see you again. I was not sure if you would still be in Parse."

"Yet here I am," I say. "It is nice to see you too. May I introduce you to my friend Cuyler Trent?"

Tirzah allows Trent to clasp her hand in greeting. "It is a pleasure, Cuyler."

Trent gives her his most winsome smile. "The pleasure is mine."

My cheeks hurt from the effort to not grimace. Must all men be snared by a pretty face and full figure?

We talk of small things until Leelah comes to take charge of the conversation and invites Tirzah to come to the noon meal three days hence. Though I feel his gaze, Valor lingers over his conversation with the men before finally joining us. The dynamic in the group instantly changes when Valor enters the circle. Trent throws me an amused look.

"Tirzah," Valor greets her with a reserved smile. "It is good to see you."

"Valor." She draws out the syllables of his name in a way that chafes my ears. "I am pleased to see you returned safely."

I can't stop myself from rolling my eyes. Everyone is so accursed "pleased" to see everyone else. What rot.

They continue exchanging the usual pleasantries, but the longer it goes on, the more awkward it becomes. Though not for Tirzah, it seems. She eyes Valor with a great deal of amusement as if they share a particular secret. Maybe they do.

After an insufferably long time, Tirzah excuses herself and continues on her way, greeting other friends.

Trent closes the circle, staring fish-eyed between all of us. "*That* is Tirzah? *Your* Tirzah?" He asks of Valor.

My fingers twitch in the folds of my skirt.

"My nothing," Valor denies.

"But she is—" Trent's gaze swings back to the woman until she is lost in the crowd. With absolute seriousness, he says, "Leelah. I need you to find me a wife."

Trent does not have time to block the bruising punches Leelah and I sink into his ribs. He holds his sides, chuckling.

"May I bring you something to eat?" Valor offers me.

Icy indignation shores up my pride. *That he would offer to care for me a breath after speaking with his Tirzah!* "I can manage. Shall we?" I ask Trent.

Trent needs no more encouragement to lead the way to the long table laden with a wide assortment of foods. Trent heaps his plate full while I remain choosy. I feel Valor's hand brush my arm, calling my attention to some food or other. I quickly step away.

"Anna, will you help me?" Nev asks, providing me an escape.

I give my plate to Trent with a request to add dessert to it and gladly go to Nev, all the while adamantly ignoring Valor's probing stare.

"Was that as awkward as it looked from here?" She whispers.

"Worse than," I reply, making a face.

She snickers. "Just remember, 'Queens do not pull hair.'"

We titter and pass the remainder of the meal in happy company.

※ ※ ※

VALOR

Tirzah's inquisitive glances follow me for the rest of the fellowship meal. I must find the time to speak to her privately and explain that I am no longer interested in courting her.

I flinch.

That sounds harsh. But what to say? That Anna is Malesiir's Queen in the guise of a commoner? That she has my heart?

I must think of something. Maybe I should return to my original plan from weeks ago and tell her that we are not well suited. That seems the most considerate and reasonable thing to do.

Erianna is reluctant to leave Nev's side when I come to collect her. Without looking up from the food she is bundling, she says, "I think it would be best if I ride home with the Tareth's to collect Sacha before heading over to Col's farm."

Does she not want to ride with me? "The Tareth's will be here letting the children play with their friends for most of the day. If you wait on them, you will have to forego your plans."

She huffs and carries the bundle to the end of the table.

"If we hurry, I can take you to get Sacha," I offer.

She sets to work repacking another bowl of food into a waxed cloth to benefit the struggling members of our community.

Nev intervenes, taking the bowl from her. "You know, Silla would approve."

"Silla also wore my handprint, did she not?" Erianna sourly replies.

"So do not antagonize, and it should go better for you," Nev challenges.

I do not follow a bit of what they are saying, but I do not think I am meant to. Is Nev encouraging Erianna or chastising her?

Nev's words take effect on the queen who stares her down. Erianna then gives me a hard look. What I did to anger her, I cannot imagine, but she is clearly piqued. I remain impassive, resisting the strong temptation to further rub her fur the wrong way by giving her a pleasant smile.

Erianna senses it about me regardless. "Churl."

"If I am going to be called names for things I think but do not do, then I am going to start doing them," I warn her. But not all of them. Some of them could see us back where we were this morning—in a bedroom with the house to ourselves for hours. Not that I think she would have been receptive to me, but I was sorely tempted to find out.

"Churl," she snips again.

I give her the unctuous smile I held in reserve and watch her hackles rise. There are too many witness to act on the ways I would like to pester her or for her to voice the curses spewing from her eyes, so I head toward Granite, certain she will follow. When I turn to lift her to the saddle, she is not nearby. Instead, she is headed the opposite direction with Trent who lifts her to the fore of *his* saddle. With that, Erianna's ire becomes mine.

She is nonsensical! I ride over to Nev as they lope away.

"Do you want to tell me what that was about?" I demand.

Nev does not deign to look up from her work. "I told you everything you needed to know last night. If you are so dense that you cannot understand her justified frustration, then I cannot help you."

So be it. I grind my teeth and gallop down the road. As I draw nearer, Erianna's melodic laugh floats back to me. My anger is too consuming to think reasonably about what Nev hinted. That will have to wait until later.

Trent is in the stable saddling Sacha when I arrive at the Tareth's home. "Do you truly want to stand unarmed in the middle of a battle?"

Trent laughs. "I was asked by my queen to escort her home. She said you were preoccupied. I did not realize I was maneuvered until it was too late."

"Where is the termagant?"

"She said she needed to freshen—"

A shrill scream breaks off his words and ices my blood. We sprint toward the house and pound into the great room, drawing swords.

"Hold!" The giant embracing my queen barks with a laugh. "I only spooked the little 'un. Though you both ought to know better than to let our queen enter an unguarded home before you. Where are your heads?"

Erianna laughs at our expressions of fury and raised swords. "I am sorry! I did not mean to frighten you. He thought I saw him, but I did not. The next moment I was being attacked by a bear."

Anders crushes the diminutive queen against him with a growl that elicits another burst of laughter. I fit my sword to its scabbard to remove the temptation of walloping them both with the flat of my blade.

Some of my anger at Trent revives. I thump him on the arm. "Never let a woman enter a room before ascertaining if it is safe!"

"Aye, Commander," he nods, knowing this reprimand carries with it double intent for the one that was cut short.

"When did you arrive?" I ask Anders.

"Long enough to have made a run at the larder. Where's that red head with a spoon? I need one of her stews to fill the empty places crusty bread won't reach." His thick black eyebrows wag.

"We were at Gathering," I explain.

"Is it the last day of the week already?" He asks in surprise.

"Aye. Did you lose a day somewhere between Malsihra and here?" Trent jests.

Anders scratches his bushy beard. "Must've. That bawd in Chiselm lightened my purse more than I intended."

Erianna gasps and slaps the giant. "Anders, you will remember you are in the presence of polite company and adjust your uncouth manners to accommodate!"

The fool looks at her then at us. "I see no one polite here."

She rears back to smack him, but he tweaks her nose, diverting her temper.

Anders brightens with a question that he puts to Trent. "Say! If today was Gathering, did you get to meet that tasty little dish Leelah served up for Valor?"

This time Anders does get clobbered with a force that makes him double over, right before Erianna spins on her heel and tromps up the stairs.

"I think she hits harder than she used to," Anders grunts, catching his breath.

I run my fingers through my hair, scratching my head. "That's it then?" I ask Trent.

He laughs at me and slaps Anders on the back, heading for the kitchen.

The pieces fall into place, and I begin to recognize the mire my feet are in. Not only must I resolve things amicably with Tirzah, but I must not cause Erianna unnecessary jealousy. But how do I spare her from that without declaring myself to her and imposing on her very real grief for her husband and child? She has not believed me sincere when I have said several different ways that I have no intentions toward Tirzah. How can I make her understand the unbreakable hold she herself has on me?

I turn for the door to finish tacking Sacha. Whatever news Anders brings from Malsihra will keep.

※ ※ ※

Along with a fresh dress, Erianna also dusted off her royal manners while she was above-stairs. I take my cue from her and cease pestering, opting for my own best behavior, though it falls far short of hers. The ride to the farm is pleasant yet quiet. I worry Erianna has become caught in the web of her memories, but the questions I ask her are answered promptly, if succinctly, so I let her be.

We are greeted warmly by Thad and Col who are enjoying the day of rest by carving new handles for tools with some of the younger brothers. Col is not given the opportunity to help Erianna dismount as she is in a self-sufficient mood. We leave the horses near the water trough, and I fall into conversation with Thad while Col eagerly motions Erianna forward to begin the tour. I let them gain enough lead that Erianna will not think I am hovering, but Col will most certainly know I am. I nod to Thad to follow along. If he thinks it curious, he does not mention it.

After the third time that Col glances back to see me persistently chaperoning, I hear Erianna say, "I hope you do not mind that Valor comes along. My family entrusted me to his care during my stay, and he will not neglect that responsibility."

Oh, is that what we have come back to, my Queen? Do you once again tell yourself that is all you are to me?

Col shrugs. "It makes no difference. How do you like Parse Kítaran thus far?"

Erianna replies in the positive then directs the conversation back around to her own interest regarding the farm. Col answers her questions with pride. He will inherit all of it, one day. Erianna takes her time admiring the pair of draft horses used to work the farm, and her questions become so particular regarding the care and training of them that Col begins to flounder. She alleviates his discomfort at lacking the knowledge by shifting her line of questioning elsewhere but tosses me a look that demands her questions be answered later, which I incline my head to.

Erianna's genuine desire to understand the workings of the farm, the amount of production it can yield, and a myriad of other questions regarding the economics of farming is noted by Thad. When we enter the barns, our two groups unify into one. The queen in Erianna is revealed more and more with the passing minutes as she draws Thad into the conversation, broadening her inquiries to take advantage of his experience.

Here is Grandileer's wife, the Queen of the Malesiirian court. She is intelligent, attentive, and mature beyond her age that is only two years ahead of Col's. To my amusement, her Limban accent seems to be tied to her royal manners. Her phrasing is more formal, and her vowels round similarly while her consonants become pronounced. She does not acknowledge my silent, amused warning that the common garb cannot conceal the queen any longer.

Col's infatuated eyes are full of her, and he willfully overlooks anything beyond what he wishes her to be, but Thad is not blind. He halts me from following them back into the fields and asks, "You are not bothered by my son's interest in Anna?"

"She is not bothered by it, so I am not either."

Thad's gaze settles upon the woman gracefully walking his pasture. "But it is not necessary for me to seek out her family on Col's behalf, is it?"

"It is not," I confirm.

"Does anyone else know your charge's identity?"

"Only those from Malsihra, though, no one has spent much time in her company. I believe it will be more difficult to conceal her full name than she imagines."

Feeling that the distance between us has stretched out, Erianna turns to locate me amid the shadowed interior of the barn. I step into the sunlight, assuring her that I still have her in sight. Her subtle concern prompts my conversation onward.

"I must asks you not to reveal her to anyone, including Col. Her anonymity is for her safety. Please allow her to make her identity known at the time of her choosing."

Thad readily agrees. "Of course. I am curious though. Why did she agree to visit if she has no interest in Col?"

"She wished to better understand the people she serves. She said that knowing how they live will enable her to make the best decisions possible on their behalf." Which I hope is an indicator that she means to return to Malsihra, even if she has not yet acknowledged it to herself. But I have seen despair press so heavily on her that I still worry she might harm herself to try to escape it.

Erianna surveys the land, committing the details to memory. She is regal. Only a fool could not see it.

"She is younger than I imagined her to be," Thad comments.

"In years only, not in experience," I assert.

"That is quite obvious in speaking with her," Thad concurs. "If it is appropriate, please tell her that I am honored she came to visit my farm. It is a distinction that humbles me."

"She would thank you for the invitation and for tolerating her questions. She would also say that there is no need to feel humbled by her. She believes no one is beneath her company. Not even the destitute children she regularly visits and sups with in the capital." I cannot help but brag about the woman I respect and esteem.

"Truly?" His brows disappear into his hair.

I incline my head.

"Then we are most fortunate to have been given a royal with a heart for her people." Thad's sincerity blends with compassion, watching Erianna's dignified approach. "Please give her our deepest condolences for the loss of her husband. We grieve with her."

"Thank you," I accept them on her behalf. "You were notified of the meeting this week to inform the heads of family?"

He nods.

"The elders wish to pair the rumors with fact so the gossip ends," I needlessly explain.

"Wise," he agrees.

Erianna returns with a pleasant smile. "Thad, I thank you for affording me the opportunity to tour your farm and learn from your knowledge. It has been an enlightening visit."

"You are most welcome. I hope you will come again," Thad replies earnestly.

We depart the farm discussing all she learned and still has questions on. We head for my house by unspoken agreement only to realize as we walk up the steps that we have no reason for being here. Rather than admit that we came here because it felt natural to do so, Erianna makes an excuse about wanting a book, and I claim to need a change of clothes before we return to the Tareth's home.

CHAPTER SEVENTEEN

ERIANNA

Upon returning to the Tareth house, I learn Nev decided to stay with Salome to help with the chores that have piled up in her absence. Trent is also staying there to guard Nev. I cannot begrudge her for her sensitive heart, but I am loath to be separated from her. Though nothing can replace the security of my husband's arms around me or his rich voice singing away my nightmares, I prefer waking with my friend next to me rather than waking alone. It is difficult to convince myself I am safe with vivid nightmares of cold steel caressing my face and violent hands moving over my body.

Dinner is a light affair this eve to provide Leelah rest after a week full of cooking plus preparing for the Gathering. We linger in the kitchen while Kragorn and Leelah tuck their children into bed. I set the tea on.

"What news from Malsihra?" Valor asks after I pass out filled tea mugs curling tendrils of steam.

Anders slaps a palm to the table. "I nearly forgot."

He produces a letter for me stamped with Lorennt's seal. I sip in a breath and crack it open.

Sister,

Come home. We miss you. We have laid him to rest next to your daughter but hold the funeral until your return so that we can mourn as a family. I know you are still hurting. We are too. I do not know why you are in hiding. I hope it is not from me. I regret what happened that day more than you know. I am sorry I was not here for you when you needed me most.

Please, come home. I need your help. I cannot do this without you. I do not know how he managed alone for so long.

I have garrisoned a company three hundred strong to secure your return.
Let it be soon.

Your loving Brother

Lorennt's pleas shake my resolve to remain in Parse and make me question what I am still doing here.

My eyes land upon one line in particular. *Am I hiding from Lorennt?* Memories of his rage as he battered Leer nigh unto death assault me. My vision blurs his formally scribed letters. Hot tears blot the ink on the page.

Leer's handsome face bloodied and swollen.

Lorennt's bellows and split knuckles.

And blood. So much blood from Leer's nose, his mouth.

But his eyes, contrite and pleading. "Is this enough? Will you absolve me after this? What must I do?"

My own guilt grinds my spirit beneath the weight of what my presence brought upon the Rodiharian family.

That is the reason. That is why I am hiding. How much worse will their lives be if I return? Death and turmoil are chained to my heels. Where my feet tread, lives are destroyed. That is why I tried to leave them that day. That is why I am afraid to return to them now.

The prickling awareness of Valor's eyes upon me guides me back to the kitchen.

Are you with me? Valor wordlessly asks.

I note Leelah and Kragorn at the table and the cup of cooled tea before me. Paper crumples in my fist. I stride across the room and chuck Lorennt's letter into the heart of the cook fire. It blackens and shrivels, disintegrating into unrecognizable embers. "What news of the Ruphiri?"

Conversation halts and reorders itself around my question.

"A few sightings, here and there. Wolf tracks where they should not be," Anders answers.

"Where have they been sighted?" I ask.

"Most everywhere," he vaguely replies.

"Concentrated where?" I know Zavaan better than that.

Valor's tight voice delivers the news. "The roads between where Jarmuth found us and the surrounding cities."

"In Malsihra?"

"Not that anyone has seen," Valor says.

"Where, exactly, has Lorennt told the people I am?"

The bench beneath Anders creaks. "Story is you are in deep mourning at the seaside castle. There was some evidence of the Wolves searching thereabouts, but they must've figured it was a ruse. We have heard 'em as far as the Northern Province, but they're concentrated here."

I find it difficult to believe that the Ruphiri are suddenly so easy to track and sight when they dwelt in Malesiir for nearly a year without our knowledge. "What evidence have you?"

An uncomfortable silence falls on those behind me. *Just as I thought.* Zavaan wants me to know he is searching for me.

"Your Queen asked you a question," I remind them.

"The people hear wolves howling then find livestock slaughtered the next day." Valor informs me. "At first it was only a lamb and its ewe. The number has slowly increased to include small flocks."

"He is sending me a message," I intone. "The longer I make him wait, the more blood he will let from my people." The hilts of the daggers riding my hips leave impressions in my hands. "Where is my escort garrisoned?"

"At Chishelm," Kragorn tells. "They are there under the auspices of hastening the completion of the new fortress. I can have them here in two days when you are ready to depart."

"Lorennt knows where I am."

"He suspects," Valor affirms.

"Then it is only a matter of time before Zavaan discovers my whereabouts."

"He cannot find you here," Leelah declares.

"I do not wish to shatter your illusions of safety, Leelah, but Zavaan has tracked me across the Continent. I have no doubt that he is both properly motivated and capable of finding me. Even here." I raise a hand, silencing her ignorant protests. She does not know Zavaan like I do. He will have me no matter the cost. And that is a frightening amount of determination.

"I would know what you are plotting, my Queen," Valor quietly requests.

I finally turn round so that he may know my determination when I respond. "I know what it is you are trying not to say. He is close. He is somewhere around Chishelm, orchestrating the movements of the Ruphiri, and they will not be found by our patrols unless he wills it. They move like wraiths through the forest, covering impassable ground at a speed that astounds. If our troops could arrive here in two days, he could achieve it in a third of that time. I do not want to wait for that to happen. I want the *Král Vragh* quartered like my people's livestock that he so callously slaughters. Bringing him to justice means trapping him, and that trap requires bait."

"No." Valor's eyes are gathering thunderheads, warning of the storm in him I ought to calm, but his feelings on the matter are not my concern.

"This is not a discussion. This is an order, Commander. We will take Zavaan before he takes us unawares. The longer we wait—"

"You are not bait." His lethally soft voice hints at his fury.

"There is nothing else he wants. If we lay a snare, then—"

"I said no!" Valor growls, staring me down.

I stalk closer, planting my hands on the table between us. "You do not have the final say. That responsibility rests upon me. If I say that we will do this, then this is what we will do."

Valor's posture stiffens then relaxes as he tries to swallow the orders of his queen, but he rejects them at the last. With whip-like speed, Valor's long fingers close around my neck, lift me off my feet, and slam my back to the table, scattering clay mugs that are dashed upon the floor.

"And what happens to the bait!" He roars in my face. "This! The Wolf shall earn the title of *Královna Vragh* before we bring him down!"

"So be it!" I scream, not bothering to fight his unyielding but painless grip. "Let the *Vraghan* die together! I will not let his desecration of my kingdom continue!"

His thumb lingers over my pulse, reminding us both there is life in me. "I will not figure into your wish for an early grave! Nor are you a murderer."

"You are so certain?" My whispered words float over Valor's face that is no longer the more terrifying one. "Know you how easily a woman's bones break? Certainly, you do. It is told in the gentleness of your grip on me even now." My fingers fit over his as I illustrate the edge that I was pushed over. But I will not reveal everything that pushed me. Not even in this benighted state could I expose Leer's sins to another. But mine? Those ought to be known. Then he will tie me up and leave me as Zavaan's bait himself.

"I was so surprised after only fighting men and striving to wield sufficient force against one of your braun. But a woman? The force that would slow a man can break bones in a woman." My index finger tracks up his arm, indicating what my words depict. "Break first the hands to prevent retaliation. Then these two in the forearm. Then mayhap this." My finger grazes his collarbone. "I can attest to the pain of that. Every breath is painful, screaming more so." My hands grip his sides. "A few ribs, such a fiery torture." My booted toe finds his calf and eases up the back of his leg. "Much harder to break this, but proper leverage makes it possible. And motivation!" I hiss. "Let us not forget. Motivation makes all the difference."

A sneer disfigures my face nearer what it was while I committed the atrocity. "But what could motivate one to do such a deed? Would you think vengeance turned murder justified the breaking of a defenseless woman? No? What if the avenger had been violated in the most heinous of ways? What if she had been drugged and made defenseless with what should have been a lethal dose of opium and pennyroyal that forced from her womb that most precious?

"What if I lived through your blood soaked nightmare while my enemy gloated her victory then left me alone, desperately trying to keep my babe inside me?" My intended taunting turns shrill. "Is murder justified if I held my tiny daughter and watched her heartbeat flutter her chest but could not save her while life fled my own body from my ruined womb?

"Does that justify me!" I wail, distantly aware that Valor no longer presses me against the table but holds me to him. "Or is it all undone by learning that Reuel claims responsibility for placing the poison in the woman's hands? Should I not be named a murderer for having tortured a woman to the edge of death that my husband's sword was forced to grant her?" I fist Valor's shirt. "Do you not see it yet? Bait Zavaan's trap with me and consign us both to the unmarked graves where we belong! Murderers deserve no better end."

"There is a demarcation line between what you did and becoming a murderer," Valor says. "That line is the conscience that knows what you did was wrong and heaps guilt upon you for doing it. A murderer has so far passed that line that he has strangled the life from his own conscience. He feels no remorse. He feels no guilt."

Valor's hand at the nape of my neck lifts my gaze to his, filled not with condemnation, but sympathy. "Are you justified for your actions? No? But by the depths, I understand. I have taken vengeance when it was justice I should have served. Though the Deceiver would have us believe there is satisfaction in vengeance, and for a moment there may be, conviction finds us ere long demanding repayment for the wrongs we have wrought."

"I would pay it!" I exclaim. "And with it bring an end to death's surge around me. How many more lives must be lost because I live?"

"You are not the cause of the lost lives. Zavaan is. And if it was not him, it would be another. It is the evil of the Creator's enemy at work in this world. Killing. Stealing. Destroying all that is precious and dear. What holds me to the side of justice is knowing that when I take up my sword, I am fighting against the Evil One and those who serve him. It is for the Creator to mete out righteous punishment to those who oppose Him and harm His people. When my heart strays toward taking vengeance into my own hands, I pray that I can let go of the desire and ask His holy wrath to fall on the wicked. When I am forced to kill, I pray that the Spirit of Truth would guard my heart from wrong motives so that I do not become the evil I war against.

"You have seen me cross the line too," he reminds me. "Did I bring Jarmuth down as quickly as I could, or did I make him hurt? Did I not inflict more pain on him than necessary and draw out his screams? Aye. He hurt you, and I wanted retribution, but I did not get it. Instead, I debased myself and caused you more pain, for which I am sorry. As I asked the Creator for forgiveness, so must you. We cannot make payment for the wrongs that we have done. We need Him for that too. He is our justice and our atonement. We cannot be that for ourselves."

In my anger, I push away from Valor and demand, "Where is the justice in all that has been done to me and those that I love? Your own people were purged from the Continent and your family slaughtered. How can you claim that the Creator is just?"

"Because I have seen His justice, and I believe His promises given to us in the Holy Texts. He says, '*I put to death and I bring to life, I have wounded and I will heal, and no one can deliver out of my hand. I lift my hand to heaven and declare: As surely as I live forever, when I sharpen my flashing sword and my hand grasps it in judgment, I will take vengeance on my adversaries and repay those who hate me. I will make my arrows drunk with blood, while my sword devours flesh: the blood of the slain and the captives, the heads of the enemy leaders.*' Those are not the words of a weak or unfeeling Creator. Those are the promises of an Almighty Avenging King who will not idly let His people be destroyed. As enraged as I am at your enemies, I swear to you, He is more so. You were not alone that day. Your Creator saw what was done to you, and He is livid. The same as He was outraged when His people were slaughtered without cause."

"Then why not prevent those crimes in the first place?"

Valor weighs his words. "There is unimaginable evil in our world that seeks to lay waste to everything the Creator loves. He has defeated His enemy, so the enemy has turned its attacks on us. But in His mercy, He has preserved you and I one thousand times over when we, too, should have been destroyed. Though my sight is imperfect to understand the grand scope of His plans, I trust Him to fulfill his promises to us. His plans will bring just punishment to the wicked. His plans will work everything out for my good, for His people's good, because we love Him and He loves us. But that promise only extends to those who are following Him and have been forgiven by Him, accepting the gift of His righteousness as their own."

Valor takes my hand in his, earnestly beseeching me to take his words to heart. "If you want to be able to look back one day on the darkest hours of your life and see that they were miraculously used for your good, then you must entrust your life to the Creator and ask Him to cleanse you of the blood on your hands and the sin in your heart."

Lies! The Insidious Voice whispers. *He lies to you and plays you for a fool, just as Leer did. He wants something from you.*

Not Valor, I argue. *He has never misrepresented himself to me. He would not do that.*

Would he not? What of his precious Creator? He makes promises that He does not keep. He is an oath-breaker.

"Do not listen to the Deceiver's voice!" Valor takes hold of my chin. "He lulls you to your death. Ask the Spirit of Truth to cast Him from your mind."

The Accusing Voice chuckles. *Maybe the Creator will keep His promises to Valor. He is worthy of upholding. But you are not, Erianna Zavaan Vrock. You are not enough for the Creator. And you are not enough for Valor.*

I jerk back as if slapped, deaf to Valor's calls as I flee up the stairs to my room.

That I know to be true.

Erianna-who-is-not-enough.

She could not save her people.

She could not keep her husband.

She could not protect her daughter.

She could not save herself.

And she most certainly could never be worthy of Valor Ironforge's love or that of his Creator.

CHAPTER EIGHTEEN

VALOR

August 26th

"But I like all of my hairs! Why are you gonna take 'em away?" Micah whines with his hands pressed to his head.

Leelah's patience wanes after already cutting Kragorn and the girls' hair, who were fidgety during the activity. Nevertheless, she draws out patience from a well that has deepened over the years from what was once a puddle. "Micah love, I promise you will get to keep most of what you have, I only intend to shorten it so you may see without shaking your head like Tamraz every few moments."

"You cannot cut Tamraz's fur too! He would look like a cat! I'm not letting you steal my hairs!" Micah shouts, darting under the kitchen table.

"Micah!" Leelah snaps as her bucket scrapes the bottom of the well.

I hold up a staying hand and fold myself under the table with the boy. "You are not scared are you?" I ask, getting to the heart of the matter. "It does not hurt."

"I am not scared of nothing!" Micah proudly declares. "I'm a warrior. Warriors are not afraid!"

"Sometimes we are, and we are allowed to be. The important thing is that our fear should not keep us from doing the things we ought to do. And you ought to listen to your mother. She wants what is best for you."

"You do not have to cut your hair." He tugs on the length that falls into my eyes.

"I do. Your mother told me I must cut my hair, or I do not get to eat at her table anymore," I soberly inform the child.

"You have to do what Mother says too?" His eyes widen.

"Everyone has to do what your mother says."

He folds his arms stubbornly.

"The sooner tis done, the sooner you can cross swords with Anders," I cajole.

He brightens and scrambles out from under the table. I place my hands on the ground to crawl out after him. Porridge squelches beneath my palm. With a grimace I glance at the cobblestone floor. "Leelah, when was the last time you swept?"

"Two days ago," she answers. "Thank you for noticing it needs doing. You can take care of it after your haircut."

I should have kept my mouth shut.

❋ ❋ ❋

I sweep the willow broom across the floor in the empty kitchen. The pile of hair that accumulated could stuff a large pillow. I take my time cleaning the corners of the room the girls tend to miss and find poultry feathers from the last brood that was housed here. A desiccated frog, one of Micah's escaped pets no doubt, is swept out from beneath the cupboard.

The door from the great room opens, admitting one late-rising queen. She goes straight to the kettle, but only dregs drip into her mug. Grumbling, she sets more water to boil and goes to the cupboard, stepping over a pile of hair.

"What happened here?" She asks while rummaging through the jars of herbs. She rejects anything that has mint in the blend and settles on a floral brew.

"We were informed by the general that today was haircutting day. Anders ran away before she could get ahold of him, but the rest of us did not escape her shears." It is understood that within these walls "the general" is Leelah's title, not her husband's. Kragorn asserts that this is her domain to govern as she sees fit and made it clear long ago that his wife is due the same respect as the general of this household that he is afforded in the military. When we asked what that made him, Leelah grinned and said, "The king."

I chuckle at the memory and sweep the piles out the garden door. When I turn around, Erianna is staring at me over crossed arms.

"Leelah cut your hair?" She asks, arching a brow.

"It was not the other general," I tease.

She shrugs and turns to remove the boiling water from the stove pouring it into the pot.

"There are sweet rolls left from breakfast." I open the cupboard and retrieve the stash I saved for her. "How many would you like?"

"None, thank you."

I turn around at that, but her back is to me. "Are you feeling well?"

Two spoonfuls of honey go into her mug. "Fine. I may have some later."

A blatant lie. She never turns down sweet things. I take up a mug, pour tea for myself, and sit at the table across from her. Her eyes are lowered to the mug that her fingers are wrapped around. Dark circles bruise the pale skin beneath her lashes.

"You slept poorly," I state.

She does not deny it, but neither does she elaborate.

"If you ever want company, I still keep a deck of cards—"

"I thank you for the offer, but I have the book I borrowed." Frost edges her gaze and tone.

The past few days have been strained since her revelations. I know that her guilt and anger got the better of her that night. She never intended to tell me what she did, much less reveal it to Kragorn, Leelah and Anders who sat in stunned silence for nearly all of the exchange before slipping out of the kitchen.

When I lost my temper and threw Erianna to the table, I felt Leelah at my back, trying to break my hold on her until Kragorn told his wife to sit back down. She later told me, after the evil that had been done to Erianna was thoroughly discussed, that I must wed Erianna. She could not imagine another woman capable of unflinchingly meeting the potent force of my anger. Having seen us together over the past week in lighthearted and serious moments, Leelah declared us well matched. Erianna is not even at her best and brightest, when she is the one soothing my temper or bringing light into a room with nothing more than a genuine smile. I want that woman back. I am on my knees daily asking the Spirit of Truth to break Death's grip on my friend.

The silence between us is tense with what I perceive as an unspoken grievance. "Something on your mind, my Queen?"

She drums her fingers on the table then narrows her eyes on me. "Kragorn knew his wife cut your hair?"

His wife. Is she overlaying her husband's jealousy onto Kragorn? "He was the first one to fall victim to Leelah's scissors and made a point to tell her not to let me escape my overdue trim," I jest while watching carefully for what her response will tell.

She shrugs and drinks her tea.

"You disapprove?" I prod, hoping to steer her closer to speaking of what Nev told me in confidence.

Erianna drums her fingers again then pushes aside her mug. She rises, purposefully making her way around the table toward me. She comes to stand behind me and pushes her fingers into my hair, slowly working them to the ends. I bite down on a moan at the effect her touch has on me. Again her nails graze my scalp and draw the shortened length of my hair around her fingers. I remind myself to breathe as she bends down to my ear.

"This has no effect on you, Valor?" She murmurs in a honeyed tone. "I think it does. Many a morning I woke my husband like this. Know you what happened next?"

Her words are iced water to the fire her touch ignited. I knock her hands aside and turn to glare at her. "Leelah is as a sister to me. I could not think of her otherwise."

Cold reproof rolls off her. "It is inappropriate. She should not touch you like that."

"You did not object when I asked Nev to assist me," I point out.

"Nev is not married, and I was there so—"

"So you would not feel jealous?" I say then immediately regret it.

Her eyes shutter, and she strides to the sink, setting her mug in it. "This has nothing to do with me. You asked what I thought, and I told you. What you do is your concern." The door to the garden closes before I can salvage our exchange.

I pound a fist on the table. Surely, I could have said something better than that! A myriad of other things I could have said come to mind, but no, I stupidly reacted from my own jealousy at the mention of what she and her husband shared. I must do better.

I follow the clashing of swords into the training yard. Kragorn and Leelah are practicing while the rest observe. Erianna notes my approach and asks something of Anders. They head into the weapon's room. I grind my teeth. One thoughtless remark added another layer of bricks to the wall between us that I have been working so hard to tear down.

"Uncle!" Micah cheers. "Wanna practice?"

I force a smile. "Only if you promise to go easy on me this time. I cannot have you besting me before all these women."

"I will not promise!" Micah grins and dashes off to retrieve a wooden sword for me.

I instruct Micah for a short while then work through a routine with Kragorn. Erianna practices her knife fighting skills with Anders, devoting her full attention to the task, not sparing me a glance.

※ ※ ※

At noon, we all go inside for the meal Leelah prepared. The rest of the day is allocated for the community meeting I have dreaded these past days. Thankfully, I do not have to be the one to inform our people. We decided that it would be best told by the leading elder, Joshen, but Kragorn and I will be available to answer any questions the people have.

"Are you sure I cannot convince you to stay here with Anders and the children?" I revive my previous discussion with Erianna as we go to the barn to tack the horses.

"I will be there to hear what is said and know my people's reaction to the death of their king." Her hard answer turns away anymore cautioning remarks from me. Not that it clarifies in my mind why she feels she needs to be there, but I will not argue with her about it.

The chapel is less full than at Gathering since the heads of family were encouraged to leave their children at home due to the nature of the discussion. Leelah takes charge of Erianna and sits at the back of the chapel with Nev and Trent. Kragorn and I move to the front to greet the elders while we wait a few more minutes for the stragglers to arrive.

Finally, it is time. Joshen steps to the front of the room. Without preamble, he presents the weighty matter. "Thank you for being here. It is with a heavy heart that I must inform you that the rumors many of you have heard are founded in truth. King Grandileer was murdered along with the entire company of soldiers guarding him and Queen Erianna as they journeyed to the seaside castle."

Horrified exclamations break the quiet. A few people who had not heard the news shake their heads in denial.

Joshen quells the mounting turmoil with raised hands. "Thankfully, the queen escaped the attack. She wishes it to be known that the king sacrificed his life to protect her. While the perpetrators are brought to justice, the queen is secluded in mourning at the seaside castle. The rest of the royal family are safe in Malsihra at this time."

"Who would do such a thing? Why?" A man calls out.

"At this time, General Tareth and Commander Ironforge are not at liberty to disclose who is behind this atrocity, though they are aware and are pursuing the ones responsible. The attack was intended to create instability in our kingdom. This group that originated outside our borders was also largely responsible for aiding the brigands who sowed dissension and stole from our Northern brethren.

"There is little else I can tell you at this time, but Commander Ironforge has assured me that though the Rodiharian family is shaken and grieved, their strong leadership will continue as they place the needs of Malesiir first."

I nod my agreement with Joshen's words.

He continues, "On a personal note. I know that several of you feel a deep gratitude toward Queen Erianna for the consideration she demonstrated to the widows and families of the soldiers who were lost in service to Malesiir. If any of you wish to show her the same compassion in her own grief, you may give your letters of sympathy to General Tareth who will forward them to her. At this time, let us beseech our Creator to show His love tangibly to the grieved Rodiharian family and grant them His protection from further harm. We must also ask that He mete out righteous vengeance against the evildoers and that the instability they attempted to sow in Malesiir is quashed."

We bow our heads as Joshen leads our community in prayer for Erianna and her family. Many people cry with deeply felt sympathy for the Rodiharians and with their own sadness for the loss of our strong king. I do not doubt it is frightening for them to know there are rogues loose in Malesiir who were able to bring down our king. A kingdom depends upon its king to provide it with safety and security, fair laws, and good relations with other countries. If Lorennt and Erianna do not rise to the occasion, the change in leadership could decimate Malesiir. This is nothing like the peaceful transition of leadership from Boldizar to Grandileer.

After the prayer, Kragorn and I rise to entertain questions that we are largely unable to give answer to at this time. We provide as much reassurance as we can and reiterate Joshen's requests for prayer.

I do not allow my eyes to linger on her, lest my attention gives her away, but I cast my gaze briefly to Erianna to judge how she fares. She sits with her head bowed, silently weeping between Leelah and Nev who hold her hands. Feeling my eyes, she meets them with hers that are filled with raw grief. Though it may draw attention, I nod to Trent, giving him the prearranged order. Trent rises discretely and draws Erianna to her feet, assisting her from the chapel.

The meeting concludes with the sobriety the occasion demands. Kragorn remains behind in hushed conversation with the elders while I head through the open doors into the late afternoon sun.

I find Erianna on the bank of the river with her head laying against Trent's shoulder. He looks around at my approach and bends his head to her. If she hears him, she does not acknowledge it. Her stare is vacant and glassy. He passes her to me, and I realize that only his arms were keeping her upright. She is cold and shaking as if the meeting loosed another wave of those earliest feelings of shock.

I whistle for Granite and drop my arm behind Erianna's knees, scooping her up before anyone else exits the chapel. I ride with her until day turns into night. Exhaustion finally takes control of her. She is in a deep sleep when I carry her up the stairs and tuck her beneath the coverlet.

If something does not change soon, I doubt even my undivided attention will be enough to prevent her from doing something irrevocable.

CHAPTER NINETEEN

VALOR

August 27th

I am up at dawn, swinging my sword against Kragorn's. Following a rigorous training session, he asks for my help cleaning out the weapon's room which has fallen into disarray with all the people coming and going. We scarf down our breakfast in the garden when Leelah bars us from entering her kitchen. Before I can ask, she assures me that she has taken charge of Majie and orders me to stay out from underfoot.

The door slamming in our face inspires Kragorn to knock again and steal a kiss from his wife who slaps his arm for interrupting her work for the second time. Kragorn gives me a sly grin and knocks on the door a third time. I return to the weapon's room, leaving Kragorn to right his wife's ill humor and make her glad for the interruption in her work. I assume he is successful when he follows along a few minutes later, dusting floured handprints from his tunic.

Cleaning the weapon's room is a larger task than we anticipate, owing to the family of mice that made a home in an infrequently used corner. They must be dealt with, then the room searched for the holes that allowed them to enter. Those are fortified, and the gnawed on weapons' hilts rewrapped in leather. We work through the noon meal to see the task finished. Not that I should expect different from the once weapons master, but I am surprised by the hoard of weaponry Kragorn has acquired over the years.

We bathe in the stream and change into the fresh clothes Karris delivered to us after breakfast. Anders is in the courtyard, laughing uproariously as we pass through to eat our late meal.

"You do not want to go in there, Commander," Anders warns me.

"Why is that?" I ask.

"'Cause Leelah, Tirzah, and Erianna are all sitting around having tea."

Wonderful.

"I have never seen our little Majie so polite. It is unnerving. I am less scared of her when she's got a blade in each hand," Anders jests. At least, I hope he is jesting

I turn my glare on Kragorn. "This is your fault. You told me to ask Leelah to find me a wife."

"It was only a suggestion and a harmless one as I never thought you would take her up on the offer." Kragorn chuckles. "You well knew who you were asking for help when you asked."

I mutter my way toward the house. Kragorn and Anders, the cowards, claim there is a section of the wall that might need repairs soon, and they rush off to tend to it.

I enter the great room through the vestibule, hoisting a polite expression and releasing the hilt of my sword that I unconsciously grasped. Charging into the brigands' nest was less intimidating than walking into the midst of these three women conversing over tea.

Erianna marks my entrance immediately, but only smiles demurely. I shudder. Anders was not jesting. Her prim demeanor *is* more chilling than the Warrior Queen wielding blades.

"Good day," I announce my presence to the other two.

They turn round, and Leelah grins like a bobcat to my mouse. "Oh Valor, won't you join us."

It was not a question, but I pretend like it was and thank her for the invitation.

Tirzah looks thoroughly amused at the turn of events and reaches for the kettle to pour out a mug for me.

I occupy the vacant seat on the couch next to Leelah then accept the cup of bitter tea Tirzah hands to me. Erianna watched her make it and did not bother to correct her when she did not sweeten it. I consider taking up the honey pot myself, but Erianna catches my eye with a saccharine smile and shakes her head.

Of course. That would be rude.

I smile and take a sip of the bitter liquid. Erianna's smile broadens when my eye twitches.

Leelah turns to me, and I have the distinct impression of being batted between her paws. It solidifies when she speaks. "We were just reminiscing. Tirzah asked how Kragorn and I met."

I choke on the tea.

"It is a lovely story." Erianna's smile is predatory though her voice is mild.

I glare at Leelah. "I hope you were telling the true version of events not your own hilarious rendition."

"I have an idea." Tirzah sets her cup on the table and folds her empty hands in her lap. "Why don't you tell us your version, and we can compare for accuracy?"

Leelah is gleeful. "I like that idea!"

"I also approve." Erianna taps a finger on her mug. It sounds like the drum to announce an execution.

I should have heeded Anders and stayed well clear of this nonsense. "There is not much to it. I met Leelah while serving under Kragorn shortly after we came to Malesiir. What was that, nine years ago?" I ask Leelah.

"Thereabouts," she affirms.

"She was a barmaid in one of the villages near where we were stationed. I courted her for a short time but quickly realized that she was far too terrifying and *conniving* for me," I emphasize the word, and Leelah snickers. "Kragorn, however, was not scared of her. They fell in love and soon wed."

"I like Leelah's version better," Tirzah declares.

"What about you?" I ask Erianna.

She looks long upon me but maintains a lighthearted tone. "I always prefer the truth."

Tirzah smirks at the mug she raises to her lips. "How hypocritical."

Erianna looks at her sharply.

I nudge Leelah's foot.

"Ah, very well," she sighs. "I may have exaggerated my story for effect."

"See there," I assure Erianna. "I never lie."

It is Tirzah who next raises her violet eyes in challenge. "Truly?"

I nod.

She shifts her attack to Erianna. "Where did you say you were from?"

"Malsihra," Erianna replies cooly.

"Of course. But before that? Your accent is not familiar to me," Tirzah presses.

No, there will be none of that. I will not allow Tirzah's irritation with

161

me to be directed at my queen. "Limba," I interject and rise, extending my hand to Erianna. "Forgive me for cutting your visit short, but if you still want to work with Sacha, then we had best get to it."

We discussed it a few days ago but never set a definite time. If she wishes to take the escape I am giving her, then she may. Erianna hesitates for a moment, catching her lower lip in her teeth, then places her hand in mine.

I draw her around the table and toward the stairs. "I will tack Sacha. Meet me in the barn when you are ready."

I wait until Erianna has ascended the stairs and the door to her room closes before I return to the others. "Tirzah, would you allow me to escort you home after you are finished visiting with Leelah? There are some matters we need to discuss."

"Aye. There are," she agrees impassively.

"Thank you," I bow slightly and stride out the door.

※ ※ ※

"She knows," Erianna declares as I exit the tack room.

The sight of her in her training gear still heats my blood. Unfortunately, she seems to have forgotten her decision to acquire some new clothes. "I will take care of it."

"But if she knows then she will tell others. That cannot happen if I am to remain here," Erianna asserts.

"I do not believe she will. I shall impress upon her the importance of keeping the secret when I take her home today."

"Fine." Erianna lets it drop and swings into the saddle.

We enter the training yard which is just large enough for what we intend. She warms up Sacha and demonstrates what she was mastering last winter. She has done well with Sacha and continued to develop her skills as a rider with Lorennt as her partner in training the mare. I wonder why Grandileer did not take more of an interest in this pursuit of hers. I can understand why he did not wish to spar with her —not that I agree. But why not ride with her? Grandileer was not inexperienced with horses. He trained his own destrier. This he could have shared with his wife.

"Did you and your husband go riding often?" I ask as she walks Sacha through the pattern I have laid out for her.

Erianna intends to lean into Sacha's agile nature and train her to obstacles. We have a few hay bales set in the ring for her to run the mare around. She wants to practice jumping the mare, but I asked her to do this first to build their confidence and Erianna's ability to stay in the saddle.

"On occasion. He was much occupied with the trade officials and the brigands and all his other responsibilities. Riding was mostly a means of traveling to somewhere, not just for the pleasure of it. When we did ride for pleasure, he thought I rode too fast. He complained that I could never find a nice, sedate hobby. He thought I was infatuated with danger."

To one who does not know her well, it could appear that way, but I know her to be adventurous. Her dreary existence in Limba lit within her a desire to explore and experience all things invigorating. Did Grandileer know his wife so little that he could not understand this facet of her character?

I turn aside from the topic before the murky waters can float up a memory that incapacitates her, but I mull over each detail she reveals, trying to build a picture. I wonder how much of her fear is founded in Grandileer's fear for her? Did she spend the past ten months second-guessing every decision she made because of his reaction?

"She has the feel of it. Go ahead and lope her through the turns," I instruct from the fence.

They manage very well until we increase the speed.

"Turn her sooner," I correct as she goes wide of a turn. "Let her look at the bale. You look through the turn and be directing her placement and setting her course for the next one." Erianna takes a few laps of the ring, considering the obstacles.

"Run it again," I call out as Tirzah approaches and comes to lean against the fence with me. The basket she always carries hangs from her arm.

Erianna is focused entirely on her mount. She kicks Sacha forward, rounding the first bale perfectly. I am caught up in her victory. "Go! Push her!" She lands the second turn, heading for the third. "Don't let up! Go! Go! Go!" She slides around the third beautifully and kicks the mare into gallop, running her around the ring, whooping her success. I cheer with her.

"So, that is the Warrior Queen," Tirzah muses.

I nod with pride. "Aye."

"You are not the least bit curious what gave her away?" Tirzah baits me.

"I am, but I can think of many possibilities," I reply, not interested in games.

"Beyond her accent, formal bearing, sudden appearance, and your presence here when you should be off serving the remaining Rodiharians at this dark hour," Tirzah ticks off the details she noticed, "my brother saw the queen when he was stationed in Malsihra. He described her as fair of skin, dark of hair, and quite lovely."

"All true," I agree.

Because I am watching her, I discern the moment Erianna notices Tirzah. Her back stiffens, and her smile hardens. I expect her to ignore Tirzah, but she slows the mare to a walk, drawing her up next to us. "Thank you for visiting us today, Tirzah. I am sure we shall see each other again soon."

"It was my pleasure, Erianna," Tirzah acknowledges, inclining her head.

The queen reveals herself in force. "I trust that you will not spread word of my presence here. It would be detrimental to my well-being as well as my companions."

"If you stay here for any length of time, I will not have to say a thing. You will give yourself away," Tirzah counters.

"I have no plans of staying here long. I would have your word that you will keep the knowledge to yourself," the queen demands.

"Of course," Tirzah agrees.

Erianna notes the missing honorific, so I add it. "Your Majesty."

Tirzah tosses me an amused smile. "After being simply *Anna*, you cannot mean to institute all that pointless formality now?"

The queen's smile is all teeth. "I would not. Besides, I expect we will be addressing each other with given names for years to come."

With that, Erianna moves the mare to the center of the ring to practice her footwork.

"Imperious and aloof, just as I expected the queen to be," Tirzah says.

I bite my tongue. If this facade is how Erianna wants Tirzah to think of her, then I will not undermine her. It is enough for me to know the true version of Erianna, the woman who threw a horse apple at my face.

"Would you like to ride or walk home?" I ask.

"Let us walk," Tirzah replies, setting the pace.

She launches into the conversation once we reach the tree lined path without giving me a chance to initiate it. "Before the king's death, there was something I planned to ask you, but the answer has become so obvious that the question no longer matters."

"I would like to hear it anyway," I invite.

"My brother told me some interesting stories of the illicit romance between the commander and the queen. I would have asked for your version of events to know if I had anything to worry about between you and her."

"I do not doubt that whatever rumors you heard were exaggerated. However, there was some truth to it," I confess.

"How much truth?" She arches a brow.

"Enough that we recently agreed that if I plan to marry, I cannot serve as her Hand," I explain.

"I do not need to guess which you chose," Tirzah states with only a hint of condemnation.

"I wish to continue serving as her Hand," I say to have it done with. She nods.

"Are you disappointed?"

She shifts her basket to her other arm. "We hardly know each other, Valor. Though I entertained the possibility of being your wife, my heart was not set on it."

"I ask your forgiveness for initiating something that I will not see to its conclusion, whatever that may have been. I hope I have not hurt you."

"You are thoughtful," she pats my arm. "I assure you, I am fine."

I sigh in relief. "Good."

"Will you pursue the queen?"

"We are a long way from anything near that. She is deeply grieved by the loss of her husband."

"Once she is recovered?"

Will she recover? That is a much more pressing question. "I cannot say."

"I believe you will. You still admire her greatly."

"It is so obvious?" I wryly ask.

"Oh Valor," she looks pityingly at me. "If you had shown half as much admiration for me, then I would be fighting to keep your attention."

"I am sorry, Tirzah," I repeat, feeling guilt afresh.

She waves it off. "As told, I am not. I wish to snare a man as thoroughly as she has captured you. I do not want someone else's man."

I give her statement some thought. Tirzah is a desirable woman, but there are few suitors here for her to chose from. Unless her brother decides to move her to a larger city, it is unlikely her options will improve. "Would you like to visit court this winter? I would be happy to bring you as my guest. You could have your pick of a hundred eligible men."

"Are you sincere?" She hedges.

"I am. I will even buy you a dress for the winter solstice," I offer, knowing such would be far outside her means.

Tirzah's smile is wide, placing a dimple in her cheek. "I accept."

CHAPTER TWENTY

ERIANNA

August 28th

The children bounce through their chores with unusual levity this morning. They have a scheme planned for the day and will not tell me what it is, only that we are going out and I must bring a change of clothes. If Nev was present, she would tell me what was afoot, but she is still with Salome. Valor is also being rather close-lipped about the plans and will only tell that the day promises to be fun. I resolve myself to trust them.

I am waiting in the courtyard with Valor when Trent returns. Anders relieved him from guarding Nev so that Trent could take a turn scouting the woods for signs of the Ruphiri. A young boar is slung over the back of his destrier. His face is at ease, but I hold my breath until I hear the report from him.

"Good hunting?" Valor asks, intentionally vague.

"Excellent hunting," Trent replies placidly.

I loose my held breath. Still no sign of the Wolves. Good.

"Will you be joining us wherever it is we are going?" I ask, knowing the importance of every extra sword.

Trent grins. "They have not given away the surprise yet? Then I must come along. I shall hang this and return."

Valor leads the destrier to the barn while Trent lugs the field dressed boar to cool in the cellar.

Leelah exits the house with Fialla asleep and wrapped to her chest. "Tell me, Warrior Queen, does the babe detract from my credibility?" Like myself, she wears her weapons belt bearing her dual swords.

"Perhaps on some women, but you look all the more terrifying for your ability to protect yourself and your babe." I only wish I had been able to do the same. Leelah is more deserving of my title than I. "May I see your swords?"

"Of course, but I want them back. They were a wedding present from Kragorn." With a fierce smile she unsheathes both blades without waking Fialla.

"I, too, think weapons make the best gifts." I take a firm hold on the happiness in the memory and shove past the pain. "This was my wedding present to Leer. This was his birthday present to me." I tap the pommels of each dagger in turn.

Leelah's amber eyes gleam in the morning light. "You see, Erianna. I knew we were kindred spirits." She demonstrates how to wield the swords then passes them to me. They are double-edged, surprisingly light, and well balanced. The fuller runs nearly the length of the blade, contributing to the lighter weight. At her encouragement, I gain some distance and practice swinging the blades. They do not feel like an extension of my arms the way my daggers or short staves do. That means I have a goodly amount of practice ahead of me to become passably competent with swords.

I cast my gaze to Valor as he returns from the barn and waggle my brows. "We have work to do, Commander."

He approves my plan with a nod. This week, I will take up swords.

I return them to Leelah and wrap my hands around the comforting hilts of my daggers as the rest of the family join us.

Kragorn and Micah lead the way on our adventure. The lad imitates his father's watchful posture and grips the hilt of his own diminutive wooden sword. Karris, Ivy, and Lois also have weapons belts with small daggers fastened to them. Kragorn believes in teaching his women to defend themselves from a young age. After spending two weeks with his family, my lofty respect and admiration for the man has only grown.

As we hike along the well traveled path, my gaze remains on the trees, picking apart shadows. Though Trent scouted ahead, I cannot forget how easily the Ruphiri move through the woods. It is conceivable that Trent missed the signs of their presence. I grip my hilts tighter, focusing all my senses on the forest until Valor's eyes upon my back gain my notice. I slow my pace, dropping back to walk with him.

"Is something amiss, my Queen?"

"Not that I can tell. Have you noticed anything?"

"No. I do not expect to, but I will not lower my guard." He pushes a reaching branch out of the path for me, holding it while I pass.

"Nor will I. Too many times I have been taken unawares. I will not let it happen again."

Ahead, Kragorn takes Leelah's hand to assist her over a rotting log in the path. He continues holding his wife's hand as they walk. The children clamber on the log making a balancing game of it. After glancing in Trent's direction, Karris tries to climb over the log gracefully, but Lois spoils it for her with a shove that further humiliates Karris when her skirt snags, forcing her to untangle it. Poor thing. For all her worry, Trent's eyes were trained on the woods, not paying the children any mind.

I decide that it is time to resurrect the topic that took a wretched turn the other night. "I still want to lay a trap for Zavaan. I know you disagree, but we cannot allow him to make the first move. We know he is close. We know what he wants. The time to strike is now."

"You are so eager to return to being his prisoner?" Valor tries to deter me.

I shove back those petrifying memories and stay the course. "I am counting on you to help me craft the trap to ensure that does not happen."

Valor steps over the log then takes my hand, helping me over. "If we can devise a workable plan that does not include you being the bait, then I will see it done."

"There is nothing else that he wants," I argue. "He will not gamble for anything less than me. However," I drawl, "I have decided that I want to ensure I survive the encounter."

"Why the sudden change of heart?"

"A thought occurred to me that has so much merit I cannot ignore it. I wish to know if Arcto was helping orchestrate the death of our king."

Valor's complete lack of surprise demonstrates that he has already considered this likelihood. My murderous father united with my murderous betrothed made an enemy of the kingdom that should have been their ally.

"If Arcto did, what then?" He wonders.

"Then we know just how large our enemy is." *And that will determine if I must commit patricide after I bring down Zavaan.*

"Could you do it?" Valor asks as if I had spoken aloud.

"Do what?" I ask innocently. It falls flat. It has been far too long since I thought myself innocent to feign it with conviction.

"Kill Arcto," Valor answers with forced patience.

It rides him like a bur that I pretend we must speak our complete thoughts instead of allowing half of what we say to go unspoken. It is as if our thoughts are boats on the same river. Occasionally we disagree and bump into each other, but ultimately we are going in the same direction. I must act as if I have forgotten that. It feels disrespectful to Leer if I do otherwise. He taught me to speak my every blessed thought so he could know my mind. More often than not, our thoughts were not on a parallel course. They were in direct opposition with each other. But we were trying. We were forging a new path together.

Valor's hand on my face brings me around. His understanding smile causes me to take stock of my surroundings. The others have disappeared from sight. Valor and I are stopped at a bend in the path.

"Was I doing it again?" I ask, tasting blood on my lip.

"You were lost in thought." Valor's thumb wipes away the blood. I shiver under his touch and make myself step away rather than lean into him. It is unnecessary since he breaks the contact first.

"We can speak more on this later," Valor suggests. "The children are anxious to show you the surprise."

So anxious that I hear them calling my name to hurry me along.

Valor prods me forward. "Come along, Majie."

The bend in the path opens revealing the edge of the forest drenched in sunlight. Beyond the forest is a pebble strewn beach leading down to a breathtaking mountain lake glittering amidst the lush forest.

"Surprise!" The children shout, running forward to take my hands. "Isn't this the best surprise? We get to stay all day and picnic and swim!"

Hold! Hold to here! I desperately counsel myself. *This is different. Not the ocean, not the hope of what might have been. This is real. A beautiful day at the lake with your friends.*

Staring at my blank expression, Micah asks, "It is a good surprise isn't it, Majie?"

I affect the most pleased expression I can manage. "I am stunned! What a perfect surprise this is! Thank you!"

They cheer. Without any more hesitation, they drop their belongings into an open sided lean-to constructed of split logs. I force a laugh and go to Leelah, helping her spread a blanket. We lay out food for the children soon to be ravenous from their play.

"This is my favorite place," Leelah grins, laying a hand over her heart. "Kragorn and Valor built the lean-to for me three years ago. Whenever we can, Kragorn and I escape here to be alone together. I love sleeping under the stars."

"I can see why. I could not imagine a more tranquil place," I reply with such perfect affectation that even Leelah believes me.

We chatter while Fialla crawls on the blanket until Valor interrupts, dropping his boots and collection of weapons in a heap in the shelter. "Walk down to the water with me?" His smile is mischievous, but his eyes are concerned. He does not find my act believable.

I unlace my boots and set them near Valor's then stand.

"The steel too," he chides.

I roll my eyes, but mostly obey, leaving my cuirass and weapons belt atop my boots.

"And the other," Valor insists then looks away while I slip my hands up my skirt to remove the dagger strapped to my thigh.

Leelah cackles. "Are you sure you are not *Queen of the Armory*?"

"Not yet. But we are going to add swords next. Then perhaps a mace. And a shield too. Then you may add *Queen of the Armory* to my growing list of 'a-dear-mens,'" I tease.

Valor takes hold of my arm when my feet slide on the steep bank. My world is swinging so wildly I barely notice. Leer's lies and his love, his deceit and his kept promises—they leave me dizzy. It is too much to sort through on my own.

When we have put adequate space between us and the others, Valor asks, "What is wrong? What is it about this place that has upset you?"

Valor is a rock amidst my chaos. I want to confide in him, to throw myself upon his solid ground and let him balance me. But he is not my fortress. He belongs to another. I watched him walk her home last night.

That recollection spins me faster. "Naught that need concern you."

His steadying hand on my arm tightens, tugging me toward him. Curse my weakness, I want to fall against him. If he persists, then I will. I must erect a facade so impermeable that even he cannot see through it—never mind the cost to me.

My mouth forms a teasing smile. "The bank is not so steep as that. I can manage."

"Do not lie to me. I know you are hurting."

"Of course I am. But there is nothing for you to do." At the stubbornness that firms his already chiseled features, I decide I must

171

salt my lies to make them go down easier. "I cannot swim. Leer was to teach me at the coast. The sudden reminder of that which will never happen..." I shrug as if the ground beneath me is not eroding with every earth-quaking memory. "Allow me my grief, Valor. I will come right eventually."

His concern that was shifting to acceptance leaps to the far side of disbelief. The salt of the truth did not blend with the sweet of the lie. I do not believe I will ever come right. No matter, I will force him to swallow my words. "Leave me be, Valor. I do not want you to trespass on this."

He allows me to pull away. "As you will. But you know that if you need—"

"I know. And I thank you."

My feet carry me quickly from Valor to the water's edge where I am as alone as I ought to be. From the moment Valor admitted he could not wed and be my Hand, I knew I was on my own. It is disrespectful of Valor and of Leer's memory to wish otherwise.

The mountain water is frigid on my toes. I exaggerate a squeal for the benefit of the children who swim a little ways out.

"How can you bear it?" I ask them. "You must be freezing!"

Micah splashes water my direction, and I dodge the spray. "You hafta jump in! Then it's not so bad."

I wade up to my knees, watching my skirt pool on the surface of the water. Maybe, if I try hard enough, I can fool myself into being happy. Maybe I can forget. I have done it before. I dip my fingers into the lake and send water curling at the boy. From my periphery, I see Valor wade into the shallows then disappear beneath the rippling waves. He reappears in deeper water, swimming parallel to the shore. He looks to be an expert swimmer too.

I return my gaze to the children and gasp in fright for Lois when Karris jumps on her back shoving the girl under the water. She shoots up spluttering a moment later and seeks to return the favor. Lois is no match for her bigger sister, but Kragorn—submerged except for his head—sneaks up behind his unsuspecting eldest. The next instant, Karris is hurled into the air, screaming like anything. Water cascades upward in a magnificent spray where she lands.

"Me too! Me too!" The other children clamor. Kragorn gives them each a turn, tossing them high. Valor joins in, and a contest of who can throw the children the farthest begins. I hold my sides from laughing so hard and am repaid for my negligence by Trent who curls water at me soaking the front of my dress. A water fight ensues that results in a drenched queen despite my never leaving the shallows.

When the sun is at its peak, I return to Leelah and assist her in handing out food to the hungry swimmers.

"It is so good to see you laugh," Leelah declares. "What a day it is!" Her attention is drawn away from me to her husband striding up the beach. She whistles appreciatively, giving him a look so heated that I blush and turn my attention elsewhere.

"Mother," Karris groans. "You embarrass yourself."

"Leave her be, Karris," I quietly reprimand. "We should all wish to be so fortunate to have a marriage like your parents."

"Did you?" She inquires, unintentionally stabbing the invisible knife deeper into my heart.

"Do not pry," Leelah is quick to correct her daughter.

"It is alright." I smile sadly, twirling my wedding ring. "I loved my husband very much. Given time, we may have had what your parents do."

"How long were you married?" Karris asks.

"Not long enough." I sense a curiosity in her for which I am unprepared.

A stern look from Leelah cuts off any further questions. Valor drops next to me, shaking his hair like a dog. I laugh, wiping the water from my face and hand out second helpings to the men.

After a time, Kragorn declares. "Wife, do you intend to continue holding up this finely crafted shelter all the day or will you come swimming?"

Leelah waves him off from where she leans against the wall. "I cannot leave Fialla. Besides, the water is too cool."

"I can watch her, Leelah," I volunteer.

She dismisses me too. "I am perfectly happy here."

The more the children beg, the more Leelah refuses until Kragorn barks in his general's voice, "Leelah Tareth! You are going swimming!" He hauls his protesting wife up and carries her down to the water kicking and screaming with the children running behind them cheering. He wades into the water then throws the tall woman as easily as one of the children.

Leelah emerges, brushing wine red hair from her face and looking frightfully akin to an enraged mountain lion. Kragorn, however, is not the least bit intimidated. Valor and Trent clap and whoop encouragement as he marches straight toward her in the waist deep water and makes good on the kiss she invited earlier. Leelah resists for all of a second before her arms uncross from her chest and lock around her husband's neck. Kragorn lifts her, taking her into deeper water, never letting go of his bride.

Trent chortles as Kragorn and Leelah disappear around a bend in the lake. "I hope you are content to watch the babe for quite a while, Majie."

I stare down at the overflow of Kragorn and Leelah's love who is currently chewing on her toes. "I am well with it." I kiss Fialla's feet, and she giggles.

Valor rises and extends his hands to Trent and Karris. "Let's go see if Kragorn fixed the rope swing. You will be fine with the children?"

"Certainly."

Karris holds her chin higher at not being included with the children. The trio set off on the path through the woods.

I loose my long held sigh and relax my forced smile. My bodice has dried sufficiently that I bring Fialla to rest against my shoulder, snuggling her close. She pats my shoulder and amuses herself with my messy braid. I stroll down to watch the children from the top of the bank. My thoughts drift over the sunny day, skipping past the clouds on the horizon.

This has been a lovely day.

A shout turns my head in time to see Trent swinging from the promontory out over the water while tucking his legs up. The water splashes in an impressive column. As men do, Valor tries to outdo him, but Karris judges Trent the victor with a heavy bias. I chuckle at Valor's outrage that can be seen from this distance.

The children, for the most part, play happily in the shallows while I watch over them. Fialla has fallen asleep by the time Karris huffs her way over to me, wiping angry tears from her face, and plops onto the bank.

"What happened?" I ask, shifting Fialla to my other shoulder.

"Trent thinks I am just a girl and not worth his notice," she says, brushing away more tears. "He does not see me any differently than Lois or Ivy. I am almost a woman, and he cannot see it."

"How old are you?"

"Twelve years." She defiantly tilts her head, expecting me to argue that she *is* more a girl than a woman.

I only shrug. "You are older than I was when my betrothal was signed."

Her head whips around. "How old were you?"

"I was ten, but it was a long time before I wed." *Too long.* "Do you know how old Trent is?"

"He is twenty-five."

"That puts thirteen years between you. In a few more years, age will not be a difficulty for you. My own husband was eighteen years older than me. That was not much of a problem when we married as I had grown into a woman by then, but he was slower to look upon me as marriageable because of the disparity."

"But I do not want Trent to be slow to see me as a woman," Karris worries.

"Let us think of it from Trent's perspective." I try to explain in a way that may be more effective. "He is used to keeping company with women closer to his age. He would not be a good man at all if he looked upon a young woman of your age with interest. Most men would agree a woman of sixteen or seventeen years acceptable to take to wife if they are of a closer age to the woman. So, in five more years, if you have not attracted the interest of others you prefer like I suspect you will, then you may be justifiably offended if Trent still thinks of you as a child, and I will help you take him to task if you like." I bump my shoulder into hers, and she grins.

"How old were you when your husband thought you a woman?" Karris asks.

I think of what Leer told me and what he admitted to Lorennt and I. Objectively, I try to blend the two stories to be able to give Karris the truth. Rather, as much truth as her young ears can hear. "I was seventeen when he realized that he needed to make good on our betrothal or I might be married off elsewhere, but we did not marry until last autumn, when I was nineteen."

Karris's eyes widen. "You were betrothed since you were ten, but married for less than a year? That is tragic!"

I nod. We might have built so much together given more time.

Karris opens her mouth to ask me something else but snaps it shut. After a moment she says, "Mother told me I must not ask you questions, because it would made you sad."

I wrap an arm around the girl's shoulders. "Thank you for your consideration, but I am already sad. I do not think your questions could add to it."

"Mother says that talking about the difficult memories can make them easier to carry and make them not hurt so much," Karris recommends. As one of Leelah's three adopted daughters who were rescued from abuse or abandonment, I do not doubt the girl knows of what she speaks.

"I believe she is right. What would you like to know?"

She sucks on her teeth, deciding what to ask first, then starts with what should be a simple question. "What was your husband's name?"

"His name was Leer."

"If you were betrothed for so long, you must both be noble, but your sister Nev is not. How did that happen?" She pieces together much from little.

"My husband and Nev's lover were brothers, so you could say that we are sisters by marriage, in a way."

"Oh. I see. That is why Lor did not marry her." She then snickers. "Leer and Lor. That is funny."

I smile. "I suppose it is." Maybe I should not say more, but I cannot let the mark against Lorennt's character stand. He made mistakes, but not that one. "Lor wanted to marry Nev. He was broken-hearted when she left."

"Then why did he not?" Karris asks, thoroughly confused.

"There were circumstances outside of either of their control that prevented them from marrying. That is all I can say about it," I forestall any more questions.

She nods once, acknowledging the fairness. "So, Leer was old enough to be your father?"

"He was. In fact, he first met my family when he was seventeen, and I was in my mother's womb."

Karris's jaw falls open, making me laugh.

"Aye. Quite a difference. And not one I would recommend to a woman with choices unless there was first love and similarity of temperaments." I take the opportunity to plant a seed dissuading her from her admiration of Trent. "Even though I was a woman when we married, we still had difficulties that had to do with maturity and temperament. My husband was a pensive man given to pursuits of the mind, whereas I was constantly getting into mischief and wanting to be out of doors though my duties required me to be within."

Valor and Trent come into view, swimming their way back from the promontory.

"Was Leer fat?" Karris asks.

I laugh loudly, realizing that she inferred something I did not mean. Though, it was a reasonable assumption since I did describe him as a man of an age to be my father and given to sedentary activities.

"Nothing could be further from the truth. My husband was the most handsome of men. He had dark hair and rich brown eyes. He was tall —"

"As tall as Uncle?" She interjects, looking at the man heading toward us.

I shake my head, motioning him and Trent to stay with the children. Karris and I walk back toward the shelter to continue our conversation.

"He was not that tall. About your father's height though. He also served as a general for a time, and he never neglected his sword. He was well built." I waggle my brows, making the girl giggle.

"So, he was very handsome. Did you like being married to him even though you were so different?" Karris asks. It is good that Leelah has managed to instill in her daughter the truth that physical appearance is not the measure of a man, but it would have been simpler for me if she had taken my word that Leer was handsome and assumed that our life must have been perfect.

"Leer and I got along well and loved each other, but we disagreed as often as we agreed." I swallow the words that I want to be true that simply are not. *He was a good and faithful man. There was nothing we could not overcome together. We were happy.*

Karris touches my shoulder. "Anna, did you hear me?"

I force a smile. "I would have liked to be married to him for the rest of my life."

That is a lie, the Insidious Voice says, dragging forth a memory that discredits my assertion.

"I am your Queen, Grandileer. I am done being your wife," I hear myself *say with the finality of a death knell.*

"Excuse me, Karris. I must see to my needs." I pass Fialla to the girl and stumble blindly toward the woods.

CHAPTER TWENTY-ONE

VALOR

"You could have said that kinder," I reprimand Trent after Karris stomps off through the woods.

"Better the girl gets over this childish infatuation than I am beaten by her father for encouraging it," Trent jests, but his tone shifts to disparagement when he adds, "Besides, I want nothing in common with those..." He struggles to choose just one word when a string of curses would better suit. "Those whoresons we rescued Ivy from."

"I agree. But you could have been gentler than that." I grasp the rope instead of shoving Trent off the ledge for causing Karris, who I consider my niece, to cry. For I am certain that the girl cut from Leelah's cloth was using indignation to hide her hurt.

Trent changes the subject. "Is Erianna well? She is making so great an effort to appear normal that I fear she is far from it."

I look toward the beach where the children are still playing. Erianna is watching over them from the shore. "The lake has stirred up her grief." From this distance I cannot discern her expression or the truth behind it, nor would she want me to attempt to. Each time I believe I have finally crossed the distance between us, she retreats faster than I can catch hold of her. What will it take to gain her confidence? I am terrified that I may not reach her in time. If the darkness devours her and she goes where I cannot follow...

The wind blows against my skin, lifting my thoughts heavenward, higher than my fears. *Courage. The light shines in the darkness, and the darkness has not overcome it.*

"I am curious," Trent says. "Why have you left her alone? She has always thrived when she is close to you."

"She does not wish me to be close. I am trying to respect a widow's grief." Which is accursed difficult to do when she alternates between wanting my solace and wanting to be alone with her misery.

Trent comes alongside me, observing Erianna. "Does her reticence have to do with Tirzah?"

I meet his inquisitive gaze. "Why should it? I have no intentions toward Tirzah."

"Does Erianna know that?"

"I have made it as clear as I can without trespassing on her grief." As she told me I did this day.

Trent's grin is incongruous with my thoughts. "Then perhaps I shall pursue Tirzah. A woman formed like that was designed to be held by a man."

I chuckle. "You fall in fast with beautiful women until you realize their wits are lacking."

"Is Tirzah a lackwit?"

"No. She is clever."

He toys with the idea. "Even if she were a lackwit, the fall would be enjoyable."

Before I can caution him that Tirzah's desires are rooted in marriage not a flirtation, he plunges into the cold lake.

❋ ❋ ❋

I come upon the beach determined to see how Erianna is faring behind her forced pleasantness. She and Karris are deep in conversation, but something Karris says makes her laugh genuinely, and they retire to the lean-to. She must not be as despondent as feared.

I do not intrude where my interference is not wanted. Instead, I keep watch over the children, waiting for Kragorn and Leelah's return. When next I glance back, Erianna is gone.

Probably just needed a moment, I decide. The minutes stretch on, but Erianna does not return though Kragorn and Leelah do.

I leave the little ones in Trent's care and stride up the bank. "Did you see Erianna?" I ask of the pair. Karris's brows wrinkle at the name I let slip.

"Anna went to the woods a while ago, but I think..." Karris glances at her mother with a guilty look. "We were talking about Leer, and she said she did not mind if I asked her questions, and it is like you always say, Mother, it is better to talk about things than keep them locked inside, and—"

"Karris." Leelah draws out the girl's name, but I do not stay for the lecture.

The path into the woods veers into many directions around the lake. She left her weapons, thus, I doubt she went far.

"Erianna!" I call to her, hoping she hears me. Hoping she chooses to answer me. I scan slowly then call again.

She could be anywhere. She is unarmed. Fear spikes through me. "Erianna!"

I search the edges of the leaf strewn path. Too many of us have come and gone to be able to isolate her footprints in the muddle.

Running steps and the jingle of metal sound behind me. "Can you see which way she went?" Trent asks and hands me my weapons belt.

"No. You try." I step aside and fasten my belt.

The map of earth and leaves is legible to him. "This way." He turns down the path that ends at the rope swing.

Fear grips me afresh. I want to run to the promontory. To ensure that the stricken woman who cannot swim is not leaning over the edge of a depthless lake. Trent insists on a slower pace to follow her tracks lest she turned from the path into the woods.

If not for Trent's measured pace and his catching hold of my sleeve, I would have tripped over her. Nearly invisible at the edge of the glade overlooking the lake is Erianna.

She is huddled into a ball, hugging her knees. I step around her and lower to my haunches while Trent edges around the glade to ensure she is safe from attack.

My relief at finding her is blunted by anger that she strayed from the safety of the beach and our weapons. "What are you doing here, Erianna?"

"I need a moment," she says quietly.

I push and shove at my anger until it reluctantly stands aside. "I told you that wherever you wished to go, I would go with you. You simply need to tell me." When I rub the backs of my fingers on her arm to comfort her, she flinches away.

"I just need a moment." She bristles calling to my mind an injured badger hiding in the underbrush to nurse its wounds. "Leave me be!"

I sit down in the dirt, getting comfortable.

"Commander?" Trent asks for his orders. I dismiss him with a jerk of my head.

It is time—perhaps, past time. The wounds dealt by Grandileer must be revealed so I may suture them. She will succumb to them if she does not begin to heal. "I know you are hurting though you try to conceal the depths of that pain. Let me be near you."

Erianna hides her face against her knees. "You cannot be alone with me. It is improper."

I will not allow her to rebuff me again, no matter the walls she puts between us. "It is not improper. But this might be." I wrap my hands around her ankles and gently pull, untucking her legs from her so she must look at me.

"I can manage without you!" she snarls, resisting.

"I know that. It is I who need you," I admit.

She laughs bitterly. "That is a lie I have heard before. I was a fool for believing it then."

I cannot be sure if she is speaking of me or Grandileer, nor can I ask her when she opposes my very presence. "You do not have to believe me. Ask Trent. He will tell you what state I was in without you. Anders knows, too, as does Kragorn."

"You survived. You moved on." Her head rises, giving expression to the sharpness of her tongue. "Go away before you offend your woman."

This again. Perhaps Trent's musing was not far from the origin of her anger. What must I do to convince her? "The only woman I have made a commitment to sits before me." I open my left palm to show her the scar that matches her own. "This is not something that can be undone, nor do I want it to be." I take her left hand and lace her fingers with mine. "My life is bound to yours. As long as the choice is mine to make, I am not going anywhere."

Though I know this is what she desires, the mistrust clouding her eyes will not allow her to see the devotion in mine. Again, I vow, "I am here, Erianna. I am not going anywhere. Take solace in that. In me."

She stares at our entwined hands. "Solace."

"Aye."

The peacefulness of the forest seeps into the space between us. I give Erianna time to feel it, to want that calm for herself. The waiting proves fruitful when the breeze carries away her defiance.

"What do you have in mind?"

I smile slowly, choosing to take the well trodden path between us. It has never failed to lead me past her defenses. "Fun. The sort that makes you laugh till you cannot breathe."

Her skepticism bespeaks weariness. I rise and tug her to her feet.

"Ready?"

Her shoulders bob her indifference. I interpret it to mean acquiescence.

With one smooth motion, I pull her toward me, hook my arm around her waist, and lift her off her feet. She is startled, but her hands grip my shoulders, and she offers no protest as I carry her across the glade.

When I unfasten my weapons belt and let it drop to the ground, Erianna quirks a brow. "You take so little care with your sword?"

"I won't risk losing hold of something immeasurably more precious."

She casts her eyes over her shoulder toward the trees then back to me. Her voice is breathless as she asks, "What are you doing, Valor?"

Almighty. I enjoy the sound of my name on her lips.

I grasp the rope, leaning against it with our combined weight, then the protests begin.

"Valor, no! I cannot swim!"

"But I can." I hold her tightly. "Deep breath."

We plummet through open air to the depthless water below.

CHAPTER TWENTY-TWO

VALOR

Erianna gasps at the surface of the cold lake, wiping her eyes. I tread water and adjust her arms to free mine. The gentle current in the lake pulls at her legs. Frightened, she wraps them tightly around my waist.

"Easy." I chuckle. "Use your arms only."

She shakes her head vehemently. "I will drown!"

I huff a laugh. "Erianna. I have not lost you to assassins, wolves, scorching heat, bitter cold, a villainous king and a rogue nation. Do you truly think that after all that, a bit of water will be able to wrest you from me?"

I set my cheek against hers and feel her teeth chattering from the cold. "Would you have my word that I will not let go of you until you tell me to?"

Her breath wobbles through her, but she nods.

I bring one arm beneath the surface to hold her. "Then you have it. But it will be easier on me if you help me swim."

"How?"

"Bring your legs down to mine. Do you feel how I tread water? It is similar to walking but circular."

She kicks fast, bobbing us in the water, and I am forced to block the perilous aim of her knees.

"Gently. Slowly," I instruct. "The water wants to float you. See what it does to your skirt?"

Erianna looks down to discover her skirt floating at her waist. "Woe's sakes!" She tries to push the fabric down to no avail.

"Never mind that. I will keep my hands and eyes where they belong, as always," I say to settle her. "With a bit of encouragement,

183

the water will lift you too." I demonstrate the motions again, patiently teaching her. Convinced that I will not let her sink to the bottom, she looses one arm to swim. Slowly, we make our way to shallower water.

When my feet touch the silty bottom, I walk forward until the water is chest deep on me. Erianna stretches out her legs, but her toes only brush the bottom.

"I cannot stand," she complains.

"I know. You do not need to."

"If you wish to let go of me I do."

I grin roguishly to answer that question.

Rather than giving me a sharp reply or pinching me, she simply says, "Valor."

Play with me, Erianna. I won't let you suffer these wounds alone. "I suppose if you insist I let you go, then I ought to." I spread my arms wide.

She yelps and grabs hold of me. "Do not be a churl."

I give the contrary woman something to argue. "Deny it if you must, but you like this churl. See how tight you hold me?"

A spark returns to her eyes. "I do deny it."

"That is unkind and a lie." I spit a mouthful of lake water in her face.

She pinches my side.

I grin and dip my chin into the water. *Best run, Erianna. Your defenses are crumbling.*

She gives me a stern look. "Do not—"

I spew the water.

Her noisy fit of temper is beautiful. "You insufferable, arrogant—"

"Childish, churlish," I mock, imitating her voice, and walk her into shallower water.

She turns feisty, splashing and pinching.

My hands grip her narrow waist. "Do you know what happens to saucy women?"

She stills, putting all her defiance into three syllables. "You wouldn't."

I lift my queen and hurl her through the air like a child.

Water folds around her, stifling her shrieks. She springs to the surface, spitting and vengeful. "Oaf!" She launches herself at me while naming me several choice things that I only smile pleasantly at.

I steal the ribbon that was clinging to the remaining stubborn crossings of her braid. I pester her like a boy to her girl—spitting water, making faces, taunting and teasing. It is apt since I cannot tell this woman that I love her no better than a boy could communicate it to a girl.

The girl in her instinctively understands. She chases me through the shallows, howling and splashing and lunging at me when I let her get close. The boy I act becomes too confident in his ability to retreat, or perhaps it is the man who returns thinking it would be a fine thing to be tackled by his woman in a gown that clings to her every soft curve.

Erianna shouts her triumph as she throws herself at me, shoving me backward into the water. I wrap my arms around her, dragging her beneath the waves with me. The boy is satisfied for provoking his girl, the man is more-so for holding his woman.

We surface, laughing and sputtering. Erianna is hidden beneath the tangled mess of her hair. Incapacitated by giggling, she is useless to help herself.

I clumsily push it back from her face. "Hold! I shall find you, my Queen!"

Erianna uses both hands to lift the rest of her hair from her face.

While smiling.

And laughing.

That melodic laugh I have longed to hear dulls the sharp edges inside me that have been honed by worry. "See. This is good medicine."

Her arms lace loosely around my neck. "No, Valor. *You* are good medicine."

No restraints hinder her adoring smile nor hide the truth in her eyes. Nevertheless, she pairs it with words to ensure I understand. "You are my favorite person."

My thumb touches the corner of her smiling lips. As if knowing what I wanted but dared not, she turns her head, brushing her lips across the pad of my thumb. Her eyes return to mine, seeking encouragement. Again, she easily interprets my desire. Floating in my arms, she anchors herself to me with her legs. I allot a man's portion of self-control into not brushing a hand up the bare calf, knee, and thigh gripping my waist. Erianna's own restraint seems to have vanished. One hand pushes into my hair. The other rests on my chest where mere bones separate my pounding heart from being held in her palm.

She angles her head to the side, inviting my kiss. I lean toward her, but caution clangs a warning that I must not ignore. Not a half-hour past Erianna would not look at me. She was hiding. Trembling.

Do not trespass on my grief.

I set my brow against hers, denying myself the sweet of her mouth. "Do I wrong you, Erianna?"

"Wrong me? In what way?" Her breath blends with mine, tickling my wet skin while her fingertips press gently on the back of my neck, urging me to kiss her.

I nuzzle my nose against her cheek, and her breath catches on a little sigh. My hands flex against her waist, wanting to pull her closer, to know her better.

That warning resonates again.

Almighty, she makes it difficult to think!

I set my cheek against her temple, putting distance between my mouth and temptation. "Will you regret this? In the dark of tonight. In the light of tomorrow. Will you regret my kisses?"

She does not need to answer. All that was soft and pliant about her tenses.

"You will."

Her breaths come faster. Though she clings to me, it is not an act of desire. It feels as if she fears drowning.

My hands that were ready to stoke passion, spread wide to rub soothing lines on her back. "Steady. You have nothing to regret. Naught has happened. Solace only."

Her head drops to my shoulder, muffling her words. "It is as I feared. Your solace."

I think backwards to assure myself I did not initiate more than our play. It was mostly her. "What did you fear?"

"I forget myself when I am with you. You make the world disappear." She shudders then whispers, "I feared I would betray him."

The wretched, selfish side of me wants to point out that it is impossible to betray a dead man, but my honor quashes that side. "You have not betrayed his memory."

"But I might. I want to claim any moment of happiness if it will shift this pain off me. To let you erase the world."

"You will hate yourself for it later."

"I do not care anymore."

My hand cups the back of her head. "I do. I care about you in this moment, and the next, and the one after."

Her grip on me loosens. "Then you had best let me return to my solitude."

I lower her to stand on the silty lake bottom and take hold of her hands before she can retreat. "You do not need to isolate yourself to preserve your grief or your control." The weight I will bear on her behalf settles heavily. The consequences will be unfathomable if I fail. "I will be your control. I will ensure you do not betray his memory."

Her remorseful eyes find mine. "That is not fair to you."

"*'Love does not seek its own.'*" I tug her gently back into my arms and hold her as a friend. "*'Love bears all things...It endures all things.'*" Erianna's shoulders shake with her restrained tears. "Besides," I say in a teasing tone though I am perfectly serious, "you do not have the strength to fight your battles and rebuff me. Better to let me stay your side and fight with you."

A chuckle breaks through her tears. "You are insufferable."

"That is my point." I tilt her chin up and swipe my thumbs under her eyes, banishing her tears.

As if it is of no great consequence to either of us, she says, "If you insist, I suppose you may stay."

"Magnanimous of you."

She steps away from me, but keeps hold of my hand. Our attention turns toward the shore to watch the children play in the shallows. They are akin to fishes for how well they love the water.

"Will you teach me to swim?"

Surprise swings my head toward her. Though this was part of her plans with Grandileer, I do not question if she knows her own mind. The sad surety written on her face speaks plainly of her decision. Her husband is gone. If she wishes to learn to swim, it must come by way of another.

Still holding her hand, I begin her instruction. Erianna dedicates herself to the lesson. Before long, she can paddle and swim short distances.

She sets her feet to the bottom and stands with a genuine smile. "This is exhausting!"

"It is, especially if you are not accustomed to it. You are doing very well," I praise her. "Come here, and I shall teach you something else."

"What?" She asks warily.

"I shall teach you to float."

She quirks a brow, dubious to my suggestion, but returns to my side.

I stretch her out on the surface of the water, instructing her to calm her breaths and go limp against my arms. She battles inwardly to release control of the situation to me, but eventually, she relaxes. I move a hand to support her head and the other to the middle of her back lifting her slightly. When her ears submerge she folds in half, shooting upright.

"That is supposed to happen," I assure her.

"Show me how," she requests.

I shake my head. "You have seen the children floating all day. It is not something you can learn by watching. You must feel it."

She hesitantly returns to my arms.

We begin again, more slowly this time. Bit by bit, she eases, sinking into the water, closing her eyes, and floating on the surface. She looks so peaceful she might be asleep. Sadly, I know she is not. Her sleep is fraught with more turmoil than her waking hours.

I begin to lower my hands from beneath her, but she whispers, "Do not let me go."

"You are doing just fine. You do not need me to hold you anymore," I assure her then add, "Unless you want me to."

She tenses but admits, "I want you to."

My answer is the return of my hands.

Quietly, I ask, "What memories did the lake stir up? What was the significance of learning to swim at the coast?"

Her eyes tighten. "Is this the cost you will charge for fighting at my side?"

"I am not fighting at your side if you keep me outside your walls."

Long minutes pass before she decides to let me draw nearer. "I cannot tell you everything."

"Tell me what you can." I value the trust she gives me, knowing she trusts so sparingly.

Erianna gathers thoughts around her, struggling to encompass something grand and complex with the simplicity of words. "It was a promise. One made early in our marriage. We were afraid to be honest with each other, and both of us dealt in half truths. As a result of that and our vastly different temperaments, we struggled to understand one another. Eventually, we learned to make concessions for each other, but neither of us were who we wanted the other to be, and our responsibilities—" She winces and corrects herself. "Our *choices*, kept us apart. Even when we were at our best, when you saw us together in the spring, it was less than we both wanted from the other. Leer was my king. My husband. My lover." Her voice breaks, "But he was never my friend. Though he tried to accept me for who I was—perhaps he came to—still, he would have had me be different." Salty hot tears glide from the corners of her eyes to be engulfed in the fresh mountain lake.

This woman that I love and esteem above all others was made to feel inferior to a standard she could not become. I press my hands against her to remind her she is not alone. "What was the promise?"

Her voice is choked. "In the spring we will go to our seaside castle. We will simply be. Erianna and Leer. No titles. No duties. No obligations. We will play and enjoy being together." A sob caves her chest inward, and she loses her ability to hold herself afloat. I compensate, lifting her in the water.

"We were going to see what we could make of our marriage. But it was all a fairytale. Our lives crumbled in the spring. Our marriage fell apart. Our relationships with Lorennt were torn." The darkness of those memories spreads across her face. "At the last, when Leer saw how badly I wanted to be free of the constant agony and guilt, he was taking me to the coast to try to mend us."

To save you, I silently correct her. My thoughts drift to the summons tucked away at my house. Since finding her, I have debated the merits of revealing it to her. I do not want her to think that I am using it to manipulate her feelings. I worry that is how she will interpret it. If I show it to her, she must be honest with me first, of her own volition. "What was it that ruined your lives? You have said enough for me to know it was more than the loss of Illyanna."

She shakes her head. "I cannot tell you."

"Why not?"

"Leer gave his life for mine. Before that, he shielded my reputation with his. The least that I can do is preserve everyone's good opinion of him."

"You are certain his wrongs are that damaging to his character?"

"I began to hope they were not," she admits. "I wanted Lorennt to show me how to forgive him or to explain away what he did. So I made him confess to Lorennt." She grimaces at the memory she sees behind her lids. "In my selfishness, I did not see the impact Leer's actions had on Lorennt. But Leer knew. That is why he did not defend himself. For the pain he caused us both, he would have allowed Lorennt to beat him to death. Had I not laid atop him, Zavaan would not have killed Leer. Lorennt would have. Verily, he nearly did."

I have no words to reassure her. There is nothing that I can do to make this all come out right. But as Leelah is quick to remind us, prayer is mightier than the sword. *Almighty Father. Only You can save this woman from the horrors she has endured. Please rescue her.*

"To my knowledge the brothers never reconciled," she concludes. "Just as Leer and I never reconciled." The expression in her winter eyes punctuates her words. Gouged. Bereft. Hollow. "Though it is not the same, being here made me realize that I will never know what we might have had together. There is no going back. There is no mending us."

No, there is not. Death is final. All must be reconciled to their Creator and those they love before their unknown day of reckoning. I bear Erianna into shallower water and lead her to shore distant from the others. She needs time to collect herself.

We sit in the sunshine against a warmed rock. Instead of blundering the help I wish to give her by acting in haste, I give Erianna my shoulder to rest her head.

"You were right," Erianna concedes when our clothes are nearly dry. "I do like floating. And swimming." Softer, she murmurs, "I am glad you are at my side."

I lay my head atop hers, grateful that she shared her burdens with me.

CHAPTER TWENTY-THREE

ERIANNA

September 4th

Another week passes, and with it, Anders returns to Malsihra ferrying my brief message to Lorennt.

I will return. I simply need more time. I love you all.

More time to train. More time to formulate a plan. More time to satisfy that indefinable need keeping me in this place.

We make much of each day. All morning and late into the afternoon is spent training at swords, sparring, and riding. Our evenings are occupied with cards and talk of how to snare our enemy. Thus far, nothing has come of it but a pile of rubble from ideas constructed then demolished. Nev comes to visit for a day here and there but is often with Salome. I worry that, given the chance, she will not want to return to Malsihra, preferring the life she has found here over the certain difficulties of returning. More, I worry that I will have to make it a royal command that moves her feet that direction, thereby ending our friendship.

Much to my relief, a heavy rain prevented us from attending Gathering this week, but I was not permitted to escape laundering day the following morn. Mercifully, Tirzah was not present. Being in her company would have been trying. Leelah introduced me to many more of her friends, and I listened while the talk of women swirled around families and children and daily life.

It occurred to me that even if I had wanted to participate in the conversation, I could not offer much. My family is unlike any other in the kingdom. My occupation, singular. My hobbies more befitting a man than a woman. I am an oddity here.

Though I like it little, I am at least conversant with the nobles at court. Their privileged lives have something in common with mine. They know of ordering large holdings, managing servants, and menu approving. I can easily converse with the common folk in Malsihra because they know who I am and do not expect me to relate to them. Our subjects are broader and centered around holidays, business, personal anecdotes of their families, and general goings on.

More unsettling than my inner ostracizing was the shifting of conversation to talk of the widowed queen and royal family. Not one unkind word was said, but it was awkward to be an eavesdropper when I was the topic of choice. A stack of condolence letters were also entrusted to Leelah for Kragorn to forward to Queen Erianna. They have sat in a basket in my room, as of yet, unopened.

Strange as it may be, I do not think I am ready for them. I am still reliving the last year in my mind, trying to make sense of it all. To that end, I attack my journaling with renewed vigor, writing late into the night in my room. This morning, I woke too early and brought my task out of doors.

Valor finds me at dawn atop the wall-walk. "What are you doing?"

I lie before the stack of papers filled front and back with the story I wish had a happy ending. Setting aside my pen, I explain, "I journal. Leelah suggested it. Beyond her feeding me well, this helped me to reorder my mind when speaking was difficult."

"What do you write about?" He sits near me, leaning back against the low wall.

I shuffle through the pages until I find something worth sharing. It tells of the night Leer rode into the city with me, and we played cards at a tavern. I pass it to Valor, granting him permission to read it. "I have told you much of the bad and abrading between Leer and I, but there was also good."

Valor's expression is wary at first, then it eases, lifting the corners of his mouth. He passes the page back to me with a smirk. "Here I thought Grandileer incapable of fun."

"He was. Only as *my Leer* could he match my good humor at times. Most often, we found a middle ground between us that was comfortable and pleasant. I taught him to make time for fun, and he gave me his logic and guidance when I needed perspective—which was often," I drolly admit, shuffling the page back into the chronologically ordered stack.

Valor grins. "I cannot imagine why that would be necessary. I have never seen you overreact."

I shove his outstretched leg. "I deport myself very well when need be and have everyone fooled into thinking I am well-mannered and poised."

"Aye, you do. Until you discard your royal manners and share every blessed thought that you did not say aloud at the time," he teases.

I make a face at his too accurate description, and he laughs. I am lost in his eyes for a moment, taking solace in his company.

I have done my best not to dwell on thoughts of my undeniable attraction to him or vividly remembering the press of his body against mine at the lake. It felt wonderful to be in his arms. A blush of embarrassment rapidly warms my face when I recall my brazen behavior. A lesser man would not have hesitated to kiss me and discover how much of myself I would willingly yield.

But not Valor. He cares too much for me to do something I would regret. Instead, he asked me about Leer and urged me to unburden my heart to him. I trust him all the more for it. What allure I hold for him, I will never understand. He is far too good for me. I know he will realize that truth one day.

I distract myself by glancing at where I paused in my journal, but it affords me no such reprieve.

I told Nev he was here. I felt him watching me. The sensation was so strong that I could have held on like a rope and traced it to its origin. I nearly did and would have if Leer had not called to me. If I discovered Valor watching me and Leer learned of it, I do not want to imagine what would have happened. Thus, I gave up before finding him. At the time, I convinced myself I was simply missing my friend worse than usual and had imagined everything. But I did not.

Guilt bows my head between my shoulders. Was it my fault all along? Could I not reconcile with Leer because I only fooled myself into believing my husband held all of my heart?

No. Leer and I loved each other deeply—so deeply that the loss of him steals the breath from my lungs and threatens to wring more tears out of me.

"How long has it been?" I wonder aloud.

"Do you know the date he died?" Valor asks. He keeps pace with my thoughts better than I can.

I shake my head. I could only hazard a guess at the month. Time became meaningless to me when I lost Illyanna. That date is the last one I remember.

"Lorennt thought you would not, so he and I deduced based on the day you should have arrived at the coast and the—" Valor grimaces, turning aside the callous words. *The decay of the bodies.*

I loose a ragged breath, recoiling from the thought. *My Leer.*

"I am sorry," Valor interjects, circling his hand around my arm to drag me out of the gruesome images. I overlay my hand on his, nodding that he should continue.

"We estimate that he died on July Eleventh."

"An estimate," I bitterly spew from the well of my anguish. "As if it does not make a difference whether he lived one day past that or left the world a day before. My king husband's every hour was significant!"

Remorse sets grooves on Valor's face. "Forgive me. I—"

"I am angry with myself!" I surge to my feet, rustling the pages. Valor stops them from being tossed the length and breadth of the courtyard below. "I am the only one that survived that day! I should know what benighted day it was!" I storm the remaining expanse of wall before me, reach the corner, and turn back.

Valor's eyes are upon me, but he looks through me, transforming thoughts into something actionable. "You are not the only one that knows the exact day."

Zavaan. That day is etched in his memory as a day of victory.

"And his merry band likely know as well. I will get you the exact date, my Queen."

This warrior never accepts that a thing is impossible. He will throw all of himself at an obstacle until it gives way. I forgot how much I appreciate this aspect of his character.

Valor's words reorient my thoughts from where they should not have strayed. "Today is September Fourth."

I add the days in my head then sit down hard. "Fifty-five days." Nearly two months. My mind rearranges the days into a different measure of time. "Eight weeks." It took me the first six weeks of our marriage to realize Leer had claimed a piece of my heart from Valor. Now, only eight weeks after Leer's death—my husband's death—my heart is rapidly swinging back toward Valor. What a faithless, fickle creature I am!

I prop my brow on my knees. "Oh, my Leer. I am divided again, and you are not here to set me straight."

Into the silence stretching out after my words, Valor asks, "Would you like to talk about it?"

Would you like to? Not what Leer would have said. His words would have been, and often were, *Tell me.*

I do not like the contest taking shape in my mind. I know the victor before it starts. Guilt heaps coals on the pyre of my grief and self-loathing.

"I want to cross blades." I need the heft and action of a weapon in my hand to turn me from thoughts that do not matter. The lay of my heart does not change what I must do as long as it does not influence my actions or deter me from my purpose. I can exist attracted to Valor and desperately missing Leer. I got on well enough with their roles reversed.

No, that is a lie. I correct myself. *I was a mess then too.*

Pretending not to see the hand Valor extends to help me gain my feet, I rise, shake out my skirt, and set my mind to the training ahead. "Maybe today will be the day my sword arm does not fail me, *hmm?*" In the previous days, long before the rest of me is exhausted, my arms shake so badly that I can no longer raise my sword. I knew I had much to learn, but I did not expect it would be so physically strenuous.

Valor collects the stack of papers and hands them to me without glancing at the page he would find his name upon. "Perhaps. Or perhaps you will be whining by noon. Again."

"I do not whine! I assert my opinion."

"When you start 'asserting your opinion,' let us ask Micah to name what you are doing. I wager he will say you are whining."

※ ※ ※

At noon, I sit on a bench in the kitchen while Leelah finishes preparing the meal. "Why is this so difficult? I have no difficulty with quarterstaves *or* short staves *or* daggers *or* sparring! Swordplay should be no different!"

"Why is Majie whining?" Micah asks his father.

I glower at the face of the warrior above me. *Not one word.*

"Would not dream of it," he grins, battling laughter. "Now hold still and tell me where it hurts the worst."

"What qualifies you to determine the extent of my injury?" I ask to delay the examination.

"You know the answer," he replies, seeing through my scheme. "Now face forward."

I do know. Besides earning his keep by assisting Hellah in the apothecary shop as a youth, Jessup encouraged Valor to train as a physician. For several months, Valor learned anatomy and healing from Jessup before deciding the profession did not suit him. Valor is restless as a man and says that he was downright fidgety as a youth. He did not have the patience for the studious nature of healing or spending hours in the work room, though he greatly enjoyed the parts that he now classifies as battlefield medicine—setting bones, suturing, applying bandages, and the like.

Valor's fingers probe the muscles around my shoulder blade and down my back. Fortunately, my sore muscles counteract the tingling sensation caused by his hands upon me. He begins again at my neck then down my sword arm. He asks me to extend my arm and keep it stationary as he exerts gentle pressure downward. I grunt, yielding too easily to his force.

That was what caused the injury this day. I caught the arc of his blade against mine to block his attack and felt intense pain in my shoulder and the surrounding muscles. It knocked the blade from my hands and brought me to my knees.

"Well?" Valor asks.

"It all hurts," I grumble.

"Turn toward me."

I straddle the bench and hold very, very still as his fingers walk across my collar bone, lingering over the healed break that can still be felt though, thankfully, not seen. He moves lower to the muscles across the top of my chest. His touch is distractingly pleasant until he nears my right shoulder. I hiss in pain, pulling away from him. He braces a hand behind my shoulder and a hand at the front while ordering me to rotate my arm.

"This is the shoulder you dislocated," he states. "Did you injure it again this past year?"

"No. It has not bothered me until now," I grit out between clenched teeth.

Lines form between his brows as his hands steady my shoulder, ascertaining the extent of the injury that cannot be seen. "If any bruising develops, you must tell me, but I believe you only strained the muscles. Nothing feels torn or out of place. You will need to rest it for several days then rebuild your muscle strength slowly. Until that time, no swords."

I quirk a brow. "I do have two arms, you know. I will simply train with my off hand."

"Not until you have rested your shoulder." The heaviness behind his words suggests there is more to it.

"Why do you think that is not a good idea?"

Instead of answering my question, he raises a silent observation of his own. *I thought we were not talking like this.*

I shrug my left shoulder. "We are not."

His half-smile full of trouble makes an appearance. *Whatever you say, my Queen.*

I cross my eyes at him, and his easy laugh bursts out. The tether between us that was not severed by our will or the passing of time goes taught. I want to lean into him and feel his laugh roll through me.

Instead, I shove him and yelp at the pain that shoots through my shoulder. The oaf does not even budge. "You—"

His hand covers my mouth to prevent the expulsion of all the things I intend to name him for provoking me. He *tsks*. "Mind what leaves that pretty mouth of yours. There are children present."

I can think of something better I can do with it. I flaunt with my eyes the memory he only alluded to. Heat fills his gaze, much to my delight, then I sink my teeth into his palm.

Valor yanks his hand back with a shout and knocks over the bowl of stew Leelah placed before him. The kitchen is thrown into chaos as the stew spills over the edge of the table. The girls scream while clambering out of the way, Leelah berates Valor for his carelessness, and Micah adds to the noise by banging his spoon on the table and hollering for the fun of it.

I calmly take up my spoon with a satisfied smile and enjoy my meal.

CHAPTER TWENTY-FOUR

ERIANNA

September 6th

Somehow, I find myself riding Sacha to Gathering after promising myself I would find a way to escape what is sure to be an unpleasant day rife with talk of Leer's death. Perhaps I could sneak off with Trent to guard me while Valor watches over Nev. Aye. That is what I shall do. I must simply time it correctly so that Valor has no choice but to agree with my plan. Trent wants to be here no more than I do, thus, he will side with me. When the family is entering the chapel, I will nab Trent and make a dash before Valor can object.

Ivy peeks over the side of the cart. "Will you sit with me today, Majie?" Her hopeful doe-eyes turn aside all my plans with a single bat of her lashes.

"Thank you, I would like that," I reply.

"Foiled," Valor snickers on my other side. "The next time I need your cooperation, I shall ask the children to make the request on my behalf."

I sniff, tossing my braid over my shoulder. "I have not the slightest idea what you are referring to."

"Of course not," he mollifies me.

Everyone mingles outside the chapel, greeting each other as the best of friends. To my surprise, I also receive such welcome. Col and his family greet me warmly. When no one is looking, Thad bows his head respectfully. Part of me is irked to have once again been found out, but I squelch my irritation and wink at the man instead. He grins and makes no more of my identity than that.

"Anna!"

I cringe then turn about, presenting a pleasant smile. "Good morn, Tirzah."

"Oh, none of that," she waves aside my offered hand and embraces me. I pick up my jaw only to have it fall open again at her words. "I hope you will forgive me for my pique when it was not your due."

Shock colors my voice. "It was not?"

Tirzah chuckles. "Not at all. Valor has soothed my feathers sufficiently that I hope we may all be friends. I believe you and I could be good company for one another."

"I... am pleased to hear it," I stammer.

She gives me an arch smile and leans in. "I do hope you will not keep him in suspense for too long."

"In what way?"

She saunters toward a group of women, leaving me to wonder what exactly Valor told her.

"She is a good one." Leelah appears at my side. "I do hope Valor can introduce her to some worthy men at court this winter. It would be good of you to also take up her cause, Majie. With you and Valor aiding her, she is sure to marry well."

"I... What?" I ask, still trying to keep pace.

Singing spills out of the open doors to the chapel. Leelah hooks my arm with hers. "Never mind. It is time." She picks up the melody as do those around us who file into the building with a song on their lips.

Ivy happily plants herself between Leelah and I then lifts the sweetest voice I have ever heard. My heart skips as her hand slips into mine, and she encourages me to sing the refrain. The tune and words are simple, so I sing along to please her, hoping that my voice does not overly offend the Creator since the words that leave my mouth are not heartfelt.

"You are forgiving and good, Eternal Father, abounding in love to all who call to You. Hear my prayer, Saving King; listen to my cry for mercy. In the day of my trouble I will call to You, for You will answer me."

When we sit, Ivy tugs me down to whisper in my ear, though it is not much of a whisper since whispering seems not to be a skill children possess.

"That is one of my favorite songs," she says.

"Why is that?" I ask.

She smiles brightly. "Because He heard me when I used to cry for help. He sent Uncle to rescue me and bring me home to Mother and Father."

My eyes meet Leelah's tearful ones overtop her adopted daughter's head. She squeezes the girl. "That is right, Child-mine. We do not always know why we must cross through hell before being caught up in grace, but for certain, our cries were heard by a good and loving Father."

Ivy agrees, hugging her mother. I kiss the top of her head, moved beyond words at her faith. A thought sends out fragile roots in my heart.

Is it possible He heard me too? Would He call me His own?

Not with all the wicked things you have done, the Accuser reminds me. *You are no innocent child. The blood on your hands cannot be washed away. He would reject you, Erianna-who-is-not-enough.*

Pain slashes my heart. This joy and hope are not meant for someone like me.

"Good morning, Friends," the teaching elder greets the Gathering after the invocation that included uplifting the Rodiharian family in prayer and beseeching the Righteous One to take revenge on the evil doers. "In this time of uncertainty, let our hearts take courage and find assurance in the words given to all those who trust in Him as their salvation.

'*And we know that in all things the Almighty works for the good of those who love Him, who have been called according to His purpose...*'"

The memory of Valor speaking that exact thing to me two weeks ago springs forth. "Your words!" I hiss at Valor. "You told him what was said between us?"

"I did not. I had no hand in this," Valor earnestly replies. "These words are not from man. They are from the Creator to His people. *To you*, Erianna."

I return my gaze to the front, to the elder reading from the Holy Texts. "'*...And those He predestined, He also called; those He called, He also justified; those He justified, He also glorified.*' Friends, this promise is ours. Each of us were chosen by the Creator to be His children. His Spirit calls out to ours and when we respond to His call, He washes us clean and makes us new. This is something we can never do for ourselves. None of us can ever earn forgiveness or atone for the wrongs we have done. It is all Him. All because of His love for the wretched men and women we were. He removes the stain of guilt from our lives and clothes us in His righteousness. That is His justification. The Spirit of Truth then resides in us, never to be taken away, but sealed in our hearts as the mark of His promise that when we die in this life, our spirits are reunited with our Creator. This is our promised glory."

"Oh, Friends," the elder says with glistening eyes. "Are we not all eternally grateful for the forgiveness we have received that lifted the crushing burden of our guilt?"

"It is so!" The people say as one.

"'What, then, shall we say in response to this? If the Almighty is for us, who can be against us? He who did not spare His own Son, but gave Him up for us all—how will He not also, along with Him, graciously give us all things? Who will bring any charge against those whom the Creator has chosen? It is the Almighty who justifies...' Friends! The Creator loves you! He sent His Son to die for you and has forgiven you. Do not let the Accuser remind you of your past sins. They hold no sway on you once you have been justified by the Almighty. You have been forgiven and shown mercy. Your hope is secure no matter who we were or what we did."

I cannot breathe for the weight of all the wrong and selfish things that I have done. How the Accuser mounts them up before me, reminding me of them all! My hands again feel sticky and slick with the blood I spilled to satisfy the pain in my heart. But it did not satisfy. Revenge was a trap that only added more stones to the burden of guilt.

My head bows in shame, but there, quieter and more insistent and irrepressible than the condemnation of the Accuser, is the Voice that my heart longs to hear.

Come to me, Erianna. You are mine.

You are wicked! The Accuser shouts.

I love you still, He assures me.

"'Who shall separate us from the love of the Son? Shall trouble or hardship or persecution or famine or nakedness or danger or sword? As it is written: "For Your sake we face death all the day long; we are considered as sheep to be slaughtered."' Did we not endure all of that twenty years ago? Were we not slaughtered because of the Creator whom we represented? Aye and aye. Have we faced more since then? Aye. But we were not alone! We were not separated from His love! He was with us and heard our cries. He went before us, giving us favor and bringing us to Parse Kítaran. And for it we are thankful. Let us proclaim these last verses in one voice and strike back at the Accuser—the Deceiver who tempts us to believe we are forgotten and unloved."

The people wholeheartedly declare, *"'No, in all these things we are more than conquerors through Him who loved us. For I am convinced that neither death nor life, neither angels nor demons, neither the present nor the future, nor any powers, neither height nor depth, nor anything else in all creation, will be able to separate us from the love of the Creator that is ours through the Saving Son.'"*

I am undone.

I do not understand how, but suddenly, it becomes overwhelming clear that all this time, the Creator has been calling fervently to my heart. Echoed over and over through the words of my family, my friends, and even these people—my people who have prayed over me and extended kindnesses to me at every turn—all bore witness to the Creator's love for me, in spite of me. Not that I am worthy. I am as guilty as one can be. Even so, He loves me.

Come now, and let us reason together, says the Voice of Truth. *Though your sins are like scarlet, they shall be as white as snow; though they are red like crimson, they shall be as wool.*

The elder's gaze drifts around the room and seems to land right upon me before continuing, "If there are any who have not yet received forgiveness, hear the Spirit of Truth calling to your heart. Your Heavenly Father loves you. He has already paid the penalty for your sins with His own precious blood through the death of His Son. His sacrifice will atone for what you have done, and His righteousness will cover you. If He is calling to you, will you respond to His call by stepping forward?"

Here I freeze, holding my breath and utterly terrified of what is being asked of me. Before all these people, my people, some who know that I am their queen, can I own to what I have done? Will they see the guilt on my hands and the stain on my soul? I am too ashamed. But how can I not respond? I cannot go on like this any longer. If there is even the remotest chance that the Creator will redeem me, then I must take it. But I am stuck fast to my seat.

"Breathe, Dry Bones. Leave the grave behind." Valor's deep voice against my ear shakes me into action.

I nod. I want to. "Will you come with me?"

He extends his hand to me but waits for me choose. This must be my decision.

I place my hand in his and rise on leaden feet. I step past him into the aisle and make my way to the front of the room that did not seem so large when I first entered. But I cannot turn back now, not even if I wanted to. The call to my soul moves me forward and will not let me go.

Finally, I stand before the elder. Valor squeezes my hand then takes a seat on the nearest bench. "Welcome, Daughter. What is your name?"

Do not hide from Me or them, the Spirit of Truth instructs. *Falsities have no place here.*

"Erianna Rodiharian," I reply unwaveringly.

A murmur goes through the room, but it is not my concern right now.

The elder beams. "I ask you, Erianna, do you wish to be forgiven of your sins?"

"I do. So badly."

He nods with empathy. "Do you acknowledge that you cannot atone for them in your own power or through good works?"

My voice cracks. "This I know."

"There is only one way that you can be saved and receive forgiveness. It is by believing that through the death of the Saving Son your sins were paid for in totality. His death purchased your life."

I nod my understanding as tears pour from my eyes. I have known such love. Liddy's and Leer's deaths were echoes of what the Creator did for me. But more than giving me a chance to go on living in this present life, the Son took the punishment for my sins with his death and offers me new life, now and for eternity.

"And his resurrection from the dead secured yours into His everlasting arms. When you die, your spirit will not be condemned to hell for your sins, but you will be freed from your mortal body, and you will dwell with your Creator in heaven for eternity. Do you understand?"

Again, I nod.

"Very good. Now, aloud or silently in your heart, call out to the Creator and ask for His forgiveness for your sins, and verily, this day, your life will begin anew."

I bow my head to pray, but my guilt bears down mightily on me. In humility, I lower to my knees, contrite and broken.

Creator, I am sorry. I am so sorry. I have been selfish. I have lied and deceived and sinned. I have taken revenge into my own hands and done terrible things. My hands are soaked with blood, and I loathe what I am.

But if you will it, I believe that You alone can wash away my scarlet stains. Please cleanse me of all my sin and wickedness. Please make me clean through the death of Your Son. Please give me new life right now. I cannot carry these burdens any longer.

The Creator that is everything beautiful, matchless, and eternal answers my plea. *I will take them from you, Child-mine. Your sins are forgiven. Receive your new life.*

With that, I am freed. The guilt vanishes. The burdens are no more. For the first time, my hands are clean. I am clean.

This I promise you, the Spirit of Truth declares, not from without but from within my being, *Never will I leave you. Never will I forsake you. As one of my children, you will face persecution. But take heart! I have overcome the world. And surely, I am with you always, until the very end of the age.*

The fear that has dogged my steps for a decade, so much that it has become a tangible presence, is flung far from me. I will never be alone. Never *have* I been alone.

Something between a laugh and a sob of relief shakes out of me. I am so light from the burdens lifted that I am overcome with dizziness as I stand.

One realization after another washes over me. Where all the wretchedness was taken from me, it was replaced. My despair for His hope. My fear for His peace. My shame for His righteousness. My sorrow for His joy. My rejection for His love.

The elder takes my hands in his and says for my ears, "No more tears today, Majesty. Today is for rejoicing."

I laugh quietly and wipe away the tears.

The elder turns me toward the Gathering whose faces reflect the joy on my own. Valor must not have heard the admonishment about tears, for though his face is radiant with joy, tears flow unabashedly down his cheeks.

So I tell him, *No more tears. Our prayers were answered this day.*

Valor laughs and wipes them away.

"Friends," the elder declares with arms spread wide. "Today you bear witness that Erianna has passed from death into eternal life. Let us praise the Almighty for what He has done and welcome her into the kingdom of the Everlasting King on this, her day of redemption."

The Gathering rises, clapping and cheering, except for Valor who wryly admits, *I need a moment, else I will keel over from relief.*

With a smile that springs from the hope within me, I go to him and take his hand in mine while a song of rejoicing is raised with such enthusiasm that it can be heard throughout the valley.

"Surely this is our Creator; we trusted in Him, and He saved us. This is the Almighty; we trusted in Him, and He redeemed us. Let us rejoice and be glad in His salvation."

* * *

※ ※ ※

VALOR

Gratitude overflows from my heart all day long. The dry bones are alive, filled with the breath of the Almighty. Vibrant unquenchable life is displayed in the beauty of her full smile, the melody of her laugh, the droll humor she liberally shares, and in the sparkle of her wintry eyes that flash my way.

Erianna's mouth quirks to the side. *You are staring again.*

I am not sorry, I declare from across the meadow.

You are distracting me. Cease!

Make me.

Her eyes flit to the horses then back to me, naming her missile of choice.

I dare you.

Erianna giggles, and the women she converses with turn to see what elicited her reaction. I feign interest in the food until Nev gains my side, wrapping an arm around my waist. I squeeze her close, watching Thad's family approach their queen and bow deeply.

Erianna takes their hands warmly, brushing aside their formality. "I will only tolerate that nonsense at court," she declares.

Col is particularly affected by the revelation of her identity and stammers when he addresses her. She places a hand on his arm, and I read the words that pass her lips as she whispers to him. "I am still the same person, but I hope you now understand why I cannot accept the generous offer of your suit?"

Col nods vigorously, and red colors the back of his neck.

"Good," Erianna says. "Let us be friends."

Nev nudges my side. "You see. I told you she was a dab at gently setting aside the interest of young men."

"So she is," I chuckle.

Micah runs at Erianna, and the solid lad nearly takes her legs out from under her. She only laughs and kneels down to him.

"She is free," Nev says. "And joyful. It gladdens my heart."

"Mine as well," I agree. "You were much the same when you were freed of your burdens the day your belief was made into personal faith." It was a privilege to witness Nev's heart that had been wrapped in grief from leaving behind Lorennt and her home suddenly unburdened when she was welcomed into the Creator's family.

She nods. "This community has been a blessing to me. More than that, it is liberating to know that I do not need to strive to be a good person to earn forgiveness. Especially carrying my sin so publicly."

Grasping her shoulders, I turn Nev to face me. "Your child is not sin. This babe is a gift from the Creator. The sins that led to his conception are forgiven, the same sins I also stand forgiven of. None of us can hide our sins from the Creator. Everyone here knows that. Just because this one past sin of yours is known, no one thinks any less of you. They know how much they have been forgiven. That personal knowledge removes the desire to judge others."

"I know, but not everyone in Malsihra feels that way. It will be so hard to return and be scorned by all."

"Their opinion does not change how the Creator sees you. Nor can it take away your friends' support. We will be there for you."

"I have no doubt Erianna will quell as much gossip as she can..." Nev presses a hand to her heart. "He does not know he is going to be a father. Oh, how I wronged him by not telling him! I cannot fathom how badly this will hurt him. And what if he has taken a new lover? I could not survive his rejection."

"You are borrowing trouble," I assure her. "I do not doubt he will be hurt and angered. But if you return, you stand a chance at making all of it right."

"I hope so. That is why, when Erianna returns, I will return also," Nev informs me with much resignation.

I smile, knowing what this will mean to all involved. Once Lorennt overcomes his shock, I do not doubt he will do what is right. "You are making the wise decision. Erianna will be overjoyed to have you at her side."

"You mean in her service?" She corrects me. "I will not suddenly come into a title when I return. I am merely a lady's maid."

The vaguest outline of an idea forms. "Do not worry, Nev. I am certain Erianna has a plan." And if she does not, then we will craft one together.

Trent joins us, licking his fingers clean. "I hope we are going on a campaign soon. All this good food is taking a toll. This one," he winks at Nev, "cooks even better than the general."

Nev smiles. "Do not let her hear you say that."

Trent feigns terror then glances around in jest but starts violently at finding Leelah standing just behind him with crossed arms.

"I am pleased to know I will not have to feed you my inferior meals anytime soon," Leelah says.

Trent takes a step back. "Do you have paws for feet?"

Leelah unleashes her most feline grin in answer.

"I was merely being polite to Nev," Trent scrambles out of his self-made hole. "I adore your cooking. I would eat in your kitchen every day if I could."

Her eyes narrow before disregarding the soldier. Like removing an apron, her ire vanishes revealing a pleasant expression when she turns to Nev. "We are celebrating tonight. Would you consider joining us?"

"I would be delighted, thank you," Nev accepts.

"Come along then, you may ride home with us." Leelah rounds on Trent. "*You* may scout the woods around our home. Tamraz was a bit tetchy this morning, and I want to know why."

"Yes, General," he bows his head remorsefully.

"A word of warning," I advise after the women depart. "Do not eat or drink anything she gives you."

Trent shudders. "Aye, Commander."

His eyes are pulled toward our queen whose demeanor reveals how lighthearted she is. "I am relieved to see her happy."

"She is more than happy. She is joyful."

"I hope it lasts."

"It will," I vow. "This joy is founded on hope and faith in the Creator. It is not derived from herself or circumstances."

"So you say." Trent eyes me skeptically. "But when Zavaan is found, when she must return to Malsihra and her burdens, do you think she will still be joyful?"

"I do. That is not to say all her grief is gone or that she will never be sad again, but she will always be able to come back to this day when she was redeemed and given eternal hope. Some of what weighed her down was circumstances, grief, and all that she has lost. But even had none of that occurred, she would still have been burdened with the wrong that she herself has done. That weight is crushing. We cannot move it ourselves. It must be lifted from us."

Trent stares long at her, feeling the weight on his shoulders. I have witnessed the knowledge of his own guilt increase steadily during these past years. When we first met, he thought I was ludicrous for what he called *an overdeveloped sense of morality*. He could not fathom my dedication to prayer and striving to control my anger, to never boast, lie, cheat, become drunk, or bed women. Eventually, he began to respect me for all but the last. That earned me the moniker "vestal," and many jokes have been made at my expense wondering why I abstain from slaking that powerful desire.

Trent's mind was altered nearly three years past when we found Ivy in a dilapidated tavern being peddled by her uncles. They intended to sell her to a bawd once a price could be agreed upon. She was seven years old at the time. As the law in Malesiir is quite clear on what is to be done with those found abusing children in such a way, I carried out justice as the Hand of the Prince then delivered Ivy to Leelah. Seeing justice satisfied and no more was an exercise in self-control the likes of which I had never experienced.

Trent was angered with me for not working revenge on the men, but as time passed, he revealed that he was also disgusted with himself. Though Kragorn and I warned our soldiers of the evils of the industry they spent coin upon, it became personal for Trent when we rescued Ivy. He lamented Ivy's life and the fate of others like her who had been sold to brothels. More, he wondered how many women he had gratified himself with whose lives began as enslaved girls. He hated himself for being a man who unwittingly added to their misery.

In Trent's eyes, no longer was I the needless vestal. I was to be commended and imitated. For the most part, he has stayed far away from the bawds who lure men in their doors. But when he succumbs to lust, he loathes himself afterward.

"None of us is perfect, Trent. If being my friend for the last year has demonstrated anything, it is that we all make profound mistakes. You saw me selfishly initiate an inappropriate relationship with a betrothed woman then become a drunken sot when I lost her. I deviated from what I knew to be truth and reaped the consequences of my decisions. But all the while, the Spirit of Truth beckoned me to repentance. He did not withhold it from me or turn me away. He restored me and set my feet on firm ground once again. That was not something I could do for myself, just as Erianna could not set herself free from the guilt and grief weighing on her soul. It is undeniably the Almighty who gives us His strength in our weakness. Erianna's changed heart will prove that to you."

Trent's expression hardens as he turns to his destrier. "Time will tell."

My heart is heavy for my friend still wandering in darkness. *Father, You have called one of Your children to repentance today and changed her life forever. Please, do it also for Trent. Let Erianna's life bear witness for You.*

PART THREE

RESTORED

CHAPTER TWENTY-FIVE

ERIANNA

September 8th

Rain sluices down slate roofs and stone walls, muddying the courtyard and preventing us from leaving the house. I am told summer is officially at an end. This will bring in the cool harvest season before the snows of winter grip the Haven Mountains. The rain does not suit me or the rest of this family who much prefer being out of doors, but since it could last for days, Leelah puts us all to work cleaning the house top to bottom. Drying lines are strung up before the fire in the great room and laundry is washed in the kitchen. After the work of scrubbing the house is done, the work of washing people begins. Nev, who was caught here at the onset of the rain, helps me wash my hair in the laundry tub that is not large enough for a grown person. Maneuvering Nev into the small tub is comical with little Melon preventing her from bending at the waist. Water sloshes onto the floor in slippery puddles while we laugh like ninnies.

When finally we exit the kitchen—washed, dressed and the floor dried—I declare, "Leelah Tareth, as compensation for housing and caring for your queen these past weeks, I shall commission a bathing room and tub to be built for you at your earliest convenience."

Leelah gleefully hugs me then dances across the great room and up the stairs to retrieve paper to draft the design.

"A shame it is not already built," Valor complains from where he huddles by the fire.

"What happened to you three?" I ask the shivering men with towel-dried hair.

Trent jabs an accusing thumb toward Kragorn. "This one said we ought to bathe in the rain to have done with it. If he was not such a miser we could have enjoyed a nice, hot, tub bath."

Kragorn stoically defends himself. "When you are housing, feeding, and providing for seven people plus guests you may name me a miser all you wish."

Pulling a blanket tighter around his shoulders, Trent retorts, "You cannot include yourself in the counting as you are housed and fed by Her Majesty's army most of the time."

Kragorn blinks once. "Aye. But it is still a goodly number."

Valor, Nev, and I exchange knowing looks.

"Unless congratulations need to be given because the Tareth family is increasing," Valor muses, eyeing his brother.

The corners of Kragorn's mouth twitch.

Valor claps him on the shoulder while Nev and I enthusiastically throw ourselves at Leelah just coming down the stairs.

"Oh, you cannot keep a secret for anything, can you?" She chides her husband without any true reproach and sits across his knees, placing a stack of paper on the table. "Aye, your gift is wonderfully timed since hauling tubs of water around will likely become taxing for me. It is early to be certain, but we expect another babe come summer."

Warmest congratulations are given to Leelah and Kragorn, but she does not wish to linger on the subject and begins sketching the shape of a room on paper. "I want a large bathing room with a tub as big as Valor's."

"I thought that was not necessary," Valor contests.

Leelah dismisses him. "When I tried to convince Kragorn to buy me a tub it was not. The queen is gifting this to me. It is necessary."

"I agree. That is why I will be purchasing myself a much larger tub also." I look down my royal nose at Valor.

He grins at me with blue tinged lips and chattering teeth. "How generous of you, Majesty."

"Quite generous," I agree and sit alongside him, leaning my back against his shivering chest. "You are chilled such that looking at you makes me cold. Warm yourself."

Valor hesitates, then slips his arms around my waist, hunching his shoulders against mine to best soak in my heat. "Generous, indeed."

Trent grumbles under his breath, and Nev laughs. "Poor Trent. Shall I join you?"

"Thank you, but no," he replies. "I witnessed Lorennt knock Anders unconscious for saying something crass about his woman. Almighty spare me if he ever learned that I put my arms around you."

"He did?" Nev drops to the couch next to me.

"To be fair, Nev," Valor's deep voice rumbles through my back, "Anders did not know you at the time. He was merely baiting Lorennt."

"And got what he deserved," Leelah interjects. "Anders ought to pay the cost for not minding his mouth."

"Minding one's mouth is very important," Valor intones for my ears, sending heat to my cheeks.

"Tell me more about your bathing room, Leelah," I request and subtly pinch Valor's arm. His silent laugh shakes me, and I think what a very foolish thing I have done in toeing this blurred line with him. There is too much emotion from both of us. I can only hope he has the fortitude to be my control and his own.

"I want a large tub and shelves for towels." Leelah jots down her plans.

"Might I suggest a drain in the floor? It would prevent you from cleaning up water if the tub is overfilled," I recommend from experience.

Nev bursts out laughing. "From someone unexpectedly joining a bath already occupied, *hmm*?"

She ignores my warning look.

"Do you remember how many towels it took to dry your bathing room?" Nev adds.

"No, I do not remember, and you do not either," I say, but Leelah demands the story. "If you must know, one time Leer pretended to have a sense of humor," I begin. I play upon the jocularity in the story, and everyone laughs, but I cannot forget that was the first time Leer told me he loved me. I lace my hand with Valor's as grief pierces my heart. The emotion is not jagged with my own guilt since the Creator lifted those burdens from me, but a more pure feeling of the loss of my husband and wishing that his love for me had not demanded such a sacrifice.

We continue planning Leelah's bathing room, intermingling good stories late into the evening. Though Valor is sufficiently warmed, his constancy is a balm to me that I welcome, so I remain close alongside him. Our companions drift off to bed, excepting Trent who snores in the chair closest to the fire that burns low once again despite the log added by Kragorn before he went above-stairs.

"What was the rest of the story you told?" Valor murmurs.

Softly, I relate the whole of it, explaining what it meant to me, though Nev did not know.

"Did you record all of those significant moments in your journal?"

"I did."

He does not make his request lightly, rather, he knows the weight of what he asks. "If you feel comfortable with me doing so, I would like to read all of it."

I am conflicted. In some ways—many ways—I want Valor to understand. I would trust no other to know so much of me. If it was only my story, then I might. But it reveals much of Leer too, and he was never transparent. "There may come a time that I can allow you to read it, but not yet. I hope you understand."

"I do. What I have asked of you is extremely personal. But if I could make one more request, it is this. When you reach the darkest parts of your story, those days when you no longer wished to live, I would like to give you a few pages to incorporate into your journal. Will you allow that?"

What could he want to add? Instead of asking, I decide to trust he has a reason for doing so. "I will."

I shudder thinking on what I next have to write. I do not want to do it, but if the rain lasts as long as they seem to think it will, I ought to have it done with. Then maybe, perhaps finally, I will see what I could not at the time.

I stretch my newfound faith as Leelah instructed me to, bringing my hurt to the Healer. *Please be near. Please help me see what went wrong, where it all fell apart. I need to make peace with the end, but I am scared to relive it.*

I am with you, the Ever-present One reassures me.

My heart settles, but my arms are so empty they ache. "You once told me to ask you for what I need. May I still do so?"

Valor does not rush his answer, but neither do I feel uncertainty in him, only caution that does not offend. "You may. But I will tell you now what I should have then. I will do my very best to do what you ask, but I shall endeavor to place your honor first and uphold you so that we are above reproach for our actions. What your people think of you does matter. I was wrong to argue otherwise."

"You are worthy of my trust," I assure him, blinking back tears. "We have both learned from our previous mistakes."

"I am imperfect, Erianna. Do not falsely trust that I am incapable of sinning with you. It would be an outrageous lie to say that I do not desire you. I believe it will be even more challenging for us to be close going forward. In the past, your fear, naivety, and betrothal made a barrier that I walked the boundary of but did not attempt to cross. All that is gone now. I will proceed far more cautiously than I did previously and try to stay far away from tempting either of us where we should not go. Though we are friends, I will not excuse all in the name of friendship that could quickly become more. I vowed that I would be your control and not allow you to betray his memory. This is how I will uphold that vow. Do you understand?"

I nod against his shoulder, grateful that he shared his thoughts with me. For certain, we must be cautious.

"What do you need from me, my Sweetest Friend?" He murmurs against my hair.

My breath wobbles out of me. "Please hold me? I need your solace."

Valor's arms come around me, bringing me against his chest and tucking my head under his chin. His hand that bears the mark of our entwined lives rubs slow circles over my back.

The wave of grief ebbs away after a time, leaving me exhausted.

Valor's hand smooths my hair down my back, moving me closer to sleep. "Do you know that I would never have chosen this for you? My heart aches for all that you have lost."

"I know." I place my hand on his chest. "If by some miracle we lay hold of that which I previously deemed unattainable, it will be because the Almighty creates life from the ashes."

"As only He can do," Valor concurs. "I will not press you. You must be allowed to grieve and heal. If there is one thing I can do, it will be to encourage you to draw near to your Heavenly Father. That relationship is the most significant one in your life. Build that and give Him the control to work out all the rest. His plans are always better than ours."

"Thank you," I breathe. "Thank you for pushing me toward Him so that I could be redeemed. My life has been saved and forever changed. Thank you for interceding for me. Thank you for fighting for me like you promised."

Valor's holds me to him. "It has been my honor. For all that He has done, I am inexpressibly grateful."

Peace wraps around me. When I begin to doze, Valor rouses me gently, helping me to my feet and seeing me up the stairs. As I slip beneath the covers already warmed by Nev's presence, my heartfelt gratitude carries me into restful slumber.

CHAPTER TWENTY-SIX

ERIANNA

September 9th

The pain gathering low in my belly forewarns that the vulnerability I felt last night may not have been entirely within my ability to control. This will be my first flux since I lost Illyanna, and I am dreading it.

I find Leelah in the above-stairs hallway seated in the window casing, staring out the open shutters into the dreary morning. I set a hand on her shoulder. She looks around slowly with none of her usual good humor.

"Are you well, Leelah?"

"For the moment," she says, again looking into the rain. "I try not to set my hopes on a babe this early in the pregnancy. I have been disappointed before."

I hug her in sympathy. "I shall add my prayers to yours that this one fills your arms not only your heart."

"Thank you. There is no stronger remedy than that. Was there something you needed?"

"Actually, I shall soon need cloths."

"A word of warning," she says, walking toward a closet. "It is my experience this cycle shall be more unpleasant than most."

"Delightful," I grumble, stowing the cloths in my room.

"I think we need a task to distract us. Have you baked bread before?" She marches down the stairs.

"No, but I am willing to learn."

"You are going to love it. It involves a great deal of hitting the dough."

I chuckle. "We truly are kindred spirits."

"Maybe one day sisters?" She casts a meddlesome glance my way. "Or was I much mistaken in how late it was when you finally trundled up to bed last eve?"

My face flames. "Maybe one day. But I do not doubt that babe of yours will be walking before such a thing is even discussed with any amount of probability."

"So you say, but mark my words, longing to share his bed will get the better of you, and you will be speaking vows inside of a year."

"Leelah Tareth! What a thing to say!" My astonishment with the outspoken woman is quickly supplanted by mortification as we push through the kitchen door to find Kragorn, Valor, Trent and Karris having tea.

Three of them stare into their mugs trying to pretend they did not hear what they undoubtedly did, but the oaf under discussion takes the afforded opportunity to attempt to deepen the scarlet hue of my complexion. "From your lips to the Creator's ears, Leelah."

Kragorn and Trent slap palms to the table, guffawing. Valor proudly admires the effect of his words.

"Leelah," I say with deadly calm. "I require your largest wooden spoon." She slaps it into my palm without hesitation.

Instead of taking his deserved beating like a man, Valor springs from the table and grabs a rolling pin to fend off my onslaught. Nevertheless, I wallop him and the other two troublemakers for encouraging him.

"Well done," Leelah approves as the men flee the room. "A woman is the master of her kitchen and need never take sass from anyone in here."

"To be fair, Mother," Karris says, "you do not take sass from anyone anywhere."

"Rightly so." Leelah bustles about, grabbing large bowls and a crock of bubbly goop from near the stove, then enters the larder to retrieve the flour.

"May we make sweet buns?" Karris asks, arranging the bowls on the table.

"Of course! There would be no point in the trouble of making bread if we did not reward our labor with sweet buns. Get the sugar, Love," Leelah calls from inside the larder.

Karris pushes a chair against the cupboard and reaches far to the back of it, withdrawing a sack of maple sugar and the costly spices—cinnamon and nutmeg—that are imported from the Sutherlands.

We talk and laugh, sinking our hands into the sticky dough. Nev joins us, bringing her sewing into the kitchen, and sets a second basket on the table. "Erianna, here is Valor's mending."

"Excuse me?" I exclaim.

Nev's brows wrinkle. "He said that you exchanged him caring for Sacha for you doing his mending."

So that is why he was so quick to take over my chores while I was resting my shoulder the week past!

"Oh, I have been tricked, haven't I?" Nev huffs at her own gullibility. "I knew that did not sound right. You stitch so slowly that this will take you the better part of a day. Never mind. I will see to it."

"There is no need." I assure her. "I will see to it."

Nev is well acquainted with my schemes and hears this one in my voice. "What are you planning to do?"

"You shall see." And so shall everyone else.

✳ ✳ ✳

September 10th

My cycle arrives the next day, and I remain abed for most of it. Since I cannot think around it, I take up my pen and document the day I lost Illyanna. My heart breaks again for my tiny daughter. I bring my grief to the Creator, asking Him to work something good from this atrocity and reveal why He permitted her to die. Though I hoped to be given an immediate revelation, I am not. But I am given peace that is illogical in the midst of this situation, and my heart is comforted.

I take up the basket of mending, finding a morsel of amusement in the task. Karris joins me on the bed with her own sewing projects. A concerned looking Valor appears shortly thereafter wanting to know what he may do to help me feel better. Of course it is said lightheartedly with a hefty amount of teasing, but his request is genuine.

"Mending is dull work," I complain. "Will you read to us while we sew?"

He readily agrees. "What would you like to hear?"

Karris requests a story from the Holy Texts of a queen who was chosen by the Creator to save her people. I listen with rapt attention, unaware that there are such stories in the Texts. The woman's bravery and sacrifice stun me. She was forced to give up all that she knew to enter into a harem and was chosen to be queen because of her beauty.

Through her humility and faith in the Almighty's plan, her people were saved.

Did she also lie awake at nights wondering how the Creator could make something good of her life that had been chosen for her? She was made the queen of a powerful nation, she was favored by her king husband, and her people were saved. Her life was spared, but what happened to her? Did her husband love her? Was she blessed with children? Was she content with her lot? The story does not say.

"The Queen Esther was a brave and selfless woman. For it, her people were saved and the wicked man was punished. The Creator chose well the one He wanted to use," I comment while tugging the green thread through the blue fabric.

"I knew you would like that story," Karris smiles. "Queen Esther and you are much alike."

I quirk an eyebrow at the girl. "I thank you for the compliment, but I must posit that the only thing we share is the title of queen."

"Father told us stories of you when he came home after your coronation. He said that Queen Erianna was very brave and gave up something she wanted greatly so that she could help her people. He said that she made good decisions for Malesiir, and we were blessed to have her as our queen. And he said that after months of combatting the brigands, the idea that finally worked to win back the North was the queen's. He told me lots of stories like that about you."

"They are all true," Valor confirms. "We are blessed to have Erianna as our queen."

My heart quickens as I stare at Karris. Though the subtle sensation is new to me, I know that it is the Spirit of Truth leading me home to Malsihra. But like Esther, I ask Him, *Why me? Why have you chosen me for this? This path could be the death of me.*

I hug Karris tightly. "Thank you for your encouragement."

"May I ask, what was it you gave up for your people? The thing you wanted greatly."

"Can I trust you not to speak of this with your friends or anyone outside of your family? It is not something I wish for my people to know."

Karris nods solemnly, pleased that I think her worthy of trusting with sensitive information.

Quietly I say, "I never wanted to be queen. I wished to dissolve my betrothal with Leer so that I could lead a simple life with the man I loved."

Karris's eyes widen in astonishment, then she glances at Valor, undoubtedly piecing together bits of many conversations she has overheard. Her uncle stares steadily back at her and nods, verifying everything she is thinking.

Before she can ask anymore questions or make premature suggestions, I request, "Would you please bring me more of that tea your mother made?"

"The willow bark for the pain? Of course," Karris agrees and clambers off the bed, heading for the kitchen.

I fix my gaze on that which I wanted so greatly.

Valor's storm cloud eyes are soft upon me. "Karris spoke true. You and the ancient queen have much in common. The most significant of which is being placed into your roles by the Creator. Despite wanting a different life for yourself, He has something greater for you and has made you capable of more than you think."

"I feel Him calling me back to Malsihra." I remove my signet ring, holding it between my fingers. "Though I would be content to hide in Parse Kítaran for the rest of my life, I know it is not what He has planned." I give the ring to my Hand. "Please make the arrangements. I would like to set out as soon as the roads are passable."

Valor bows his head, accepting my order.

I set my heart upon finding joy in the Creator's sustaining love and endeavor to trust that He knows best. I want to be satisfied no matter what His plans are, but I cannot help asking, "The Creator's plans for Queen Esther were indisputably good. But do you think it was also in His plan for her to be happy?"

Valor rises from his chair and squeezes my shoulder. "I do."

I set aside the mending to take up my pen once more. *Father, give me the strength to see this done.* "I am nearly ready for those additional pages."

Valor pauses in the doorway. "I am proud of you."

❋ ❋ ❋

The rain has turned to sleet by evening, freezing the muddy ground. I worry for Trent who set out for Chishelm with letters drafted by Valor —one summoning the company to escort me home and another that will be carried by messenger to Lorennt in advance of my arrival. If the weather clears on the morrow, I could be headed home in as little as two days.

Returning stirs a hundred thoughts and feelings—some happy, some indifferent, most trepidatious. I bring them all to the Creator and ask for clarity to sort myself out. I lie awake long after Nev has come above-stairs and fallen asleep. The news that she plans to return with me gladdens my heart, but I am anxious for Lorennt.

As wronged as I feel, poor Lorennt was lied to by all of us. He was loyal to a fault, and I repaid him by hiding his child and lover. Though I know I stand forgiven of all wrongdoing, I tell the Creator I am sorry for my lies and ask for wisdom in making them right and pray Lorennt will be willing to listen to us.

I wander below-stairs on the off chance that Valor is still awake. I find him sitting by the fire with his head bowed over loosely folded hands. I curl into an armchair, tightening my robe around me against the chill in the air.

"The pages for you are on the table," Valor says without looking up.

"Before we get to that, I would speak with you of Nev," I say and get to the crux of the matter. "I will not allow her to return into service as a maid. If Lorennt is amenable to it, I wish them to marry. Even if he is not, I mean to keep her in my court, but I am not sure what is required to do that without setting the castle on its ear. How can I legally make Nev a lady?"

Valor leans back in his chair with a contemplative smile. "It is remarkable how similar our thoughts run. As it happens, I was going to propose an idea to you on how to accomplish precisely that."

Valor outlines his plan, and I improve upon it. Together we see even more benefits than previously realized. It also has the perk of being indisputably legal though the stuffy court will no doubt complain regardless.

That settled, we speak of lesser things until the papers on the table between us dominate our interlude. The utter solemnity and care with which Valor approaches the topic breeds apprehension in me.

"When I told you that Hagan sent for me, that was the truth." Valor picks up the folded pages. "What I did not tell you was that Grandileer also sent for me."

My heart stumbles. "He did?" I flounder to make sense of why Leer would have summoned Valor at such a time.

"My intention was always to do whatever I could to help you and encourage you to forgive your husband." Valor hands the pages to me.

"Forgive him?" I repeat, feeling affronted and embarrassed and relieved all at once. "You know?"

He shakes his head. "Read it."

The first page is Hagan's summons, that most loyal castle guard and Valor's friend. I shall ever be thankful for him saving my life and for how he faithfully watched over me. Only a few days after summoning Valor, Hagan gave his life in service.

The second summons is Leer's.

Valor,

I would have you know that I do not make this request lightly, but make it I must. I need your help.

Something awful has transpired as a result of my actions. Though I have tried for months to reach her, Erianna is withdrawn and will not hear me. I hid the truth from her in an effort to protect her, not comprehending how deeply my lies would cut her until it was too late to be honest. She will not believe a word I say anymore, but I hope that she will listen to one who never lies.

Though it was within my rights to claim her as my bride, I have come to believe I wronged you both by not releasing her from the betrothal when she asked, especially considering what I have done, of which I shall reveal all in hopes that you can reach her where I cannot. I did not appreciate the lengths you went to save her life and help her recover from the abuse she suffered. Seeing her brokenness now gives insight to her state when you brought her out of Limba. It rends my heart to see her like this. I cannot allow it to go on. I will do anything to save her.

My hope is that you will be able to help her find her way out of the darkness that has sway on her and see her restored. I love my wife wholeheartedly and ever shall. She has been a blessing the likes of which I do not deserve. I pray that she will find it in her heart to forgive me, but if she cannot and still wishes our marriage dissolved, I will allow it. I would rather lose her than have her be lost.

If you have ever truly cared for Erianna, then please come to the seaside castle. We depart Malsihra on the morrow. I ask that you proceed with all haste.

Grandileer

I read the letter until I can recite it perfectly. The Spirit of Truth brings to my mind the promise Leer made me on the day he died.

"I will do anything to bring you back to life. Anything for you, my Dear. This I promise you. Remember it so that you know I kept my word to you. There will come a day that you can see how much I love you."

This is what he meant. He loved me enough to do anything to save me, even if that meant returning me to Valor. Or laying down his life for mine.

The man that spoke vows anew to me was not the same one that callously left me in Limba or took another woman to our marriage bed. My Leer was imperfect, but he loved me. He was a good king, a good man. He was a loving husband to me.

That is why I cannot reconcile his actions from before with those after. He hated what he did and was perfectly genuine when he said he wished he had brought me to Malesiir as soon as he returned from his general's command. That man would have made different decisions than those made by the cunning general.

I cannot reconcile his prior actions, because my Leer did not do them.

My longing to return to Malsihra increases tenfold. Even if Leer cannot hear me, I wish to be as close to him as the divide will allow when I return to him and speak the words lodged in my heart.

CHAPTER TWENTY-SEVEN

ERIANNA

September 13th

I hate saying goodbye to Leelah and the children. I want to bring them with me, but I know things will be miserable in the coming weeks. "Winter solstice," I promise them. "You must stay with me for winter solstice. It will be so wonderful. There are games and ridiculous amounts of food that you do not have to prepare," I wink at Leelah, "dancing, and the whole place looks like a rainbow. We even hold a tournament."

"We would not miss it," Leelah agrees, hugging me tightly. "I require regular letters from you until then, Majie."

"Likewise, General," I tease. "And you too," I call upon Karris, embracing her. "I want letters. I also charge you with sending me water paintings from all the children. My room has far too much black decor. It needs some color."

"What should I send you, Majie?" Micah asks.

I kneel next to the boy that I have considered sneaking home in my saddle bag. No one can stay sad for very long with Micah underfoot. "Since I will not be here to harvest apples with you like we planned, will you save me seeds from the very best one that you eat and help me find a place to plant them at the castle when you come visit?"

He holds up all his fingers. "I'll save you this many!"

"Perfect." I gather him to me and Lois and Ivy also. "Behave for your mother. Thank you for sharing your home with me. I love you all."

I hold Fialla, soaking in every last snuggle, while Leelah and Kragorn say goodbye. I tried to convince him to stay with Leelah a few more weeks, but they both argued that they were well with his departure and reminded me we have a villain to hunt down.

Leelah hugs Valor next saying, "You had better not let my friends come to harm, or I will take it out of your hide."

"Can you not simply say 'farewell' without all the threats against my person?" Valor complains, then quietly, "I will look after them all and fill every moment I am not doing that praying this babe stays."

Leelah squeezes her eyes shut, swallowing tears. Valor holds her a second more, letting her collect herself before releasing her to Nev.

The grey skies portend more bad weather before the day is out, but we must depart in the window we have been given. Trent brought back news from Chishelm that Zavaan is becoming impatient and orchestrating more destruction against my people. Besides raiding livestock and burning fields, he set fire to a barn that caused the death of the farmer who ran into the burning building attempting to rescue his livestock. I cannot allow Zavaan to continue terrorizing my people.

For the continued privacy of the Judges, Anders handpicked only a dozen of the three hundred soldiers to enter Parse Kítaran to retrieve us. They await us at the end of the winding path into the valley. At my insistence, Nev will take turns riding with one of our soldiers. She is not the horsewoman I am, and I will not risk her taking a spill. Presently, Valor hands Nev up to Trent before coming to my side.

"Good-byes do not get easier, in case you were wondering," he informs me, swinging into the saddle.

"No, I do not imagine they will."

With many a backward glance to the family on the wall-walk, we cross the grass lawn and pass Tamraz, watching over his herd. The tree lined path opens to a gloomy autumn day, nothing like the beautiful morning Valor and I raced across the high valley. But now, unlike then, the bleak skies cannot dampen the expectant hope burning brightly in my heart.

※ ※ ※

Valor was determined that the Ruphiri would not be served the opportunity to ambush us a third time. Three hundred soldiers hem us in on all sides. It necessitates moving slowly along the road to allow the soldiers guarding our flank to pick their way through the forests and fields bordering the road into the capital. Our procession has created more than a few inconveniences for fellow Malesiirians traveling this road. Despite my protests, Kragorn ordered my people to pull their carts off the road while we passed. Travelers behind our procession were warned to go by a different road if possible. Those that could not were stuck moving slowly in our wake until we made camp for the night thereby clearing the road and allowing them to pass.

Traveling with an escort of three hundred soldiers seemed a grand, safe way to return to the capital. In practice, it is tedious and frustrating. Valor vows that it will only add a single day and night to our travel, because we are riding from dawn till dusk. I tried to bargain that he and I could ride at a gallop to reach the city within a day if we abandoned the rest. He did not believe my suggestion was sincere, or chose not to believe it.

"I admit, it is a comfort to be surrounded by so many soldiers," Nev says from our shared perch by the fire. Hearing her comment, Valor smirks at me. I pretend not to notice.

"I feel watched from the darkness," Nev continues, shuddering.

Trent tosses a stick into the fire, shooting sparks into the air. "You are watched only by our soldiers. You have naught to fear."

The lie rolls easily off Trent's tongue. Earlier, he brought word to Valor that we are being tracked, likely watched at this moment, by the Ruphiri.

Nev looks to me then Valor for confirmation. Can she hear Trent's lie?

"You are safe, Nev," Valor assures her.

His words do not finish vibrating on the air before the night is pierced by a long, blood-chilling howl. Another answers it from across our camp. The hunting cries of dozens of wolves send our camp into turmoil.

I leap to my feet, drawing daggers. Valor and Trent form a wall of steel and muscle before Nev and I with the fire at our backs. Kragorn's gruff voice rises above the tumult, ordering men into their places. Concentric circles of soldiers surround us. Unless Zavaan has acquired an army to fight his way through three hundred of Malesiir's cavalry, he has no chance of reaching us.

Nev whimpers at my side, wrapping her arms around Melon. The sight distracts me momentarily. Did I look so helpless to Jaleh?

I edge my shoulder in front of Nev. "You are safe. I will not let him near you."

"I fear for you, too, Erianna." She leans her shoulder into mine.

"Don't. I am not afra—"

The buzz of arrows is immediately drowned by the screams of soldiers. A soldier near us falls to the ground with a gurgling scream as an arrow spears his throat.

"Shields!" Valor bellows.

Most soldiers raise bucklers or heater shields to protect their exposed faces and necks, but a handful of soldiers run toward us raising door-sized shields.

"Get to the center!" Valor commands us, not waiting for compliance before pushing Nev and I into the middle of the shield fortress. I hastily sheath my daggers lest I impale the backs of the soldiers pressing against me. Nev clings to me, alternately crying and screaming. The thunk of an arrow lands on the shield above us that blots out the night. The reek of sweat from the shield bearers assaults my senses. I cling to the present with a desperate grip.

"Return fire!" I hear the order amidst the rain of arrows and screams of the wounded.

The twang of bowstrings shakes our camp. With each of our volleys, the incoming attack lessens.

The noise from men, animals, and weapons turns into a chaotic song that makes my ears ring until I cannot discern a single noise, only the overarching din. One of the shield bearers stumbles into me, yowling. An arrow protrudes from the leather top of his boot. I steady him with a hand at his back. Before he regains his place in our shield wall, I glimpse Valor bent behind his shield, a snarl on his face, with more arrows protruding from his heater shield than a hedgehog has spines. A scream jerks his gaze then his body toward mine. I do not understand why until Nev's mouth presses against my ear asking if I am hurt.

"I am fine!" I shout to Nev and to Valor who has taken a position on the other side of our shield wall. I fix my eyes on his boots to keep my gasping breaths moving between my lips.

As suddenly as it began, the hail of arrows stops.

"Captain Anders, mount a pursuit!" Valor orders.

The shields around us begin to lower till Valor says, "Hold!" They snap back into place.

Nev trembles fiercely in my arms. I hold her tight, feeling Melon press against my belly. "It is over." I say, though I cannot know that to be true. "You are safe."

She cries through her fear. My response is utter silence. Hiding places last longer if the pursued is silent. Breathless.

Blackness touches the edge of my vision. I drag air through my nose and immediately regret it. The stench is oppressive.

"Valor?" I query.

"A little longer, my Queen."

The sound of his voice is air to my tight chest. "What goes?"

"Anders is in pursuit. As soon as he gives the signal, you may come out."

"Casualties?"

"Some, but not many."

I hear him exchange words with Kragorn, assessing damage and bringing the wounded near the center of camp. I tie my breaths to the cadence of his voice. The confidence. The control. Even the ire soothes me.

A three pronged whistle advances the cracking open of the wooden shell holding us captive. Valor's armored arms and sweat streaked face fill my eyes. Time spins around us in a flurry of meaningless noise. The arrow laden shield lays at his feet, its purpose served. A rope of fear unwinds from my chest even as my heart pounds more determinedly in my chest. Valor's cuirass heaves with the breadth of his relief at finding me likewise unharmed before his eyes find mine again. His tempestuous gaze holds me secure, pouring strength into my soul, making promises more binding than words. It sustains me.

I shift Nev forward, giving her into the safety of Valor's embrace as more of her tears shake loose, but his eyes do not let me go.

CHAPTER TWENTY-EIGHT

September 16th

"The next time I ride into my city, can we please make it a joyous occasion?" I say to Valor where we stand overlooking Malsihra. The city is shrouded in mist thicker than the mourning veil covering my face. Only the spires of the castle are visible above the haze despite being near noon.

"From a certain perspective, it is joyous," Valor replies. "By nightfall, Lorennt will be reunited with all of his family."

"Let us hope enough time has passed to allow that fact to outshine the betrayal part of it." Still, I fret that Lorennt's temperament and shock will bring him to say or do something he will mightily regret.

"We can do more than hope," Valor says and takes my hand in his. With his eyes on the city and his other hand upon his sword, Valor brings this matter to the Creator along with all our concerns and hopes. He places them at the feet of the Almighty, trusting Him with the outcome, whatever it may be.

I breathe deeply of the peace that surpasses understanding that comes from knowing the future does not depend on me or my abilities. It is, and has always, depended solely on our all powerful, all knowing Heavenly Father who is working everything out for our good.

Even these moments shadowed with grief.

☀ ☀ ☀

Anders leads our mounted procession into the city at a slow, somber walk. Not far back in the line, Valor and I ride side by side over the cobbled streets. Nev rides near the back with Trent, hidden amongst the ranks of soldiers.

231

I sit straight in the saddle with my head raised and gaze fixed before me. My people come out of their homes and shops to line the streets, guiding me home. The city is adorned in mourning grey. The friends I have made, like Mari the baker and Daan the cobbler, raised grey sashes outside their shops when I lost Illyanna and have not taken them down since.

The whole city has been in abeyance since its king's death, waiting for its queen to return so we may hold the funeral and mourn together. It is good that I am home, though my heart aches moving toward the castle.

It happens suddenly the further we go through the market district. My eyes are drawn to the tavern where we played cards and Leer counted the ways I was his *goodwife*. There is the alley he dragged me down when he finally riled me into hitting him and convinced me to yield to the love that was growing between us. The smith who made our daggers and called our marriage blessed stands on the corner with sympathy shining from his eyes.

I sip a breath slowly, letting the chill air steel me.

Sacha's hooves echo as I cross over the bridge and through the gatehouse into the lower bailey. Having delivered me safely home, the lines of soldiers break aside, and I move forward with Valor. The trumpeters blow a low, single note, announcing my arrival as I cross into the castle proper. The doors to the entrance hall open wide and... *Leer* runs down the steps toward me.

I gasp, moving to swing from the saddle, but Valor's hand settles over mine on the pommel. "Tis Lorennt."

I blink, looking closer. The man's features resolve into those of my brother.

I can hold myself together no longer and begin to cry.

Lorennt reaches my side and lifts me down, bringing me to his chest. We cling to each other, weeping in the courtyard, and the words I have needed to say to him pour out of me. "I am so sorry! There was nothing I could do. I could not help him."

"I know. It was not your fault. I am sorry too. I should have been here. I never should have run."

"Not your fault. We hurt you too. I should never have—"

He cuts me off. "I am sorry I did not kill that lying bastard Chase from the first! Then he never would have had a chance to—" Lorennt tilts my face up and lifts the veil from it, searching my eyes. "Are you going to be alright? I am so sorry he hurt you."

I nod. "I am alright. We can talk about that later."

Lorennt agrees and takes me under his arm, leading me toward the castle. Mother Celiea and Father are waiting at the top of the steps. Through my tears I discern how much these tragedies have aged them, Mother especially. She is wan in the muted daylight.

Mother embraces me, and Father holds us both as more tears shake free. Somehow we make our way inside through the heavy, iron-clad doors into the great hall. A collection of the nobility are in attendance and bow deeply as I enter.

I touch my hand to my heart, but feel uncertain as to what I should do. What happens now? Do I join them in the noon meal? Can I go up to our... *my* room? What should I do?

I need Leer to tell me what to do.

I stare at his vacant seat at the high table. I should not do it, but I search the room for him though I know he is not here. It feels so wrong. He is always here. He has never *not* been here.

"He should be here," I murmur to my family.

Lorennt squeezes my shoulder. "I know. It still feels wrong to me too."

"Come." Mother Celiea guides me toward the far stairs. "Let us eat in our parlor as a family."

"Thank you."

I glance over my shoulder to where Valor stands with the guards at the entrance.

He nods, reassuring me he will bring Nev in quietly just as we planned, and adds, *I am so sorry.*

Me too, I say and ascend the stairs with my family.

❋ ❋ ❋

This day only grows harder as the hours tick by. Our noon meal cannot proceed until we deal with the obvious. They want to know what happened beyond the amount Valor told Lorennt when he was here weeks past, which was more of what he deduced than the little I was able to communicate at the time. I look to Father and Lorennt, unsure how honest I ought to be while Mother is in the room. We have always shielded her from the ugliest details.

As I dither, she declares, "I want to know everything this time, Erianna. Tell us as much as you are able."

With a quick prayer for wisdom, I begin by explaining how we were ambushed at the coast. I gloss over the details of what Zavaan did to me since it is not essential for them to know, but the vindictive gleam in Lorennt's eye says he wants to know exactly how much Zavaan has to answer for. I acknowledge him, and move on.

I explain why I did not want to come back, some of which had to do with the erroneous belief planted by Zavaan that I would be pressed to remarry, something my family heartily rejects as false.

With quiet joy, I tell them how the Creator redeemed me and freed me from all the guilt and sin crushing me. Father and Mother could not be more pleased.

They all take turns relating what transpired in my absence which occupies another hour of the day, moving us into late afternoon by the time our noon meal is concluded.

Lorennt takes me on his arm as we make our way slowly through the corridors, and I tell him in private what I held in reserve. Though I know I stand forgiven by the Almighty for all my wrongdoings and that Valor spoke true in saying I was transposing my own revulsion onto others, hearing Lorennt say that he holds Zavaan and *only* Zavaan accountable eases a tension bound up in my chest.

"Thank you for sending the cavalry to bring me home. We would have had trouble without them."

"How so?" Lorennt asks.

"By nightfall on the first day, the Ruphiri discovered us."

Lorennt draws up short, turning me to face him.

"We never saw them," I calmly explain, "but they were in the woods nearby. The wolves surrounded us and howled almost continuously each night. On the first night, some of our soldiers were killed when they rained arrows upon us." I shudder, remembering it. Nev was so frightened that she cried and sat tucked into Valor's side the remainder of the night. I wanted to be there too, but I had the unnerving sensation that Reuel could see me. I determined to never cower before him again, so I sat in plain view near the fire, sharpening my daggers on a whetstone each night despite my trepidation.

"I pressed Valor and Kragorn to use me as bait to draw them out during the day. We had the advantage of numbers after all, but they refused. I am hoping that you will—"

"Absolutely not!" Lorennt roars. "Did you recover from one extreme of mental illness to return to your prior version of brash recklessness?"

I am taken aback by his outburst. For some reason, I thought it would be reasonably simple to convince him to enact my plan. "But

Lorennt—"

"No! You are under my care now, and so help me Erianna, if you push me to it, I will use whatever means necessary to prevent you from endangering yourself again. Do I make myself clear?"

Fear for my wellbeing underlies most of what Lorennt says, but he has a point. If all of these seasoned military men agree that my plan is nonsensical, I will have to trust them. Again, I wish for Leer's presence. He was the greatest strategist of us all and had unwavering logic that I have need of.

I relent, hanging my head. "Aye, Brother."

Lorennt hugs me. "I cannot lose you too. Promise you will be careful. We have lost too much already."

"I promise." This is as good a transition as I could hope for. I hook my arm with his, steering him toward a distant section of the castle near Valor's room. "Lorennt, I must confess something to you that I did."

I push through the story quickly before he can interrupt. "Months back, when Nev asked me to help her leave, I told you that I sent her to the Commonwealth. That was a lie. I did not know where he was at the time, but I ordered Anders to take her to Valor. He has been looking after her in Parse Kítaran until now. I brought her back with me."

"Nev is here?" The hope in his eyes lifts mine.

I smile genuinely. "Yes."

"Where?"

"I am taking you to her. She is anxious to see you as well, but I want you to promise me that when you see her, you will give her a chance to explain why she left before you say something regrettable."

Lorennt's steps falter. "She and Valor are not..."

"No, nothing like that," I rush to assure him, once again inwardly praising Valor for being smarter than I. "Valor has protected her and provided for her, though I of course made sure she was well-off to begin with."

Lorennt's unease is still marked, so I say with all sincerity, "Nev's heart still belongs to you. Whether or not you two resolve things, I have every intention of keeping her at court. Valor and I crafted a plan to legally make Nev a landed noblewoman."

"You... *How?* But, then that means..."

"As of this moment, she is now Lady Nev of Limba."

"Limba?"

"I have titled her with the dower lands that were bound to me and my descendants as part of my marriage to Leer. Since I am now..." I still cannot bring myself to say that wretched word. "The lands are solely my property. Valor drafted the document to transfer the title of the lands to Nev, a substantial amount for any noble. All that awaits is my signature and seal on the original property deed. This will ensure the lands stay in the Rodiharian family, securing our ties to Limba."

Lorennt lifts me off my feet, spinning me around. "You are brilliant! Thank you again and again! All is forgiven!"

"I will understand if you change you mind, but I have kept you in suspense long enough." I guide him down the halls at a near trot and tug him to a standstill outside the parlor door. "Remember what I said, Lorennt. You must let her explain."

My insistence dims his eagerness to a modest amount.

I knock on the door. Valor answers it, stepping aside to admit Lorennt. Nev is seated, facing away from the door, and looks around with her heart in her eyes. That is all Lorennt needs to go to her, drawing her into his embrace. He steps back instantly, looking down to confirm with his eyes what he felt.

"Tis yours, Lorennt," Nev shakily tells him. "I was two months along when I left. I am so sorry. I am so sorry I did not tell you."

Lorennt stares dumbfounded then shifts his gaze to me.

"She speaks true. Listen," I remind him.

He nods mutely and sits down on the couch. Happy tears prick my eyes as Lorennt reaches for Nev's hand, bringing her down next to him.

I glance up to Valor who winks at me and motions me out of the room. I want to stay and see this all resolved, but it is a private matter, so I follow him out of the room, close the door, and sit down on the floor to eavesdrop.

For shame, Valor silently chides.

Was it not you who pointed out this bright spot in my horrendously gloomy day? I challenge. *Either take a seat or take your morals elsewhere.*

He sits next to me.

We listen as Nev explains why she hid the babe from him and again asks forgiveness for having done so.

"Were you afraid that I would make you get rid of our babe or that I would cast you aside?" Lorennt asks.

"No, Lor. Of course not that. I did not want you to give up your family to be with us or to feud with your family to keep us here. What kind of life would that have been for Melon, growing up in the shadow of Leer and Erianna's twice royal babe?"

My heart fists in my chest. Illyanna's and Leer's passing reunited this family.

Valor tugs me into his side and whispers in my ear, "Do not think there. You kept Nev as close as you could. No matter what happened, you would have made a way to bring this about."

I lay my head on his shoulder.

"Melon?" Lorennt asks.

Nev explains the name given by the Tareth girls, and Lorennt laughs.

"May I?" Lorennt asks.

There is a smile in Nev's voice. "A father does not need to ask permission to hold his babe. Here. If you place your hand just so, that is the babe's back. And here, you will feel the feet kicking."

I sink my teeth into my lower lip, remembering this same conversation between Leer and I. He came to know his daughter so well in my womb that he did not need my explanation to know how she lie.

Lorennt's pleased laugh floats through the door. "Was that a kick? When will Melon arrive?"

"Near winter solstice."

"Is the babe growing well? You are much smaller than Erianna was."

"Aye, all is well. The babe quickened when it should. Women just carry their babes differently."

I do not realize I am crying until Valor's thumb brushes away the tears. His hand slips to my waist, lifting me to my feet, unwilling to let me continue torturing myself. "I think we can be assured they will resolve things."

I lean into his arm, trying to savor the good in those hopeful memories that ended in profound heartache. Though I did not get to keep her, I do have a daughter. I knew her and loved her, and so did her father. I will never forget her or cease saying her name in remembrance.

I know I ought to go wash and change for dinner, but dread fills me at the prospect of facing my empty room filled with Leer's and Illyanna's belongings. "Have you had a wash basin delivered to your room?"

"Nev and I went on a little hunt and selected a few dresses you may need. They are in my room along with whatever other things Nev deemed essential."

I sigh in relief. "You are my favorite person."

※ ※ ※

After checking on Nev and Lorennt still contentedly sequestered in the parlor, Valor and I go to dinner.

Helplessness finds a foothold in me as we enter the great hall and begin approaching the dais. Where am I supposed to sit without Leer as the focal point?

Having never seen Valor in this setting, I forget that he is acquainted with court propriety. He does not hesitate in crossing the room that contains a larger amount of nobility than usual for this time of year.

The funeral. That is why they are here, probably have been here for some time. Everyone has been waiting for me.

Valor settles me into my usual seat then walks past Leer's chair and sits at the left. It is the place of honor for whomever had Leer's ear for the evening. Being the king's Hand, that position would belong to Valor. Thus begins the period of mourning for our slain king, honoring his life by noting his absence with his unoccupied chair.

Lady Silla is in residence, and I call upon her to join me, filling Lorennt's empty seat to my right. She apprises me of the temperature amongst the nobility since Leer's death, a conversation that engrosses us till the end of meal. I schedule a meeting with her tomorrow to go over all of this information again with Valor and Lorennt, if he is available. I also need to know everything she knows about Chase-turned-Zavaan. Her connections and gossip have always been the choicest. She might know something useful.

The combination of the taxing day and the sleepless nights since departing Leelah's home force me to cover one yawn after another. I conclude the meal, grateful Silla whispered to me that no one expects the usual cards and drinks before bed due to our state of mourning, and bid the nobility good night.

With the rumors of our history being common knowledge, Valor and I decided that he should not be seen walking me up to my room at nights. His exact words were, "Henceforth, we will be above reproach in our conduct." We bid each other a very formal good night amid the rest of the nobility.

Part of the new security measures include two guards stationed at the bottom of the stairs that lead solely to the royal suites. I pass between them and trudge upward alone. I stop before the door to my old room, having taken the coward's way in avoiding entering my and Leer's room this eve. But I must do it eventually. Maybe tomorrow.

This room is only slightly better since it is the room Leer and I shared on our wedding night and for the first six weeks thereafter. Still, it always felt more mine than ours. It also has a glaring benefit compared to my other room for the time being.

Company.

"How was dinner?" Nev asks from the parlor.

"Wretched."

Her face reshapes into a softer expression, concealing her obvious joy at a reunion she both anticipated and dreaded in nearly equal measure.

"But to be fair, I do not like the castle at all without Leer. It feels empty to me."

Nev does not push platitudes on me. She simply listens.

I have already said more than I care to in one day on the subject and instead ask, "Did Lorennt take the news well?" I heard enough to know he did, and her glowing expression tells the rest.

"He is overjoyed," she gushes, following me into the dressing room. "He is hurt by what I did, but he said he will not waste our time together on unforgiveness. He is thrilled with you making me a lady and easing my way into noble society. Not that it is necessary. He vows to marry me and will do so, lady or not, but it will be a better transition and—how did he say it? 'Spread the blame around nicely.' Oh, how I have missed him!"

Nev's fingers work the laces on my dress, then I help her out of hers, listening to all her happy musings. It soothes my heart and paints a bright end to this morose day. "What did he say when you explained you would not be sharing his bed until your wedding?" I ask while blowing out all the candles and lamps save one.

Nev sighs, climbing under the covers. She asked me to hold her accountable to this and expected I would ask her. "He thought it was unnecessary to be separated since we have been together so often before, and it is quite obvious because of the babe, so what difference does it make?"

"Yet here you are. So what did you tell him?" I press her while climbing into bed.

"I told him that even if no one else knows, we will know, and the

239

Creator will know. That is enough reason to do what is right and abstain until we are wed rather than going back to what we were before." Nev says it with conviction but still huffs at the end.

I grin at her. "You are not my first choice of bedmate either."

"Or your second, *hmm*?" She teases.

"Nor my second," I admit. "But there is a wide gulf between my first and second choice."

"As there should be. For now, anyways."

CHAPTER TWENTY-NINE

VALOR

September 17th

My sleep does not last as long as I hoped it would. Before dawn I am at my desk, addressing the work that has piled up these past months. Even without the additional responsibilities of assisting Erianna and Lorennt, it is past time to appoint new trade officials for the provinces and follow-up with the cities in the North.

The tasks occupy my attention for a few hours until my eyes begin to cross on the papers that all look the same. I push away from the desk, donning my mantle then heading out of doors to clear my head before breakfast. The sharp air does wonders for mind and body. I take the stairs to the ramparts, circling the castle to the forest overlook. Evergreens dominate the landscape, stretching toward the grey sky, concealing the paths through the forest with which I am well acquainted. In the past when I was in residence at the castle, I began each day with a run, usually with Grandileer, before setting about the day's responsibilities. I would like to take up the habit again and may try to engage Lorennt.

Approaching from the opposite direction at a leisurely pace is a woman whose beauty is shrouded with grey veils. The back of the veil conceals the midnight tresses of her hair. The front portion is customarily lowered to shield a widow's face out of doors, because the light of day is thought to intrude upon her grief. Erianna honors the tradition.

"Does the queen reacquaint herself with her castle?" I ask, gaining her side. The personal guard assigned to follow her at all times drops back.

"Let's pretend that is why I have been up here ere dawn. It sounds far less pathetic," she says wryly.

"But the truth is…?" I turn around, making her course mine.

"My wing of the castle is lonely." Her huffed breath flutters the smokey veil that falls to her waist. "I took for granted so many kindnesses Leer showed me. His presence was one of them."

"How so?"

"The first several weeks of our marriage, I lamented never having a moment to be alone or to drop all pretense, as you suspected I would. Even when I intentionally sought solitude, Leer seemed to be everywhere. He pursued me, and I did not make it easy for him." She shakes her head. "Why must I only appreciate what I was given when it is gone?"

I refrain from offering more condolences, knowing it is not pity she seeks. She is only voicing her thoughts.

"Did you need me for something?"

"I found you by happy coincidence. Dozens of things vie for my attention on my desk, so I abandoned them all with the purpose of returning to them with a clear mind."

She chuckles. "Oh, this kingdom is going to fall to pieces if even you, who is far more devoted to your work than Lorennt or I, can leave a stack of obligations incomplete in favor of a walk. What will we do without our king ordering us all to attend to task?"

"Likely eat pastries from dawn till dark and play cards from dark till dawn," I tease.

Her laugh is unhindered.

I offer her my arm at the stairs. "I know that you are daunted by this transition, but you forget that I was here when Grandileer took the reins from Boldizar. I have done this before. Besides, Grandileer instructed you and Lorennt for the last year. You are prepared for your responsibilities. You also have Boldizar's wisdom to fall back on. We will get through this."

She hugs my arm. "Thank you for the encouragement. I will need lots of it, I think. And laughter. Give me plenty of reasons to laugh."

"I can do both. *Without* neglecting my responsibilities." I flick her hand on my arm.

"Good. Because I already have a meeting scheduled for you today."

"Oh, do you now?"

She nods assertively. "But first, breakfast."

"Will there be pastries?"

"If there are not this morning, there will be once I reclaim the menu planning."

※ ※ ※

Erianna hesitates outside the door to Grandileer's office after breakfast. She removes her hand from the handle, shaking it at her side.

"Take your time," I encourage. "We are not in a rush."

She tries again, this time pushing the door open.

Erianna moves through the room as if greeting an old friend. She rearranges various objects, straightens stacks of paper, then stands over the map of the kingdom. With a deep breath, she turns to the desk, running her hand over its surface. She stares hard at the chair behind it. "We always intended to have a matching chair made for me, but..." She covers her eyes. "Valor, this is miserable."

I place my hands on her shoulders in lieu of words that are inadequate.

"Lorennt has made a mess of things," she remarks, stepping around the desk and settling into the chair. She pulls open a drawer and slips her hand inside, feeling around. She frowns, opening another drawer and again reaching inside. "Confound it, Lorennt," she grumbles pulling open another drawer. She slams it closed as tears gather on her lower lashes then searches under the desk.

"Erianna."

"He moved the accursed key! The stupid, meddlesome fool! Why would he move the key?" She rises from the desk to search behind the paintings and wall hangings.

"Just wait to ask him. It is not essential—"

"He had no right to move Leer's things! He should not have touched anything!"

Lorennt slams the door to the office closed. "Someone had to hold the kingdom together while you were hiding from your family and your responsibilities!"

The remark stings Erianna, provoking a rejoinder. "Was it necessary to make such a mess of things? Nothing is where it ought to be!"

"Forgive me for not tidying up before your return! I was somewhat preoccupied with the burial of my brother!" Lorennt's acerbic tongue cuts through Erianna's paper thin frustration, exposing her grief.

She slumps into the chair. "I am sorry I was not here."

Lorennt hangs his head, regretting his sharpness. "Let me get that key for you." Reaching to the top of the ornate cabinet, he retrieves the key and places it in Erianna's palm. "I had to move it because I could not sit in the king and queen's chair."

She squeezes his arm before unlocking the cabinet. Locating what she seeks, she returns to the desk, passing me a stack of papers written in my hand. It was an eternity ago that I drafted them. I sift through her marriage documents until I find the one pertaining to the dower lands. After making the necessary changes, I return it.

"It only needs your signature and seal, my Queen."

She adds both then passes it and the transfer deed to Lorennt. "Nev is now and forevermore a Limban noble." Before Lorennt can express his gratitude, Erianna presses on. "We have much to do. Be seated and let us decide the best way to tell Mother and Father that you will be taking a wife and determine when we ought to introduce her to the court."

They tackle the introduction to Boldizar and Celiea first, intending to see it done tomorrow. Depending on how that goes, an introduction to the court will take place in the evening. They both agree that although the somber atmosphere of the castle is not appropriate for a wedding announcement, it is better to do it immediately so that Nev can be present at the funeral as Lorennt's intended.

"Which brings us to setting a date for the funeral," Lorennt presents the next order of business.

The spine goes out of Erianna. "You decide. It makes no difference to me."

"You must have an opinion," Lorennt insists. "He was your husband."

Erianna stares through the desk, swallowing tears. "This chair is too big." She shifts from side to side, rests her arms upon the desk. "I cannot easily reach to write."

"Should I have the seat altered for you?" I ask softly. Lorennt's head snaps around, having forgotten that I am present due to my prolonged silence.

Erianna considers it, sitting taller then resting back into the upholstery. "No. Then my feet will not touch the ground."

"Taller boots?" I suggest.

She smirks. "Or a shorter desk."

"So all three then." I grin.

"Very likely," she concurs. "How does this desk suit you, Lorennt?"

He huffs his annoyance. "What are you on about, Sister?"

"If you and I are responsible for all this, then we had better make it our own instead of sitting in Leer's seat, at his desk, in his office, pretending we are merely occupying his place until he returns."

"Well said," I commend her.

"And that begins with new furnishings?" Lorennt drily questions.

"It is a start," she replies and takes a sheet of paper from a drawer, glancing around the room. "So, do you want this desk or another?"

"Do what you want," he dismisses her query.

"There is space enough for us each to have a desk. It seems foolish not to share the office, do you not agree? I would rather do this together and be able to immediately consult you on issues than be forced to arrange meetings."

Lorennt's shoulders lift slightly. "As I hoped."

"Valor, please arrange for the funeral and tell me when it is."

I nod.

A knock on the door pulls Erianna that direction. Lorennt stiffens as Lady Silla glides into the office.

"You are right on time," Erianna greets her.

I rise, giving her my chair.

Lorennt does not attempt to conceal his annoyance. "What have you done?"

"Oh, Lorennt," Silla simpers. "There is no need to be piqued. I am here to help."

"Said the fox to the hare." Lorennt crosses his arms.

Silla touches a hand to her chest. "You flatter me, Lorennt. By the way, I hear congratulations are due you."

My brows rise. Erianna did not exaggerate. Her unofficial spymaster is better than mine.

"Good. You know." Erianna motions her to a seat. "What you likely do not know is that I have made Nev a landed noble of Limba."

Silla is impressed. "A bold move. But I do not think the Malesiirian nobility will much care for it. Especially with the waters muddied by this one's restructuring of the trade officials." She flicks her fingers my direction.

"*Hmm...*" Erianna pulls her hair around from beneath the veil hanging down her back and begins separating it. She does her best thinking while her fingers are occupied, though I have not seen her sufficiently at ease to succumb to this mindless habit for quite some time. "I had not considered the two being linked in their eyes. What else am I not seeing?"

Silla glances around the room, considering us. Her eyes land on me with unnerving perceptivity, then she smiles. If this is the woman Lorennt's mother was pushing at him, it is no wonder he chose the exact opposite in Nev. "Well, a few things, I think. You know Celiea has always cared a great deal about noble blood. That has not changed."

"My mother will be fine, thank you," Lorennt interjects.

"Either listen and learn, or go away." Erianna stops mid-plait, glaring at her brother.

Lorennt excuses himself. "See you at noon."

Erianna rolls her eyes, dragging her fingers through her hair and beginning anew.

Rather than being offended by Lorennt's obvious dislike, Silla is pleased. "He is never going to forgive me for that kiss, is he?"

Erianna snickers. "We can both take responsibility for that. No, I think it was more what you said to Nev that one day. He tolerated you well enough before then."

Silla is contrite. "I regret few things, but having any association with that murderous whore is something I do regret."

I am surprised by her strong words and more confused than ever.

Erianna's mask is so perfect that even I cannot tell what goes behind it. Her resolute words give no clue either. "Let us leave it all in the past. Nev may never be a bosom friend of yours, but she is the forgiving sort. It would help me greatly if you make peace with her."

"It is the least I can do," Silla readily agrees.

"Now, back to the task. Where were you headed with the topic of Celiea?"

"Well," Silla drawls, "If you cannot thoroughly bring her around, the court will take note of her distaste for the commoner and mimic it. I do not envy Nev having to live in constant tension with her mother-in-law and the entire court."

"You are right. I hope Celiea will be eased by learning that she will be a grandmother and forgive all, especially considering what she has already lost."

"Possibly. Or it will make it more difficult for her. A word of caution," Silla somberly lowers her voice. "Do not give Illyanna's gowns to Nev without Celiea's blessing. She was nearly as heartbroken as you by the loss of the babe. I know you probably do not know this, but Celiea held your babe for the hours the physician worked to save your life. It was all Boldizar could do to convince Celiea to give her granddaughter to me to dress her for burial."

Erianna is pained beyond words for a long moment. "I did not know that. Thank you for telling me."

I am riled with Silla for bringing more grief to Erianna, but there is nothing I can do prevent her from feeling this acute pain.

"As to what we discussed last night," Silla resumes her languid tone, "I think Lorennt should present the changes to the trade officials at meal. You should share the responsibilities for the changes and let it be known this is not all coming from you. It was begun under Grandileer's orders, thus it continues."

"What do the nobility know of my absence?" Erianna asks, combing her fingers through her hair.

"Most believed you were at the coast. That story will not hold much longer since three hundred soldiers know you were in the mountains, so be prepared for questions."

I lean my shoulder against the wall. "That is not a problem. Her Majesty was in a time of deep mourning as told, and the misdirect was for her protection," I supply the information I already told the Judges.

"Very good." Silla continues discussing the minutia of the nobility with a touch of combativeness that engages Erianna, lifting her mood to what it was in Leelah's company, but with less good naturedness and a bit more antagonism from both women. It is interesting to see her in this capacity. This is more like what she became around Tirzah the few times I witnessed their exchanges.

Throwing a mischievous glance my way, Silla scolds, "Erianna, have a care. You are driving the poor commander to distraction by playing with your hair."

I chuckle at the truth of it.

Erianna colors, replying, "Do not start that nonsense. I have a new playmate arriving for you at any moment if you have bored with us."

Silla perks up. "Oh?"

"Indeed," Erianna affirms and not much later Trent arrives. "Lady Silla Hugler, this is Cuyler Trent. He serves as—"

"The commander's elusive spymaster. I have seen you at work but have not had the pleasure of an introduction." Silla extends her hand with a coy smile.

Much of Trent's work is dependent on charming those he wheedles for information. He applies that charm to Silla, winsomely bowing over her hand. "Lady Silla. I did not realize you were the one pulling the strings of the servants. It is no wonder they are reluctant to feed me more than morsels. They are used to a far prettier face."

Silla quirks a brow, appraising him. "Do not sell yourself short, Cuyler. I think you are quite pretty."

Trent laughs genuinely and releases Silla's hand, taking the empty seat alongside hers.

"You see," Erianna grins deviously. "I knew you would have fun. Your task is to work together to maintain constant awareness of the climate of my kingdom among commoners, nobility, and soldiers. I want to know of a problem before it arrises. I do not want to allow discontent or mistrust to fester until it becomes large enough to garner my attention."

Trent accepts the order with a nod, but Silla cocks her head to the side. "Not that I do not have fun with our little games, but this is far grander and will require much effort."

"So, what is the incentive for you?" Erianna shrewdly voices the unasked question.

Silla bats her lashes. "I am curious."

"I have two thoughts." The queen names her incentives, "We could make this a monetary exchange, as it is with Trent."

Silla folds her hands primly. "Then I will take the second option."

Erianna huffs. "Very well. You may name a reasonable favor from me in exchange for useful information."

Silla toys with Erianna. "Who is to say what is reasonable?"

I state, "I will decide what is reasonable. All the information that goes to Her Majesty will be filtered through me. I want regular updates from you both."

Silla pouts. "That I like less. The queen is much more fun."

I shrug. "Take pleasure in your work and do it well. That is plenty of fun."

Silla obviously disagrees and slides her gaze to Trent, taking his measure. "What of you, Cuyler? Are you a bore also?"

I watch Trent step willingly into the woman's snare. "A bore? That is not something I have been accused of. But I anticipate hearing your determination after a few weeks in my company."

Silla's eyes glitter. "I can assure you, I will not hesitate to tell you precisely what I think."

"Then it is settled," Erianna brings the matter to a close, gathering the papers on the desk. "Oh, one more thing, Silla. There is something critical I must tell you that cannot yet be known by the rest. I need you to think back on every encounter you had with Gavin Chase and relate it to Trent. I want to know everything that man did while he was in Malesiir, everywhere he went in my castle, who he spoke with, what he did with his days."

"Why?" Silla asks.

Erianna's words are chilling even to me. "Because I watched Gavin Chase kill Grandileer."

Silla pales, visibly struck by the news. "*Chase* murdered the king? Why would he do such a thing?"

"Trent will explain everything. The important thing is, I want that murderer brought to justice. He also had a hand in poisoning me. Please discover how he was connected to *her*. It may be significant."

"Aye, Your Majesty." Silla inclines her head. "I will do all that I can to assist you."

Her absolute compliance and sincerity make me question what part she played in grieving Erianna. I hope my queen decides to make all known to me soon. Despite her forgiveness of her husband, whatever happened between them seems to be far reaching.

"I thank you," Erianna replies, dismissing them.

Trent offers Lady Silla his hand, drawing her to her feet and leading her out the door.

I whistle low. "That woman is trouble."

Erianna props her elbows on the desk. "Aye. Thus I keep her on my side. Life was much more difficult when we were opponents."

"Trent is taken with her," I point out. With our constant assignments over the past year and a half, Trent has gone longer than is typical for him between flirtations.

"I noticed."

"This cannot end well."

"In certain disaster only."

CHAPTER THIRTY

ERIANNA

September 18th

Lorennt escorts me from the dais after I conclude breakfast. It is a relief to leave the great hall, even knowing the trials the day holds.

"Has this become easier for you? Mealtimes, I mean," I ask my brother.

"I know what you want me to say, but it would be a lie," he answers.

Leer was the focal point of our kingdom, our court, and my very existence. Life revolved around the King of Malesiir. He was our conductor. And we loved him.

"May I suggest," Valor politely interjects, "that after your time of mourning, when Her Majesty sits upon the high seat on the dais and your lady wife is at your side—in other words—once you have both fully assumed your roles, this will become expected and therefore easier?"

"More time then," Lorennt surmises and affectionately squeezes my hand before passing me off to Valor. "I go to prepare my intended for the introduction. I shall see you there in an hour?"

"I would not miss my time of reckoning," I archly declare.

Lorennt heads up the stairs with a smile I have not seen in five long months. Nev will soon be at his side as she should have been all along.

"You are very good at this," Valor says, watching Lorennt take the stairs two at a time.

"At what? Righting my wrongs? I have some practice."

He elbows my side. "Being queen. I know you are anxious, but no one else can see it."

It is true. My stomach is in knots. I tug Valor toward the outer doors, postponing my impending work until I can attend to the tasks. Once we are on the path to the gardens, I give credit where it is due. "I am the product of the exceptional people that have poured into me, chiefly the Rodiharians and you. The only thing I bring to the table is my un-queenly attitude."

Valor knows I am not begging for compliments. I am searching for banter to distract me, which he is only too happy to provide. "There is also your diminutive stature. That also works to your advantage"

"How so?" I drawl.

"Like coming upon a badger in the woods, some unsuspecting fool will mistakenly think they can impose their will on you. Then you show your teeth." Which he does with an animal growl.

I laugh. "A badger, *hmm*? I think I prefer being compared to a chipmunk. It painted me as something sweet."

A roguish gleam lights Valor's eyes while he discards several comments, searching for something more appropriate.

I glance over my shoulder, ensuring my guard is not in earshot. "Out with it."

His smile makes my heart race. "You are unquestionably the sweetest thing I have ever tasted, but that does not negate your teeth."

My blush is instant and thorough, but he is not done. "Not that I recall the times we *danced* very often. Only four, maybe five times a day at the most."

I set my palm to my cheek, attempting to cool the flame, but the mourning veil prevents the action from having the fully desired effect, though it checks my blush for another reason. "That will do."

"I could go on," he teases.

"No, no. I need to return to my normal complexion by the time I face my parents."

Valor's attention gratifies me as it should not, nor should I crave it like I do.

Before my guilt can grow legs, he gently says, "You needn't feel guilty for wanting to be reminded that someone knows the woman you are beyond your titles and state of mourning."

He knows me so well. That makes me wonder, "What of you? Do you ever need to hear that you are known and admired?"

Valor considers me with a half-smile. "Anders tells me often that I have a fine face and figure, but any praise you feel inclined to throw my way is appreciated."

I burst into laughter. Anders has never done anything of the sort. "I shall try to do better than Anders. When I am feeling generous, that is."

"I like when you are generous." Valor grins. "So much so that I might go stand out in the next rain in hopes that you will generously warm me again."

I will never rid the blush from my cheeks at this rate.

※ ※ ※

Lorennt and I plan to carry out this introduction similarly to the way we went about reuniting him with Nev. We congregate in a nearby alcove and leave Nev with Valor while Lorennt and I prepare our parents.

"It is going to be fine," I reassure him.

"Your optimism is hollow," he observes, knocking on the door.

"You are marrying her whether they like it or not. Take comfort in that fact."

A servant answers the door, and I dismiss her as we enter Mother Celiea's solar.

Leer's caution that his mother was the truly crafty one in the family resonates as she invites us to be seated. Her eyes are keen this day despite of her pallor. She does not allow us to make any pretense of dancing around the matter. "Look, Boldizar. Our children have finally come to tell us about the lady's maid hiding in their wing of the castle. Did you hear that she is heavy with child?"

Lorennt's expression falters, but I have enough battle experience against my king husband to know not to flinch. Instead, I smile. "Clever as always, Mother. Now, I am going to tell you why that is and confess to what I did." I get right to it, informing them of everything. Not waiting for them to question the babe's legitimacy, I assure them it is so. Thankfully, they do not argue this point.

Father listens without interruption, but Mother does not. "Lorennt! How could you be so careless! Getting a child on a maid and allowing her to entrap you. I will not stand for it!"

Lorennt firmly states, "Nev did not entrap me. Verily, she left so that I would not be at odds with you over my child's half royal blood. She only came back at Erianna's urging, and I am glad that she did."

"And you!" Mother turns on me. "Keeping such a thing from Leer. That was wrong for so many reasons. Outright lying to him about it!"

I hold steady under her gaze though I ache inside.

Father steps in. "Celiea. Let us not bring up faults between Leer and Erianna. Almighty knows that he gave her reason not to trust him. Furthermore, though her reasoning was not flawless, I do not doubt that the man who worked evil against Erianna and murdered our granddaughter would have done the same to Nev and this grandchild. Erianna's secreting away of Nev surely saved her life and that of Lorennt's babe."

"Do not compare our Illyanna to this ill-gotten, baseborn child!" Mother lurches to her feet, upsetting her cup. I watch the tea soak into the rug like the words she cannot take back.

Lorennt wraps an arm around my shoulders, both of us shaking with hurt and anger. "Let me be very clear," he enunciates. "We are all grieved by Illyanna's death. My child cannot replace her in our hearts. However, my child is as much a Rodiharian as Leer's child and will be treated as such in this family and in this kingdom. To make that easier for everyone to swallow, Erianna has made Nev a landed Limban noblewoman, investing Nev with her own dower lands."

Celiea breaks her own cardinal rule and raises her voice. I hope that Valor kept Nev well away from the door. "Leer intended those to stay in the Rodiharian family! What were you thinking, bestowing those on a commoner?"

My voice remains steady as I explain, "They are now assured to stay in this family with Nev's marriage to Lorennt and the birth of their child. I strengthened the bonds between Limba and Malesiir."

"Marriage!" Celiea shrieks.

"Enough, Celiea." Boldizar guides his wife back to her chair. "You knew that was where this was headed when Nev returned. Erianna has made a wise decision. Do not chastise her for so sensible an action."

"Erianna is a Rodiharian. There was no need to undue what was done." Mother's eyes land sharply upon me. "Unless she kept something else from us. Do you already have plans to take on another's name and disrespect my son only weeks after his death?"

I shake my head as my composure fractures.

"Enough, Mother!" Lorennt declares, surging to his feet. "You grieve us with your prejudice. Erianna lost her husband and daughter. Do not attack her for trying to salvage the broken pieces of our family. I will not allow it."

"Try to see the good in this," Father encourages. "Though we have lost much, the Creator is also giving—not to replace, but to console and build anew."

Mother goes to the window, turning away from all of us. Father squeezes her shoulder then offers us a kind smile. "Please send for Nev and let me greet my new daughter."

Lorennt hugs his father then retrieves Nev. She enters with all the mildness and sincerity I have come to know in her. I find an encouraging smile for her as she is greeted warmly by Father, but she notices the coldness emanating from Mother. As they talk, Celiea glances at Nev from the corner of her eye. So much anguish is there with glimpses of frightened hope and jealousy that I begin to understand.

I go to my heart-mother, wrapping my arms around her waist and setting my head on her shoulder. I whisper encouragements to her, telling her I also am scared to hope for this babe we affectionately call Melon and that I sometimes feel jealous for what we have lost. She listens receptively until a knock on the door disrupts the moment.

"Come," Lorennt calls.

Valor halts on the threshold with a letter in his hand. "Forgive the intrusion, Majesty, but a letter has arrived for you that requires your attention."

I kiss Mother's cheek and depart with haste at Valor's grim expression. He guides me down the hall a ways before handing over the letter.

It is addressed to Queen Erianna Zavaan. I break the seal, flipping it around to read while Valor looks over my shoulder. My hands shake so badly that he places his around mine to steady the paper.

Greetings Wife,

It was good to see you a few days past. You are looking well, though I was disappointed you did not come to me as you should have, but a reluctant bride will be so much more amusing when we finally partake of the rest of our wedding night.

Was that Nev I saw with you? And got with the prince's child, no less? You are keeping secrets from me, my Little Queen. We shall talk about that soon.

Though I have no doubt you will hear of the welcome feast I prepared in honor of your return to Malsihra, I wanted to personally tell you, lest you think I was taking you for granted. In your honor, I butchered five hundred sheep and roasted them at Klaptin. You remember Klaptin, do you not? That insignificant town Ironforge rushed off to at my behest after abandoning you. Unfortunately, the messenger I conscripted last time was recalcitrant to our little feast. He and ten others thought to prevent us from celebrating. Thus, they became part of the bonfire. How his wife cried! Did you know her name is Anna? I thought it delightfully ironic.

I hope you know that I am thinking of you and anxiously awaiting your return to me.

Sincerely,

Your Reuel

Valor's wrath builds like a thunderstorm over the grasslands. My skin prickles with the intensity of it.

I am frozen by my own fury.

Each line is a mockery of me and my marriage to Leer. My people are being slaughtered, their livelihoods taken, and Malesiir abused. Not to mention what he means to do to my family, to Nev specifically, if he catches them.

The ice in me explodes into shards. I crumple the letter in my hand and stalk through stone corridors and into the bailey. My destination is unknown even to me until I reach the training rooms near the barracks.

I enter the largest of the rooms equipped with short staves and pels. I rip the mourning veil from my head, discarding my cloak and sash and every bit of finery that can be removed. I catch the staves Valor tosses to me and whirl to engage him, pouring all of my strength into the movements. My screamed rage harmonizes with the warrior's bellowed ire as we clash again and again.

More blood. More widows. More orphans. More life snuffed out by the scourge of the Ruphiri.

I hate Zavaan.

I hate him. I hate him. I hate him.

I scream it over and over without words. Valor catches my anguish on his wooden staves and redirects it like a conversation. My staves become my words, articulating every answer to his questions without restraint.

Would you go for Zavaan's neck? Valor leaves his own unguarded.

I swing my staves there. *I will behead him!*

Would you prevent Zavaan's escape? Valor sidesteps me.

Ripping fabric sounds as I drop to a crouch, sweeping my leg out to fell him. *I will cut his legs from beneath him!*

On and on we go. Such a clamor do we raise that the door to the training room is flung open by Lorennt, charging in with a drawn sword. Given over to the venting of our mutual fury at our enemy, Valor sees only the flash of steel and another warrior surging toward his queen. He roars, propelling me behind him and relieving his opponent of his weapon.

I chase after Valor, wrapping my arms tightly around his waist. "Tis Lorennt! Do not harm him!"

Valor's back heaves beneath my cheek. His tunic is drenched. But his staff does not lower from Lorennt's neck.

Lorennt is not as concerned as he ought to be. Rather, he is but for the wrong reason. He swears vociferously until something intelligible comes forth. "What goes in here, Commander!"

I remove my hands from Valor's waist, setting them on his back, willing calm into him. I feel him exhale, stepping away from Lorennt toward my pile of belongings. Lorennt's gaze rakes over me, and I follow it. My gown is dusty and torn in several places and hangs close to my legs. I look across the room to find I must have discarded my layered underskirt so my legs would not be hindered by the bulk.

Before Lorennt can form any wrong conclusions, Valor presents him with the letter. While he reads it, Valor guides me across the room and scoops up his mantle. With unparalleled tenderness, he cups my face and uses the corner of the fabric to wipe away the streaks of dirt, sweat, and angry tears. Lorennt's curses accompany his crushing of the letter beneath his boot. He sheaths his sword, picks up my dropped staves and launches himself at the pel.

I lean into Valor's touch, gathering my frayed emotions. I worked out most of the volatility I felt, but staring at Valor, I know he is no where near spent.

"Go," I encourage him. "I will be fine."

The creases around his eyes deepen. "I have never agreed with your definition of 'fine.'"

A brittle laugh escapes me. I take Valor's mantle and continue dusting myself off while he retrieves his own short staves. He battles Lorennt with strength he never unleashed against me. I would shatter myself against such undiluted potency.

I gather my belongings and slip on my underskirt beneath my dress while the men are focused on their match. I shake out my mourning veil and do my best to affix it then wait patiently while Lorennt and Valor blunt their anger.

It is well past noon when we make our way toward the castle. "How did you come by the letter?" I ask.

"It was sent by regular courier. He was uncertain of the surname but only knew one Queen Erianna," Valor explains.

"Do not believe a word of his taunts," Lorennt insists. "He will not lay hands on you again."

"Regardless, he is killing our people. What Zavaan means to do to me, his men have undoubtedly done to other women. They are so vile that he did not even trust them alone with me."

"He was manipulating you, making you dependent on him," Lorennt argues.

"No," Valor backs me. "He was ensuring his property was not claimed by a usurper."

Lorennt rounds on him. "What did you call her?"

Valor raises a hand. "I know. It disgusts me as well. But that is still the way of the barbaric peoples and one of the reasons he is so determined to have her. If he can subdue our queen, he believes he can lay claim to Limba and upend Malesiir."

"He *could* have Limba," I assert. "It would be that simple. And," I shudder, "this has become personal to him. He genuinely believes I am his." Shadowed caves rise up in my mind.

"Little Queen," Reuel drawls. "You are mine, Erianna Zavaan. I will find you."

Valor's hand catches mine, wrapping it around his arm, reminding me I am with him beneath an overcast sky, far from the repulsive caves.

I hold tightly to Valor and steady my voice. "Let us use this to our advantage. Silla and Trent should have had ample time to review what she learned of Gavin Chase. I want a meeting arranged on the morrow with our military leaders, and we are not going to leave the war room until we have something actionable to use against Zavaan."

"I will arrange it," Valor agrees as we mount the steps into the castle. "But first I shall order a bath sent up to your room straightaway."

"Bless you," I release him to his tasks.

Intentionally shifting my thoughts away from that which I can do nothing more about, I fall into step with Lorennt, heading toward our stairs. "What happened after I left the solar?"

"Father welcomed Nev into our family, and they were doing well. Eventually, Mother joined them on the couch. What did you say to her?"

"It does not matter." I do not want Lorennt to understand this pain of ours that could distract from his own joy.

"I think it does, because she was polite to Nev thereafter. So for whatever you said, thank you."

My heart swells with gratitude to the Creator. *Thank You for giving Nev and Melon to us. We need them.*

"There is still more that could be improved upon, but it is a start." Lorennt stops me outside my door. "Do not tell Nev about the letter. She was badly frightened on the journey here by the encounter with the Ruphiri."

Soberly, I intone, "Brother. If there is one thing that I learned from my marriage, it is this. It is far better to be honest and face your trials together than it is to lie and go it alone."

Lorennt pinches the bridge of his nose in a gesture so like Leer's my heart constricts. *Oh, how I miss my husband.*

"You are right, of course," Lorennt concedes. "If you do not tell her, I will."

"It is for the best," I hug him.

※ ※ ※

Nev is understandably shaken by the letter from Zavaan when I recount it to her. Valor kept it in its abused state, insisting it might reveal more than taunting upon careful inspection. I doubt it is so, but I would have gained nothing by gainsaying him.

Unfortunately, this day has been an emotional one for Nev as well, and it is not over yet. I work her hair into a Limban style that Liddy often twisted my hair into for formal events. Nev wears it well, along with a formal, high-waisted gown that I never wore during my short pregnancy. I sent Lorennt to retrieve it from my closet since I still have not gathered my courage to return to my room where Leer is not.

"Should I not also be in grey?" Nev questions with a glance at the plain satin gown I donned.

"Not for tonight. I want you introduced to the court as the lovely lady you are. Besides, you are announcing your wedding. It is a joyous occasion. You should not be in mourning clothes." I wrap a black sash around my waist to take in the slack in the bodice. I should order some grey gowns made to my measurements or, at the very least, tailor the ones I do have.

I grimace. Dress fittings will be much less fun without Leer. It became one of our regular outings. He said the results of him attending my fittings were much better than when I saw to them alone. Mostly, he enjoyed flirting with me, and I dramatized my need for his opinion to give him the opportunity.

Lorennt knocks on our door to collect us for dinner. I stare hard at it, willing my heart to give up the belief that eventually, when I open this door, Leer will be standing on the other side with his flawless demeanor and handsome face. I can count on one hand the number of times I attended a meal without him. Until now. The number now occupies two hands.

Cease! I order myself, taking a deep breath and smoothing my expression. I open the door for Lorennt, ushering him into the foyer. Waiting in the hall, flipping a knife into the air and catching it by the blade, is Valor.

He pauses, quirking a brow at me. "You forgot your shoes."

My expression wobbles. I cross the floor, crashing against his broad, solid chest. I fill my arms with him, breathing deeply of his scent that reminds me of the grasslands and open skies. He hides me in his embrace that was no small part of what made that time crossing the Continent freeing to me. How is it that being in Valor's arms feels safe and sheltered while also unburdening? It is as if my troubles cannot find me here. Or perhaps he takes my burdens upon himself, giving me respite from the load.

"Can we ride across the Hillcountry someday? Maybe camp in the pine forest?" That time with Valor was the closest thing I have ever felt to freedom from my crowns.

Valor's deep voice is fervent. "I do not hold the future, my Sweetest Friend. But if the choice is mine, I will take you back there. And to a hundred more places I know you would love."

I find his eyes, needing to see hope.

Compassionately, he assures me, "This grief will not last forever. There is life ahead of you."

"The getting there is miserable."

"I know." He rubs my back. "Are you ready to announce Nev and Lorennt's wedding?"

"I need to find my happy face first," I drolly reply.

"That I can help you with." He dips his head to mine to whisper in my ear. "Were you as filthy as I after sparring in the training room? You would never believe where I found sand."

I snicker, pushing away from him. "That is inappropriate."

"It is not," he indignantly declares. "I found sand between my toes. Where did you think I meant?" He dares me.

I blush, but say it anyway, refusing to back down from a dare.

He barks a laugh. "Mind your mouth, my Queen."

I am tired of this hole in my heart, tired of feeling lonely. So I step closer, inviting trouble. "You could mind it for me."

Valor's smile does not waver. "When you actually mean that, I shall. But for now, go find your shoes."

The pang of rejection I feel is my own fault. It is not fair for me to use his affection like a bandage when it is not truly Valor I want. I pass by Lorennt who is reassuring Nev without words in the foyer.

"Enough," I growl at them. "We shall be late for dinner if you do not control yourselves."

Nev steps away from him, blushing. "Of course."

From the dressing room I hear Lorennt murmur to his love, "That makes a dozen. You still owe me a hundred and thirty two more."

I puzzle at the number then make a face when I understand. A kiss for each day they were apart.

Happy. Not jealous. Happy, I remind myself.

"I think I can clear most of my debt on our wedding night," Nev whispers.

I shove my feet into slippers instead of lacing on boots to faster escape their lover's talk and dart past Lorennt stealing a thirteenth kiss.

"Come along, you Churlish Oaf." I roughly snag Valor's arm and decide, henceforth, I will be taking myself to dinner. A queen does not require an escort.

Nor do I need the sort of affection that my heart weeps is lost.

I will be just fine on my own.

Just. Fine.

※ ※ ※

I make an excellent show of introducing Nev as a member of our court and announcing the wedding. For the most part, I simply repeat Leer's words when he announced our wedding. No one here remembers those exact words except me, so the nobility do not know I am borrowing from my king husband's formality.

A steady murmur of dissent runs through the room when I state that I have given Nev the title of a lady and placed her on equal footing with them. I am a tad beyond caring for their ruffled plumage after the day I have had and let it slip into my address. "I am certain I can count on you, one and all, to greet Nev with the same warmth you bestowed upon me at my introduction to court." The threat in my voice is too obvious, and Silla affects a pleasant expression, encouraging me to do the same.

I soften my tone, smiling sweetly. "My family is overjoyed at the news we will be celebrating Prince Lorennt's wedding in four weeks time and welcoming his babe near winter solstice. We need something to look forward to in our time of grief. Lady Nev's return is nothing less than a blessing from the Creator. Please make her feel welcome." I lead the nobility in applauding the happy couple while gaining my seat.

"Well done," Lorennt commends me. "And thank you again." He shifts his gaze to his right where Nev is seated, looking positively amazed that she is sitting next to him on this side of the high table.

"A toast! To Lady Nev and Prince Lorennt," Valor raises his water goblet on the other side of Leer's vacant chair. "May you continue overcoming all the odds together and your love deepen in the days to come."

"Hear, hear," I raise my goblet then drink deeply.

My eyes fall on the empty chair at my left as I return my goblet to the table. *Oh, Leer. Why could you not do this for them?*

CHAPTER THIRTY-ONE

VALOR

September 19th

The nobility congregate before breakfast to gossip over all that has transpired. I watch from an alcove as Silla and Trent meander through the crowd, fleecing the people for information. Ever so casually they meet, redirecting each other to pick up conversations without drawing notice. I laud Erianna for matching the two. They seem to be working well together.

Erianna's other match descends from the royal wing of the castle, making their rounds. The nobility must have taken the queen's strong recommendation to make the new lady feel welcome for they great Nev with equanimity. I expect Erianna will follow behind them, but she does not.

I catch Nev's eye, pressing a questioning look at her. She winks in response. What is my queen up to now?

Anders and most of the military officials participating in the meeting after breakfast trickle into the great hall, mingling with the nobility. A courier also enters, seeking a particular nobleman. At the direction of a guard, he goes to Lord Mortin, the trade official responsible for Klaptin's district in which his family holdings also lie. The whispered words of the courier and discreet letter are all for naught with Lord Mortin's exclamations. "Five hundred sheep burned! Who is responsible? I want them hanged!

Conversation swells through the room, repeating over and over. *Klaptin was attacked. People were killed and flocks destroyed. It is a heavy financial burden for the district to shoulder alone.*

Lorennt and Nev drift across the room, distancing themselves from the conversation that is building to a clamor.

Is this to be the first of increasing attacks on our cities? Who are these men responsible for the destruction? What do they want? Were they the ones who killed the king? What does the queen have to say about it? Is she capable of facing this enemy? Is the prince?

The answer to their questions and mine strides through the entrance hall, confident and capable, garbed in her training clothes and armed with her cuirass, daggers, and a sword. She is striking. Kragorn follows close behind the Warrior Queen, imposing and scowling as ever.

The crowd hushes, parting before her, clearing a path to the dais. Without hesitation, she takes her place in the high seat amid incredulous stares. Lorennt and Nev follow, taking their new places as well. Boldizar and Celiea do not appear surprised by any of this, but they are accustomed to maintaining their unwavering calm after years of practice. My queen crooks a finger, summoning me. I bow deeply upon reaching her side.

"My generals have arrived?" She asks without lowering her voice.

"They have, Your Majesty."

"Very well." She motions me to be seated on her left. With another wave of her hand, she commences breakfast and servants enter bearing viands.

The nobility gape as they find their seats, but not Lord Mortin. He stomps up the dais, brandishing the letter. "Your Majesty! My district was attacked and five hundred of my flock were destroyed by the same men and their wolves that have been plaguing the kingdom in your absence."

"I am aware," she declares.

Exasperation twists his face. "What do you intend to do? My family's money was invested in those flocks!"

"The district and your family will be compensated for their losses, and the perpetrators will be brought to justice." She takes up her spoon to begin eating her porridge, but Lord Mortin is not satisfied.

He steps forward to slam the missive on the table but finds the point of my dagger at his throat. "Your queen has spoken. Remove yourself."

"Was there something else, Lord Mortin?" Erianna asks, spooning honey over her porridge as if the man were politely engaging her.

"Do you even know who these knaves are? How do you intend to bring them to justice when you don't know what happened? I was informed moments ago. It is impossible you knew about this," he challenges.

Erianna rises to face the lord's accusations. "I am well acquainted with the criminals—too well. I saw them murder my king husband, after all."

Astonished gasps echo throughout the great hall. The nobles lean forward, anxious for whatever previously withheld details the queen will reveal.

Mortin formulates his response but utters not more than three syllables before Erianna snarls, "I am not finished! I know who they are and what they intend. Be assured, I will bring them to justice. Besides the sheep they slaughtered and burned, do you know how many men died as a result of their actions?"

He yields a step to the queen's ire. "Nine men were killed."

"But do you know *who* they were? Do you know what roles they served in your district?"

"Shepherds," he states, but it is only a guess.

"There were six shepherds. Leiff, Maar and Míek—three brothers and fathers who left behind widows and children—an elder named Aaen, his son Dion, and the grandson named for his grandfather. The other three were Hoff the tanner, Gierd the thatcher, and Nate Bevins, a farmer. They heard the commotion and ran to aid their neighbors in fighting thirty lethal men while armed with only a pitchfork, club and scythe. Their bodies were cast into the bonfire of sheep while their wives and children wept. The villains pillaged their homes and assaulted their women."

Erianna plunges her dagger into the center of the table. "Make no mistake, Lord Mortin, I am livid at the atrocities committed against my people and will not allow this or the death of my king husband to go unpunished!"

Prince Lorennt's understated rage drives the nobleman the rest of the way from the dais. "What none of you realize is that Queen Erianna spent ten days as a captive of these savages before escaping. She knows each of them by sight." Lorennt allows that information to sink into the soil of fertile minds then continues, "These men call themselves the Ruphiri. They are a rogue nation intent on destabilizing Malesiir and becoming a dominant power on the Continent. We will not allow it."

"To that end," Erianna declares, "our generals and captains have been assembled so that we may eradicate these vermin."

Lorennt's eyes drift over the hall. "We shall also continue the work King Grandileer began in strengthening our kingdom through trade with Limba and the Commonwealth. That includes replacing the weak links in our trade districts, namely those trade officials whose priorities are first their purses, not their people. Commander Ironforge shall continue that work after King Grandileer's funeral. In fact, I believe today has been elucidating for him."

I offer Lord Mortin a chilling smile. He pales and seeks his place at a table. Lorennt nods at me, and I scoot the queen's chair beneath her as she sits then take my seat.

"Cream, Sister?"

She accepts the pitcher from Lorennt and returns to her breakfast as though it had not been disturbed.

But her dagger remains embedded in the high table throughout the meal.

❊ ❊ ❊

Immediately following breakfast, Lorennt entrusts Nev to his mother's care while the Warrior Queen leads the way to the war room. She goes to the window, bracing her hands on the stone sill to gaze upon another gloomy day while we await the rest of the party's arrival.

"Do you have anymore surprises in store, my Queen?" I ask, leaning against the wall next to her.

Defensively, she replies, "Silla informed me that some of the nobles thought you were pulling my strings and that I was not in control of the kingdom. I needed them to see that was not the case and head off the anticipated trouble when the nobles learned what transpired in Klaptin, though I was unsure what form it would take."

I shift my attention from guarding her back to study her guarded expression. "I commend you for your excellent thoughts and execution of them. You displayed your strength and capacity to sort out this problem." With daylight upon her face, I discern her bright complexion is achieved by cosmetics meant to conceal her wakeful night.

"You are not upset that I did not inform you of my plans?" She asks, presuming she knows my answer.

"No. You do not need my approval to make decisions and act on them, though I am pleased you included Lorennt as you said you would. You two presented a perfectly united front."

Some of stiffness leaves her shoulders but not the tension. She gnaws on her lip. "Did I do the right thing in taking Leer's place? We have not even mourned him yet."

"You have been mourning him for two months. Today, you did what was best for the kingdom by demonstrating that a strong monarch reigns. The king's symbolically empty chair, though appropriate, would have been demoralizing to your people. Grandileer would have made the same decision. Above all, he was a pragmatist."

She sighs through her nose. "To a fault."

"Here they come," I inform her as the generals begin to file in.

"Almighty, grant us wisdom," she murmurs.

"Amen," I second her plea.

The meeting opens with a candid dispersal of information by Lorennt. He explains who and what we are facing, the atrocities they have already committed, and their intentions. Another hour of questions and clarifications follow. Finally, we get to the meat of things.

I take charge of this portion of the discussion. "The queen would like to hear your ideas on how we are going to bring the Ruphiri to justice and prevent future attacks."

Silence long and taught is their answer.

"Generals," the queen prompts, "I am willing to entertain any and all suggestions, and I should warn you, we are not leaving this room until we have something workable."

The first half dozen ideas were already considered and discarded by our small circle in Parse Kítaran, but we work our way through them again, hoping that the additional military minds will have something new to offer. The conclusions of each plan turn out the same way.

Things deteriorate after another hour, and the queen dispatches Trent to have the late noon meal delivered. While the men dig into their meal and talk amongst themselves, Erianna picks at her food then abandons it to stand over a chess board in a far corner of the room. She thoughtfully plays out a game with herself, moving the pieces around without regard to the rules restricting their movements. The food is cleared away from the table, and she returns. A lull in conversation descends over the room into which Erianna speaks. "I am going to present an idea that may be unpopular, but I think it should be considered nonetheless."

I tense, knowing where this is headed. So does Lorennt.

"Zavaan wants me. How can we use that to draw him out?"

The air in the room becomes uncomfortable as the generals and officials spurn the idea on principal but cannot disregard it entirely. I grit my teeth and feign calm by way of stillness as I remember the state of Erianna when I found her in the woods. She was feral, could not even speak. I fix my eyes on her now, whole and safe. Redeemed and hopeful. But the scars are still there. So is the cuirass Zavaan laced her into.

Kragorn is the first to offer a suggestion. "Could we lure them into an area, a valley that we have surrounded? Turn their own scheme against them?"

My mounting anger toward him dissolves. He knows that would never work. He is simply appeasing her to formally kill this plan so she will cease suggesting it.

The topic is discussed thoroughly but all with the same premise. The idea is to lure Zavaan somewhere by convincing him that the queen is there but she is not. Kragorn eventually points out that Zavaan had the best opportunity to lay hands on the queen since she escaped him on the way to Malsihra, but he did not take it because he was outnumbered ten to one. Furthermore, if we attempted such a ruse he would likely arrange an ambush as he has done with great success in the past.

Lorennt is closing the matter when a general on the far side of the room speaks up. "What if we simply give them what they want?"

All heads swivel to General Kannik who has been orchestrating the hunt for the Wolves in the Central Province. He stares down the queen across the table. "By your own account, the Ruphiri were retreating to the Ascent like hellhounds once they captured you. If we turn you over to Zavaan as a peace offering, they will leave, and Malesiir is spared further losses."

Lorennt growls, "Do you understand that you would be consigning your queen to ravishment, lifelong enslavement, and every sort of abuse?"

General Kannik's expression does not falter. "She tamed one king. Perhaps she could do it again and spare herself such unpleasantness."

Lorennt's choler reaches the level of mine. We are not the only ones whose anger begins to boil. Many sight Kannik as if looking for the best place to begin gutting him.

Kannik shrugs. "Forgive me, Your Highness, but I cannot say I have been altogether impressed with Queen Erianna's rule. Her every decision has been based on emotion at the expense of our safety and economic security. The banishment of General Tergehn was wasteful of an excellent military mind and served only to uplift her own tarnished reputation. Her murder of the king's mistress was barbarous and self-serving. Just this morning, she pointed out the value of a few people over the well-being of the whole district which will be strained by the loss of livestock and buildings. Emotion drives her every decision, and it makes her unfit to rule Malesiir."

Lorennt's outraged bellows are drowned out by the roaring in my ears. *The king's mistress.* Grandileer's unforgivable offense. He kept a woman while married to Erianna. I had considered it, but it seemed implausible since he was so obviously in love with his wife. Now knowing it as fact, the pieces come together too well.

Grandileer kept a woman, likely a common woman, but would not allow Lorennt to be with Nev. Silla repented having any association with the whore. The whore that tried to murder Erianna and her babe out of jealousy. Grandileer's letter admitted he wronged her so greatly he would have released her from her marriage vows. Because he was unfaithful to her. Lied to her. Was partly responsible for the death of their child.

Even Erianna's disproportionate response to Tirzah! It was not because she learned jealousy from her husband. It was because he scorned her, and she wanted nothing to do with me if there was the remotest chance it could happen to her again.

I cannot stymie the rush of details. All I could not understand at the time is given clarity by this explanation. Such turmoil is in my own head that I do not perceive the chaos in the room until I feel Erianna's hand on my knee beneath the table. Prince Lorennt and the generals are on their feet, raging at General Kannik. Kragorn has a grip on Anders who curses and threatens with increasing probability that he will act on his threats.

But I only see winter eyes. The grieved eyes of my promised wife.

Are you with me? She asks as I have asked her dozens of times these past weeks.

I laugh bitterly.

I am sorry. I would have told you had I known it would come out like this. I understand now.

Her eyes are sadder still. *You do not. But you will soon.*

Blazing depths! There is more?

She squeezes my knee and returns her attention to the room, raising her voice to be heard. "Generals, be seated."

Her command takes a moment to register, but the men—soldiers at heart one and all—obey the order of their queen.

"General Kannik." Erianna's voice is cold. "I thank you for your input. For a number of reasons that are not founded solely in emotion, I will not be surrendering myself to the Ruphiri. Furthermore, I do not simply want them gone from Malesiir. I want them punished for the death of our king and the heir to the throne as well as countless others. You may name that *emotionally driven* if you wish, but I think a desire to see justice satisfied is a worthy cause."

The general inclines his head.

"Now. I have one more idea I would like to present." She rises and begins to outline the details of her plan while circling the table. "I would like to engage the help of our people to find the Ruphiri hiding in our midst. It was with the providential help of two young boys that Commander Ironforge and Sergeant Trent located the brigands in the North. I would like to empower each of our citizens to be able to provide the same aid. I also would like to engage every soldier in Malesiir, whether they be currently in service or retired, to form a net of troops across our kingdom. Is that feasible?"

"In a word?" One of the older generals replies, "Aye. It can be done. But the financial strain of such a thing would be heavy."

Lorennt explains, "After the last year and a half of significantly higher expenditures and the losses from the brigands, now from the Ruphiri, plus the succor you have and will give the widows and orphans, I am not sure it would be wise to bring our coffers so low. This winter also seems to be an early one. Less production will in turn mean less revenue from taxes."

Erianna considers it, nodding along as she paces around the room. "I want figures. How much will it cost to do this? I also want to see the estimated production yields for this season. Beyond that, I will tighten the purse strings in meaningful ways in our castle and explore ideas for alternative incomes. That might mean serving pottage at your wedding, Brother, but we all must make sacrifices."

The generals chuckle, believing it is an empty threat. I know her better. She might very well do it.

Erianna talks with her hands, emphasizing her words. "I am thinking aloud, of course, but I want us to be of one mind. For your part, I am depending upon you all to create a web that threatens to snare the Ruphiri at every turn. I do not want what occurred in Klaptin to be repeated. I want them to fear venturing into our cities. I want them to become desperate and make a mistake. When that happens, I want the full force of the Malesiirian army to be waiting for them."

Murmurs of bloodthirsty assent rumble around the table. Erianna sets a hand on my chair as she passes. "Commander. As part of your restructuring of the trade districts, I would like you to ensure two additional things. One, that the districts have a reasonable military presence and the people have been educated on the Ruphiri. Ensure procedures are in place to defend them from that threat and any further threats from opportunistic brigands. We cannot afford more losses."

I am still reeling, and it only now occurs when I see Trent's pen moving rapidly over the paper before him that I should have been the one taking notes as the queen's Hand. I owe Trent yet again.

"And two?" I ask to let her know I am with her.

"I want a comprehensive audit conducted within each district. I want to compare the past years' production against the years to come. It will be a means of holding the trade officials accountable in the future."

"Aye, my Queen."

"Very good." She stops behind her chair, wrapping her hands around the ornate back. "I am content that we have accomplished something today. Prince Lorennt, are you satisfied?"

He glares at General Kannik but gives his assent.

"Then let us hone the details of these plans on the morrow."

"Tomorrow is the day of rest, Majesty," I interject.

"Oh. Then the day after," she says.

It is an uncomfortable moment, but Lorennt says gently, "That is the day of the funeral."

Erianna closes her eyes, attempting to conceal her pain. She lost track of the days.

Lorennt goes to his sister's side. "I will inform you when we are prepared to convene again. You are dismissed." When it is only the three of us, Lorennt pulls Erianna into a hug. "You did so well. All those chess matches paid off, even with you hiding the pieces."

She laughs through her tears. "It seems Leer made a queen out of me against my best efforts to remain feckless."

He chortles. "We would have been the most indolent rulers on the Continent without his insistence we make something of ourselves."

"But oh, the tournaments and card games we would have had," she says wistfully.

"The Court of Folly," he concurs then holds her at arms length. "I must go to Nev. Will you come with me?"

She shakes her head. "I must tell Valor about Jaleh. I have put it off far too long."

Lorennt's gaze is pitying. "I will do it if you do not wish to."

Erianna shakes her head. "Go. Rescue Nev from sewing or whatever sinfully boring occupation with which Mother has engaged her. I can personally attest to the welcome you will receive from her. I think Leer encouraged me to go to the solar just so he could rescue me with his company."

Lorennt grins. "He did. He sometimes arranged the times of his meetings for that purpose entirely."

Her face crumples, and he pulls her close again.

"Have you forgiven him?" She asks.

"I am trying. More than what he did, I regret what I did," Lorennt confesses.

"I understand perfectly. I wish so badly I had not wasted those last months on hurtful words and pushing him away."

Lorennt hangs his head. "The last time I saw him, just before you left for the coast, I told him that I hated him and never wished to see him again," his voice breaks, "that he was not my brother."

Erianna wraps her arms around her brother as regret of the worst sort carves his face. "Oh, Lorennt. I am so sorry."

"A hundred thousand times since I have recanted those words but to no avail. That I had learned the value of not speaking in anger sooner! There is no relief from this guilt."

"There is," she says. "Ask the Almighty to forgive you and give you a new beginning. You will find relief you never believed possible."

"That is what Father says as well."

"He is right, and I am proof. Am I not?" Erianna turns to me.

"Incontrovertible proof."

Lorennt sighs. "I shall give it some thought. But now, to find my intended."

Erianna gains my side but calls out to Lorennt, stopping him at the door. "You will honor her wishes, will you not?"

"Regarding?" He frowns.

Erianna flushes but presses on. "Waiting to take her back into your bed."

Lorennt casts his eyes at the ceiling, escaping this uncomfortable topic. "I would never do anything she did not wish to do."

"Help her do what is right rather than what she wishes," Erianna urges, burning scarlet.

Lorennt hastily exits before she can say anything more.

"Was that overly personal?" She asks me.

"No. It was a thoughtful admonishment out of love for both of them." I reach behind her and pull her chair closer to mine before we sit.

Erianna unlaces her boots then brings her bare feet beneath her in the chair. She shifts to get comfortable, cannot, sits forward to pluck loose the laces down the front of her cuirass, and sets it atop her boots.

Eyeing the offensive garment, I ask, "Would you mind if buy a new cuirass for you?"

"I would much rather wear something from you than him," she says, pulling her cloak around her like a blanket. "Actually, it is something I have meant to purchase myself, but I only think of it when I must don it."

"Then I will see to it."

Erianna gathers her thoughts for minutes. "How much do you want to know?"

I do not have to think about my answer. "Everything."

"Alright. I am going to tell you what happened in the order it happened, not how I learned of it. Considering things from Leer's point of view makes his actions much more forgivable when you see what I have come to realize—the cunning general that thought only pragmatically and sinned against me was not the good king that loved me and sang me to sleep with lullabies when nightmares woke me."

With a deep breath, she begins. "When Leer returned from serving as a general, he took up with a maid named Jaleh."

CHAPTER THIRTY-TWO

VALOR

Sleep is elusive this night. Giving up on it entirely, I take to stalking the ramparts. The overcast sky blots out the stars. The light of the moon dispersed by the clouds appears as a smudge high above the mountain peaks. My hands clench into fists at my sides, distracting me from the serene view. My king's actions foment rage within me such that I cannot reason my way out of the turmoil.

A large part of Erianna's resolution comes from disassociating Grandileer, the cunning general, from Leer, her loving husband. I am glad that she has that, and I cannot deny its merit since being her husband did change him.

But that was not the man I loyally served. I served Grandileer, the cunning general prince. That was the man I knew, that I swore fealty to. He is the man who betrayed me and made a liar out of me. I promised Erianna that he was a good man who would look after her and protect her, all the while, he had abandoned her to every abuse in Limba then planned in advance to be unfaithful to her when they wed.

Erianna did not voice her feelings regarding his infidelity or all the details of what transpired. She related the events dispassionately, so I know she withheld much, choosing not to reveal the extent of her hurt. But it is there, in her hidden scars.

My fist connects with the stone battlement, splitting my knuckles. I may as well thrash his gravestone for all the good it will do. I know precisely how Lorennt feels. Without consideration for either of us, only his own selfish motives cloaked in the guise of making wise decisions for Malesiir, he denied us the women we loved. We served unquestioningly, and he betrayed us.

You must forgive him, the Spirit of Truth speaks to my heart.

I shake my head, watching the blood trickle down my hand. *How? The woman I cherish who will one day be my wife was wronged again. The man I gave allegiance to is culpable in the worst things that were done to her. How can I forgive that? I am not even sure I want to.* I speak from the roiling of my heart, baring my distress to the One who knows my every thought.

In the wake of my unburdening, I am still and quiet, listening.

His answer does not come suddenly, nor does it come loudly. But it sinks through the turbulence like a lodestone, drawing away all the doubt plaguing me.

My grace is sufficient for you. My work of redemption is absolute.

※ ※ ※

On my way back through the great hall to seek what remains of the night on my bed, I notice only one guard at the bottom of the stairs to the royal wing. My questions of the remaining guard divert me down an adjacent hall. I find the missing guard stationed outside the queen's office.

I push into the room and am met with organized chaos. Erianna sits barefoot and cross legged on the floor amidst crates stacked high and piles of papers. A teetering tower of books sits atop one of two new desks that now occupy space in the room.

She does not glance up from frowning over the papers in her hands. "Shut the door. You are letting in the cold." Clad in only her tunic and pants, I am sure she is already cold.

I close it and pick my way around the room. "You are not surprised to see me."

"You were preoccupied at dinner. You sleep no better than I when that is the case." She flips the paper over to the back then passes it to me. "Is this something I ought to keep?"

I glance at the document. "No."

"Good. Add it to the fire."

I wad the paper and toss it across the room into the fireplace where a large pile of ashes attests to her having been at this for some time.

"The steward was expedient in replacing the old furnishings with the new, but that has necessitated cleaning out decades worth of accumulated documents. Grab a stack and lend me a hand."

I help her sort through several piles, clearing space on the floor and filing the papers into the cabinet. "Why can you not sleep?"

She shrugs. "Nightmares. I decided I may as well be productive since I am going to be awake. You?"

"Making sense of what you told me. I went for a walk."

Her eyes flit to my spilt knuckles, but she does not inquire.

"Why did you allow General Kannik to go unchallenged?" I ask, selecting another crate to sort.

"I wanted to see how much support I could expect from the generals. Before the meeting, I asked Trent to take note of those who were the most supportive and those most opposed to my leadership."

Though her logic is sound, that is the sort of thing she usually discusses with me. I begin to wonder if there is more to her not informing me of her plans earlier. "Have I offended you?"

"Of course not." She slides a crate of papers to be filed my way and changes the subject. "Did you hear what happened in the solar today?"

"I did not."

"Some of the ladies made snide remarks about Nev. No one is willing to tell me exactly what was said or who said it, but they made Nev cry. Then Mother Celiea did something delightful and reminded the ladies that just as I can bestow titles on people of extraordinary character, I can strip titles from those underserving of them." Erianna holds her head high. I do not doubt it is a source of personal pride to have grown from being defenseless in the Limban court to being the defender of the defenseless in this one. "Silla said it was a sight to behold. Mother Celiea took an interest in Nev for the rest of the time and even became acquainted with Melon."

I add the emptied crate to a stack against the wall. "That is a dramatic improvement from yesterday's introduction. I am relieved."

"The day *before* yesterday. We are well after middle night," she contradicts, definitely piqued with me about something.

I chuckle. "Fine. The day *before* yesterday."

Erianna points at the next crate to sort. I heft it over to her. Her eyes linger on my arm, and she snickers.

"What?" I ask.

"Nothing. Nothing at all." She contains a smile, catching her lip in her teeth while reaching into the crate. But the mischievous glint in her eyes distracts me from my work.

One more chuckle to herself has me carefully inspecting my shirt. I notice the tear in the sleeve that she mended, but that should cause her irritation, if anything. Erianna grins wickedly as I further examine my sleeve. I turn it to the side and catch sight of green thread in the dark blue fabric. Pulling it around, I discover a series of embroidered green roses on the back of the sleeve. Not noticeable to me wearing the shirt, but certainly obvious to anyone standing behind me.

"I thought your clothing could use some embellishments. What do you think?" She innocently asks.

I glare at her. "You did this to multiple things I own?"

She flips her plait over her shoulder. "Only on everything you tricked me into mending for you."

My gaze on her narrows.

"And whatever items of yours I could find in the laundry."

Without thinking through my actions, I chuck a book at her. She cackles, leaning to the side, and throws a slipper back at me. An instant later, missiles of all sorts fly across the office. Erianna reaches the stack of books atop the desk first, and I take cover behind a chair.

"Surrender!" She demands, hurling a book at me.

"I will never yield!" I mock in an exaggerated Limban falsetto while lobbing the book back and gaining the superior protection of the opposite desk.

"I warn you, Commander. I am in no mood to take prisoners!" A flurry of leather bound volumes soar over the desk.

"Unfortunately for you, I am!" I seize my chance, skirting the desk and sprinting toward her.

Erianna squeals, throwing the books faster, but I press on until I have the subdued the rebel. I trap her against the desk making a cage of my arms. Unfettered laughter signals the end of her ire for the moment. She hops onto the desk, swinging her bare feet. I do not release my prisoner but remain with my hands braced to either side. This playful spirit of hers lures me in, tempting me to cross the barrier I swore to respect. Repressing the temptation and choosing what is better, I bide with her to discern the source of the friction between us.

In the space between my arms, she lifts unguarded winter eyes. "Will you promise to be careful while you are gone?"

So this is where her pique comes from. She dreads the coming weeks apart perhaps as much as I.

"Careful like you are careful?" I tease.

She sneers, causing me to chuckle again.

"How about we strike a bargain?" I suggest. "Let us both be careful while we are apart and save recklessness for when we are together and can look after each other."

Erianna wraps her arms around my neck, bringing me down to her. "I will make that bargain. But I need you to return in two weeks. Someone must protect me from the angry horde when I serve pottage at a royal wedding."

I relish the feel of her in my arms, sensing this will be our last moment like this for a long while. "A horde? I think you had better practice your swordplay between now and then. It will take both of us to fend off a horde."

"Deal."

CHAPTER THIRTY-THREE

ERIANNA

September 21st

Our people crowd under the portcullis, filing silently onto the castle grounds. The guards have orders to turn back anyone bearing weapons to prevent the Ruphiri from adding another layer of sadness to this day of mourning.

The day we buried Illyanna was the brightest blue heralding the beginning of summer. This autumn day is bleak portending rain. It does not feel any more appropriate for a funeral. Perhaps no day feels appropriate for a funeral.

My gown drags over the ground, measuring my steps like it did on the days of my wedding and coronation. Unlike those days, if I fall, Leer is not at my side to catch me. But I will be at his side soon. I made a promise.

Lorennt and the family quietly buried Leer after Anders retrieved him from the coast. As such, there is no casket to follow to the graveyard. Instead, the king's Hand leads Leer's destrier, saddled and riderless, with his dagger hanging from the pommel. Reaper is not easy to manage. Like me, the person he was bound to was taken from him. He tosses his head and flattens his ears, trying to bolt. Maybe we will run together from the utter wrongness of this day.

Valor turns Reaper aside at the gate to the cemetery. I lead the procession into the graveyard with my family following behind. I have not been here since Illyanna's funeral. Next to her is where I will find her father.

I hear Mother Celiea sob as the most recent graves come into view. I feel frozen inside. This should not be happening. I stop at the foot of my husband's grave, staring through my widow's veil.

Widow.

The word has never felt more mine than it does now. Suddenly, it does not offend as it once did. It encompasses what I am. What I feel. My loss. My grief.

I stand motionless as my people pass through the graveyard casting sprigs of evergreen upon their king's grave, paying their last respects to him. Grandileer was a good king to them.

Valor makes his way to my side. Like me, he wishes to speak to his king in private.

Lady Silla casts her sprig upon the grave then comes to me. She curtsies deeply with tears in her eyes. "My heartfelt condolences, Majesty." She continues on with the mourners, not waiting for a response from me, perhaps knowing that my words are held in reserve for one man today.

The king's grave overflows with greenery as does Illyanna's. Many people brought tokens for the king's heir too.

It is customary for the closest relative to address the mourners, but I deferred the responsibility to Lorennt to speak on behalf of our family. His words are steady and reassuring. Mine would not have been.

He honors Grandileer's life and speaks of his love for his brother. Nev slips her hand in his when his voice shakes. He and I both carry the pain of the many horrible words we spoke to Leer echoing in our memories today. It certainly does not make this trying day any easier.

My family returns to the castle to begin the wake. They will light candles in the great hall to honor the fallen king that will stay lit through the night into the morrow.

It is late afternoon when the last of the mourners depart. Valor and I have remained all this time until we are the only ones left in the graveyard. My guards are stationed outside the perimeter, affording us solitude.

Valor steps forward, kneeling at the foot of his king's grave. After service in the chapel yesterday, he told me that he is working toward forgiving Grandileer for what he did, but he admitted that it is accursed difficult. "Forgiveness is often a process wherein we must continually choose to let go of the past and submit our emotions to Truth. I strive to forgive like the Almighty has forgiven me, instantaneously and completely, but I am imperfect. Forgiving him will take time." Valor's honesty was better than platitudes or empty reassurances. He promised to tell me where he is on that road and support me on the days that I struggle with the same.

Valor bows his head in reverence and removes Grandileer's signet from his finger. He stares at it, then places it upon the king's gravestone. The act brings tears to my eyes. Valor has worn the ring continuously since entering Leer's service and even after his death, fulfilling his last vows to his king. Valor found me and protected me from the Ruphiri. He has seen me restored to my Creator and now to my husband's side, helping me fulfill my promise to Leer too. Valor's service to King Grandileer is complete.

He walks around my husband's grave and kneels beside my daughter's. Somberly, he touches Illyanna's name carved upon the stone. I can only guess at his thoughts. Maybe they are on that night in the woods with the snow falling silently around us when he laid his hand over my barren womb and asked the Creator to heal me.

Valor returns to me. With doleful eyes he murmurs, "This is not what I had in mind."

I touch his cheek, accepting his sympathy and offering him mine. My friend moves alongside me, standing vigil for as long as I need.

It is time to keep my promise.

After seventy-two days, I return to my husband's side.

I tread upon the evergreens then lower to the ground, laying a hand on my daughter's grave and a hand upon my husband's. In the entire world, these are the two people I want most in my arms. But I cannot cross this divide. This is as close as I can come. Tears crawl down my face to be caught in my widow's veil. It feels symbolic of this divide between us. I am divided from the world by my loss that has divided me from those I love most.

"I told you I would come back to you. I am sorry it took me so long." The inscription on his headstone that proclaims who he was to all of us. The final line reads *My Leer*.

"You know it was not supposed to be this way. All those times that we talked about what a year could bring, it was not supposed to bring this." Almost a year ago today, I arrived in Malsihra and met my husband. Our beginning was challenging, but our ending was horrible. I hate that. It gouges my heart.

"I am sorry, Leer. I am so sorry that I did not cherish you in those last months we had together. I am sorry I was not alive for you. I miss you desperately. I would do anything to bring you back to life. Anything for you, my Leer." I echo his words back to him, wondering if he felt a fraction as separated from me as I now feel from him.

"I would not have left you. Even given the choice to be with Valor, I would not have left you. I loved you then, every bit as much as I love you now. I want you to know that I forgive you. I know your heart. I know who you became to me. Our marriage was not perfect, but it was sweet. You were good to me, and, in spite of what I said in the midst of my deepest pain, I would have been content to stay with you. I am sorry for all those hateful words I threw at you. I wish that we could have reconciled. I wish that your love had not demanded such a price."

I sink my fingers into the heaps of evergreen. The overwhelming scent of pine reminds me of the time we made love in the woods. "You were right, my Leer. We were broken, but we could have been mended just as you promised." I weep from the sea of regret that seems boundless. "I am sorry I did not hear you. I have sought the words you spoke to me after we lost Illyanna, but no matter how hard I try, I cannot hear you. I am so angry with myself for shutting you out. I am sorry I did not mourn our daughter with you. I am sorry I forced you to face everything alone. Being alone is miserable. I am sorry for punishing you with that."

I fold over my knees, mourning Leer late into the night. Now that I am finally returned to his side, I do not want to be parted from him again. I wish so badly for his arms to come around me. To smell the spice of his skin. To hear his mellifluous laugh. To simply be with him.

Boldizar finds me beneath the starless sky, alternately pleading with the Almighty and speaking my every thought to Leer while Valor spares me from being truly alone.

"I want him back," I say to my Father as he joins me between their graves. "I would do anything to bring him back."

Father wraps his arms around me. "I would too."

"Why did it have to be like this?"

"I have been asking that question of the Creator most of my life." Father points to the left of Illyanna's grave.

The headstone is dark with age. The inscription reads *Lianara Rodiharian* and is dated thirty-six years ago. It is Leer's stillborn sister.

"My first daughter," Father says. "Celiea's heart nearly did not recover from that loss. Mine either."

Why? Why do this to them again? I ask the Creator.

"I cannot see with the Creator's sight to know the full scope of His plans. But I know that He loves us more than we can fathom. And He loves them too." Father sweeps his hand to all those he lost. His mother, father, and step-mother rest next to his daughter.

Valor said much the same thing to me. My gaze returns to my husband's grave. More tears flow from my eyes. "But Leer did not believe in Him. Leer trusted in himself."

"You do not know what happened? Ah, of course you do not. You were not yourself then."

I search Father's eyes that are so like Leer's—deepest brown flecked with black.

"During our afternoon talks, after Leer and Lorennt had their falling out," a mild description for what happened, "Leer told me everything. He told me what he did and the ways he wronged you. He told me of his guilt for not releasing you from the betrothal and the consequences of his actions."

I suspected Leer told him much, but I did not know he told him everything.

"You see, Leer's guilt was crushing him. He loved you with his whole heart and hated himself for what he did to you. Until you, he prided himself on never making a mistake so large that he could not atone for it, or so he thought. He confessed all to me and persisted in asking what he needed to do to atone for his sins. However, when you tried to end your life, he realized that nothing he could do would make up for the ways he had wronged you. He was finally broken. In abject humility, he asked the Almighty to lift the burden of his sin. He realized that he could not atone for what he did. He needed forgiveness."

"He had hope again," I say, marveling at this revelation. "I could see it in his eyes when we journeyed to the coast. He asked me for forgiveness, something he almost never did."

Father smiles. "Aye. He was changed. It was heartening to see. After decades of praying for my son to be redeemed, it was Leer's love for you that finally moved him from his complacency." Father kisses my brow. "You, Daughter, were used by the Almighty as an instrument of grace in Leer's life. His path to redemption was not easy, nor was it short. But he was redeemed. There is no doubt in my mind that he is in the arms of our Heavenly Father with Illyanna. My heart aches for what we have lost, but it is overjoyed at what was gained. Everyday I thank the Almighty for bringing you into our lives. You have been a blessing to us in a thousand ways. You were a blessing to your husband that reached into eternity."

I return my Father's embrace with tears of joy. Leer was redeemed.

He has everlasting life. Praise pours from my heart.

This is more evidence of the Almighty's good plans. In spite of the evil worked against us, He used everything bad and everything good to ultimately bring about my and Leer's redemption. And the Creator gave us a precious daughter. Though she is not here with me, Illyanna is with her father and her Creator.

Not even death can separate us from the love of our Heavenly Father.

Or from each other.

CHAPTER THIRTY-FOUR

ERIANNA

October 6th

I return from breakfast to find that the courier has already delivered my letters for the day. I sit on Leer's favorite couch in our parlor to open them. To my delight, a thick letter from Leelah resides in the stack. I discard the more necessary bits of business and settle in for this dessert before attending to my responsibilities. I devour the anecdotes she tells of the children and feel the miles between us fall away. Mercy, I would like to be in the valley with my friends! Though they are all hale, my heart constricts for Leelah as I read her last words.

My hope has grown to unreasonable levels. All is well so far, but please pray.

She has not lost her babe. *Almighty, be praised.*

Karris also sent me a letter and an assortment of pictures painted by her and the children. I head into my bedroom past Leer and my large poster bed to stare at the far wall. The tapestry of an ancient battle can take up residence in the lowest level of the castle to make way for these happy pictures. I especially like Micah's picture of a frog. With an eye to the clock, I pull down the tapestry, loosing a heap of dust, and manage to knock myself from the chair on which I was precariously balanced. A smart rap at the door is all the warning I have to hurry out from under the tapestry before Silla strolls into my foyer, calling for me.

"Already redecorating, I see." Silla glances about our room. "The king's taste was austere."

"I added my own touches to our parlor months back, but I never got around to addressing this room." Were she of a kinder disposition, I would also admit that I am now hesitant to change much of anything. Our memories are tied to these rooms. I am unwilling to reveal that much of my heart to Silla.

"Adorable," she says dryly of the artwork I hold up to the wall, deciding the best way to arrange it.

"I think so," I shoot back. "What brings you to my humble residence?"

"The menu for your brother's wedding has found its way to the nobility. Rumor has it that you do not favor him and his intended if you are truly planning on serving pottage."

My mouth twists wryly. *The horde gathers.* If only my Hand would return to my side to aid me in turning back the onslaught.

"Pottage is *one* of the courses on the menu." One Mother Celiea swooned over. "We have a kingdom to defend. I will spare no expenses on that front, but doing so means I must be frugal elsewhere."

Silla arches a brow. "I am not the one that needs convincing. Tis your court."

"You are my subtle connection to them. You could make my intentions known."

She considers her nails. "That would cost you extra, I am afraid."

Of course it would.

I return to my parlor and the stack of letters. The first round of requested audits arrived from Valor yesterday along with a note that simply said, *I miss you.*

Not nearly as much as I miss him, I would wager.

A notice from a business I have never patronized catches my attention. Apparently, my order is complete.

"Silla, do you know this shop?" I pass the note to her.

She glances at the paper. "It is a saddler's shop. He works almost exclusively with the military, constructing saddles and light armor."

A grin splits my face. "Does he?" I glance at the clock and decide that if I hurry, I can make the time to ride into the city today. "Feel like an outing?"

"Always," Silla's smile is more controlled than mine.

"Excellent. Tell your counterpart that we require his escort. No extensive guard will be needed."

Silla dips her chin to me and quickly turns away but not before I catch sight of the unaffected smile she tries to hide at the prospect of venturing into the city with Trent.

I straighten my parlor then enter my dressing room to affix my veil before the mirror. Nev and I help each other dress in the mornings since I refuse to take on a new lady's maid and she will not need one in less than a week. She will have a husband to assist her.

I fight back a surge of longing as my eyes drift to Leer's side of the dressing room. With no one to see, I allow myself a poignant relief and bury my face in his tunics that hang neatly. The spicy musk I grew to love clings faintly to his clothes. It was one of the first things I realized when I took refuge in our room after the funeral. The second was how cursed cold our bed is without him. What I would not give for his warmth at my back and arms to come around me!

I indulge my aching heart a moment longer then straighten my royal spine and set my mind to the tasks of the day. The clock has no compassion for my grief.

※ ※ ※

"What about my instructions was so difficult to understand?" I grumble to Trent. A contingent of no less than twenty soldiers crowds the street hemming us in. I cannot proceed through my city in the usual way with the excessive number of soldiers.

"Nothing. But you were overruled, Majesty."

I fix the dolt with a pointed look. "You do understand that I am the only person in this kingdom that cannot be overruled?"

"The head of your security disagreed." Trent's grin makes it plain who is to blame.

I roll my eyes behind my veil. Only two men in this kingdom would presume to tell me what to do, and I can still bring Lorennt to heel when necessary. "You may tell the self-proclaimed *head of my security* that I take exception to his interference."

"Are you certain? He said that if you cooperated I was to purchase you a treat for good behavior."

"Do not patronize me!" I bark.

"So you don't want the treat?"

"Of course I do you fool of a—"

"Language, Majesty," Silla cautions for my benefit. "There are many people in this city who still have a good opinion of you. Don't ruin it by speaking with the vulgarity of a soldier."

I settle for glaring daggers at Trent. Unfortunately, he has known me too long and is not cowed. He fixes me with a mocking rendition of the look I gave him.

"As fun as it would be to see her Majesty lose her temper in the middle of the street, we have arrived." Silla looses her arms from Trent's waist so he may dismount. She still doggedly asserts that she is incapable of riding a horse of her own. I have my doubts about the veracity of that. Trent takes his sweet time lowering Silla to the ground and releasing her. Neither does she hurry to remove her hands from his shoulders.

I swear under my breath, striding for the door of the saddler's shop only to be cut-off by one of my guards who enters before me to ensure no threats to my person are within. Valor had better return soon, because if not I am going back on my word and doing something decidedly reckless.

The saddler is unmoved by my title and speaks to me as he would to anyone else. I like him instantly. "I see you are quite anxious for your order, Majesty. I did not expect you for several days."

"I must admit, I am curious to see the results." Of which I can only guess.

The man gives a jerk of his head and retrieves a canvas wrapped bundle from the back of his shop. "Commander Ironforge assured me you would appreciate the design, though if it is too elaborate…"

I barely contain my excitement as I watch him untie the laces concealing my armor. I gasp as it is revealed. "May I try it on?"

He ushers me to a corner with a hazy mirror. I quickly remove my veil and sash. With efficient movements, the saddler teaches me how to fit the cuirass in place, something I am easily able to do without assistance. It laces under my arms to best protect my vitals. The rich brown leather is hardened and molded to my figure without hindering my movements. The shoulders are wide and protective. The body of the cuirass is decorated with feminine scrollwork that matches the scabbard of my dagger. Blue stitching pieces the armor together. It is so beautiful.

"The commander told me that your other cuirass had sheaths for knives sewn into it. I dissuaded him from such a design 'cause it weakens the leather protecting your vitals. Instead, he purchased these." He extends matching vambraces to protect my forearms with a knife sheath riveted in each. "These are solid pieces of armor."

I strap the vambraces in place, admiring my reflection. The saddler inspects the fit, nodding to himself. I draw the knives. They are perfectly balanced and could double as fighting daggers if need be.

The saddler takes a step back and crosses his arms. "There was one more thing."

I sheath the daggers, giving him my attention.

He swears under his breath then without meeting my eyes says, "The commander also said I was to make you some greaves to protect your fine legs."

Trent barks a laugh.

I flush. "His words, I assume?"

"Aye, Majesty. That I was ordered to repeat exactly." The tanner eyes my blades apprehensively, but they remain in their scabbards.

That thoughtful rogue. "Well I do not have my pants with me, so I shall save that fitting for another day."

"As you will, Majesty." The saddler bows and returns to the back of his shop.

"What do you think?" I turn to Silla.

She tilts her head to the side. "About the commander's unabashed admiration of you or the armor?"

Trent snickers.

"Careful, Silla. My retribution is tenfold," I remind her with a meaningful glance at Trent.

She grins. "It is good to have you back, Majesty."

❋ ❋ ❋

VALOR

October 9th

Eighteen blessed days and not a minute of rest among them. I am looking forward to a full night's sleep nearly as much as I am looking forward to being named a churlish oaf.

"So you gonna wrangle me an invitation to the wedding tomorrow?" Anders asks as we hand our destriers into the care of the stable lads. Granite makes a loud entrance, whistling and prancing down the aisle, waking the animals that have already bedded down for the night.

"If you promise to bathe between now and then. You will offend her majesty's delicate sensibilities otherwise," I quip with a critical eye to the mud-caked woodsman.

Anders snorts.

Though Malsihra and its occupants have shed their mourning grey in favor of vibrant gold and crimson to honor the prince's wedding, I find a petite shadow lurking in an alcove, observing the gaiety. I train my eyes upon her as I cross the great hall and see her expression soften though she has not yet shifted her focus to me. I wonder if she truly can feel my eyes on her or if she would still know I am near if I withheld my gaze. It is a question that will likely never have an answer, because I cannot prevent my eyes from settling on her when we are in the same space.

"Should I always expect an eleventh hour entrance from you because you are incapable of reading a calendar, or is this simply a more elaborate means of pestering me?" Erianna's frosty words do not match the repose of her stance.

"I must say, I liked your last greeting much better." I reprove her with a scowl. "You could at least pretend to care whether or not I have returned with all my limbs attached."

With a long suffering sigh, she shifts her attention to me. "You seem fine."

"That is all you have to say? I bring you another soldier to aid in the Great Pottage War and you cannot even manage a 'good eve' for my trouble?"

"You are late to the war, I am afraid. Thankfully, I did not sustain fatal injuries." Erianna looks past me. "If you mean to stay in my castle, Anders, I will not tolerate you muddying the floor like a dog. Get down to the kitchen and have baths ordered for you and the commander."

Anders sketches a bow. "With all haste, Majie. I can see you've a commander to take to task." Flakes of dried mud fall off the bushy eyebrows he wags at her.

"Indeed." She mutters darkly then strides across the great hall, motioning one of her guards to follow.

I close the door to her office that has been restored to order and tastefully decorated since our skirmish. Erianna stands in the middle of the room with her back to me. "Woman, if you do not greet me properly, I am afraid you are going to have another reason to be put out with me for the liberty I intend to take."

"Then we had best get this over with," she resignedly says then turns a bright smile on me and runs into my arms.

I catch her, lifting her off her feet. *Home. This is what home feels like.*

"Tell me you are well," she pleads against my neck. "Tell me you are not late because you were set upon."

"I am well. We were not set upon. But we did take an opportunity to kill a few wolves when they attempted to harry our mounts."

She pulls back, and I set her on her feet although I would rather hold her close till dawn.

"Wipe away that concern." I touch her porcelain face, smoothing the worry lines. "None of your soldiers were harmed, and we only lost one pack horse. The cowardly Ruphiri did not dare show their faces but sent the wolves to attack the horses in the night. We slept half-awake at all times and met their only attack decisively, felling many of their dogs before they retreated."

"How does that not qualify as being set upon!" She slaps my arm.

I grunt. "None of that. I am spent."

Concern returns to her face. Her hands grasp mine, leading me to a plush chair. I drop into it, feeling the last hundred miles in every weary muscle. I prop my elbow and drop my head in my hand, viewing her through bleary eyes. The motivation that kept me beating a path toward this moment is satisfied. The exhaustion I relegated quickly becomes vengeful, overwhelming my faculties. "Did you have any adventures while I was away?"

"No. However, would you mind telling me why I had a veritable army of guards while on a simple errand in my own city?"

"Your knack for finding trouble in the safest of places necessitates preventative measures." I packaged that response the moment I adjusted the number of guards assigned to her weeks ago.

Her temper sparks. "Which I was willing to tolerate until a saddler relayed a compliment about my 'fine legs' in front of absolutely everyone, you churlish oaf!"

I chuckle into my hand. *Now, I can sleep.*

"You made the poor saddler horribly uncomfortable. Though Trent and Silla found it funny."

"Are they still working out if they want to be combatants or lovers?" I mutter my question.

"Silla is leading him on a merry chase, but they are leaning toward the latter."

My eyes are heavy when honeyed lips kiss my cheek. "Thank you for my armor. It is perfect."

I smile without opening my eyes. "I want your 'thank you' when I am awake and can thoroughly enjoy it."

"Rogue," she whispers and kisses me again. "Come. Your bath is ready by now. Then you may sleep."

My groggy mind blends her into those actions. "It is an ancient tradition for the lady of the castle to aid her honored guests in bathing. Let's revive it."

Erianna snorts. "Oh, you have no decency when you are tired, do you?"

"Sorry." I would not have been sorry had she agreed.

"I shall grant you mercy just this once." Erianna's hands find mine as she pulls me to my feet.

"Knew you were generous."

CHAPTER THIRTY-FIVE

VALOR

October 10th

The wedding is a lavish event. More than one noble is forced to swallow their words about the queen not favoring the bride and groom. It seems her majesty favors them highly. This wedding is declared to be every bit as extravagant as her own. Only a few of us know that in addition to her heavy load these past weeks, she worked tirelessly to find ways to reuse and make-do, achieving these results at a fraction of the normal expenditures for such an event. Even the course of pottage is delicious, and Kragorn knows why.

"This is Leelah's recipe," he declares after a bite.

"Your wife is a wonderful cook," Erianna says. "I returned to the castle with several of her recipes to help me do more with less. She is a wonder with such things."

Kragorn proudly agrees and tucks into the soup with enthusiasm.

Erianna offered to send for his family to attend the wedding, but Kragorn declined the offer since Leelah prefers to avoid rigorous activity during the beginning of her pregnancies. Erianna understood her caution.

Dinner concludes with appreciative sounds all around. Lorennt and Nev have eyes only for each other as the queen calls the musicians to play. The prince leads his bride to the dance floor amidst polite applause. Their joy is a sight to behold, though the queen's eyes drift continuously around the room with a calculating gleam.

"What are you looking for?" I ask her.

She forces a pleasant smile to cover her sharp words. "Noting anyone who does not appear pleased for my brother and his bride."

"Wise," I reply and join her in the task. Unfortunately, there are quite a few that fall into that category.

When the nobility join the prince and his bride for the second set of dances, the queen politely but resolutely declines several offers to dance. She places herself between Kragorn and I to dissuade anyone else from approaching her. The strategy works against the noblemen, however, it does not intimidate her royal brother.

"Have you ever seen such a radiant bride as mine?" Lorennt declares, kissing Nev's cheek. "None could possibly compare to her."

Erianna is all smiles for them. "Without question, there has never been such a beautiful bride."

Lorennt is pleased with his sister's praise, but ever sensitive Nev will not allow anything that could be a slight to someone else. "Lorennt, that is quite an exaggeration. Erianna was a more beautiful bride to be sure."

Erianna turns the compliment back to Nev without hesitation. "Any of my beauty was owing to you, Nev. You are a wonder with cosmetics."

Having seen Erianna on her wedding day, I know without a doubt she was a vision, but underneath it, she was falling apart. The greater amount of Nev's radiance this day comes from her joy and love. She nearly glows.

Lorennt placates his wife with a smile. "You are right. Erianna was *comely*, indeed."

Erianna gives an exaggerated eye roll. "A split lip on your wedding day, Brother? Tell me you are not so foolish as that."

Her retort seems exactly was Lorennt was aiming for. "It seems I have a beating to talk my way out of. Commander, I entrust you with the safekeeping of my bride until my return." He takes Erianna in hand, dragging her toward the dancing couples.

"Lorennt, I do not wish to dance," she hisses, all trace of her smile vanishing. She goes so far as to dig her heels in while trying not to draw more attention to herself.

Lorent insists. "Nonsense. You have never turned me down. I will not allow you to begin now."

The rest of their disagreement is drowned by the music echoing in the great hall as they begin to dance. Lorennt deftly turns what seems to be an emotional point for Erianna into a challenge, knowing precisely how to goad her into action. Their movements around the room, though flawless, present as a sort of battle. It is a sight to behold.

Lorennt leads Erianna through increasingly complex patterns that she executes without a single misstep. I had no idea she was this accomplished.

"They dance so well," Nev sighs. "I am glad Lorennt coerced her. Dancing is one of her favorite things."

"Then why did she fight him?"

Nev's sympathy for her friend dims her joy. "Because she finally gave her heart to Leer when they were dancing."

Lorennt says something that pushes Erianna to this side of happiness, but the contrary woman would rather be cross, so she fights a smile. Lorennt continues plucking whatever chords he found with her until Erianna's melodic laugh floats on the air.

Nev's smile echoes hers as she continues her explanation. "When Leer and Erianna danced, they became the focal point of the evening, though they did not notice. It was more than skill. The affection they held for each other was always subdued in company. But when they danced, they seemed unable to conceal their love. It was expressed through their movements and the music, a rare moment in which they were in perfect harmony. He flawlessly led, and she faithfully followed."

"But now her dance partner is gone," I conclude.

"I think there is another for her," Nev says pointedly.

"I am out of my element. I cannot compare to that." I nod toward the queen and prince who execute a series of whirls too intricate to follow. A decade of practice would be insufficient to bring me up to their skill.

"You are missing the point I am trying to make. Ability has nothing to do with it. Erianna's heart shows when she dances. That is what was mesmerizing. Look around. Though Erianna and Lorennt are laughing and showing off to a degree of which Leer would have disapproved, they have not stolen the room."

Nev is right. If anything, some of the court looks upon the queen and prince with disapproval for their flamboyance.

"Valor, I am going to tell you something that she would probably not be pleased with me for saying on her behalf, but her sadness in the moments she believes no one is looking breaks my heart. I want her to have love again." Nev lowers her voice so that I barely catch her words. "I was there when she placed the treasure box in your room. Though she was committed to her marriage and loved her husband, she came alive in a way I had never seen when she spoke of you. You are her other half. She needs you."

The dance concludes with a round of applause.

I have no idea how we have circled back around to this topic over something as innocuous as asking *why does Erianna not want to dance*? I refute it in the same way now as when Nev has cornered me here before. "She will not welcome my pursuit. She is in mourning."

"Then bring her out of it," Nev hurries her words. "You love a woman whose loyalty and stubbornness will not make it easy for her to let go of her self-imposed segregation. She needs your help."

Nev's words muddy the water that I thought clear when I vowed to help her maintain her state of mourning. How long does that promise stand? Until she indicates her mourning is over? Or would she cling to it even to the point that she does herself emotional harm?

I tuck away what Nev said for closer examination later. My all too perceptive friend is eyeing me. I use humor to set aside the intensity of Nev and my conversation as they join us. "Who won? It seemed my queen took an early victory, but his highness rallied."

"I won," they both declare then size each other up.

"Clearly, I was the favorite," Erianna asserts.

"Could you not simply give me my due without argument?" Lorennt retorts. "It is my wedding day."

Erianna croons, "I did not realize you were so desperate for a victory. Of course I will give it to you. Consider it a wedding gift."

Lorennt grimaces. "Now I do not want it. Take your ill gotten victory and be gone with you."

The queen grins, including me in her fun. "Isn't it adorable that he thinks he can toss me from my castle?"

Nev giggles, steering her outraged husband toward the dancers.

I mockingly whisper, "Best let him thinks he has such power. He might throw a tantrum that could make yours seem mild."

"Do you mean to imply that *I* throw tantrums?" Erianna arches a threatening brow.

"The likes of which might incite a lesser man to tie you up."

She leans closer, winter eyes sparkling. "I still have not paid you back for that bit of humiliation. Perhaps I ought to start wearing that scarf again to have a means at the ready when an opportunity presents itself."

I catch a silken lock of her hair twisting it around my finger and testing the line between us. "I hope you do. I brought it with me—for practical reasons, you understand. My hair can be quite unruly at times."

Erianna's laugh is a bit breathless. "I have noticed."

"But I could return it to you for safe keeping. In fact, I am incredibly optimistic that your hair will need it again." I slowly release the raven lock. "Eventually."

Sadness edges out the sparkle in her eyes. "Maybe you could keep it a while longer? I am not the most trustworthy with scarves right now. I would hate to tear it."

I trace the edge of the veil framing her face. "I imagine it would be difficult to be responsible for the demands of a scarf." I open my left hand to her in the scant space between us. "Maybe you could manage something less demanding? Like safe-keeping my hand for a few minutes. I am about to do something incredibly daunting. I could use the help of a friend with far more experience."

She catches her lip in her teeth, vacillating. I remain steady, giving her all the time she needs to make her decision. Emotions war on her face. I know I could easily prod her into dancing the same way Lorennt did. I am a self-made expert at heckling her. But I want her to know this means more to me too. It could be a cornerstone in building a future with her. This is the woman I want to protect and cherish for the rest of my life. I refuse to rush her and ruin our beginning.

Uncertainty tugs her away from me, so I make one last plea. "Since we met, you are the only one I have entrusted with this particular activity, in all its various iterations," I add with a wink. A becoming blush tinges her exquisite face. "I am quite certain no one else is equal to the task. It must be you or no one."

Hope briefly flickers in her eyes then is snuffed by her past. "You might come to reconsider your choice after a time. You may prefer another woman to me."

A prayer for wisdom caps the surge of rage at her faithless husband. Anger would undermine what I need to instill. I draw on our history and the trust she once gave me. "My Erianna. That is not a wound I dealt you. But know this. It will be my hand that pulls the glass from your side and sutures you."

Her lip quivers on an exhale while my own breath is bated. Then she raises her hand to mine.

Hurried footsteps register a moment before Trent blocks the dancers from view. "I need to speak with you both."

My beholden thoughts to the man are burned up in an instant. Erianna's hand drops to her side, and the queen reappears, concealing the woman I love.

My teeth threaten to crack from the force of my temper grinding them. "Trent, the city had better be on fire or you are going to receive the beating of your life."

"You will wish you hadn't said that," Trent tightly replies. "The Ruphiri have invaded the city and are setting fire to the west side."

CHAPTER THIRTY-SIX

ERIANNA

My heart drops into my stomach. Not the west side of the city. It is the poorer, more populace section located far from the military barracks and any kind of meaningful aid. The faces of those that live there flash before my eyes. My people.

Valor recovers quickly. "Is the portcullis closed and the castle secure?"

"Aye. The city guard is engaging the Ruphiri. Do we tell the prince?" Trent asks.

"I do not see how we can avoid it," Valor says.

"No."

They both look at me. One thought rises above the tumult in my mind. *Protect them.* "These are my people. This is my family. I will not allow my enemy to ruin this day for them. We take care of this quietly."

"He would want to know," Valor argues.

"If he knows now, he will want to ride into the city with us, and Zavaan will target him. The Vragh takes sick pleasure in destroying families. I will tell him tomorrow, after his wedding and after we have driven them from our city."

"You are not coming," Valor snaps.

I hold my ground. "You will not gainsay me, Commander. Ensure the castle is secure and rally as many soldiers as we can spare from the castle without leaving it vulnerable."

"Anders is doing that now, Your Majesty," Trent says.

"The guests should not leave tonight. It will not be safe," Valor states.

I nod while forming a plan. My servants will all resign tomorrow from the overwhelming work I am about to cause them, but there is no way around it. "Alright. Get Kragorn. I will handle everything here then meet you in the lower bailey."

Terse acknowledgment precedes action.

Now, to manage Lorennt.

※ ※ ※

The concentration of horses and men in the lower bailey raises a cloud of steam in the frigid night air. I push my cloak behind my shoulders to free my movements then tighten the buckles of my vambraces. I have not practiced in my new armor yet. I was waiting for Valor's return and had planned on using my unoccupied day tomorrow to acquaint myself with every particular of fighting in it. While going into battle with unfamiliar gear is a risk, going without it is a larger one.

I easily discern Valor from the other soldiers by his size. He moves among them, doling out orders. "Disable them only. We need prisoners, but be prepared. They are lethal, without conscience. Do not underestimate them."

I gain his side, exuding more confidence than I feel.

"Do you have anything to add, Your Majesty?" If Valor resents my presence, he masks it well. I can only hope that the gift of my new armor was not merely symbolic. I shall know soon enough.

I gaze upon the faces of men who will likely not all return to the castle alive. I do not want to sound like I am giving them a farewell speech, but neither do I want them to think they are merely bodies to throw at my problems. I see them.

"I thank you for your courage." Intensity of feeling carries my voice to each man here. "I have every confidence that you will oust these murderers from our city. We do not yield to terror in the night. We meet it with swift justice. The Almighty goes before us. We will not fail."

My words harden the steel of their will. I can feel it in the air.

Valor's words put a razor sharp edge on it. "Your queen rides with you into this battle. Ensure she returns. I will not live to see her captured again."

The portcullis is raised, permitting our egress. I ordered that the gate not be opened for anyone going or coming until our return. Only Valor, Kragorn, and I have the authority to open the gate. I specifically ordered that should Prince Lorennt seek to leave, he be turned back on my order. I know what Zavaan means by attacking on this day. I will not give him the satisfaction of destroying the Rodiharian line.

The sky over the west side of my city glows orange against the low hanging clouds. We move toward it as quickly as is safe down the cobbled streets, and I prepare myself for what awaits. I have seen contingents of soldiers ravaged by the Ruphiri, my own husband murdered before my eyes. Foolishly, I expect something like that carnage. I am utterly wrong.

Buildings burn and collapse, shooting sparks into the sky. Falling snow turns to vapor far above the heat of the blaze. Acrid smoke chokes the air that is filled with my people's screams as they flee the marauders. Black cowled wraiths move through the chaos, cutting the defenseless down as indiscriminately as the few brave souls who resist. The high pitched wails of infants and children pierce my heart.

Waves of emotion surge through me.

Disbelief. Terror. Horror. Anger. Rage. Bloodlust.

The last pounds a drum beat in my heart.

Bloodlust.

What I felt toward Tergehn was only the crust of the molten ore pouring through my veins.

"*Vreh Král Vragh!*" I command Valor. "This ends tonight!"

"Agreed." The glow of the fire writhes across the face of my warrior, describing his wrath with crimson hues. "Form an escape route for the women and children. Defend them. Let the soldiers engage the enemy."

"You have my word," I give him the vow he needs to free him from the distraction of my presence.

Valor draws his sword and enters the melee with Trent while the guard fifty strong turns with me. We create a wall at the fringe of the chaos providing our people somewhere safe to flee. The Ruphiri stay far back from our line, cutting off our people's escape. Anders and the rest of our soldiers launch themselves at the enemy who are more intent on murdering my people than challenging my soldiers.

The terrified screams of children draw my attention. Three wolves corner a mother and her brood against a building. She passes her infant to her eldest, hiding her children behind her with arms spread wide, using her body as a shield.

They will be ravaged.

Revolted by what I am about to behold, I dig my heels into Sacha's sides, drawing daggers. Sacha is no warhorse and tosses her head in fear, but obeys me regardless. I slide her around an abandoned cart, guiding her through the crush. The wolves taunt and snap at the little family while drawing ever closer. One lunges at the mother, but she kicks the animal. It catches her skirt in its teeth, shaking viciously, dragging her away from her babes.

A savage battle cry tears out of my throat. I hurl my dagger the moment I am in range. It sinks into the spine of the wolf, killing it instantly. I charge Sacha at the remaining two who narrowly evade her shod hooves. I loose a second then third dagger, felling them. "Run!" I order the mother, pointing her in the direction of our defensive wall.

She obeys without hesitation, herding her children to safety. I scan my immediate vicinity then swing to the ground, keeping a tight hold on Sacha's reins while I retrieve my daggers. I hastily wipe the blood on my pants and sheath them, hearing more terrified screams and snarling wolves. I swing to the saddle, searching out others, urging Sacha through the fray. Around the edges of the battle, wolves prey on those fortunate enough to elude the flashing steel of the Ruphiri.

My eyes skip over the children I was too late to help, refusing to let that horror sink into my heart yet.

I am never going to sleep again.

A gargantuan soldier fights his way to my side, cutting down wolves with his sword while I take a wailing child whose leg is torn open on the fore of my saddle. I hold the boy close and shepherd him and his family back to the wall of soldiers that has swelled with reinforcements. I hand the boy down to his father who balances the injured child in one arm while clutching a toddler in the other.

Anders stands between me and the frenzy. "You look to need a personal guard, Majie."

"I will not watch idly while my people die!"

He grins despite the gore dripping from his blade. "Good. I'd be disappointed if you did. Back to it then?"

My contention is thrown off course.

"Think this belongs to you." Anders extends the hilt of my throwing dagger, wiped clean. I slide it into my left vambrace. "You are frighteningly good with those. Might even be able to outdo the commander."

The sounds of battle clamor against my senses. "Of course I can," I bluster, wheeling Sacha into the battle.

Anders wields his sword at my side while I hurl daggers and ferry my people out of this nightmare. All our hours training together pay off in dividends. We easily anticipate each other's movements and settle into a rhythm.

Hustle. Throw. Hack. Retreat. Over and again.

Shrieks behind me, deeper in the frenzy, turn me from our current rescue. A flaming building is near collapse. Sooty figures dart from an alley stalked by a Ruphiri. My gut intuition propels me toward them before my mind overlays meaning to what I see.

The building engulfed in flames is Mistress Getty's dress shop.

The figures are those of Jace, his mother Tessie, and his sister Bett.

The Ruphiri is Bronis.

Panic whips my bloodlust into recklessness. The building groans as I race past. With deafening noise, it disintegrates into a heap of burning rubble, expelling thick smoke and tiny bits of scorched fabric into the air.

"Jace! Bett!" I frantically call. I cannot see past Sacha's ears. I cough violently from the smoke burning a path down my throat into my lungs.

"Jace!" Another voice shouts for the boy. I guide Sacha that direction, but she is so frightened she balks. I leap to the ground, leading her forward.

I nearly trip over the prone form of Bett. Her mother Tessie kneels at her side.

"Majesty!" Tessie exclaims. "We lost Jace!"

Bett sobs on the ground, clutching her leg that is bent at a sickening angle. I force my watering eyes to stay open, searching for the boy, but I cannot see him. Sacha wheezes and chokes on the smoke. I make a snap decision. "Tessie, help me put Bett in the saddle."

"But Jace!" The desperate mother argues.

I shake her. "Do as I say! I will find Jace. You must get Bett out of here, or she will die."

Tessie turns to her daughter. With as little jostling as possible, we heft the girl into the saddle. I turn Sacha's reins over to Tessie. "That way," I point. "I will bring Jace out. Go to our soldiers, they will take you to safety."

They weep but obey. I pat Sacha in gratitude and call for Jace, not forgetting for a second who was in pursuit of this precious family as I unsheathe the dagger from my leg.

"Jace!" I pray my voice carries on the smoky air. Slowly, I walk toward the collapsed building, eyes roving the darkness.

I pick out a child's voice crying for his mother amid the greedy roar of the fire. I breathe through the cloth tied around my face, pressing it closer to prevent the soot from entering my lungs. I remain quiet to follow his voice.

Silhouetted in the smoke is Jace. Frantically, I call to him. He spins in a circle at my familiar voice. I close the distance between us with my hand outstretched. "Are you hurt?"

"I lost mother and Bett!" He wails.

"I found them. They are safe and charged me with bringing you out." I take hold of his small hand, leading him back the way I came, but everywhere is smoke. I scan ahead and behind, unsure where to go. I was so focused on finding Jace that I forgot to mind where I was.

Racking coughs shake the boy.

"Tuck your nose inside your shirt. Breathe through the fabric," I instruct, but it does not seem to help him. With one hand, I keep a firm hold on Jace and walk with my dagger outstretched in the other until I come upon a brick wall. I follow it around a corner until it gives way to the front of a building. *Thank you, Heavenly Father! Please lead us out of this!*

As the smoke thins, I risk a bit more speed to sooner deliver us from its oppression. The outlines of buildings and rubble come into view as I drag Jace along behind me. Blessedly, we emerge from the worst of it though we are on the opposite side of the battle, far from the protection of Anders and our wall of soldiers. The soldiers here are intent on pursuing the Ruphiri and have not formed a defensive wall.

"We must double back." I search for a street I recognize then dash for it.

"What about mother and Bett?"

"We will search for them after—"

My words are cut off as lightning flashes across my vision, and I fly backward. I lose my grip on Jace and my dagger, but the ground is only too willing to catch my body on its unforgiving surface.

I blink, disoriented. I cannot see out of my left eye. My fingers search for the cause. My eye is still there, but my fingers are slick with blood. I move them higher. Sharp pain lances across my face. I force myself to probe the injury. A gash splits open my brow surrounded by unbearable throbbing. What happened?

"Jace," I croak, rolling to my hands and knees.

It is a tactical error I was warned never to make. The boot that stomps me into the cobblestones proves it.

A guttural chuckle casts me into a well of fear. "That makes three

303

times I have caught you, little Queen. But it will not be the third time you escape me."

CHAPTER THIRTY-SEVEN

ERIANNA

Bronis grabs a fistful of my braided hair, arching my head back to see him—not that I can see for the pain painting my vision black. My hearing, however, still works perfectly well. "This time, I will make sure you cannot even crawl before delivering you to your master." The barbaric Ruphiri dialect of Limban grates in my ears.

Not bothering to take a less painful hold on me, Bronis drags me by my hair over stone and debris down an alley. I claw at his hand, screaming at the pain and praying the noise brings aid running before I am completely hidden from the view of my soldiers further down the street. In the clamor of the night, it seems unlikely. Momentary relief stalls my willful struggle as he drops me to the ground.

I cannot draw breath before Bronis attacks, kicking my ribs. My hardened cuirass blunts the bone-breaking force, which he all too soon realizes. He flips me to my back, considering me.

My head aches fiercely, causing my vision to waver. *Almighty, keep me lucid! Show me what to do!*

Bronis circles me, perverse delight in his expression. "How has your shoulder fared? I dislocated it at our last encounter."

"Your memory is flawed. I dislocated it *myself* during my escape. I wonder which of the scars on your face I dealt you? I hope I did not bring you to tears against the heel of my boot." My gibe lands with the confidence of a woman armed and on her feet, neither of which I am.

"A pity the *Král Vragh* likes your tongue so much. I would enjoy feeding it to you after I sever it."

"Try," I dare, hoping he takes the bait and comes close enough for me to put a dagger through his temple.

"Someday. But first, I will hear you say 'Master Reuel' a few thousand times."

That is a more chilling threat, to be sure. I hide my fear with defiance. "I will never say it again."

"You will say it this very night. He awaits you on the edge of the city."

Zavaan is not here?

Bronis stands at my feet, eyeing me. I realize what he intends a second before he stomps a boot on my lower leg. I jerk aside before he can snap my bone and retaliate with a kick of my own to his opposite knee. I do not wait to see him stumble but vault to my feet. The earth pitches violently, hurling me into the wall of the alley. I grapple along the bricks toward the orange hazed street but not quickly enough.

Bronis smacks my head against the stone and pins me between the wall and his body before I collapse. "Fight, little Queen. I enjoy the struggle."

I spit in his face that is inches from mine.

Malevolent laughter rather than outrage coils through the air. "It seems I must remove a few of your claws before turning you over to Zavaan."

I cannot abide that.

The defiance in my eyes elicits a pleased chortle. Then his hands loose me. "Go ahead. Show me your claws."

The steel of my and Leer's daggers sing as I bring them to hand. I know without a doubt I am no match for Bronis. Even so, I am not going quietly, this night or any other.

Bronis does not draw his own weapons. His venomous appraisal is, in itself, a weapon. I want to run. I want to hide. But I raise my daggers instead.

I relegate the throbbing in my head and launch myself at my enemy. Bronis's delight makes me search for a way out. I know he is only toying with me as he deflects my attacks. He does not restrain himself as Valor and Anders do. I feel the full force of each defensive block as if I am striking the curtain wall around the city, not a man made of flesh. I am so far outmatched it seeds fear. My mind plays out the conclusion of this match even as I give my all to change the ending.

Bronis's laughter at my impotence makes me cringe. I strike with what could have been a gut-spilling cut, but he deflects and punches with such power that my bones shudder. I am thrown off balance and cannot right myself before Bronis's hands clamp on my wrists. He brings me to ground none too gently, jarring loose a scream I cannot hold back.

It is over, Erianna who is not enough, the Deceiver's insidious voice spears my courage. *You only make it worse for yourself by resisting.*

I scream again as Bronis's elbow connects with my thigh. My leg jerks with pain then goes numb. I will never be able to run like this. If I cannot run, I cannot escape.

My head pounds with renewed intensity. My limbs shake from exhaustion. The might of my enemy is unconquerable. I am beaten.

The Spirit of Truth proclaims, *My grace is sufficient for you. My strength is made perfect in your weakness. I chose the weak things of the world to shame the strong.*

A sharp crack sounds in my ears then Bronis's hands fall away.

"Let her go!" Jace courageously shouts from the mouth of the alley then hurls another rock. Bronis has no choice but to duck to the side to avoid the missile. Jace reaches for another rock from the pile at his feet. The bravery of the sweet boy resoundingly proves that the might of the Almighty at work in us far exceeds what evil men possess.

Give me Your strength, I ask, believing He is able.

Bronis reaches for a dagger, but mine is faster. I cross my body, cutting a deep line of crimson across his face. I bring my knee up between his legs with everything I have and roll from beneath him as he loses his grasp on me. Bronis bellows with murderous rage. If we do not escape, I have no more cause to fear Zavaan's retribution. My life will end this night.

I dart away, half crawling, as I try and fail to get my feet beneath me. The earth pitches, my leg muscle seizes, and I stumble. Jace rushes to me, taking my hand in his little ones to guide me in a straight line while I focus all my concentration on keeping my legs moving. Bronis's guttural fury at the humiliation of being bested by a woman and a child shakes the brick walls. He has no idea that it is the Almighty's strength in us he fights against.

We break from the shadows of the alley, racing for freedom. Bronis's growls raise the hair on my nape. I glance over my shoulder to see him charge from the alley like a ferocious beast roused from its den. He fairly flies at us, so quickly does he overtake the precious steps of freedom we gained.

"Help!" I scream, praying our soldiers hear me. I nearly cry when the reassuring warmth of Valor's gaze lands heavy on me.

Before I can call to him, Bronis yanks me off my feet and slams me to the ground, expelling the breath from my lungs. Stars burst in my eyes when the back of my head connects with stone then again as knuckles like rocks hit my cheek before I can guard against them. When Bronis finishes with me, Jace will pay with his life for helping me.

"Run!" I grunt between punches to my armored sides.

My plea is drowned as a thunderclap booms ahead of a storm. It explodes with unparalleled wrath at my enemy.

Steel flashes. Rage thunders. I close my eyes against the tempest, drawing an arm over my aching head.

Let him be righteous, I pray. *Help him be just.*

"Do not watch," I command Jace when he kneels at my side. He does not obey.

A velvet whiskered nose *wuffs* against my arm and soft lips nibble my shirt. I bat it away, but the bossy animal is insistent.

"You may as well be useful." I fumble my way from Granite's muzzle up to his neck, using him to pull myself to sitting. The helpful destrier lifts his head and hoists me to my feet. I bury my fingers in his mane, leaning against his powerful neck to hold myself upright while the world spins around me. I extend my hand to Jace, hugging him against my waist, urging his head to look away from the bloodshed.

The storm abates with a final clash. Steel whines as it is reunited with its scabbard. I feel Valor's gaze wash over me, and I turn to meet it. Soot blackens his imposing form, obscuring even the golden brown of his hair. Perspiration streaks down his face, exposing the flesh of the thunderous warrior. Blood darkens his armor and the legs of his pants where he cleaned his sword more than a few times this night. He has never looked more menacing, yet all I want to do is run into him and be held in the safest arms I have ever known.

The boy clinging to me is terrified. He hides half concealed behind me as Valor approaches. "Jace, this is my very best friend. We are safe with him." The boy tenses until another bout of coughing seizes him.

I reach for the water skin on Granite's saddle, but I cannot get my eyes and hands to agree where it is. Sure hands slip around me and free it from the saddle, transferring it to the child who gulps the water.

I relax as Valor probes my tender scalp, locating the other knots on my head. When he finishes his perusal, I release my steadying grip on the horse in favor of the embrace of the man. He looses a held breath, carefully supporting me.

"The Vragh is not in the city," I croak. "That was Bronis, his second." The body of that man lies in a heap.

Valor's voice is gruff and raw from the smoke. "Your uncanny ability to find the worst trouble in any situation astounds me."

"A hidden talent," I quip.

"A heart stopping talent," he corrects.

"Sorts of flattery goes to your head." That rejoinder did not come out quite right. "You know what I meant."

"You, my Girl, are concussed." Valor's tone is tinged with worry.

"Must be. Thought I heard you say 'my Girl.' I know that cannot be right."

"When I said earlier that I needed you to help me through something daunting, this is not what I meant."

"To be fair," I smirk, "I also thought dancing would be the most frightening thing I did this night."

"Frightening..." He intones then shakes his head. "The Ruphiri are on the run. Our soldiers are assisting with the rescue efforts and putting out fires. It is time you return to the castle. Is—"

"Jace too," I interject. "Till we find his mother and sister."

"Jace too," he agrees. "Is Sacha nearby?"

"I lent her to Jace's mother. They cannot be far."

Jace coughs fitfully in the choking air.

"We cannot stay here any longer," Valor declares then lifts me from the ground to Granite's saddle and swings up behind me. Valor extends his hand to Jace, but the boy refuses to ride with us.

"Please, Jace. Only until we—" Coughing interrupts my plea, burning my chest and my throat like fire, but that pain is mild compared to what it does to my concussed head. My vision blackens, and I sway, desperately grabbing a fistful of Valor's sleeve. I needn't have worried. His arm wrapped around my waist holds me secure. I feel small hands press the water skin into my hand.

"Jace," Valor's commander voice brings a conclusion to the matter, "Our queen is injured. I must return her to the castle, but she will not leave you. You must come with us so the physician can tend her."

The boy is convinced. Valor lifts Jace to Granite's rump.

The Ruphiri have gone, but my city is desecrated. Bodies litter the streets. A few are my soldiers. Most are common folk driven from their beds when their homes were set on fire. Too many are children.

Overwhelmed, I lay my head against Valor's chest. "Much of the west side is uninhabitable. Our people need somewhere to go."

"Kragorn ordered tents set up in the training yards of the city barracks and is directing all the people there."

"Good. They will need provisions, blankets, and..." My thoughts scatter under the pounding in my head.

"It will be taken care of."

I do not allow my eyes to close against the horror of what the Ruphiri did. I look upon it as the one person in this kingdom most responsible for protecting its people.

I failed them.

Of all the cities in the kingdom, this one should not have been breached. It is walled. It is heavily patrolled. It is defended.

I hold tightly to the one question that demands an answer. *How did the Ruphiri invade Malsihra?*

※ ※ ※

VALOR

I rally a contingent to escort us back to the castle. There is much to be done this night, but until I ensure my queen safe and cared for, I cannot attend to any of it. The full measure of the destruction will not be known till the morrow. The death toll will take even longer to be reckoned. The rubble must first be carted out of the city to uncover the bodies trapped inside the collapsed buildings. There are also those who have yet to die from smoke inhalation but will soon succumb. I fear Erianna's little friend Jace might be among them.

I thank the Creator again that I was close when she ran from the alley, barely staying upright, her face covered in blood. My heart nearly beat out of my chest between hearing her cry for help and impaling the murderous villain on my sword.

"By order of the Queen, raise the portcullis!" I call out when Granite's hooves alight on the bridge into the castle.

Erianna moans at my raised voice. The physician shall be summoned immediately to give his opinion on her concussion and treat the wheezing lad behind me. I need to learn the best ways to counteract the effects of smoke in the lungs. Hopefully, some of the people taking refuge in the barracks across the city can be saved.

The castle is eerily quiet compared to the tumult in the city. I marvel at the extent of Erianna's powers to calm upheaval. So I do not aggravate her aching head, I ask softly, "What did you say to the wedding guests to convince them to stay without a fight?"

Moonlight exposes her bloodied, battered face as she tilts her head back to see me. I know I did right by bringing Bronis down as quickly as possible, but violence thrums in my veins, making me wish that he was alive and I alone with him to carve my own vengeance into his festering hide.

"After I sent Lorennt and Nev above-stairs, I 'invited' all the guests to seek beds in the castle this eve so that 'our celebrations may continue into the breaking of our fast together.'" She attempts an eye roll at the formal nonsense then swears at the pain it exacerbates.

"Brilliant. How did you manage to send the wedded couple from their own celebration?"

"That was rather simple." She drolly explains, "With their own best interests in mind, I noted how tired Nev was looking and reminded my brother that pregnant women tend to fall asleep early in the evening. Without delay, Lorennt escorted his bride to their nuptial chamber."

I chuckle and kiss her sooty head. "You, my Queen, are quite persuasive."

"I am glad you approve. Because I charge you with protecting me from Lorennt and I when he learns that I once again kept something of monumental importance from him." Her expression becomes pained as she lays her head on my shoulder.

"Erianna?"

"It is not easy being queen. My sympathy for Leer grows each day."

I neither agree nor disagree with the last part, but place another kiss on her head. I am gaining ground in forgiving Grandileer, but my heart is nowhere near sympathetic. "I will always protect you."

Everything is discreetly set in motion, including the changing of the guard to send fresh troops into the city to replace those that I withdrew and those that were killed. That number was not so great since the Ruphiri were far more interested in slaughtering common folk than engaging us. Repeatedly, they slipped away from the ends of our swords to murder the defenseless. If Zavaan was not in the city as Erianna claimed, then their primary purpose was not to capture her. It was to do what they did. What did they have to gain from it? They paid in blood too.

With Jace on our heels, I carry the queen inside despite her protests. Silla paces the great hall before the roaring hearth.

I call to her, but it is unnecessary. She dashes across the room to intersect us. "Erianna! What happened?"

"In a moment," I say. "Have baths brought to the—"

"No," Erianna objects. "Have them set up a bath in the kitchen and post a guard. It will be quicker. Will you assist me?" She asks her enemy turned friend.

"Of course," Silla agrees. "The physician?"

"Already sent for," I assure her. Worry tightens her face as she glances back to the oaken doors that lead into the great hall. On an impulse, I say, "My Queen, I ought to have told you earlier. Trent carried word to Anders that you were found and then was going to the barracks to assist Kragorn. He will bring an update back to you by dawn on the rescue efforts."

Tension slides off of Silla's face replaced by genuine relief. There is nothing like mortal peril to bring one's feelings into sharp clarity. I imagine Trent will learn that very soon.

"I will gather your clothes," Silla offers. "Is the boy staying?"

"Aye." Erianna confirms. "Set him up in my parlor. Thank you, Silla."

CHAPTER THIRTY-EIGHT

VALOR

October 12th

"How did so few cause so much damage?" Lorennt halts his destrier, surveying the blackened ruins of the west side. Though the steady snowfall cleansed the air from ash and choking smoke that would have otherwise afflicted the entire city, this street remains oppressive. We may as well be trying to draw breath with a piece of charred wood stuffed up each nostril.

My gaze skitters over the cleanup efforts currently focused on locating bodies within the rubble. I point to the place the survivors told me of in the course of our continuing investigation. "The fires were strategically set in the old thatched buildings to cause the most damage with the least effort. Fire spread outward from there and jumped the street while the Ruphiri and wolves slaughtered our people as they escaped from the burning buildings."

"From the fire to the sword," he intones. "What is the current death toll?"

"A hundred and eighty seven. And rising." I am intimately familiar with the number. Each time I arrive at the west side or at the barracks I am informed of more fatalities. The tisane the physician prescribed has blessedly stymied the deaths from smoke inhalation. Even little Jace is slowly improving. But some people were beyond recovery. Their slow, suffocating deaths have been demoralizing and painful to watch.

Lorennt pinches the bridge of his nose, squeezing his eyes shut. Though I was here to witness the atrocity on that night, a day and half later I still struggle to comprehend the scope of it. For that reason, I sent a message to Lorennt early this morning that it was imperative I speak with him. We rode into the city before the castle had fully roused so he could see the destruction for himself. Yesterday, he spent the entirety of the day in his rooms with his wife, sparing us from giving an immediate account.

"We saved as many as we could. The Ruphiri did not make it easy for us. They repeatedly disengaged themselves from skirmishes with us to cut down the defenseless." I flex my hands on the reins. "It was brutal."

"You should not have kept this from me! I should have been here!" It is the guilt we knew he would feel, and his anger toward us is our due.

But I have learned to trust Erianna's intuitive decisions and find the logic in them later. In this instance, I have had ample time to think on her decision to keep this hidden from Lorennt. "You could be feeling guilt of a different sort if Erianna had not done what she did. Beyond the possibility that you could have been targeted and left Nev widowed on her wedding day, your sister bought you time with your bride. She was adamant that the joy of your wedding not be stolen from you."

"Nev would have understood. She loves these people as much as we do."

"I think this had as much to do with Erianna herself as it did with you two."

Lorennt shifts his muddled eyes to me.

"She wanted to protect the sanctity of your marriage while allowing us to tend to the needs of Malesiir."

His expression resolves into one of disparagement as he draws the same conclusion I did. Erianna did not want Lorennt's duty to Malesiir to come before his wife. "Leer never should have sacrificed her on the altar of *For the Good of the Many*. Malesiir was first in his heart until it was too late to salvage his marriage."

I have not heard him speak so bluntly about what his brother did. It heartens me to know that Lorennt does not share Grandileer's beliefs when it comes to the importance of the individual weighed against the needs of the whole. Lorennt has the potential to be a greater king than Grandileer, even though he does not see it.

Lorennt focuses a measure of his disapproval on me. "I am still angered that you allowed Erianna to ride out with you. She is not equipped for such battles."

"I would have had to tie her up to make her stay behind." That is something I will never do to her again. It nearly destroyed her and our relationship. "Besides, I think Jace and the dozens of children she saved from the mouths of the wolves would disagree. You will hear her people singing her praise when we go to the barracks."

"But *she* was injured. *She* could have been killed," Lorennt retorts.

My mind revisits the memory of her being thrown to the ground and beaten by Bronis. I wipe a hand over my face, but the memory will not be erased so easily. Erianna told me what happened in the span of time between Anders losing sight of her and me finding her. Imaginings of those minutes ignite vengeance in my veins. Jace was not sure how to respond to my overwhelming gratitude for his throwing rocks at the villain. I made it clear that I was personally in his debt for the aid he gave to our queen and would ensure his mother knew of his bravery.

"Valor?"

I return my attention to the prince. "Sorry. Say again?"

He repeats himself. "Was Physician Cervil confident that Erianna would make a full recovery?"

Erianna insisted that she was far more disturbed by what happened to her people than Bronis's assault. Time will tell. "He was. Though I will warn you, she looks worse for her heroics. She has a nasty bruise on her thigh, two black eyes, and a handful of stitches in her brow that will add stigma to the Warrior Queen."

Lorennt shakes his head. "She will enjoy that."

"Probably," I agree. "She is also mildly concussed. Cervil gave her strict orders to sleep for a day or two then take brisk walks on the ramparts to speed along her recovery. He also gave her a tisane for smoke inhalation that we replicated and distributed at the barracks. Silla remained with Erianna for the first day, waking her every four hours to ensure she could be easily roused."

"Could she?"

"Aye." Even in this ruined place, thoughts of her lift the corners of my mouth. "Silla said that Erianna mustered some threats of bodily harm each time she was woken. Apparently, the queen did not appreciate her sleep being interrupted."

Lorennt heaves a sigh of relief. He knows that if Erianna is trading barbs, she will be in fighting form in no time. "What of Jace's mother and sister?"

"They are at the barracks. The girl's leg was badly broken, so Erianna offered to keep Jace in the castle for a few days while his mother cares for Bett."

"Nev will be delighted to have Jace around. She is quite fond of the lad."

Lorennt leads on, surveying every damaged portion of his city. We discuss the process of rebuilding and the steep costs. The displaced people will not be able to contribute monetarily, but their labor will be invaluable. As for all the belongings that were lost and businesses that were destroyed, without direct interference from the kingdom's coffers, the impoverished will become destitute.

I hope the Spirit of Truth sees fit to whisper some more unconventional wisdom in my queen's ear. If the Ruphiri attacks take this form across the kingdom, Malesiir may go from being the wealthiest kingdom to the poorest kingdom in less than a year.

※ ※ ※

Upon returning to the castle sometime after midday, we enter the great hall to find Erianna embroiled in a verbal tussle with her guards.

"You will escort me to the city or I shall go without escort!"

"I thought you said she was injured," Lorennt mutters to me.

Unfortunately, years of physical abuse raised Erianna's pain tolerance and ability to function while injured to the point that she cannot be trusted to know her own limits.

"With all due respect, Your Majesty," the guard says with the strained patience of one who has already argued this backwards and forwards, "Commander Ironforge said that you were not permitted without until he returned."

"And I say again," Erianna snaps, "your orders come from me, not my insubordinate Hand!"

I extend the reach of my stride and speak over the words of the queen's guard. "Excepting in matters of your safety, Majesty, as always."

Erianna rounds on me, planting her feet in a fighting stance. Her choler does not diminish the blow Lorennt and I feel at seeing her stitched and swollen face.

Lorennt reaches for her arm, tucking it around his. "I have saved you the necessity of venturing into the city this day. Come, let us speak."

She tries to flatten her brows to glare at him but pales at the attempt that tugs on the stitches. Lorennt takes advantage of his ornery sister's aching head and steers her toward their office without waiting for her assent.

The moment the door closes she shoves him away. Her irate gaze lands on me. "I will not be locked in this castle! You have no authority to make such decisions!"

I draw breath, but Lorennt beats me to the sparring line. "The responsibility of keeping you safe is absolutely within our rights. You, Dearest, are too reckless for your own good."

Erianna bares her teeth. "Do not name me that!"

Lorennt has no qualms about wielding her vulnerabilities. "You are still dear even if Leer cannot name you such. To me. To Nev. To our parents. To Valor." He surprises us by including my name in the list. "You are *dear* to us. You must take care with yourself for our sakes, if not for your own."

Erianna's anger loosens its hold, but not entirely. "That does not excuse you from locking me in the castle," she rebukes us both.

I calmly explain, "I only asked the guards to hold you up until I could personally escort you."

Lorennt takes a seat, pressing the conversation forward without giving Erianna time to kindle her argument. "Valor has apprised me of all that transpired the night of my wedding and since. We have just returned from riding through the west side and to the barracks. I personally spoke with our people to assure myself they were as well as could be expected." Lorennt offers her a smile. "They have much to say in praise of their Warrior Queen."

"But *how are they*?" She asks, finally settling into a chair opposite him.

Lorennt leans into the cushions. "They have lost much. They are hurting. They are sad. They fear they are now destitute though I have assured them we will not allow it."

"Are their needs being met?"

"They are," I say. "In addition to the provisions allocated, donations of food, clothing, and necessities are pouring into the barracks. Already, a roster is posted of generous souls who have opened their homes to orphans and families with young children."

She sighs and rests her head on her fingertips. "We must rebuild. Soon. Winter is not the time to be living in tents."

Lorennt acknowledges that worry. "I have already set the rebuilding in motion. Skilled masons have been contacted to expedite the process. It will not be long before we have estimates on the construction."

"Jace's family?" She asks.

"Lorennt and I sought them this morning and ensured they were on the waiting list for temporary housing. Bett suffers from smoke inhalation the same as Jace, and her broken leg keeps her immobile. It will be a week at least before she is healed enough for crutches. Tessie sends her thanks for allowing Jace to remain here until she is better able to look after him."

Another sigh, then her weary eyes find mine. So much anguish and guilt rests in them that my concern for her deepens.

"Has Physician Cervil seen you today?"

A deep blush of embarrassment colors her cheeks, and she quickly looks away from me. "Aye. He says I will be fine."

Lorennt picks up on her discomfort. "What else did he say?"

"Nothing of significance." The blush runs down her neck.

Lorennt narrows his eyes. "I do not believe you."

"Believe whatever you like." She lifts her chin defiantly, revealing more flushed skin.

Lorennt opens his mouth to press an answer from her, but I have a vague notion of what she might tell and interrupt him. "Leave it be, Lorennt."

He glares at me for usurping his role as his sister's guardian, but Erianna flicks grateful eyes to me.

"We have more important things to discuss, Lorennt." Erianna masters her expression. "The largest of which is how the Ruphiri invaded our city."

"Kragorn is leading the investigation, but it remains a mystery," I grudgingly admit.

"How many Ruphiri were killed?"

"Not many," Lorennt informs. "We have nine bodies, though you and Anders took down quite a few wolves. It would not surprise if they have less than half the pack with which they arrived."

The reminder sets a grim shadow across Erianna's face. "It was not enough."

"Your people are grateful you rode to their aid. *I* am grateful," Lorennt impresses upon her.

She lifts doubtful eyes.

"You did Nev and I a great kindness. Thank you."

"You are not angry with me?"

"No. I am not. When I was at the barracks, our people were profuse in their gratitude to you."

The shadow darkens to despair. "There were so many I could not reach—too many children. Why did they do it?"

The letter in Lorennt's pocket must feel like a lead weight for how he shifts in his chair.

"What is it?" Erianna asks.

Lorennt glances at me. The look I return urges him to tell her.

Erianna sharpens her gaze on him. "You know why."

Lorennt leans forward with forearms across his thighs. "On our way into the castle, we came upon a courier with a letter for you."

Erianna smooths the wrinkles from her queen's mask and evenly demands, "Hand it over."

"Reconsider," Lorennt objects. "I will read it and if there is anything pertinent I will tell you. There is no need for you to suffer his words."

Erianna's unwavering stare matches Lorennt's.

I feel as he does, wanting to shield her from whatever bile Zavaan spews at her, but I know she will not allow it. The best we can do is to be here after.

Lorennt finally surrenders the letter. Like the last one, it is addressed to *Queen Erianna Zavaan*. Unlike last time, she reads it alone. Seconds after breaking the seal and unfolding it, Erianna rises and tosses it upon the fire.

Lorennt barks his surprise.

"One of our generals aided them," Erianna states from the fireplace.

"He said that?" Lorennt's temper propels him to her side. "Why would he admit that?"

"Amusement."

Lorennt works his jaw. "Explain."

She stares vacantly into the fire.

"What else did he say?"

Erianna shakes her head.

"Erianna." Her name comes out as a harsh command.

"Naught," she lies.

Lorennt grips her shoulder and wheels her to face him. "Tell me what he said!"

"Lorennt!" I snarl, jumping to my feet.

He jerks his hand away as though burned. "Forgive me. I did not mean—" He takes a step back. "Forgive me."

Indifference marks her tone. "Zavaan finds amusement in proving he is smarter than we are. He says the generals assisted him to see me dethroned."

"Or just one," I suggest.

"Kannik," Lorennt agrees. If any of the generals have had opportunity, it is Kannik who has been leading the hunt for Zavaan. Or perhaps only clearing the way for him.

"Possibly." Erianna shrugs. "Or Zavaan is stirring up dissension where there is none."

"You do not believe that," I point out.

Guilt moves behind her mask.

"It was not your fault."

"No one will argue that if I had allowed them to take me from Malesiir, hundreds of people would still be alive."

"And hundreds of others killed in Limba," I contest. "Zavaan is a murderer. Whether these people or others, he will kill again. Sacrificing you to him will not prevent that."

She touches her temple and says to no one in particular, "My head aches."

Lorennt's hand returns to her shoulder with abject consideration. "Maybe you ought to lie down a while longer. Let Valor inform Kragorn of the possible involvement of the generals. There is nothing you can do at the moment."

"I must go to the city," she doggedly circles back to her purpose.

Hoping that I will be able to sway her before then, I offer, "Will you take a late noon meal with me before I escort you into the city?"

She considers then inclines her head.

"I leave you to it." Lorennt looks long on her. "Take care, dear Sister. No adventures today, please." His words resonate with her, but instead of drawing cooperation, they draw blood.

She shrugs him off with ice in her tone. "If you misappropriate my husband's words ever again, I will make you regret it."

Lorennt sourly replies, "Fine. Then have mine. Do not do anything reckless. Or else..." The office door bangs against the wall from his forceful exit. Erianna glares after him.

I wonder if their relationship has always been so turbulent. They obviously love each other, but the unrestrained way they fight cannot be good for either of them. Furthermore, how can they harmoniously rule a kingdom if they are willing to tear flesh in a fight? King Grandileer was the undisputed dominant figure between the three of them and had the final say in all matters. Erianna has made it clear that she is in control at the present, but once Lorennt takes the king's crown on the first day of the new year, who will have the weighted vote then?

With her back still to me, the Warrior Queen vows, "Commander Ironforge, if you ever undermine me to my soldiers again, I will find myself another Hand."

No, the Warrior Queen will not yield authority to the Indolent Prince. If he does not earn a new title by the time he is crowned, he will be no match for Erianna's spine of steel.

"As told, my Queen, my intention was not to undermine you. I only intended to ensure you were adequately protected before you ventured out."

"Hmm... It is funny how often people make decisions on my behalf that utterly undermine me and place me in jeopardy, supposedly with my best interests in mind."

"I see nothing humorous about that."

"Then do not become one of them!" She snaps and moves to the door.

"Aye, my Queen. So long as you remember that my name is Ironforge, not Rodiharian. I am always on your side."

I do not doubt she heard me though she gives no acknowledgement as she strides away.

No, the Warrior Queen will not yield anything easily. Including her heart.

※ ※ ※

ERIANNA

"Was it worth it? Your generals do not agree."

Zavaan's thorn digs deeper into my heart with each city block we traverse. It is hard to believe that fighting Zavaan and allowing him to wreak havoc on Malesiir is worth the cost when balanced against my enslavement and the Limban deaths that would come as a result of surrendering to him. If I had fully understood the cost in blood from the moment I broke my betrothal to him by fleeing with Valor in Limba, then I might not have run. The mass grave being dug outside the city makes me reconsider surrendering to him now. But if I do and he goes unpunished, what is the purpose in their sacrifice? I may as well have turned myself over on the way from Parse Kítaran to Malsihra a month ago.

Just as Lorennt told, the people are prolific with their thanks to me. Valor asks me to point out to him each child that I saved. I know what he means for me to see, but it is still disheartening to know how many died in spite of my efforts. Kragorn agrees to look into Zavaan's hint about the generals, but I do not believe it will bear fruit. Zavaan would not have said it if he knew it could be easily unravelled.

A whimper of pain escapes me as I pull myself to the saddle when we depart the barracks. My head is throbbing and making me dizzy. After my unkind words to him, Valor does not offer consolation or recommend returning to the castle, but he does ride close enough to catch me if I sway in the saddle.

My heart hurts all the worse for it.

Valor is not Leer or Lorennt. His gentle reminder that I am judging him as if he is one of them was not amiss. I have been unfair. But if I admit that and apologize, I will soften to him. Then I will find myself agreeing to dance with him like I did the other night. I am relieved it did not happen, glad, in fact, that Trent interrupted. I should not be dancing with anyone. I am in mourning—a fact that is not difficult to remember during the long lonely nights. It is only difficult to remember when Valor looks at me like he does and offers me things that ought to be impossible. Then my heart reminds me it is not buried between the two graves in the cemetery. It revives at Valor's touch.

I breathe through my nose and exhale on a cough.

"Was Cervil certain your lungs were improving?" Valor asks as we ride toward the west side.

"Aye. The cough is nothing to worry about."

"And the concussion?"

"A week will set me to rights."

"And your woman's health?"

My face flames.

"That is what else he discussed."

Not a question, and my embarrassment would belie a denial. "It was."

"And?"

"This is hardly appropriate, Valor."

He snorts. "It is your health, Erianna. Have you continued to improve from your loss?"

"It is too soon to say. He strongly recommended I not conceive for at least a year." I cut a look at him from the corner of my eyes, deciding he ought to share in my embarrassment since he is partly responsible. "Cervil offered me a tisane to prevent conception."

Valor's eyes darken. "He thought you would need one? Why?"

I raise an accusatory brow. "Apparently being 'above reproach' does not prevent people from making assumptions."

"Me?" He asks in a small voice.

I nod.

"I hope you told him—"

"That you would be careful not get me with child? I told him."

Valor swallows hard, bobbing his throat. "Those were your words? Do you understand what he would infer?"

"I do." I tap Sacha's sides, moving her into a trot. "I was irritated and wanted to bring an end to his impertinent questions."

"Blamed for something I do not get to enjoy," Valor grumbles. "That is hardly fair."

Though my thoughts run the same path, I do not voice them. It does not bode well for Valor to know I have reached for him in the middle of the night, thinking I might find him in my bed after a vivid dream that was anything but unpleasant. I restrict my thoughts from wandering there during my waking hours, but I cannot be held accountable for my dreams.

As we near the west side, the stench of it offends my nose before the sight of it offends my eyes. Carts of rubble pass us on their way to the city gates. Another cart bearing charred corpses follows.

I cannot brace myself for what the light of day reveals. The destruction of the west side is heart wrenching. I look to what was once Mistress Getty's dress shop. She was found inside during the excavation. I liked the woman tremendously and will miss her.

A soldier whistles for a cart to be brought to a building currently being searched. My heart shatters as the soldiers reverently collect one body after another from the collapsed building. The last body is an infant. Valor turns us back to the castle, using Granite to discreetly guide Sacha.

I do not see anything else until Valor reaches for me in the upper bailey to lift me from the saddle. I am captive to that scorched night in the city, reliving it without the benefit of a task and battle-fever to dampen my emotions. My people have been slaughtered. Again.

Valor leads me away from the castle to the adjacent chapel. The doors are opened for us then closed to hold captive the heat inside the building from the thieving grasp of winter. He walks me down the center aisle to the front of the sunlit room. I fold over myself on the bench then feel Valor bring me into his side. I cling to him, sobbing uncontrollably.

Valor's grief stricken voice blends with mine, raising prayers heavenward. Prayers for the injured to be healed. For the families that were destroyed and the lives lost in one horrific night. For the massacres to end. For wisdom in the decisions we must make. For peace in our kingdom.

When my tears are mostly spent, Valor holds me closer still and offers up praise to the Almighty for the lives that were spared. Including mine. Especially mine. I feel Valor's tears unashamedly wet my hair as he thanks the Almighty for protecting me.

CHAPTER THIRTY-NINE

VALOR

October 15th

The notice comes while we breakfast together. It is as unwelcome as it is promising.

"The Ruphiri attempted to raid the storehouses at Chishelm." Erianna passes the missive to me. "Thankfully, the townsfolk raised the alarm just as you taught them. The garrison intercepted the Ruphiri before they could destroy the storehouses or kill anyone."

I digest the rest of General Kannik's words with growing resolve.

I have held onto their trail and am pushing them west toward the Ascent. I request reinforcements be sent to Chishelm. By my count, there are twenty-odd men, all clad as Ruphiri.

"This is good news," Erianna notes. Before I can point out what else it means, she does. "You must attend to this. Have you completed the preparations for your next assignment?"

Erianna presents the appearance of a stolid queen. She is poised, collected, and controlled. The bruises on her delicate face do not negate her composure. This is the Warrior Queen of Malesiir. Her presence is like cool water with the depth and strength of a river beneath her surface.

She has changed so much in the last year. The enchanting girl I loved grew into a woman with allure and power. Her intelligence has been enhanced with experience. Her beautiful heart that was tempered with loss and grief has been made anew with life eternal. Joy lights the winter sky in her eyes.

She loves deeply. Consumingly. Someday, I will show her what it means to love passionately. But for now, our love does not breach the confines of truest friendship.

"I will complete my preparations this day and leave at first light on the morrow." My assignments will carry me hundreds of miles away, to the northernmost reaches of our kingdom. "Six weeks is not so very long. We have been parted far longer."

Erianna fidgets with the edge of her widow's veil. "It is plenty long. Does our prior agreement still stand?"

"No recklessness until we are together? I will uphold the bargain if you will. For your part, that includes taking an escort into the city." The specification seems necessary in light of her reticence to the guards.

"I will. And I promise not slip my escort to venture into the city alone," she teases.

I eye her with reproach at her hinted scheme. "See that you don't."

She makes a pretense of eating her breakfast for some minutes. I still her hand that absently taps the table. She turns her hand over to clasp mine. "Do everything that you can to come back to me. I need—" Her lips seal over words that she is not ready to speak, but I understand.

I lace our fingers together then hide our hands beneath the table. "We have much to do when I return to you. A city to rebuild, a traitor to find, a prince to crown..."

She nods, but worry lingers in her eyes.

Although she cannot yet speak her heart, I assure her of where mine remains. "And I have a queen to woo."

Erianna's cheeks blush followed by her whole face when a nobleman seated next to me coughs to cover his astonishment.

I wink at Erianna and turn to him. "Are you well, Lord Hugler?"

Silla's father grumbles, "These biscuits are stale. And presumptuous."

My queen masks her own chuckle with a cough. "I quite agree."

"Then perhaps you ought to visit Mari when you are next in the city. Part of my preparations include making a deposit at her bakery, should my queen need to steal a dessert while I am away."

Erianna's eyes dance. "Aye, you have much to do this day and when you return." She squeezes my hand in hers and makes no move to let me go.

A Note from the Author

Dear Readers, thank you for spending time with me in the world of the Redemption Saga. I hope you have enjoyed this chapter in Erianna and Valor's tale. There is nothing more transformative in a person's life than being caught up in God's grace. I pray that you too will know the awesome power of His redeeming love.

If you enjoyed this story, would you please consider leaving a review? It is the best way you can support me as an author and help fellow readers find their next great read.

Thank you!

Truth from the Holy Texts

I have included this appendix to cite some of the specific verses that answered the questions that plagued Valor, Erianna, and others in this story. Though this novel is fictional, the truth of God's Word is undeniably real. These verses have been taken from the New King James Version® of the Holy Bible.

Isaiah 1:18 *"Come now, and let us reason together," says the Lord, "Though your sins are like scarlet, they shall be as white as snow; Though they are red like crimson, they shall be as wool.*

1 Peter 1:15-16 *But as He who called you is holy, you also be holy in all your conduct, because it is written, "Be holy, for I am holy."*

Romans 12:19 *Beloved, do not avenge yourselves, but rather give place to wrath; for it is written, "Vengeance is Mine, I will repay," says the Lord.*

Ephesians 6:11-13 *Put on the whole armor of God, that you may be able to stand against the wiles of the devil. For we do not wrestle against flesh and blood, but against principalities, against powers, against the rulers of the darkness of this age, against spiritual hosts of wickedness in the heavenly places. Therefore take up the whole armor of God, that you may be able to withstand in the evil day, and having done all, to stand.*

1 Peter 5:8 *Be sober, be vigilant; because your adversary the devil walks about like a roaring lion, seeking whom he may devour.*

Deuteronomy 32:39-42 *Now see that I, even I, am He, And there is no God besides Me; I kill and I make alive; I wound and I heal; Nor is there any who can deliver from My hand. For I raise My hand to heaven, And say, "As I live forever, If I whet My glittering sword, And My hand takes hold on judgment, I will render vengeance to My enemies, And repay those who hate Me. I will make My arrows drunk with blood, And My sword shall devour flesh, With the blood of the slain and the captives, From the heads of the leaders of the enemy."*

* * *

Psalm 86:5-7 *For You, Lord, are good, and ready to forgive, And abundant in mercy to all those who call upon You. Give ear, O Lord, to my prayer; And attend to the voice of my supplications. In the day of my trouble I will call upon You, For You will answer me.*

Romans 8:28-30 & 37-39 *And we know that all things work together for good to those who love God, to those who are the called according to His purpose. For whom He foreknew, He also predestined to be conformed to the image of His Son, that He might be the firstborn among many brethren. Moreover whom He predestined, these He also called; whom He called, these He also justified; and whom He justified, these He also glorified... Yet in all these things we are more than conquerors through Him who loved us. For I am persuaded that neither death nor life, nor angels nor principalities nor powers, nor things present nor things to come, nor height nor depth, nor any other created thing, shall be able to separate us from the love of God which is in Christ Jesus our Lord.*

John 16:33 *These things I have spoken to you, that in Me you may have peace. In the world you will have tribulation; but be of good cheer, I have overcome the world.*

Matthew 28:20b *And surely I am with you always, to the very end of the age.*

Colossians 1:13-14 *He has delivered us from the power of darkness and conveyed us into the kingdom of the Son of His love, in whom we have redemption through His blood, the forgiveness of sins.*

About the Author

Erin L. Cross is a wife, homeschooling mother, author, and part-time landscaper. A native to Florida, she divides her time between reading, writing, and turning her suburban backyard into a homestead. Being a life-long learner, she is not satisfied until she has exhaustively researched a subject of interest.

This habit proved fruitful in fully developing the fictitious yet historically inspired medieval world and characters in her first novel *Redemption's Pursuit*, a story that was ten-years in the making. On that solid foundation, she dove into writing four consecutive novels in The Redemption Saga that are scheduled to release in 2021 and 2022.

Erin's deepest desire is that in whatever she does, she will do it to the the best of her ability, to the glory of God.